The Lady in Waiting

THE LADY IN WAITING

Deborah Fowler

CENTURY
LONDON SYDNEY AUCKLAND JOHANNESBURG

The right of Deborah Fowler to be identified as the author of
this work has been asserted by her in accordance with the
Copyright, Designs and Patents Act 1988.

First published in Great Britain in 1991 by
Random Century Group
20 Vauxhall Bridge Road, London SW1V 2SA

Century Hutchinson South Africa (Pty) Ltd
PO Box 337, Bergvlei 2012, South Africa

Random Century Australia Pty Ltd
20 Alfred Street, Milsons Point, Sydney, NSW 2061

Random Century New Zealand Ltd
PO Box 40–086, Glenfield, Auckland 10
New Zealand

British Library Cataloguing in Publication Data
Fowler, Deborah
The lady in waiting.
I. Title
813[F]

ISBN 0–7126–3969–1

Phototypeset by Intype, London
Printed in Great Britain by Mackays of Chatham Plc
Chatham Kent

ACKNOWLEDGEMENTS

A great many people have helped me with this book. I would like to mention especially my husband Alan, my secretary Vi Niness, and Margaret Wiltshire, who kept the children at bay while I wrote. I would also like to thank Diana Palmer, PhD, who undertook all the historical research and whose extensive knowledge and advice proved invaluable.

For Locket – my daughter and my best friend
Lots of love Mum

PROLOGUE
June 1965 – Suffolk

Nanny Fraser was going to die. Prue knew it although she had been told nothing – not even the nature of Nanny's illness. As was the way with small children, the gruesome details of pain and death intrigued as well as terrified her. She gazed out of the car window. She felt nervous and apprehensive about the visit, and wondered whether she would be sick when she saw Nanny. They had not seen her since last Christmas. She had left the Mansell household after eight years' service to be nursed by her sister in Long Melford, and this was the first time they had seen her since then. Prue shivered despite the warmth of the day.

By contrast Prue's parents were giving little thought to what lay ahead. The road from Thurston Hall to Long Melford took them past Chadbrook, and suddenly it came into sight – white walls gleaming in the morning sunlight. Sir Robert Mansell slowly eased his battered Landrover round the bend in the road, savouring the moment – this particular view of the old house always gave him pleasure. By his side his wife, Margery, was neither thinking of Nanny Fraser nor enjoying the view. She was completely absorbed with thoughts of her asparagus bed – gardening was her passion, her *raison d'être*.

They crossed Long Melford green, dipped down into the village and all too soon for Prue they reached the little thatched cottage which belonged to Nanny's sister.

'I'll see you later,' Robert called out, as mother and daughter clambered down onto the pavement. 'Why don't you meet me at the pub and we can have some lunch before going home? It will save cooking.'

'Good idea,' said Margery. 'I don't expect we shall be long.'

Forty minutes later, they emerged from the stifling gloom of the cottage into the bright sunlight. Both hesitated a moment, as if adjusting to the contrast. Not normally a demonstrative woman, Margery reached for Prue's hand and together they began walking up the village street. The scene they had just witnessed had shaken them to the core.

1

Nanny – her plump, rosy face now a death mask, the bones standing out on her skull, the skin drawn tight and thin. Nanny – her deep, throaty chuckle reduced to a rasping fight for breath, her warm grey eyes dull and clouded with drugs and pain. Margery glanced down at her daughter. The expression on Prue's face was unreadable. She looked a little pale but there was no hint of tears or emotion. What sort of impact had the visit made on her, Margery wondered, but it was not in her nature to ask. She simply held tight to the little hand in hers and began pointing out the flowers in the cottage gardens they passed.

Robert was already waiting for them at a table in the front courtyard of the pub. He rose as they arrived. 'How was Nanny?' he asked.

'Not too good,' said Margery, glancing anxiously at Prue, who said nothing.

'Well, I expect she'll be better soon,' he said with forced heartiness. 'What would you girls like to drink?'

'A dry sherry, I think,' said Margery, 'and a lemonade, Prue?'

'Yes, please.'

Prue and Margery sat down and Prue glanced at her mother hoping for the chance to discuss Nanny's illness but Margery seemed to be lost in thought. There were so many questions Prue wanted to ask about Nanny, but the irony was that the person who normally provided her with information in a form suitably digestible for a seven-year-old was Nanny herself. Her parents were not easily approachable in that way. She looked around her miserably and her attention was caught by the pub sign, hanging high above them. The Lady in Waiting, she read out slowly. What a strange name – waiting for what? She studied the crude drawing on the sign. The illustration was of a woman with thick, red hair, in a green dress with a tight bodice. Her face was both defiant and proud – not particularly likeable but interesting. Prue found herself staring at both the woman and the name. For some reason, they seemed immediately familiar. 'Why is it called The Lady in Waiting, Mummy?'

'What, dear?' Margery's gaze returned from the far distance.

'The pub, why is it called The Lady in Waiting?'

Margery frowned. 'I can't remember exactly but I think it's something to do with the woman who used to own it a long time ago.'

'What happened to her? Is that her up there?' Prue pointed to the pub sign.

'I don't know, probably.'

'I think I'll go and help Daddy get the drinks. I want to see inside.'

'Good idea.' Margery looked relieved.

Prue's initial impression as she stepped inside the pub was one of warmth and welcome. It was a large bar with a stone-flagged floor, white walls and heavy oak beams. A vast inglenook fireplace dominated one end of the room in which a fire glowed despite the warmth of the day. Brasses twinkled, glasses sparkled, the lighting was soft. Through the gloom she could see the dark shadow of her father, who was talking to a pretty barmaid. She stepped forward ready to call to him when an unseen hand seemed to stop her in her tracks and from nowhere came crashing in a series of sensations – the room was suddenly darker and the smell so strong and repulsive that it made Prue catch her breath – sweat, horse dung, roasting meat, stale beer, the air thick and cloying with wood smoke. Then the noises began, so loud as to be almost deafening – men calling out in harsh, rough voices. She swung round, bewildered, expecting to see the room suddenly filled with people but there was no one there, though the sound of clattering plates, of feet stomping, of people shouting and laughing were all about her so that she felt at any moment she would be trampled underfoot.

As she stood bewildered, the fear began. At first it was like a trickle of cold water down the back of her spine. She looked wildly about her, expecting to see the object of her fear, but there was nothing upon which to pin it. Fear, dread, the extraordinary sensation of sound and smell . . . building, building. This terrible emotion, never before experienced in her young life, grew relentlessly until at last it burst out as a wild, horrifying terror, blinding her, clawing at her. She turned and fumbled for the door. It opened and in a moment she was out and running. Her mouth was open but she could not hear her own screams, nor did the sunlight of that beautiful day make any impression on her. She simply ran and ran, straight ahead, across the road and down a long narrow path towards the river.

Robert caught her at the bridge. She had stopped running now and stood breathing heavily, staring down into the waters below. For a moment he had been paralysed by his daughter's blood-curdling screams and the mindless way in which she had run across the road, as if no traffic existed. But now he was beside her, catching hold of her flailing body, kneeling down, securing her arms by her side and forcing her to face him. She was desperately, frighteningly pale, tears streamed down her face, she was breathing heavily and the eyes that stared wildly into his did not seem to recognize him at all. 'Prue,

3

Prue, what is it?' She did not reply. He shook her gently. 'Prue, it's Daddy. What happened, what's wrong?' Her eyes slowly focused on his and as they did so she began to tremble, her body becoming limp in his arms so that he had to support her. 'Prue, are you ill?'

At that moment Margery reached them. She took the child from Robert, picking her up, holding her like a limp doll. 'What happened, I don't understand?'

'Nor do I,' said Robert. 'There's a bench over there, let's sit down for a moment.'

They sat together on the bench, Prue on Margery's lap. Prue seemed calmer now, the shaking had almost stopped, and the sun shining through the trees both warmed and calmed them. Robert took her hand. 'Tell us what happened, why you ran off screaming like that. You could have been killed on the road. Did something frighten you?'

Prue looked at him. 'I – I don't know,' she said. 'It didn't feel nice in there.'

'How do you mean?' Margery asked, her voice bleak with shock.

Prue searched her mind, trying to find the words to describe her experience, but none came. It was not simply that she could not express herself – the feeling of not wanting to share what had happened to her with anyone, even in the pursuit of comfort, was very strong. She shrugged her shoulders. 'It just felt horrible.'

'And how do you feel now?' Margery asked.

'All right.'

Both parents looked relieved. 'It's been rather a difficult morning for her,' Margery suggested.

Robert let out a sigh. 'Of course, that's it. Poor child, it was seeing Nanny so ill, wasn't it – that's what upset you? Perhaps we shouldn't have taken her to see Nanny, Margery. Come on, let's go home – you'll feel better there, poppet.'

The three of them began walking back up the path, Robert and Margery now apparently satisfied with the explanation they had found for Prue's extraordinary behaviour. But Prue knew it was nothing to do with Nanny, nothing to do with Nanny at all.

CHAPTER ONE
New York – Spring 1980

'Pam, will you come in here?'

'Yes, sir.' Pam Driver picked up her notebook, paused to check her make-up in the mirror above her desk and slipped through the door, just as Jonathan spoke again.

'Pam, where the hell are you?'

'Right here,' she said, too brightly. 'Ever at your beck and call.'

Jonathan Lindstrom was leaning back in his chair, his feet on the desk, smoking a cigarette. He smiled at her, a slow, lazy, attractive smile. Despite all her efforts to give him up, she knew she never would, not while he looked at her like that. She glanced down at her notebook so he would not see the expression on her face. He was clearly aware of her vulnerability but it was vital he did not know the extent of it.

'You won't be taking notes, Pam. I want to talk. I need your advice.'

His words had Pam staring at him in amazement. Jonathan Lindstrom never needed advice from anyone. He went his own self-indulgent way, and thanks to his charm, good looks and impeccable family background, he tended invariably to get what he wanted. She watched him now as he swung out of his chair and went to stand by the office window with its spectacular view of the Manhattan skyline. He had a tall, rangy figure, not graceful exactly but loose-limbed and fluid of movement, dark curly hair, a fresh complexion and, most startling of all, pale blue eyes – cold eyes, calculating eyes but mesmerizing nonetheless. Whatever was on his mind it had to be serious and she was instantly apprehensive.

'You know me,' she said lightly. 'Always anxious to please. What's the problem?'

He turned to her. 'Mother has made me an offer which I can very easily refuse but which nonetheless has a certain appeal.'

'What kind of offer?' Pam asked.

'You may recall that Lindstrom's Bank bought a small merchant bank in London at the end of last year. The details of the sale are

5

now complete and Gerrards Bank becomes ours next week. Edward Deckman is being sent over to run the show, but my mother has asked me if I would like to go too and head up the corporate finance division. It's kind of a challenge.'

Jonathan leaving New York – it had to mean she would lose him. She tried to shut her mind to the implications and rally as best she could, but her thoughts were racing to the very edge of panic.

'I see. It has to be a great opportunity for you, though I didn't think you cared much for Edward Deckman?' Her voice sounded surprisingly normal.

'I don't,' Jonathan agreed. 'In fact I can't stand the guy – he has no flair and absolutely no charisma, which is exactly where I reckon I can score. I don't see him being much of a success in London and if I'm right, I'd like to bet I'll be heading up the whole operation before long.'

'And in the meantime,' said Pam, fighting the desire to scream, yell, cry – anything to relieve the pain, 'what will be your duties as Head of Corporate Finance?'

Jonathan drew deeply on his cigarette and then stubbed it out – extinguishing the flame as carelessly as he is robbing me of my happiness right now, Pam thought.

'The Thatcher Government is really into promoting the entrepreneur,' he said. 'There's a lot of Government help around and so there's a real rash of new business start-ups in the UK right now. The idea is that I should take advantage of the trend.'

'It sounds quite a challenge,' said Pam, lamely. 'But I never thought of you as living any place outside New York, nor, come to that, working any place but Wall Street.'

'I guess so,' Jonathan admitted. 'But I'd sure as hell like to get out from under Mother's influence for a while and do something of my own.' He hesitated. 'So what do you think, Pam?'

Pam Driver was a beautiful girl, with a long mane of chestnut hair, clear skin and classic features. If looks were the only criterion, she could have been a top model as easily as a secretary, but she had precious little confidence in herself and right now her self-esteem was at an all-time low.

'I don't know what to say,' she said after a pause. 'I guess it's hard for me to judge since I'm well . . . kind of involved.' Jonathan stared at her, genuinely puzzled, and she suddenly realized that he had not even considered the implications his move would have upon their relationship. He was asking her opinion simply because, as his secretary, she was available to talk through what was on his mind. What he had chosen to ignore, or worse still, not even realized, was the effect his news would have upon her personally.

He rallied quickly, apparently recognizing his mistake. 'It won't be so bad, Pam, it's not as though it will be for very long. We'll call each other regularly, and in any event the guy my mother picks to replace me here might be just your type. Who knows, it could be a great opportunity for you, too.' He grinned boyishly.

The banality of his suggestion finally broke through her reserve. 'What happens to us is not even of the slightest concern to you, is it?' she burst out. 'All you can think about is you, you, you – as always. What am I supposed to do – sit around here waiting for you, in case you come back, or do as you suggest and offer my bed to your successor – all part of the perks of working for Lindstrom's Bank? You shit.' She turned and made to run from the room but Jonathan was too quick for her, grabbing her arm and swinging her round to face him. He put his hands on her shoulders and then, drawing her to him, kissed her deeply, her notebook falling uselessly onto the floor between them. She fought him briefly.

'If I do take the job and it's by no means certain that I will, I'll miss you, too, but we'll manage,' he said, his voice now full of apparent concern. Pam made a conscious decision to allow his hollow words to soothe her. She knew she was of no real significance in Jonathan Lindstrom's life. She had no major part to play, never had done, never would do. 'I tell you what,' he was saying. 'Why don't we go to lunch early today, somewhere really great, somewhere I can spoil you?'

Pam shook her head. 'You can't. Your mother's called a meeting to discuss the Stebbings account – one o'clock start – a working lunch.'

'Jesus, I wish she wouldn't do that. Why is she so hung up on these lunchtime meetings?' He released Pam, his tenderness of a moment before replaced by childish irritation.

'To keep you guys out of the bars and restaurants, I guess,' said Pam, sourly.

'I think it's a short-sighted approach. Everyone needs a break at lunchtime.'

'Not for three hours at a time,' said Pam. She never normally bitched – it was one of the things Jonathan liked about her most or so he told her.

He chose to ignore her. 'OK, so what about this evening?'

'What about this evening?'

'Shall we take in a show, have some dinner?'

'Dinner would be nice,' said Pam, forlornly, the fighting instinct already gone. She was being hopeless, she knew. This was no way to keep him.

'Just a quiet dinner and then . . .' Jonathan smiled suggestively, his good humour instantly restored.

She knew she should refuse him and at the same time she knew she never would. 'Why not?' she said.

'There's my girl. Hell, who needs London anyway?'

Pam felt tears well into her eyes and she hurried to the door. I'll just make us some coffee,' she said.

Standing by the percolator, waiting for the coffee to brew, Pam tried to quell the sense of mounting misery. Of course Jonathan would take the job. It was a challenge and an opportunity he would not be able to resist, besides which she had sensed a restlessness in him for some time, caused in no small measure by his mother.

Harriet Lindstrom was a spectacular character. Widowed at twenty-four, when her son, Jonathan, was just a few months old, Harriet had stepped into her husband's shoes and begun running Lindstrom's Bank with absolutely no experience whatsoever either of banking or the world of commerce. Not only had she managed to hold the bank together, she had made an enormous success of turning a gentlemanly, respectable but barely profitable concern into a considerable commercial force on Wall Street. Now she was a legend in the banking world, a formidable matriarch, someone to respect, admire, fear but rarely like. Jonathan was her only Achilles heel, the weak point in the armour plating she had built around herself following her husband's premature death from tuberculosis. In the early years of her widowhood there had been plenty of hopeful suitors but nowadays no one believed that Harriet Lindstrom would ever take another husband. Her world revolved round her business . . . and her son.

As she prepared Jonathan's tray of coffee, Pam wondered whether Harriet saw her son for what he was – selfish, arrogant and shallow. Probably not – what mother ever saw a beloved child in his or her true light? She must think positive, Pam told herself, she must recognize that she had no part to play in Jonathan's future. If nothing else, at least this move to London would enforce the separation which she, herself, was quite incapable of instigating.

8

'Thank you, gentlemen, that will be all.' Harriet Lindstrom sat ramrod straight at the head of the boardroom table. With her neat dark hair and the blazing blue eyes which Jonathan had inherited, no one ever noticed her tiny stature and slight build. Her indomitable spirit and natural authority more than compensated for her small frame. Obediently, like children, they all rose and began filing out of the boardroom. 'One moment, Jonathan,' Harriet called. Jonathan returned to his mother's side and sat down at the table. He was dying for a drink, or a cigarette at least, but he never smoked in front of his mother, who strongly disapproved of the habit. 'Have you thought over my offer?' she asked, without preamble, as was her way.

'Yes and no,' said Jonathan.

'What kind of answer is that?' Harriet's quick anger threatened, but Jonathan remained unruffled.

'Yes, I have thought about it a great deal, and no, I haven't come to a decision.'

'I want a decision by ten o'clock tomorrow morning,' Harriet warned.

'I know that, Mother. You made that quite clear but I'd like to use all the time I have available to make absolutely sure I'm doing the right thing.'

'You're not emigrating,' said Harriet, testily. 'We're only talking about a year or two, just to establish ourselves. By then it will be appropriate for you to return here and think of taking over my job. I won't last for ever, you know.'

Jonathan smiled. 'I have to challenge that statement.'

Harriet returned the smile. 'I'll be fifty next birthday,' she reminded him. 'I aim to take retirement soon, I deserve it after all these years.'

'I have a good mind to tape this conversation,' Jonathan said, 'and play it back to you at sixty and again at seventy, and again at seventy-five . . .'

'I'm serious, Jonathan. I've worked hard all my life and sometime before I'm too old, I intend to spend a little time enjoying myself. Besides, you should be taking over – you're older than I was when your father died.' Her voice held little conviction.

'I'm sorry, Mother, I know you too well. You'll never retire and you're never willingly going to hand over the reins to me or anyone.'

They regarded one another with the usual odd combination of emotions – frustration and guarded affection. 'What about Jo?' Harriet asked suddenly.

9

'What about her?' Jonathan was instantly on the defensive.

'I don't want to come between a man and his wife.' Harriet's voice was heavily ironic.

'Jo and I are history. You know that, Mother. Neither of us has filed for divorce because we've been so busy, but we will in our own good time.'

'A grave mistake,' said Harriet. 'That woman is right for you, Jonathan. You behaved like a fool.'

'Don't start that again, Mother. Jo is not relevant to my decision. I'm a free agent.'

'You certainly behave like one.' Harriet studied her son in silence for a moment and then her expression suddenly softened. 'Are you doing anything this evening?' she asked, unexpectedly. 'I wondered if you might like to come round for dinner.'

'Regretfully, I'm busy,' said Jonathan.

'No matter.'

The telephone rang. Harriet answered it and began what appeared to be a lengthy conversation, but Jonathan was too well trained to leave without her dismissal. His mother had her faults but he could not help admiring her. Not for the first time he wondered what kind of woman Harriet would have been if his father had lived. John Lindstrom, by all accounts, had been a pleasant, easy-going man, and it was hard to imagine that he would have been a match for Harriet in the long term. So, whether his father had lived or died, it was likely that Harriet would have been the dominant figure in his life. Oddly though, he had never missed having a father. He had never felt the need for one – in fact he positively disliked the idea. His mother more than fulfilled the role of both parents – trying to lead a life independent of her strong will was difficult enough, without the intervention of yet another influence. He felt the same about siblings – an unnecessary encumbrance.

Harriet replaced the receiver and looked at her son enquiringly. 'You clearly think I should go to London or you wouldn't have suggested it?' he asked.

'Yes, I do, on balance. I think it would be a good opportunity for you, and a chance to get away from me.' There was a twinkle in her eyes.

'Good Lord, Mother, you're surely not suggesting I need to do that?'

He was teasing her but she took his words seriously. 'Not in a personal sense, no, but commercially I think it would be a good idea.

It is the only way we'll see just how good a banker you really are, without my guiding hand.'

'Jesus,' said Jonathan, 'I don't believe what I'm hearing.'

Harriet was not amused. 'It's time you took some responsibility,' she snapped. 'You need to do a lot of growing up if you're ever to run this bank.'

'How can I?' said Jonathan, peevishly. 'Normally when I try to take any responsibility, you slap me down.'

'I can't agree with that,' said Harriet. 'But even if you're right, then this is just the opportunity you need – you'll learn a great deal. Edward Deckman's a good man, sound and loyal. He has made the last years possible for me.'

'So you've told me many times,' said Jonathan. 'And I agree he is an excellent bank clerk.'

Harriet's eyes blazed. 'I won't have you speak of Edward like that. He has a great deal of talent and you would do well to learn from him – you couldn't have a better teacher.'

'If I didn't know you better, Mother, I might think you had a kind of soft spot for Edward. Perhaps that's why you haven't married all these years.'

'I don't find that very funny, Jonathan.' The mask was down, the easy mother and son rapport of a moment before was gone.

'OK, sorry.' He stood up. 'I'll see you later.'

Jonathan wondered if he had touched a nerve as he left the room. Harriet usually enjoyed being teased by him. He couldn't imagine his mother having the slightest interest in Edward Deckman, who was by all accounts safely and boringly married, and had been for many years. Still, women were strange creatures and he supposed that somewhere, deep down, his mother was a woman in an emotional sense, though heaven knows it was hard to believe.

It was after three in the morning by the time Jonathan managed to extricate himself from Pam's bed. He dressed hurriedly, afraid of waking her, of seeing those sad, reproachful eyes asking him for things he could not give. It was a balmy night and he drove slowly with the windows open, dawdling at traffic lights, much to the irritation of other drivers. He was in no hurry to get home and nor was he tired – just restless like the City itself, he thought. Making love to Pam that night had bored him, he realized. Indeed it had been boring him for weeks, months perhaps. An affair with your secretary was so irritatingly predictable, yet it always happened. He could not remember employing a secretary whom he had not taken to bed, for he only hired girls he found physically attractive and he never had the slightest difficulty in persuading them to extend their relationship beyond the office door. At the thought, he suddenly realized how much his current way of life wearied him – the same parties, the same people, the same restaurants, the same summer trips. He was growing stale and tonight had really proved it. He had never before made love to a woman while thinking about something else entirely. So London it was to be, a change of scene, a change of pace, a change of women – it had to be right.

CHAPTER TWO
London – June 1980

Ever since 1837, when young Alexander Gerrard had inherited the bank from his father, luncheon had been served in the boardroom at one o'clock precisely. Even by City of London standards, the meal was a lavish affair and an invitation to join the directors was much sought after by customers and fellow bankers alike. When it was announced that Gerrards had been bought by Lindstrom's Bank of New York, there was considerably more interest expressed in the future of Gerrards' luncheons than in the price of their shares. On his arrival in London, it did not take Edward Deckman more than twenty-four hours to recognize that if he was ever to be accepted in the City, he could not be the man to disturb such an important tradition. So the luncheons continued in the oak-panelled room, which sported an enormous refectory table of highly polished walnut, silver candelabras, Crown Derby tableware, white damask table napkins, Waterford glass crystal and a menu in the best traditions of English cuisine. Every day at half past twelve, the directors and a few selected guests met in the little ante-room for drinks and then, loosening their belts, went on to tackle a truly splendid meal.

By the end of Jonathan's fourth week in England, he was heartily sick of London, of his job, of Edward Deckman and, above all, of the interminable luncheons. He stood now, gin and tonic in hand, half listening to an unspeakably tedious accountant regaling him with the wonders of the Government Guaranteed Loan Scheme. If these luncheons did not stop, he really would have a weight problem, he thought – that is, if he did not die of boredom first. He glanced across the room at Edward Deckman – a small dapper man with not an ounce of extra flesh on him. How the hell did he do it? He was talking animatedly to fellow banker, Benjamin Crossman. Crossman's was an American bank of similar size to Lindstrom's, and was also extending its operation into Europe. Jonathan had known the Crossman family since childhood. He knew he should be taking an interest in the conversation but Benjamin Crossman was a garrulous old man with nothing new to say.

Eventually they all filed into lunch, Jonathan already regretting the third gin and tonic – it was going to make it extremely difficult to stay awake during the afternoon. He sat down at his place and glanced at the menu card in front of him – watercress soup or smoked mackerel, gammon or roast beef, a selection of sweets, which he knew to his cost were delicious, followed by cheese and port – it was ludicrous.

The kitchen door swung open, releasing a wonderful combination of aromas. Jonathan glanced up casually and then with a sudden quickening of interest. The comfortable, middle-aged woman who usually served lunch had been replaced. The girl was tall and slim, with red-gold hair, and that perfect peachy complexion which belongs exclusively to the English. Her voice, when she spoke, was high and clear like cut glass. 'Now, gentlemen,' she said, blushing furiously. 'If you have studied the menu, perhaps you would like to give me your orders.' Jonathan smiled with pleasure. Her good looks coupled with her obvious discomfort and embarrassment were quite charming. Used to New York women who never seemed to know a moment's confusion, he found the girl's gaucheness oddly attractive.

The meal progressed. Conversation flowed after a fashion, on the usual subjects, but for once Jonathan did not mind. The girl, whoever she was, continued to fascinate him. She was dressed conventionally in a silk shirt and plain, tailored skirt, a rope of pearls around her neck. Her glorious hair was caught into a French plait, from which it kept escaping. Her pale skin became increasingly flushed as she dashed about the room and Jonathan felt an almost overwhelming desire to help her. For some reason she inspired a degree of gallantry in him which was entirely out of character. He tried to gauge her age – twenty-one or two, at the most, he supposed, judging by the firm chin line and perfect skin. With her air of innocence, she could even be a virgin.

When at last the meal ground to its inevitable halt, he appeared to leave with the others, but slowing his pace in the corridor, he doubled back to the boardroom, to find the girl already clearing the plates. 'That was a great meal,' he said, enthusiastically.

She looked up and smiled, gratefully. 'I'm glad you liked it.'

'You served it beautifully. Did you help cook it, too?'

'I did cook it,' said the girl.

'Wow . . .' Jonathan was truly impressed. 'How come I've never seen you before? I have to say our normal waitress in no way possesses your charms.'

14

The smile left her face. 'I assume you're referring to Barbara. She's off sick, which is why I had to serve the meal myself.' The blushing again. 'It also means I have to do the washing-up, so if you'll excuse me I must get on with it.'

'Can I help you?' suggested Jonathan.

'Of course not,' the girl said. 'You get back to your wheeling and dealing or whatever it is you do.'

The need to establish his position suddenly seemed very important to Jonathan. He wanted to impress the girl, needed to see the look of admiration on her face, which was how he had come to expect most women to react to him.

'I guess I can wash up if I please,' he said. 'It's pretty much up to me what I do, since I more or less own the bank.'

'Really,' she said, not pausing in her clearing and stacking of the plates.

'That's right.' Jonathan hesitated, sensing he was not making the impact he had expected. 'My name's Jonathan Lindstrom. My mother, Harriet, owns the bank, but for a few shares. It will be all mine one day and when it is I shall certainly insist upon your serving lunch every day, rather than your assistant.'

'Then I'm afraid you'll be disappointed,' said the girl, with sudden spirit. 'I hate waiting at table and having to be nice to customers, particularly when they've drunk too much. The cooking's fine, I enjoy that, so long as I can keep out of sight.'

'A girl like you is not meant to be kept out of sight,' Jonathan said, aware that he sounded banal in the extreme. The girl was starting to bug him. She wasn't responding at all how he had expected.

He opened the door to enable her to push the trolley through into the kitchen and then followed her. She stopped half-way across the room and turned to face him. 'It's been very interesting talking to you, Mr. Lindstrom, but the kitchen is my domain, even if you do own it, and I like working alone.'

Her hostility surprised him. 'OK, OK, I'm going but at least you might tell me your name – after all you know mine.'

'Prue,' she said, 'Prue Mansell.'

'Then how do you do, Prue Mansell.' Jonathan held out his hand and briefly Prue shook it. She had a surprisingly strong grip – the skin cool and smooth. Hell, he was not going to be ordered out of the kitchen like some office boy. He propped himself against the dresser, clearly indicating that he had no intention of leaving. 'I wonder if you'd do me a favour, Prue?' he said.

15

'I don't see any reason why I should,' was her uncompromising reply. She turned from him and began stacking the plates next to the sink.

'Will you have dinner with me tonight?'

'No,' she replied.

'Because you don't like me or because you have another engagement?'

Prue glanced up. 'It's not a question of liking or disliking. I don't know you and I never go out to dinner with men I don't know.'

'Then you're not doing anything tonight?' Jonathan said, triumphantly. Prue did not reply. 'Look, I've only been in town a few weeks and I'm lonely as hell. I know no one – the high spot of my social calendar so far has been dinner with Edward Deckman and his wife, and I could really use some inspiring company. Hell, it's no big deal. Put yourself in my position – supposing the situation was reversed and you found yourself in New York, knowing no one – I'd like to bet you'd accept my invitation to dinner in those circumstances.'

Prue stopped stacking and looked at him with a slight smile. 'You chose to come to London. Perhaps your loneliness is divine retribution for forcing the sale of one of the country's oldest banks. I strongly disapprove of Gerrards being bought by Americans – the bank stood for everything that was British.'

'And still does,' said Jonathan. 'We've changed nothing, even your luncheons – even if they are expensive and time-consuming.'

'And good for business. Still, I suppose I should be grateful you appreciate them or I would be out of a job.'

'I promise you won't be,' said Jonathan. 'Especially if you come out to dinner with me.'

'That sounds like bribery.'

'Christ, you're so prickly – it was a joke, right? Your job's secure. Edward and I discussed it and the luncheons stay, we recognize their importance.' In fact Jonathan had been greatly opposed to them and the argument with Edward continued unabated. For the moment, however, he chose to forget his opposition. 'You British are all the same – you take everything so seriously. I'm simply asking you out because I could use some company, some charming, intelligent company. This is not a pathetic attempt at seduction, nor indeed am I trying to pull rank as your boss. I'd just like to spend the evening with you. Is that so terrible?'

'No,' said Prue, 'I suppose not.'

16

'Then will you come?'

'All right,' she said, her reply surprising them both.

They dined in Covent Garden at an excellent French restaurant. Prue was hungry, having eaten nothing all day, but all Jonathan could do was pick at his meal, having done full justice to his lunch.

'Your career must spoil restaurants for you.'

'On the contrary,' said Prue. 'I can never eat anything I've cooked – besides which, it gives me the opportunity for a little industrial espionage. I've had no formal training, you see, so I'm always on the look-out for new tricks.'

'Taught to cook at your mother's knee,' said Jonathan. 'No better way.'

Prue laughed. 'You have to be joking. Mother can't cook to save her life. Meals at home are unspeakably dreadful – in fact, everything the poor old dear turns her hand to domestically is a disaster. She gardens for hours, in all weathers, and still the plants die, or at best look a mess. Who knows, perhaps that's what inspired me to embark on a career in catering, to try to prove I'm not similarly afflicted.'

It was difficult for Jonathan to gauge what sort of impression he was making upon Prue as the meal progressed. She was polite, apparently interested in what he was doing but really rather shy and not at all forthcoming. In many respects the past month had been something of an eye-opener to Jonathan. In New York, he had always taken for granted his established position as one of the most eligible men in town, and despite the evidence to the contrary, he could not believe that here in London he was not having the same impact. Travelling daily between the bank and his flat in the Barbican was his only contact with people outside the bank staff. He had never even visited Europe before. His mother had always been too busy working to take holidays, and so it was not entirely surprising that he found everything about London and the British strange. His rarefied Manhattan lifestyle had simply not prepared him for it, and this girl's reaction to him only added to his sense of disorientation. As he paid the bill, he glanced at Prue and asked, with none of his usual self-assurance, 'Would you care to come back to my place for coffee, or a drink?'

Prue shook her head. 'I have a meal for twenty-five to prepare for tomorrow and no Barbara, remember.'

'Great,' he said. 'So we'll be seeing you in the boardroom again tomorrow.'

She ignored him. 'There's meat to marinade, pâté to make and I

17

haven't even started on the puddings. I shouldn't have had dinner with you, really.'

Jonathan was appalled. 'You aren't going to start work now? It's nearly midnight.'

'It's now or first thing in the morning and I work better at night,' said Prue.

'Then an extra half hour won't make any difference.'

'Where do you live?' Prue asked, displaying cautious curiosity in him for the first time that evening.

'In the Barbican. It's not a great apartment, at least not by Manhattan standards, but I guess it suits my bachelor existence.'

'Then it's out of the question for me to join you for coffee. I live in Chelsea. It would take us at least half an hour just to drive from your flat to mine.'

'I could come back to your place,' Jonathan suggested.

'You could if you were invited,' said Prue, with a sweet smile.

Jonathan watched the lights of the departing taxi, feeling more disconcerted than ever. His emotions were mixed – on the one hand if the bitch wasn't interested in him then why waste time and money? At the same time the challenge was irresistible – he wanted to break down that cool reserve. He could not explain his feelings nor understand the need to reach her. He did not recognize that his self-image was in jeopardy for the first time, and that making it with Prue Mansell was the way to prove he had not lost his touch. Yes, he would have her, however long it took.

CHAPTER THREE

The alarm clock sounded unacceptably loud through the thin wall which divided Prue's bedroom from Richard's. She snapped on the bedside light, assuming the alarm was hers, then seeing the time and realizing her mistake, she groaned and put her head under the pillow. The ringing persisted. She sat up and pounded on the wall. 'Richard, for God's sake turn off that bloody alarm.'

'Sorry,' came Richard's muffled reply.

Prue sank back onto the pillows. Half past five . . . she had only been in bed for two hours. Everything ached, her eyes were gritty and she was only too aware of how much champagne she had been drinking all night. Damn Richard.

In fairness, as lodgers went, Richard was ideal in all respects except the time at which he chose to get up. As a photographer, his day was governed by the light, whereas Prue preferred to work at night. She had bought the flat a year ago. In his will, her grandfather had left her a sum of money which she had inherited on her twenty-first birthday. After searching London for a suitable property to house both home and business, she had finally settled on this basement flat in Chelsea Manor Street. Though not particularly stylish, it was roomy and central, but the only way she could meet her outgoings was to take a tenant.

There was a tentative knock on her bedroom door. 'Yes,' she said, wearily.

'I've made you some coffee as a peace-offering. Can I come in?' Richard appeared in the doorway, filling it completely. Tall and broad, with a mop of thick brown hair which always fell into his eyes, this morning he looked even more chaotic than usual. 'Hi,' he said, with forced cheerfulness. 'Here you are, this will sort you out.' Coffee slopped over the side of the mug as he crashed it down onto Prue's bedside table. He collapsed onto the bed and the springs groaned as Prue shifted hurriedly to avoid being crushed. 'Did you have a good time last night?'

'Last night and most of this morning,' Prue corrected. 'No, not

19

particularly. Jonathan didn't really enjoy it much. In fact I don't think he enjoyed it at all.'

Richard eyed her speculatively over the top of his mug. 'Tell me to mind my own business, but is this thing serious between you and Jonathan?'

Prue sat up in bed and reached for her coffee, trying to ignore the drips which fell on the duvet cover. 'No, not at the moment,' she said carefully. 'I don't really know why I invited him last night and no, there's certainly nothing going on between us.'

'Do you wish there was?' Richard asked.

Prue looked up at him sharply. His open, friendly face, suntanned and freckled like a little boy, was wrinkled with apparent concern. 'Why do you ask, Richard, don't you like him?' she asked, aware that she was avoiding the question.

'Not especially,' Richard admitted. 'I realize I'm not being fair because I don't really know him but he doesn't seem your sort, somehow.'

'You mean I'm so suburban and he's so . . . so transatlantic?' Prue suggested, seriously.

Richard grinned. 'Something like that. I don't know, maybe I've got him all wrong but he seems to me a sort of stereotype of how a successful New York banker should be. He looks good and says all the right things but there doesn't seem much warmth, or depth, to him . . . Sorry, tell me to mind my own business.'

'Mind your own business,' said Prue, cheerfully.

There was an amicable silence between them. 'Why didn't he enjoy last night?' Richard persisted, after a while.

'I don't know exactly – I had thought it would rather appeal to him. It was a charity ball at Grosvenor House. Prince Charles and Lady Diana were there, with half the world's press and most of the titles in the land. I'd fondly imagined it was just the sort of occasion an American would enjoy.'

Richard grinned. 'Your friend Jonathan has just gone up in my estimation, if he didn't enjoy that sort of bash. It's certainly not my scene.'

Prue laughed. 'To be honest, I think he found it all rather juvenile.'

'I'm not surprised,' said Richard. 'All those Hooray Henrys spraying champagne, throwing bread rolls and playing silly games. I'm starting to like the guy more and more.'

'He really couldn't stand the men and their silly games,' Prue admitted. 'But he wasn't too keen on the girls either. Apparently we

20

don't compare very favourably with New York women, who manage to be both good-looking and clever. He says English women are empty-headed, overweight and plain.'

'I hope he's not including you in that sweeping statement,' said Richard.

Prue sighed. 'I rather think he might be. He certainly makes me feel stupid. I keep saying the wrong thing and putting my foot in it. The trouble is he does know so much more about everything than I do.'

'Rubbish – it sounds as though he's doing you no good at all. You're developing a first-class complex. When's the bastard going back to New York?'

'I don't know,' said Prue. 'That's the other thing. I can't understand what he sees in me and I also can't understand why he stays in England. He doesn't seem to have any friends apart from me, he clearly doesn't think much of the country and it would appear he isn't even enjoying his job much.'

Richard nodded sagely. 'Then you watch your step, my girl. The last thing you must do is let yourself become involved in a heavy relationship if he's likely to up sticks and return to New York at any moment.' He glanced at her clock. 'Hell, is that the time?' He stood up, towering over her. 'I must fly, see you tonight. Will you be in for supper?'

'No, Jonathan's taking me out to dinner.'

'OK,' said Richard, 'have fun and remember what I said.'

Richard's words were very much in Prue's mind, as she lay in the bath that evening. This was to be her fourth date with Jonathan Lindstrom and so far, apart from a goodnight peck on the cheek, he had not touched her. It was the way Prue wanted things to stay, or so she tried to tell herself. She had reached the age of twenty-two with very little real experience of men. There had been the odd relationship but none of them were serious. After a May Ball at Oxford, she had been relieved of the burden of her virginity by a hesitant undergraduate who, to her relief, she had never met again after their single night of questionable passion, in sleazy digs off the Cowley Road. The terror that she might be pregnant that followed had put her off men for some time and it was easy to drift from one meaningless relationship to another in the circle in which she moved. Jonathan was different. He was considerably older and more experienced than any man she had been out with before, and he came from

21

a very different world from her own. These factors combined to make her feel she was not fully in charge of the relationship and it unnerved her.

The door bell ringing snapped her out of her muse. She jumped out of the bath, her hair wet, wrapped herself in a towel and went to answer the door, expecting it to be Richard, who made a habit of forgetting his key. Jonathan stood in the doorway, his arms full of parcels. Instantly Prue was aware of what a mess she must look – all hot and blotchy from the bath, her mascara running, her hair hanging in wet rats' tails. 'You're early,' she accused him.

'I know,' he said with a devastating smile. 'Are you going to let me in? You look great, by the way. I love you in that towel.'

Prue was not to be placated. 'I'm not ready to go out yet,' she said firmly.

'Hell, Prue, are you really going to stand there until my arms fall out of their sockets. I'm early because we're not going out tonight, I've brought dinner to you instead, and if you don't let me in right now, I shall drop the lot.' She stepped aside as he staggered through the door and into the kitchen. She followed, reluctantly. Jonathan deposited the carrier bags on the kitchen table. 'I bought dinner in because I guessed you might be kind of tired after last night. I hope it's OK. I went to the deli and found some melon, Parma ham, pâté, cheese, French bread, a bottle of champagne and a bottle of red wine. Will that do you, madam?'

'Lovely,' Prue said, disarmed by his thoughtfulness. 'I'll just go and get dressed.'

'You don't have to.'

'I do,' said Prue and rushed out of the kitchen.

In the privacy of her bedroom, Prue vigorously towel-dried her hair and put on jeans and a T-shirt. She stared at her reflection in the mirror as she reached for her make-up bag. Instinctively she felt that Jonathan was trying to orchestrate a change in their relationship. Dinner in her flat suggested a greater degree of intimacy than before – still, Richard would be home soon, and such was the confusion in her mind that she did not know whether she would be relieved or sorry to have his reassuring presence.

When she entered the kitchen Jonathan had made himself very much at home, having found a tray and carefully laid out the food and wine he had bought. 'It's great news about Richard, isn't it?' he said.

'What do you mean?' Prue asked.

'That he's not coming home tonight.' Jonathan grinned roguishly.

'How do you know he's not coming home?' Prue asked, alarmed.

'There's a note on the hall table. Didn't you see it?' She shook her head. Jonathan picked up a scrap of paper. ' "Weekend job has come up in Leeds. Never say mine is not a life of glamour. See you Monday. Richard." So, that means we have the whole weekend to ourselves. Come on, let's take this lot through to the living room.'

Half an hour later, the bottle of champagne drunk, they were both relaxed and Prue was beginning to enjoy herself. 'This is one hell of a lot better than last night,' Jonathan said.

Prue's growing good humour evaporated. 'I'm sorry, I wouldn't have asked you to the ball if I had thought you wouldn't enjoy it, but it occurred to me that it might be something which would amuse an American.'

Jonathan smiled. 'I guess it did, briefly, but your friends . . . Jesus, Prue, they're so, well, goddamned infantile.'

Prue was hurt. She turned away and busied herself slicing a piece of cheese so that he would not see the expression on her face. 'They're nice people, kind, they wouldn't hurt anyone and they're always around when you need them.'

Jonathan shrugged. 'Maybe, but they don't seem to have much between the ears. I guess that's the difference between our two countries – the elite, the aristocracy if you like, of New York society are the people with brains. They have brains, therefore they have money, therefore they're top of the heap. Here it's a question of inheritance and, well, I guess most of them are not too smart, I'm sure you'll agree. Perhaps your aristocracy is too interbred – some of them are really nuts – the men don't seem happy unless they're throwing stuff about and the women bray like donkeys. God, I don't know how you can stand it.'

Prue found herself laughing. 'I shouldn't agree with you,' she said.'But I suppose I do know what you mean.'

'I'm very glad to hear it. From what I understand most of them don't even work. Jesus, I thought I'd lived a privileged and sheltered life but I guess in many respects, compared with your young lords, ladies, dukes and duchesses, I've had it tough.' He reached out suddenly and took her hand. 'Seriously, Prue, why do you mix with those people?'

Prue sobered. 'I don't know, I suppose it's because I always have.'

'You know what I can't bear to contemplate?' said Jonathan. Prue shook her head. 'Your marrying one of those guys and having pink champagne sprayed all over you morning, noon and night.' Prue began to laugh. 'Hell, I'm serious, Prue, you're worth a lot more.' There was sincerity in his eyes and Prue's heart flipped.

There was silence between them for a moment, then Prue, ferociously embarrassed, hurried on. 'You haven't seen anything yet,' she said. 'You should see them in the country, at shooting parties, at the races . . . It's just the same except usually it's cold and raining as well.'

'There you are,' said Jonathan triumphantly. 'You're starting to see things my way. I just don't want you throwing yourself away on one of those buffoons, I care about you too much, I really do.' He patted the hand he still held. 'Now, eat up, I didn't stagger through the streets of London with this lot to have you rejecting it.' He frowned, suddenly. 'Something occurred to me last night, after I left you. You're not a lady or a duchess or something, are you? I never thought to ask.'

Prue laughed. 'No, though my father is a knight.'

'I knew it. Then you're a lady.'

'No,' said Prue, 'I don't have a title. My mother's a Lady, my father's a Sir but it's rather sad – the title will die with my father as he has no son or brother who can inherit. I'm their only child.'

'So, we're both only children,' said Jonathan, 'I wonder if that's significant.' He leaned forward and kissed Prue, swiftly and gently on the lips, then he drew away a little and stared at her. 'You know something, Prue, you're the first woman in a long time who's really interested me. I've been very rude about your friends, I guess, and really mine are no better. New York women are so hard and ruthless. Everything they do is motivated by what they can get out of a situation. You're so generous and kind – a caring person who's not on the make all the time. It's very relaxing.'

'You make me sound unbelievably boring,' said Prue, embarrassed by Jonathan's sudden outpouring.

'I don't mean to. What I'm trying to say is that I think we could have quite a future together.' He kissed her again, pulling her closer to him.

For a moment she gave herself into his arms, returning his kiss, then she forced herself away from him. 'I don't think this is a good idea,' she said, her voice trembling. 'You won't be in England long. I can tell you don't really enjoy it here and you don't seem very happy in your job. I'd like to be your friend, Jonathan, but that's all.'

24

'Who says I'm not staying in England long?' he replied, quietly. 'It all depends upon what, or who, keeps me here.'

They spent the weekend together, leaving the flat only once on Sunday morning, to walk in the park and collect the papers. The rest of the time they spent in Prue's bed, talking, laughing and making love. For Prue, who had never before shared such intimacy, the weekend held a magical quality. She could not believe that this handsome, sophisticated man was apparently so happy to be with her, and nor could she recognize herself in the girl who submitted to Jonathan so eagerly and without embarrassment, blossoming in response to his skilled lovemaking.

The weekend changed them both. By Monday morning Jonathan felt a great deal better. Life was back on an even keel. The seduction of Prue had proved easier than he had imagined and his ego was completely restored. His feelings for her surprised him – she was so open and generous, so warm and anxious to please. Normally, he would have found her kindness and generosity cloying but for some reason he found it oddly touching. Their affair would not last long, of course, but he had to admit that the relationship was refreshingly different. For Prue, too, things were very different – indeed her life would never be the same again, for by the end of the weekend, she was hopelessly and irrevocably in love with Jonathan Lindstrom.

CHAPTER FOUR

Monday morning began badly for Jonathan. The weekend of sex, after what for him had been a long abstinence, had made him tired and jaded. He had left Prue's flat very early, in order to go home for a shower and a change of clothes, and he was in no mood to hurry through the crowded streets to work. He was nearly an hour late, therefore, when he finally arrived at the bank. His secretary, Jean, met him at the door to his office, clearly agitated. 'Oh, there you are, Mr. Lindstrom. Mr. Deckman wants to see you urgently. He keeps telephoning and he seemed very angry when he heard you hadn't arrived.' She glanced nervously at the clock.

Jean Sinclair was an infuriating little woman, with tightly permed hair and a perpetually martyred expression. Jonathan was sure Edward Deckman had hand-picked her specially, knowing Jonathan's reputation with secretaries. 'Let him wait,' said Jonathan. 'Sometimes that guy really oversteps the mark.'

'I did promise I'd telephone him as soon as you arrived.'

'Go ahead then, but tell him I won't be free for half an hour.'

Moments later there was a tentative knocking on Jonathan's door. With exaggerated irritation, he lowered his *Financial Times* to see Jean hovering again. 'What is it and for Christ's sake come in if you have something to say.'

'It's Mr. Deckman, Mr. Lindstrom. He insists you see him now. He says . . .' she lowered her voice, 'if you're not in his office in five minutes, he'll be down here to talk to you, but he thinks you would rather hear what he has to say in private. He really is extremely cross.'

An uncomfortable feeling of disquiet pursued Jonathan through the corridors and in the ancient, creaking elevator which took him to the presidential suite on the fourth floor occupied by Edward Deckman. Angry at being summoned as though he was an office boy, and more particularly at his own nervousness, he strode through Edward's outer office, past a protesting secretary and marched straight into his room.

26

Edward looked up from some papers he was studying, his expression cold. Jonathan just had time to note how stupid a very small man looked behind such an enormous desk when Edward said, 'What the hell do you mean by charging into my office without knocking?'

'You wanted to see me so I'm here,' said Jonathan coldly. 'For some reason it doesn't seem to be a morning for affording much courtesy. I think my secretary told you I wasn't free for half an hour.'

'Sit,' said Edward.

'I'd rather stand,' said Jonathan.

'As you wish.' Edward rose and walked purposefully over to the window. He stared down at the traffic below for a moment and then turned to face Jonathan. 'I begged your mother not to give me this job but not because I wasn't grateful for the challenge it presents. I love England, she knows that – I was here during the War. She was offering me a plum job in my favourite capital city but I didn't want it.'

'Edward, if you have something to say, please say it,' said Jonathan, affecting boredom.

'I'm coming to it,' said Edward. 'The reason I didn't want this job was because I didn't want to work with you. Your mother knows you'll never make a banker but she can't accept it and I guess by sending us both here she was hoping for miracles.'

Jonathan was stunned. He knew there was no love lost between him and Edward but he had not expected such an outburst. He recovered as best he could.

'I would like to remind you that it's not a question of making me a banker, I am a banker.'

'Never,' said Edward.

'Look,' said Jonathan, 'I know you don't like me, I know you never have, but I'm busy right now. If you want to vent your spleen on someone, why not go home and take it out on Mrs. Deckman?'

'Mail Sale called in receivers this morning,' Edward said.

For a moment Jonathan could think of nothing to say; the shock was total. 'Mail Sale? Are you sure?'

'Of course I'm sure,' said Edward, wearily. 'That's five million pounds down the pan, Jonathan. Five million, and when did we sign up the deal – two weeks ago? What kind of idiots do you imagine that makes us look in the City? I've already spoken to the guy in charge of the winding up and he just can't believe it. He just can't

27

believe that bankers of our reputation could have made such a crass mistake. How come? How come we did, Jonathan?'

'I don't understand,' said Jonathan. 'They seemed sound enough.'

'Seemed sound enough.'

'They made a profit last year – I saw their balance sheet.'

'You should have looked one hell of a lot closer at that balance sheet. They didn't make a trading profit, they just acquired a massive increase in stock. Mail order is a notoriously volatile business – you should have gone through the company with a fine-tooth comb if you wanted to offer any backing. Personally, though, I'd never touch that type of business.'

'But then you're not in charge of the venture capital fund, are you?'

'No, and more's the pity. We're going to be a laughing stock. I dread to think what the papers will say tomorrow. Five million pounds and it wasn't enough to save the company. Jesus, Jonathan, a kid in diapers could have worked out it was a foolish investment.'

'As you are well aware,' said Jonathan, 'Mail Sale is just one of a number of investments I've made on the bank's behalf. Enterprise funding is a risky business – you win some, you lose some. There is an element of luck involved, there has to be.'

'This wasn't bad luck, this was crazy. As it happens, I spent all of Sunday in the office, going through your portfolio of investments, and I don't understand it. I can't figure what makes you tick. How do you rate a business worthy of investment, Jonathan? What's the criterion you use – ensuring that at least one member of the management team is worth getting your leg over?'

'How dare you speak to me like this!' Jonathan said. 'I'm well aware of why I was sent over to England even though you are clearly not. My mother knew you simply do not have the imagination or guts to be able to invest in British industry with any degree of flair. I know you're looking for ways to trip me up but I simply won't have it. You're out of your league, Deckman. You shouldn't be running this branch, you should be putting your feet up. Why you ever made it beyond bank clerk I'll never know, but it seems now your lack of talent is being joined by the onset of senility. You might at least do my mother the favour of bowing out gracefully.'

Jonathan had expected a heated exchange but he was disappointed. Edward Deckman returned to his desk, sat down heavily and briefly closed his eyes as if in pain. Then he raised his head and looked straight at Jonathan, his gaze unflinching. 'You're fired,' he said.

'What!' Jonathan thundered.

'You heard me. You're fired. You're to clear your desk and be out of here within the hour.'

'Don't be ridiculous,' said Jonathan. 'You can't fire me.'

'I just have.'

'I own this bank.'

'Not yet, you don't. You're a minority shareholder and a pompous, ignorant little jerk. Now get out of my sight.'

Jean Sinclair had used Jonathan's absence to retouch her make-up. It was a pointless exercise, her sallow complexion was not improved by the beige foundation cream she used, and what colour there was in her skin was drained by the over-red lipstick and pea-cock-blue eye shadow she used, regardless of what she was wearing. She was just applying mascara to short, stubby eyelashes already clogged with too much when Jonathan burst through the door, his face white with fury. For a moment she thought she might be the object of his anger for not being at her desk, but he headed straight for his office. 'Book me the next flight to New York,' he shouted. 'And call Mother's secretary and arrange an appointment for me to see my mother just as soon as I get in. Tell her it's urgent.' His office door slammed, and with a trembling hand Jean reached for the telephone. All the girls were very envious of her job working for handsome Mr. Lindstrom, but she hated it, and him.

Harriet Lindstrom could not remember the last time she had felt nervous. She assumed it must have been some time before John died. Since then the struggle – first to survive, then to build on that survival and finally to capitalize upon it – had toughened her. She had been such a silly girl, so frivolous, so naive. When she thought about her youth she almost blushed with embarrassment at the memory of the young woman she had once been. She glanced at her watch; it was five to twelve. Jonathan was due any moment. On impulse, she went to the drinks cabinet, kept purely for visiting customers, and poured herself a brandy. Equally, she could not remember the last time she had drunk at lunchtime. There was a knock and Tessa, who had been with her for so many years both as friend and secretary, put her head round the door. Harriet had not confided in Tessa. She did not need to – the eyes that met hers were full of compassion and understanding.

'Mr. Jonathan's here,' Tessa said. Then noting the brandy glass still in Harriet's hand, she added, 'Shall I ask him to wait a moment?'

'Yes, please,' said Harriet. 'Give me five minutes would you, Tessa.'

Always tidy and meticulous in everything she did, Harriet went into her private bathroom, washed the brandy glass and returned it to the drinks cabinet. Then she went back to the bathroom and studied her reflection in the mirror – a tired, strained old woman stared back at her. Where had she gone wrong? She sought an answer from her reflection but none came. She loved Jonathan passionately but she was not blind to his faults. He was not bad but weak, vain and full of self-deception, yet how could he have made such an idiot of himself in England, and so quickly? Edward's call the previous night had shocked her, not only because of the stupidity of her son's actions but Edward's reaction to them. He had always been a mild man, and dismissing Jonathan so abruptly was out of character. 'If you want me to resign, Harriet, I will, of course,' Edward had said. 'I went too far, I realize that, but he goaded me into it. It's what he wanted me to do. He'll never be happy until I'm out of the bank.' It was all such a mess.

Harriet heard the click of her office door, turned abruptly and went to greet her son. At once she noticed that Jonathan looked extremely tired, and in need of a shave. Normally fastidious to the point of obsessiveness when it came to his appearance, she found his slightly dishevelled look rather appealing. It made him vulnerable. She fought her feelings and offered a cool cheek to be kissed.

'Deckman's called you I suppose,' said Jonathan, throwing himself into a chair.

'Yes, of course,' said Harriet.

'The man's a fool, I've always told you that.'

'Edward Deckman is no fool,' said Harriet. 'And if we are to have a discussion at all you must understand that hurling abuse at Edward Deckman is not going to solve anything.'

'He hauled me into his office like I was some little clerk wet behind the ears, and all because one of our investments had gone wrong! What does he expect with venture capital? He was quite happy to ignore all the sound investments I have made.'

'If I understand it,' said Harriet, dryly, 'there are precious few of those.'

'That's what he would say, isn't it? I don't know what his game is exactly, but he certainly wants me out of the way. You should watch that man, Mother, he's dangerous.'

'He is not,' said Harriet. 'It's you who's dangerous, Jonathan.'

Her words surprised him so much that he was silent for a moment. Then he rose abruptly and began striding about the room. 'Are you saying you're on his side over all this?'

'I'm on the bank's side,' said Harriet. 'That's my job. The fact is you have behaved irresponsibly with the venture capital fund, and almost worse than that, made us look a laughing stock in the City of London, just at a time when we are trying to build a reputation. We could spend a fortune on public relations right now and it would not undo the harm that you have done by that foolish investment in Mail Sale. How can we possibly expect to attract large British investors, if they know we are prepared to squander their money on such foolish investments as Mail Sale?'

'Mother, Mother,' said Jonathan. 'For Christ's sake keep a sense of proportion. We are only talking about five million pounds, ten million bucks. It's nothing, a fleabite.'

'It is not a fleabite,' Harriet thundered. 'It's a very large sum of money, and you've lost it – you've lost it just two weeks after investing it. How can I ever hand this bank over to you if you seriously believe that ten million dollars is meaningless? We must have a sense of responsibility as bankers. We're custodians of other people's money – money that they have worked hard to acquire. It is our job to safeguard that money and make it work for them, not squander it on worthless investments.'

'Spare me the lecture, Mother. We're in banking to make money for ourselves, just like every other man in the street, and we don't do that by sitting on our butt playing house, like Edward Deckman. Jesus, you've taken some gambles in your time, I know that. This whole venture in England is a gamble.'

'With increasingly lengthening odds, thanks to you,' said Harriet.

'Are you trying to tell me that you're not going to dismiss Edward Deckman?'

Harriet looked at her son with genuine surprise. 'Did you seriously think I would?'

'Yes, I did. I'm a shareholder in the bank and the bank is going to be mine one day. How dare he try and sack me?'

'He didn't try and sack you, Jonathan, he did sack you.'

Jonathan stopped pacing and stared at his mother. 'You mean you're backing his decision?'

'No,' said Harriet. 'I've made the point to Edward that the bank's future is dependent upon my having somebody to hand over to and for that reason we have to give you another chance. I have therefore persuaded him to take you back.'

'Big deal,' said Jonathan, childishly.

'There is a condition though,' said Harriet. 'You will not be returning as manager of the venture capital fund but as Edward's personal assistant.'

'What!' Jonathan stared at his mother. 'You have to be joking! There's no way I'm doing that.'

'It's the only way open to you,' Harriet said. 'If you work directly under Edward's supervision for a few years and watch how he operates, it could just be that some of his skill rubs off on you.'

'I'm not working for him in those circumstances – you must be crazy to suggest it. There's no way I'm giving him the satisfaction of having me at his beck and call.'

'It won't be easy for him either,' said Harriet. 'He doesn't relish working with you any more than you do with him, but he is prepared to do it for the sake of the bank.'

'I bet the hell he is,' said Jonathan. 'He'd just love the opportunity to have me sharpening his pencils and making his coffee.'

'It's not quite what we have in mind, though if that's what needs doing at any given time, it won't do you any harm.'

'No, Mother,' said Jonathan. 'I'm not going back to England – I decided that on the flight over – it's a God-awful country, small and dirty, and the people are weird. Deckman can have it – I'll come back to my old job and give you a hand here.'

'It's filled,' said Harriet.

'What!'

'It's filled,' said Harriet. 'Your old job, we've replaced you.'

'Well kick him out, whoever he is, the Prodigal Son's returned.' Jonathan was jaunty again. The thought of taking up the threads of his former life in New York was suddenly very appealing.

'I don't think I'm making myself clear,' said Harriet. 'The only job that's available to you within the bank is that of Edward Deckman's assistant in London.'

'Is this some sort of joke?' said Jonathan.

'No joke,' said Harriet. 'I've carried you long enough. You're either going to have to pull yourself together and learn to be a banker, or you'd better find yourself another job. I've worked too damn hard building this bank to have you throw it all away.'

'You're as bad as he is,' said Jonathan. 'You want me out of the bank too, don't you?'

32

Harriet wearily shook her head. She was close to tears but she knew she must not let him see any sign of weakness. 'No, Jonathan, it's the last thing on earth I want, but the bank must come first. At the moment, for whatever reason, you are in no fit state to take any form of responsibility.'

'I don't believe this,' said Jonathan. 'My own mother!'

'There's no point in recriminations.'

'Like hell there is, Mother. I wonder what my father would think of this, of your humiliating me in this manner?'

'I've thought of that, too,' said Harriet, suddenly quiet.

'And?' Jonathan challenged.

'And I think he'd believe I was doing the right thing.'

'In which case,' said Jonathan, 'Lindstrom's Bank is being run by the last Lindstrom because there's no way I'll stay, under these circumstances. You'll just have to find someone else to run your precious bank for you, Mother, because it isn't going to be me.'

Although Harriet had expected him to be angry, she had not expected him to go this far. Despite his words, she saw him only as a petulant child stamping his foot. 'Don't be silly,' she said. 'There's a marvellous opportunity here for you, a golden future, if you just accept that if you are ever to run a. . .'

'Don't start preaching to me again,' said Jonathan. 'It's over, finished. I've played to your tune long enough. You can stuff your job, Mother, and your precious bank. I quit, as of now.'

'What will you do?' Harriet could not hide the desperation in her voice. She was no longer a bank president admonishing an erring member of staff – she was a mother losing her son, her only child.

'What's it to you?'

'I'm still your mother, Jonathan,' she said, quietly.

'I don't know,' he said. 'But I guess I'll have no problem finding a job, some place where I'll be more appreciated. I have my apartment, I have my. . .'

'Your apartment belongs to the bank, if you remember,' said Harriet.

'You mean you're going to throw me out of my apartment as well?'

'No, it's your decision to go, but you can't expect to live in bank property if you're not going to work for the bank.'

'Jesus! So now you're chucking me out of my home. OK, you've got what you want, Mother, you and your precious Edward Deckman. God knows what kind of hold he has over you, but whatever it is, it's clearly more important than your own son. To hell with you both! I don't need you, I don't need anyone.' He turned and strode out of the door, slamming it with such force that a picture hanging by the door crashed to the floor.

In the silence that followed, Harriet sat absolutely still. Then she began to shake and at last she put her head in her hands and wept. Not only had she lost her son, she had lost everything – the reason for working so hard and building the bank had been to have something to hand over to Jonathan. Somewhere deep inside her she had known for a long time that sooner or later this scene, or one very like it, would have to be played. It should have happened years ago, she thought, when he was younger, when there would have been more chance of him bouncing back, and of a reconciliation. He had been over-indulged all his life but the fault was hers, not his. Now he would have to make his own way in the real world and how had she equipped him to do so? She hadn't. In the eyes of everyone who knew them, it would seem that he had failed her, but Harriet knew it was nothing like the extent to which she had failed him.

CHAPTER FIVE

It began to rain and the dull, overcast sky perfectly suited Prue's mood. Clearly, he was not coming and to wait for him any longer would be unbearably embarrassing. She paid for the cocktail, only half drunk, wincing at the price, and once outside she felt a fleeting sense of relief at being freed from the burden of her humiliation. Ignoring the rain, she started out across the park towards the Serpentine. Prue had been due to meet Jonathan at the cocktail bar at five forty-five. It was now just after seven and not only had he not shown up, he had not even bothered to telephone. She hunched herself into her thin jacket for there was a chill dankness to the air, heralding the end of summer. The thought depressed her and she suddenly felt very weary. There was a bench beside the water ahead of her and she sank down on it gratefully. The soft rain continued to fall but it did not worry her, indeed she did not even notice it, for her mind was racing with unanswered questions.

To Prue, the weekend she had just spent with Jonathan had been magical. It had opened up a side of her nature she had not known existed, taken the lid off a well of love and warmth, which she had not even realized she had been waiting to share with someone special. Jonathan was that special person, or at least she thought he was, though perhaps she had misread the situation? Perhaps what for her had been the most wonderful experience of her life, for him had been commonplace, dull even. The thought appalled her – her life had been changed irrevocably by the experiences of the weekend. Perhaps he recognized her commitment to him and so had decided to end their relationship.

It had not surprised Prue to find that Jonathan was not with his fellow directors at lunch that day. The numbers for Lindstrom's luncheons could vary considerably at short notice and she supposed he must have become involved with a customer at the last moment. As her assistant, Barbara, was back at work, she had no cause to go into the dining room while the meal was being served and as everyone left after the meal, she was far too self-conscious to ask of Jonathan's whereabouts. It had also come as no surprise when Jonathan was late at the wine bar for she had already discovered that punctuality was not his strong point. However, as the minutes ticked by and she began to realize it was unlikely that he was going to come at all, she began to query the whole basis of their relationship, with a growing sense of unease. In a strange way, he was still such an enigma to her. He volunteered little or nothing about himself, so how could she judge what had prevented him from keeping their date? It was possible, of course, that he had been involved in an accident, but somehow Prue felt that Jonathan's sense of self-preservation was too developed to allow such a thing. She knew it was a ridiculous notion, but that was how she saw things at this moment, and as she became increasingly more miserable and unsure of herself, tears mixed with the rain began flowing down her cheeks.

She had no idea how long she sat there, but gradually it dawned on her that the infrequent passers-by were giving her strange looks and she began to feel cold as well as wet and bedraggled. Wearily, she got to her feet and began walking towards Knightsbridge. What on earth was she doing? She had never let anything get her into such a state as this before. She would go home, have a hot bath and a drink and pull herself together. Heavens, by now Jonathan might well be at the flat and wondering what on earth she had been doing. This thought sustained her during the long, damp walk home – all buses seeming to have completely disappeared off the face of the earth. It was almost dark by the time she arrived. She could see lights on in the flat window and her spirits lifted. Stupid, of course if he was running late, the sensible thing was to go direct to the flat. She unlocked the door and almost ran down the passageway into the kitchen.

Richard was standing over the electric kettle, looking tired and unshaven. 'Hello. Good grief, what on earth have you been doing? I thought I looked bad, you definitely look worse – a little drowned rat.'

'Thanks a lot,' said Prue. 'Is Jonathan around?'

'No. Should he be?' Her crestfallen expression brought a smile of sympathy from Richard. 'Hey, what's up, the man's not messing you about, is he?'

'No, no, I don't think so.' Tears were threatening again.

'Sounds to me like he is. God, you're wet. Look, I'll abandon this coffee. It seems to me what we both need is a whisky. Go and take off those clothes. I'll light the fire in the sitting room and we'll drown our sorrows.'

It was good to have someone to come home to, Prue thought, as she stripped off her soaking clothes. If only it had been Jonathan, though, not Richard waiting for her – Jonathan, with warm words and sympathy, and an apology.

Richard had poured a very generous tumbler of whisky, to which he added only the smallest splash of water. 'I could get horrendously drunk on this,' said Prue, with evident satisfaction.

'Excellent,' said Richard. 'Cheers – the toast is "don't let the buggers get you down" – right?'

'I agree,' said Prue. 'How was your weekend?'

'Gruesome in the extreme. Thousands of shots to take, mostly outside – on the moors, would you believe. The weather was stinking, the light dreadful, the models never stopped grumbling and the art director was as bent as a corkscrew and fancied me.'

'That should have made your job easier,' Prue said. 'Art directors are normally the thorn in your side, aren't they?'

'In this case, it certainly didn't make my job easier,' said Richard, 'I didn't dare turn my back on him, even for a second.'

They laughed together. 'You do me good,' said Prue.

'I'm sorry that you need someone to do you good. So what's been happening, to put you in this state? People don't wander around in the rain unless they're feeling extremely miserable, if not unhinged.'

'Oh it's nothing,' said Prue. 'It's just that I was due to meet Jonathan tonight, in a cocktail bar, and he didn't turn up. I expect he's been delayed with a customer.'

'What time were you due to meet him?'

'Five forty-five.'

Richard consulted his watch. 'And it's now eight-fifteen. He could have telephoned.'

'Don't rub it in,' said Prue. 'Maybe he tried to ring here before you got back. How long have you been home?'

Richard grimaced. 'Sorry, all afternoon, and there haven't been any calls.'

'Oh well.' Prue tossed back her whisky.

'Did you two have a good weekend?' Richard asked, shrewdly.

Prue blushed slightly. 'Yes,' she said, staring at her whisky glass.

'It must have been nice having me out of the way – very convenient I should think.'

37

His voice was gentle but Prue resented the intrusion. 'Mind your own business, Richard.'

'Sorry. Here, let me give you a top up.'

By ten o'clock they were both extremely drunk. Prue made scrambled eggs in an attempt to sober them up and it took Richard three attempts to make the toast without burning it, which at the time they found hilariously funny. Eventually they staggered off to their respective beds to sleep it off.

It was hardly surprising that the telephone ringing at half past four the following morning had little impact on Prue for several minutes. When finally she emerged from sleep and reached for the receiver, she knew immediately who it was.

'Prue, Prue, is that you?'

'Jonathan. Where are you?' Prue rubbed the sleep from her eyes, sat up in bed and switched on the light, squinting at its brightness.

'I'm at Kennedy. Look, can I come and stay?'

'Kennedy?' Prue did not understand him. 'Jonathan, we were supposed to meet this evening. What happened?'

'This evening?' He sounded confused. 'Were we?'

'Yes, I've been so worried. Where did you say you were?'

'Kennedy Airport.' Jonathan sounded tense and irritated.

'You mean . . . you mean New York?'

'Of course I mean New York. Look, I have to go, my flight's been called. Can I come and stay with you or not?'

'Yes, of course you can. But why?'

'Explanations later. When I get back to the UK, I'm going to need to crash. Can I pick up a key some place?'

'I suppose you could come to the office.'

'No,' said Jonathan, tersely. 'Can't I go straight to your flat?'

Prue's tired mind was flummoxed by his obvious ill-temper. She thought as quickly as she could. 'There's a hanging basket at the top of the area steps. I'll put the spare key at the back of it, under the leaves.'

'OK, fine. See you.' He was gone.

When Prue returned from work the following day, there was ample evidence of Jonathan's arrival – a briefcase and coat were abandoned in the hallway, the remains of a hastily prepared meal in the kitchen and his shoes in the sitting room. Pausing only to brush her hair and check her make-up in the bathroom mirror, Prue tiptoed to her bedroom door and eased it open. He lay on his side, one hand covering his face, his hair normally so neat now tousled and boyish.

He had not bothered to undress. There were dark shadows under his eyes but in sleep he looked years younger. Prue closed the door and sat down on the bed beside him.

He stirred and opened his eyes. 'Hi.' He smiled at her and her heart melted. She forgave him everything in an instant.

'What happened?' she asked.

'I'll tell you later – it's been a hell of a twenty-four hours. Come here.' He reached out for her.

She didn't need asking twice. With her head on his shoulder, their arms about one another, they both let out a sigh of contentment. 'Please tell me why you had to go back to New York?' Prue said, after a moment's silence.

'I told you I'm not ready to talk about it yet.' His voice was angry.

'I'm sorry.' Prue shifted restlessly on the bed.

'No, it's me who should be saying sorry and, hell, I do need to talk to someone. Look, would you go and fix us some coffee? I promise to be nicer to know by the time you come back.'

He was sitting up in bed when she returned. Although he seemed more cheerful, there was a weariness about him which Prue realized instantly was caused by something more than jet-lag. He sipped his coffee in silence for some moments and she had enough sense to keep silent. 'I've quit Lindstrom's Bank,' he said at last.

She stared at him. 'I don't understand.'

'I'm not sure I do either. I had an argument with Edward Deckman, over a matter of policy – our banking methods are entirely different and things finally came to a head. So I flew to New York to get my mother to arbitrate, or rather sort Deckman.'

'What happened?' said Prue.

'My mother wouldn't agree to firing Deckman. She told me to come back here and get on with the job. Prue, I just couldn't do that.'

'Why not?' said Prue.

'I can't compromise to that extent. I have my principles and I'm not about to abandon them.'

'So . . . you resigned?'

'That's about it,' said Jonathan. 'Maybe I was hasty but there really didn't seem any alternative. The trouble is, Lindstrom's Bank isn't only about a job, it's also about a home. My apartment in New York is owned by the bank, as is my flat here in London. So what did I do in my hour of need?' He tried a weak smile. 'I called you, I knew you'd be my port in a storm.'

'It doesn't make any sense,' said Prue. 'You've thrown away your whole career because of an argument?'

'It's been brewing for years,' said Jonathan. 'Look, I don't want to talk about the details – it's over. What I have to do now is to decide what happens next.'

'I suppose you'll have no problems getting a job at another bank?'

'Probably not,' said Jonathan. 'But that's not what I want.'

'What do you want?'

There was a bleak look in his expression. 'I don't know, but first thing tomorrow morning I know what I'm going to do.'

'What's that?'

'I'm going to sell my Lindstrom shares.'

Benjamin Crossman had never liked young Lindstrom, ever since he first met him as a noisy, over-indulged child. He had nearly refused to see him but then his secretary had said that Jonathan was anxious for an urgent appointment and his curiosity had got the better of him. He did not rise when Jonathan entered, considering old age gave him sufficient excuse. 'Well, young man,' he said. 'What's all the fuss?'

'Hello, Ben.' Jonathan leaned across the table with an extended hand.

Benjamin did not remember giving permission for such familiarity but he took his hand and then waved him into the visitor's chair. He studied the boy in silence for a moment – Jonathan was nervous, he could see that straight away. What the hell did he have to be nervous about? All he had to do was to sit on his backside until it was time to inherit the bank from dear mama. Fleetingly, Benjamin thought of his years of struggle and in a flash of inspiration recognized one of the reasons he so disliked Jonathan Lindstrom – Jonathan had been born to it, while he, Benjamin, had needed to work for it.

'I want to sell my shares, Ben.' Jonathan avoided his gaze, and fingered the cuff of his shirt. 'I have a five per cent holding in Lindstrom's Bank which is of no further use to me. I want to offload my shares, and I want to do it right now.'

Benjamin hid his surprise well. 'So why did you come to me?'

'Oh hell, Ben, do I have to spell it out to you? Lindstrom's and Crossman's have been scrapping for business in New York for a quarter of a century. Their profile is identical, their expansion into London is parallel. It's only a matter of time before one of them gets taken over by the other. I guess I'm offering you a head start.'

40

'Why?' said Ben.

'Because I want out.'

'I know you want out, what I want to know is *why*?'

'It's none of your goddamned business,' Jonathan said.

The temptation to show him the door was enormous, but Benjamin's mind was working overtime – this was exactly what he wanted. 'Come on, straighten out your thinking, boy,' he said in as amicable a tone as he could manage. 'I'm not going to buy into your bank unless I know the circumstances of your wanting out. What's wrong – is the bank in trouble, has your mother overstretched herself at last? I'm not being unreasonable, I have a right to know if you expect me to hand over good money for your shares.'

Jonathan opened his mouth, a prepared excuse at the ready, but suddenly he realized that nothing but the truth would do for Benjamin Crossman. The old man was too shrewd. It cost him dear to be honest. 'I'm sorry, I'm not prepared to go into the details of why I want out, but I will tell you this. As far as I am aware, the bank is in very good shape, but I can't get along with Edward Deckman. I issued my mother with an ultimatum, him or me, and she's chosen him.'

Wise woman, Benjamin thought to himself. 'OK, so it's a family feud. Five per cent you say? I'll give you six hundred thousand dollars.'

'You have to be joking,' said Jonathan. 'My shares have to be worth upwards of a million.'

'Maybe they are to you, or certainly they were when you were due to inherit the rest, but they're worthless to an outside investor. Only shares over ten per cent can be of any real interest. Incidentally, what about the rest of the shares? Have you been cut off without a cent?'

Jonathan had been thinking about very little else since leaving his mother. 'No, of course not,' he said, with a shade less conviction than he would have liked. 'My mother doesn't own them all, of course – there are a number of other shareholders, former directors, loyal staff, that kind of thing. Nonetheless, she has at least eighty per cent and I have no doubts that I will inherit the lot. It's just that there's a rift at the moment and I have to live in the meantime.' He hesitated. 'I won't be greedy, Ben, I'll accept a million.'

'I'm not offering a million, but because of our families' long association I'll split the difference with you – eight hundred thousand dollars and that's my final offer.'

Jonathan met the old man's eye. He sat hunched over his desk, gaunt and wrinkled like an aged lizard. Jonathan disliked him intensely but what was he to do? He knew Benjamin was right, the shares had little value in themselves, but he also suspected that Benjamin would not be able to resist the opportunity of owning part of Lindstrom's Bank, even a small part with no voting rights. It would irritate Harriet Lindstrom, and that fact alone gave Jonathan and Benjamin something in common. 'OK,' said Jonathan. 'Done.'

'That's marvellous news,' said Prue, 'and you sold them so quickly. You'll have to translate for me, how much is eight hundred thousand dollars?'

'Four hundred thousand pounds, give or take a pound or two,' said Jonathan.

They were sitting over dinner in the kitchen. Prue was stunned. 'That's wonderful. My God, all that money? What on earth are you going to do with it?'

'It's not enough, not nearly enough. It won't last long.'

'It's an absolute fortune. I don't understand you,' said Prue. 'If someone handed me four thousand pounds, never mind four hundred thousand, I'd be ecstatic.'

'I've no job,' Jonathan said. 'And the income isn't going to be enough to live on.'

For the first time, Prue felt a real sense of exasperation. She stood up and began clearing the plates. 'Coffee?' she asked coldly.

'Yes, please.'

'OK, so you have no job, but you've got all this money and the opportunity to start all over again, doing exactly what you please.' An awful thought suddenly struck her. 'Will you go back to New York?' she asked, tremulously.

Before Jonathan could reply, the telephone began ringing in the hall. Prue went to answer it. 'Is Jonathan Lindstrom staying with you?' The voice sounded American, female, clipped and authoritative.

'Yes,' said Prue. 'Who shall I say is calling?'

'Harriet Lindstrom.'

Prue put her hand over the mouthpiece. 'Jonathan, it's your mother. Perhaps she's changed her mind.'

'How the hell did she know I was here? Tell her I'm not in.'

'I can't do that, I've already said you are.'

'Jesus, you might have asked me first.' Jonathan stood up angrily and strode to the phone. 'Hello, Mother, how did you find me?'

'Ben Crossman gave me your address at the same time he told me he had bought your shares,' said Harriet, her voice brittle with suppressed anger.

There was a shocked silence. It was hard to believe the news had travelled so fast. 'Yes, I concluded the deal this afternoon,' Jonathan said, awkwardly. 'And before you start yelling at me, I would remind you that with no home and no job, I had to do something to realize some cash.'

'You could have simply gone out to work like everyone else.' His mother's voice sounded odd, almost shaky.

'I'll have to do that, too, Mother.'

'How much did you get for the shares, Jonathan?'

'I can't see why that matters to you, one way or the other.'

'Just answer the question.'

'A million,' he lied, cursing himself for not being able to do a better job of handling the parental interrogation.

'Is that all?'

'It's a fair price.'

'Not in the circumstances it isn't.' The contempt in Harriet's voice made his blood run cold.

'What circumstances?' he asked.

'You're not going to tell me you were unaware that Ben Crossman is already a shareholder of Lindstrom's.'

'What!' Jonathan could not even begin to cover his surprise. 'No,' he said, after a moment. 'No, I didn't know that. Why should I?'

'Because it's something we have discussed regularly in the board-room, though clearly you never listened. Benjamin Crossland has gradually acquired a seven per cent holding in the bank over a number of years, buying the odd share here and there from past employers. As of yesterday he had seven per cent, as of today he has twelve per cent. That gives him voting rights. That gives him the opportunity to make real trouble in the boardroom. How could you do this to me, Jonathan? If you wanted the cash, you know I'd have bought the shares, and at the proper price.'

'How the hell was I supposed to know that? You not only took away my job, you took away my home as well. With you in that kind of mood, I reckon I was justified in assuming there was no way you were going to bale me out over the shares.'

'I didn't take your job away,' said Harriet. 'You threw it in my face, and your apartment's not mine to give or take. It belongs to

43

the bank.' She sighed, audibly. 'I suppose the deal with Benjamin Crossman is fixed, you can't slide out of it?'

'I have his cheque,' said Jonathan. 'And in any case, I don't want to slide out of it.'

'I think there will come a time when you'll regret those words.'

'Is that some sort of threat?'

'No,' said Harriet. 'But have you considered how the rest of the New York banking world is going to view this? It is disloyalty of the worst kind, Jonathan. I think you will find it very difficult indeed to find a job, anywhere on Wall Street.'

'I guess if my own mother is going to rubbish me around the trade, that's probably true,' said Jonathan.

'No one will hear a word against you from me. You've put the nails in your own coffin, Jonathan – you didn't need any help.'

Jonathan replaced the receiver and stood in the hall for some moments. 'Are you there, Prue?' he called at last.

'Yes.' Prue, having made the coffee, had been trying hard not to eavesdrop on the conversation.

'You asked me a question just now. The answer is, I'll be staying right here in the UK.'

CHAPTER SIX
September 1980

It had rained, relentlessly, from the moment they joined the A11. Prue's mini had seen better days and continual rain had a nasty habit of causing the vehicle to seize up altogether. She gripped the steering wheel and squinted through the windscreen, praying it would not happen now. Jonathan was in no mood for a breakdown. He had done nothing but complain since leaving London and Prue was beginning to query the wisdom of her suggestion that they should spend the weekend with her parents in Suffolk.

Ever since the telephone call from his mother, Jonathan had been morose and difficult. He had hung about the flat, getting in Prue's way when she tried to work and clearly irritating Richard. He kept looking for ways to pick a quarrel, his major bone of contention being that she should give up her job.

'Why on earth should I?' she had asked.

'Out of loyalty to me,' he said, apparently confident that this was enough.

In love though she was, Prue was not swayed by his argument. 'It's not a question of being loyal or disloyal to you,' she reasoned, patiently. 'I worked for the bank long before Lindstrom's bought it, and in any event, your row with your mother is a personal matter and entirely irrelevant to my job.'

He refused to accept her view, and her leaving for work each day seemed to sink him further and further into gloom. He appeared to have no personal resources upon which to fall back, no way of moving his life forward on his own. Recognizing that she still did not know him very well, Prue was at a loss as to how to cheer him up. As the weekend approached, the thought of spending it in the flat with Jonathan and Richard resenting one another made her sufficiently desperate that her parents' home seemed an attractive alternative. It was Friday evening, the traffic dreadful, and she had worked hard all day. By contrast Jonathan, after a lie-in, had sat around the flat watching television and reading the newspapers. She loved him, she was sure of that, but she was also beginning to see a side of him which she found intensely irritating.

'How much longer?' he asked, wearily. 'This car is giving me real back trouble.'

'If you ask me that once more, I'll throw you out and you can bloody well walk,' said Prue. 'I told you the journey could take three hours if the traffic was bad, and three hours it will be – not a moment less.'

Although clearly surprised at her outburst, he didn't take the hint. 'I just can't understand why you have a car like this – it's a dumb choice. It's so small, and noisy.'

'I'll tell you why I have a car like this,' Prue said, really angry now. 'Because it's all I can afford. I have to live on what I earn, like most people, and I needed a car which was cheap to buy and cheap to run. You're the person with four hundred thousand pounds. If you were so unhappy about travelling by mini, why didn't you hire a car? After the day I've had at work, I would have been profoundly grateful to have been chauffeur-driven home.' There was silence for a moment.

'Hell, I'm sorry, I guess you're right,' Jonathan said at last. 'Would you like me to drive?'

'No, I wouldn't,' said Prue ungraciously, 'I'd like you just to be quiet.'

The journey continued in an uneasy silence, until they turned off the main road and began weaving their way through little Suffolk villages towards Thurston Hall, Prue's family home.

'This is beautiful countryside. I wish it wasn't so dark and wet, I think you'd love it.'

Jonathan put out a hand and touched her shoulder. 'I'm very glad you've asked me for the weekend, to meet your folks. I'm sorry I've been . . . well, I guess a little grouchy the last few days but it's been a difficult time for me. We'll have fun this weekend, right?'

'We certainly will,' said Prue, smiling.

'Tell me,' said Jonathan. 'Will they . . . will we be allowed to share the same room?'

'You must be joking,' said Prue.

'You mean they won't approve of me?'

'Not that,' said Prue, 'I'm sure they'll like you very much but I'm equally sure they think I'm a virgin. They really are out of touch with the modern world. You'll soon see what I mean.'

'Will I be able to come to your room later tonight, when everyone's safely asleep?'

'I don't know. It depends where they put you,' said Prue. 'It won't be easy.'

'That's rough,' Jonathan grumbled.

'Maybe, but it's how things must be done,' said Prue. 'I don't think it's unreasonable to be expected to accept their way of life, in their own home.'

'I guess not.'

Robert Mansell heard Prue's car and was already at the front door as she and Jonathan dashed through the rain. 'Thanks, Daddy. Hello. How are you?' Prue put her arms round her father's neck and gave him a kiss.

She was not normally so spontaneously affectionate. Robert Mansell was aware of the change and just the briefest look at his daughter confirmed what he had suspected ever since her phone call – she was in love. Her hair shone, her eyes sparkled, there was a vivacity about her, a glow . . . Hurriedly he turned to the man who must be responsible for Prue's transformation. His initial impression was not unfavourable – tall, dark, good-looking, very well and neatly dressed. Robert abhorred the denim revolution. 'How do you do,' he said, 'I'm Robert Mansell.'

'Jonathan Lindstrom. I am pleased to meet you, sir.'

'Ah, do I detect an American accent?' Robert asked.

Jonathan nodded. 'Yes, sir.'

'And Lindstrom . . . let me see, that has to be a Scandinavian name?'

Jonathan looked impressed. 'Yes, that's right. My family originate from Sweden. They emigrated to the US, I guess about one hundred and fifty years ago.'

'Interesting,' said Robert. 'Though of course that's not where you get your colouring from.'

'Daddy,' Prue said, 'must Jonathan have an inquisition as to his forebears here on the doorstep?'

Robert Mansell smiled. 'No, of course not. Come along in, you must be tired, I expect it was a pig of a journey.'

Prue had given Jonathan no real indication as to her family background and he was totally unprepared for the splendours of Thurston Hall as he walked through the front door. He found himself in a great baronial hall, with a wide staircase winding its way up to a gallery above. An enormous chandelier hung from the ceiling, and

47

from the wood-panelled walls, what he assumed must be Mansell ancestors stared down at him. He was impressed. 'This is just great,' he said.

'We are very privileged to live here,' replied Robert. The two men smiled at one another.

By dinner, however, disillusion was beginning to creep in. The house was certainly magnificent but Jonathan could not believe how cold it was. His bedroom, a tiny turreted room, in what seemed to be an unused part of the house, was icy. The sheets, when he felt the bed, were clammy, as well as cold. Drinks before dinner were pleasant enough, in a beautiful drawing room with faded but elegant furniture, for a log fire had been burning, but the dining room was an enormous barn of a room and extremely chilly.

It was not until dinner that Jonathan met Lady Mansell, Prue's mother. It was from her mother she had inherited her looks. Robert Mansell was a nice-looking old boy but very overweight, with a well-pronounced aquiline nose which seemed big even for his chubby face. Margery Mansell was a faded beauty, a slight woman with a pale complexion and the silvery hair of the true blonde. Her face had remained remarkably unlined and her voice and mannerisms were girlish. She had huge china-blue eyes and a sweet smile but she was preoccupied and flustered. Cook had chosen tonight to be ill, she explained. As Prue had said, it appeared that catering was not Margery Mansell's forte. The dinner was unspeakable – soup the colour of dirty washing-up water and tasteless, followed by a small joint of lamb, so overcooked that the meat had become stringy and tough, accompanied by mushy, unidentifiable vegetables and cold, lumpy gravy. Only the pudding, blackberry and apple pie, had almost survived Margery's cooking, since Cook had made it the day before, but even that was burnt, and there was no cream.

The quaint habit of the women leaving the table while he and Robert passed port cheered Jonathan a little – that and the prospect of a night with Prue. However, when they eventually joined the women for coffee in the drawing room, he was quickly disillusioned. 'How do I find your room?' he murmured to Prue, while Margery fussed over the coffee and Robert fetched brandy.

'You don't,' said Prue, firmly. She looked particularly lovely that night in a long navy-blue woollen dress, her hair caught up in a plait – very English, very demure.

'What do you mean?' he whispered.

'We can't possibly, Jonathan. You'd have to walk straight past my parents' room to get to mine.' She squeezed his arm. 'We'll make up for it on Monday night.'

So Jonathan went to bed alone. The narrow bed was damp and cold as he had anticipated – he could not remember passing a more uncomfortable night.

'What do you think of him?' Margery asked her husband. They were sitting in bed, enjoying their ritual half hour with library books.

'I'm not sure,' said Robert. 'Initially I thought he was quite a decent chap – nicely turned out, polite, but we don't seem to have anything much in common. I hope Prue doesn't want to marry him.'

'Oh, I shouldn't think so,' said Margery, reassuringly. 'I'm quite sure she wouldn't fall in love with a foreigner.'

Jonathan could not believe it. All round him people were wading across the river although in parts it was nearly reaching their waists, and they genuinely did not seem to mind. Reluctantly kitted out for the mink hunt, with wellington boots two sizes too big for him, an ancient filthy waxed jacket and matching hat, Jonathan had felt foolish enough. This was going too far. Prue had announced over breakfast that there would be a mink hunt. Jonathan had expected her to say in the next breath that it would be cancelled because of the weather. Instead Robert agreed enthusiastically and said what an excellent day it was for such an event. So far as Jonathan could see, there had been no let-up in the weather all night. It was still raining, the sky was overcast and threatening, there was a nasty wind and it was still very cold.

'Couldn't we go into the local town and have some lunch?' he suggested.

'Oh no,' said Prue. 'Mink hunting is great fun and besides which, it will be interesting for you to see an English country sport.'

A meet had been held in a barn on the Thurston estate and Jonathan had been momentarily cheered by the glasses of sloe gin everyone consumed. As local farmers and landowners met and talked, the mink hounds raced around them – great ungainly beasts, with beards and strange, webbed feet. It was a noisy affair – the mink hounds bayed, terriers barked and everyone shouted to make themselves heard above the din. All too soon they were off – forty-odd people of all ages, apparently intent on a day's enjoyment, wading about in freezing water, in torrential rain. Jonathan lasted half an hour. Then, trying to struggle up the bank of the river he slipped

49

and fell over backwards into the mud. Lying there, the ignominy of his position was increased by Prue and a gathering group of spectators laughing at his plight, and he finally lost his sense of humour. 'Jesus, Prue, if this is your idea of pleasure, you have to be out of your mind. I'm going home.'

'Oh don't be such a bad sport, Jonathan.'

'I'm not a bad sport, I've just had enough. I'll see you later.'

Thurston Hall seemed to be deserted when he eventually reached it. Still cursing under his breath, he stripped off his clothes and, wrapped in a towel, he walked down the corridor to the bathroom. So dispirited was he by this time that when the water coming out of the tap proved only lukewarm, he did not have the energy to be disappointed that there would be no hot bath. He dressed and went down to the drawing room, the one room he remembered as being cheerful from the night before. The ashes were still hot and with a little coaxing he rekindled a fire. With a sigh of relief he drew up a chair, put his feet on the fender and fell asleep, both warm and dry at last.

Jonathan was still asleep when Prue returned, a couple of hours later. She, too, had abandoned the hunt, aware that she had made a serious error in assuming Jonathan might enjoy himself. She knew she had been asking a lot for a New Yorker, born and bred, to enjoy squelching through the Suffolk countryside, but she had not expected him to give up so easily.

Having found Jonathan sleeping in front of the fire, she changed out of her wet things, made two mugs of tea and joined him in the drawing room. The sound of her coming through the door woke him. 'So you've had enough messing about for one day?' he asked, his tone belligerent.

'As a matter of fact I haven't, but I came back early because I thought it was rude to leave you here on your own.'

'Why? I was perfectly happy until you woke me up.'

Prue put down the mugs of tea by the fireplace, aware that their first major row was brewing. She was terrified of losing him but at the same time his mood of recent days had stretched even her tolerance to breaking point. 'Is there any need to be so unpleasant? OK, maybe this isn't your sort of weekend but everybody's doing their best to give you a good time. You might at least try to enjoy yourself.' She mellowed slightly. 'I've brought you some tea.'

'No, thanks. I'll have something stronger.' He got up and walked towards her father's drinks cabinet.

She watched him, and even at that moment when everything he did and said was calculated to anger her, she felt a stab of desire for him. Desire or love, she could not tell – her feelings for him were so strong, they were impossible to analyse. She watched him pour a hefty measure of whisky. He took a sip. 'This is damn good.'

'So it should be,' said Prue, dryly. 'It's an unblended malt. My father keeps it for special occasions.'

'Oh, so I'm in trouble again, am I? I'll send him a bottle on our return to London. I don't want him to feel I've been too free with his hospitality.' Jonathan's voice was heavy with sarcasm.

The slur on the character of her placid, generous father was too much for Prue. 'How dare you speak about my father like that. Of course he wouldn't resent you having a whisky, if it's what you want.'

Jonathan was not contrite. 'I've had a shit of a day, without you bitching at me and trying to tell me how I should act. I'm not prepared to have you dictating to me as to how I should feel and what I should say, like some bloody mother hen. I'm going upstairs now and I won't be coming down to another terrible dinner. Make some excuse for me, and then at least you'll be spared the embarrassment of having me around.'

'If you're not prepared to join us for dinner then I think you'd better leave.' The words were out before Prue could stop herself.

'OK, if that's the way you want it, I'll go and pack.' He walked to the door. 'How the hell do I get out of this place anyway?'

'You can borrow my car,' said Prue.

'I'm not driving that heap of junk. If you want me out so bad, perhaps you could call a cab.'

Half an hour later, Jonathan let out a sigh and leaned back against the faded, grimy upholstery of the Ford Cortina which had picked him up. He had not said goodbye to Prue, nor indeed anyone else in the house, and that was just how he wanted it.

He did not know quite how he felt about Prue. She had meant more to him than his usual women, he had to admit, but not enough to stay around while she slagged him off – he would put up with that from no woman. Besides which, if at a later date he decided he wanted her back she would come round, they always did. As he thought this, Jonathan felt an odd sense of disquiet. Prue was not in the usual mould. Perhaps he had really blown it with her and if so, would it matter? It was convenient staying in her flat, of course, but by no means essential – he could check into a hotel. Nonetheless, he would be sorry to lose her. He had become fond of her, she was his only real friend in the UK, and he suddenly recognized with surprise that he had a grudging respect for her. She was not just another empty-headed little broad – she had class and spirit, too much damned spirit. On impulse, he leaned forward. 'Do you know a bar round here?' he asked the taxi driver.

The man consulted his watch. 'The pubs will be open in a minute, mate.'

'Well drive me to a nice one, somewhere near. Maybe I won't go back to London tonight after all.'

The taxi driver glanced in the mirror and eyed the American with interest. The man was well dressed – not only would he be good for his fare but probably he would hand over a good tip as well. 'What part of America do you come from?' he began conversationally.

Ten minutes later, they dropped down into the village of Long Melford. It was nearly dusk and Jonathan peered out of the window. 'This looks a nice little place,' he said.

'It is, it's my home town. In fact I'm taking you to my local.'

Jonathan was confused by the term. 'Local what?'

'Local pub. You'll like it.'

Much to his surprise, since in his mind Jonathan had written off Suffolk, he took an instant liking to the pub. The driver would not join him and so he was the only person in the bar as it was just opening time. He ordered a large whisky from the comfortable middle-aged woman behind the bar, and looked around him appreciatively. 'This must be very old,' he said.

'It is,' the woman agreed. 'There's been an inn here for nearly four hundred years. At one stage in its life it was a really thriving business – a coaching inn and well known at that. This is the main road between London and Newmarket, or at least it was then. We have stabling out the back, in an old courtyard. The coaches used to come here and change horses, while the travellers were fed and sometimes stayed overnight. You're an American, aren't you? Are you over here on a holiday?'

'No,' said Jonathan. 'I think I might be living here more or less permanently. Do many Americans come and visit you?'

'Oh yes, a great many,' said the woman. 'It's a favourite place for the tourists. I'm sorry to be leaving. I love talking to people from foreign parts. I've never been abroad myself.'

'Leaving?' Jonathan pushed forward his glass for a refill. 'Have you lost your job?'

The woman laughed. 'No, I own the inn, at least my husband and

52

I did. Gerald died six months ago from a heart attack. Not surprising really, he drank and smoked too much, like most publicans. To start with I thought I'd stay on since I've been in the business all my life, but it's different when you're on your own, without a man. Then my sister came up with this idea – she and her husband are buying a guest house on the Broads. She's never been in catering before and she wants me to help them. I'll like that, I'll feel useful, without having the responsibility of this place. It'll be sad to leave, though.'

'Have you put the inn on the market?' Jonathan asked.

'It goes up for sale tomorrow. The estate agents have been instructed.'

Jonathan stared at her for a moment, then he felt in his jacket pocket and pulled out a card. 'My name's Jonathan Lindstrom, of Lindstrom's Bank. Could we talk about this property of yours?'

He had to be mad, out of his mind. He rested his head on the back of the car seat as the driver headed once more towards Thurston Hall. Perhaps he was drunk, but no, it would take more than a few whiskies to sink him. Still, what the hell; even if he regretted his decision in the morning, there would be no problem about selling on, if the place was properly marketed. He could probably turn forty thousand dollars on it without lifting a finger.

The house was in darkness when the taxi drew up outside. 'Wait for me here,' he said to the driver. 'We're going back to Long Melford again, just as soon as I've collected someone.'

The last thing Jonathan wanted was a confrontation with Prue's parents. Ignoring the curious stare of the taxi driver he ducked round the side of the house, to where he knew Prue's bedroom was located. 'Prue!' He spoke as loudly as he dared. 'Are you awake? Can you hear me? Prue!' He picked up a handful of gravel and threw it up at the window.

A moment later, Prue's pale face appeared at the window. 'Jonathan! What on earth are you doing?'

'Put some clothes on and come downstairs. I've got something to show you. It's really important.'

'Don't be ridiculous. It's nearly midnight.'

'So?' said Jonathan. 'Look, I'll explain in the car. I'll wait for you there.' He left her and strode round to the front of the house again, confident that curiosity would get the better of her. Sure enough, within a couple of minutes, the slim figure of Prue appeared round the side of the house, in jeans and a sweater. She climbed into the

53

car beside Jonathan. 'OK,' said Jonathan to the driver. 'Let's get going.'

'What is this?' said Prue. 'Where are we going?'

'A long way I hope,' said Jonathan. 'You and I are going into business together. It's just what you need, and me, too. We'll have a good time, Prue, and make some money – a lot, I guess, with a little luck.'

'What are you talking about? I have a business.'

'You're going to give that up. It's unhealthy for you living in London, Suffolk will do you far more good.'

At this Prue started to laugh. 'You hate Suffolk, Jonathan, you've made that perfectly clear. I thought you'd be back in London by now.'

'Well . . . maybe I've had second thoughts. You see, I've found a rather special place and as of now it's all mine.' The driver swerved at this piece of information but neither Prue nor Jonathan noticed. Jonathan slipped an arm round her shoulders and kissed her. 'I'm sorry I behaved so badly this afternoon. Will you forgive me?'

'Yes,' said Prue, without hesitation. 'But I would like to know where we're going? I haven't left my parents a note or anything.'

'We'll telephone them first thing in the morning.'

Although Long Melford was only twenty minutes' drive from Thurston Hall, it was not a village the Mansells favoured, preferring to shop in Cavendish. 'Where are we?' Prue asked, as the driver slowed the car in front of the inn.

'Long Melford, miss.'

'Oh, yes,' said Prue. 'Yes, of course, how silly of me.'

'Come on,' said Jonathan. He took her hand and pulled her out of the car. He was smiling – all his old enthusiasm and charm seemed to have returned. Whatever he was up to, Prue could not help but be pleased with the transformation in him. He reached into his wallet and drew out two ten-pound notes. 'Will this cover your fare?' he asked the driver.

'It most certainly will, thank you, sir.'

'Thank you, pal. You did me a real good turn tonight. Come, Prue, let your imagination run riot, this is really something.' Jonathan bounded ahead of her across the pavement and up to the front door of the pub. From his pocket, he took out an enormous key and inserted it in the lock of the old wooden door.

'How on earth do you have a key for this place?' Prue asked.

'Because I've just bought it,' said Jonathan. He turned the key in the lock and the door swung open. The bar was still dimly lit. Jonathan went ahead of Prue, urging her to follow. 'Come on, Prue.' Prue frowned and stepped hesitantly across the threshold. Somewhere in the back of her mind there was a sense of familiarity, and while she searched for some memory, another emotion began crowding in – fear was tugging at her sleeves. 'Prue, come on, what is it?'

Prue turned from Jonathan, fighting the sensation. She searched the deserted street outside, as if looking for an answer. Then she saw the pub sign, swinging backwards and forwards in the light breeze. Illuminated by a street lamp she read the words *The Lady in Waiting*.

CHAPTER SEVEN
Long Melford – February 1780

The inn door burst open with such force that the pewter mug Elizabeth was attempting to clean slipped through her cold fingers and fell to the floor. The sound of pewter on stone flags, of the wind accompanied by a whirling flurry of snow blowing through the open door and the suddenness of the stranger's arrival, created an instant sense of drama. They stood facing one another, the girl and the man, watching the mug as it rolled about on the floor. Only when it was still did the man turn and force the door closed against the icy blast. Then in a gesture which astonished Elizabeth, who was not used to courtesy in any form, particularly from a man, he bent and picked up the mug and handed it back to her. Their eyes met. 'I left my servant in Bishops Stortford since he has a fever and now my horse has thrown a shoe. Fetch me brandy and some food and send for the blacksmith. I have to reach Chadbrook this night.'

The girl stared at him, open-mouthed. She was not normally lost for words, but the identity of the man now stunned her into silence. At the mention of Chadbrook, she recognized him instantly. 'Yes . . . sir,' she managed at last. 'I'll fetch Father.'

'Good, and bring some logs for the fire. How can you keep such a wretchedly cold inn on a night like this? No wonder you have no custom.' He strode across the room and bending down began coaxing a flame out of the dying embers. The glow from the fire lit his harsh features – the almost jet-black hair, the strong aquiline nose, the deep brown eyes and full mouth. Elizabeth gulped. The man glanced up. 'What are you doing, girl? Don't just stand there gawping, I'm in a hurry.' She curtsied and ran.

Jem Monson had spent the evening sampling his own ale. He lolled in a chair beside the fire in the kitchen, an empty tankard dangling from his fingers. His mouth was open, displaying rotting teeth, saliva dribbled down his chin and he was snoring loudly.

'Father,' Elizabeth shouted. She shook him. 'Father, wake up. The Earl is here – here at the inn – come quickly.'

Jem's eyes opened, flickered and slowly focused on his daughter. 'What did you say?'

'Thomas, the Earl of Clare, is in the tap room. He wants a meal and a blacksmith, and some brandy, Father. He is travelling to Chadbrook tonight and has no time to waste.'

Jem's hand shot out and caught Elizabeth a glancing blow across the side of her face. Although she had been ready for it, cold and tired she did not move quickly enough. 'Don't talk nonsense. Leave me be.'

'It is true, Father. Go and see for yourself.' The urgency in Elizabeth's voice finally roused Jem. He got up, cursing, and ambled towards the tap room. 'And he wants some logs for the fire,' Elizabeth called after him, rubbing her sore cheek.

Jem, still cursing, disappeared through the door. In moments he was back. 'Mary, Mary,' he called. 'Where's that woman?' He turned on Elizabeth who was coming up the cellar stairs with a bottle of brandy. 'Where's your mother?'

'In bed, most likely,' said Elizabeth, sullenly.

'The lazy, good-for-nothing slut. Go and fetch her directly. Tell her we are entertaining the Earl of Clare, the most important man in Suffolk, indeed in the whole of England. He will pay us handsomely I shouldn't wonder, if we treat him right. Here, give me the brandy.'

The meal the Monson family set before Thomas was not one to be envied – some cold mutton, none too fresh, a wing of undercooked pigeon, bread but no butter and some very tired celery. Thomas eyed it with distaste but he was ravenously hungry and the brandy was surprisingly good. Jem hovered, with nauseating obsequiousness, wringing his hands and apologizing – blaming his daughter and his wife for the lack of good fare.

'Stop your blethering, man,' Thomas said at last when his hunger was sated. 'What I need now is the blacksmith. Go and fetch him directly. I left my horse in that shack at the back of the inn which must once have been a fine stable.' He studied Jem for a moment. 'Your inn is in a sorry state. Can you account for it?'

'We are poor folk, sir, and trade is bad. . .' Jem began.

'Enough,' said the Earl, instantly wearied by Jem's whining. 'Be off with you and fetch the blacksmith.'

The blacksmith's cottage was only a few hundred yards from the inn but it took all Jem's strength to fight his way through the snow to reach it. The wind had dropped but the snow was still falling thick and fast, transforming the village street almost beyond recognition.

He hammered on the door and after a while the blacksmith's wife, struggling against the weight of snow, managed to push it open.

'Jem Monson, what are you doing out on a night such as this? Have you trouble at the inn? Come in, do.' Maggie Hewitt's broad, rosy face beamed with good nature. Beyond her ample frame he could see into the kitchen. Two small children were playing by the hearth, a third older girl was at her spinning. The room was warm and glowing – a perfect family scene, and so much in contrast to the one he had just left.

For a moment, he was tempted to accept her offer. Then he remembered the Earl. 'No thank you, Maggie. It's Harry I want. We've a very important traveller, whose horse needs a new shoe.'

'He must be important to fetch you out on such a night, but I fear Harry's not here. He is at Juniper Farm, out Lavenham way, staying with my brother who has horses needing attention. I was expecting him in the morning, but with the weather. . .'

'But this is urgent business. My traveller is Thomas, the Earl of Clare, and he needs to be home this night.'

For a moment Maggie Hewitt looked doubtful. Jem's love affair with ale was well known but the man seemed sober enough now and was clearly desperate.

'The Earl! God preserve us, are you sure, Jem Monson?'

'Of course I am sure, and I hear the man has a terrible temper with him if he is crossed.'

Maggie considered for a moment. 'I have heard that, too. I suppose I could send my eldest boy, Jamie, to fetch his father but it will take until morning to bring him back, mind.'

Jem was very nervous as to how the Earl would react to his news. He need not have worried. Thomas had drunk most of the bottle of brandy. He lay back in a chair drawn close to the fireplace, in which a fine blaze now burned. He regarded with a benevolent eye the sorry state which was Jem Monson. 'No blacksmith until morning, you say?'

'No, sir, and the snow is very deep in parts – drifting, too. I would not be happy to see you try and reach Chadbrook tonight. It's high ground up there and it will be taking the brunt of the storm.'

'Aye,' said Thomas. 'You may well be right. What's your name?'

'Jem Monson, sir.'

'Well, Jem Monson, it seems I shall be staying under your roof this night. I have to own I have stayed in more comfortable surroundings.'

58

'There is nothing I can do about my situation, sir,' Jem whined. 'The Lion down the street takes all the coach trade. It leaves us nothing but a few vagabonds – not enough to feed us most of the year.'

Thomas cursed under his breath – if only he had stumbled upon The Lion instead of this godforsaken hole. Still, he was too tired and drunk to move now. 'If you cleaned and tidied your inn, Jem, you might well attract more custom.'

'I try, sir, but my wife and daughter are no help to me. My wife is sick much of the time and my daughter . . . well, to be truthful, sir, she is a slut with fancy ideas about book-learning and the like.' The vague idea was forming in Jem's mind that the Earl might take pity on his situation and help him in some way. Thomas did not react as he had expected.

'Book-learning, indeed. Is that red-haired wench your daughter?'

Jem nodded. 'Her mother gives her these notions.'

'Can she read and write?' Thomas asked.

'Yes, sir, so I believe – she always carries a book with her when she should be about her chores.'

'Well, I'll be damned! Fetch me some more logs for the fire – this chair will make a fine resting place. Oh, and send that wench of yours to me with more brandy.'

Elizabeth was pleased to be summoned back to Thomas's presence, for she had her own reasons for wanting to take another look at the Earl.

By the light of the fire, his boots off, his shirt open, the Earl looked younger and more approachable than when he'd first arrived. She hovered just outside the circle of light. 'Shall I pour you some more brandy, sir?'

'Yes.' Thomas looked at her slowly and smiled. 'And fetch another glass for yourself.'

Elizabeth shook her head vigorously. 'No, sir, I had better not.'

'Why not? You surely cannot tell me you are too young – what age are you, girl?'

'Sixteen.'

'And how are you called?'

'Elizabeth.'

'A good name. Come now, Elizabeth, do as I say and fetch yourself a glass.' She did as he asked, and when she returned he took the bottle from her and filled both his glass and hers. 'To what shall we drink, young Elizabeth?' he asked.

'I don't know, sir.' His friendly familiarity unnerved her and she was unsure how to react.

'Come now, surely you can think of something.'

She searched her mind. 'To the spring,' she said, 'let us drink to the spring. This winter has been long and hard.'

'A worthy toast,' said Thomas. They raised their glasses and drank. The fiery liquid made Elizabeth's eyes water but it warmed the pit of her stomach. 'Come here, girl, and let me have a better look at you,' Thomas said. Something in his manner made Elizabeth hesitate. 'Come here, I will not hurt you.'

She went and stood before him. He pulled her close to the chair. She was frightened but she met his eyes defiantly. Thomas studied her in silence for a moment. She really was an incredible-looking girl – tall, slender as a reed, with dark red hair the colour of autumn leaves, bright green eyes and a creamy skin. She was ripe for the plucking – he felt desire rise in him but he hesitated. The girl had a dignity that intrigued him. 'Tell me about yourself, Elizabeth.'

She shrugged her shoulders and moved away from him a little, relieved he had released her. 'Nothing to tell, sir. I live here with my mother and father, work in the inn all day and night – the same jobs day after day, just waiting to grow old and die.'

The bitterness in her voice surprised him. 'With your looks you'll find a young man to marry you soon enough.'

'I do not want to marry,' said Elizabeth.

'Why not, in God's name?' Thomas was genuinely interested.

'I see what marriage does to women – all that child-bearing and work. The man's only interested in them until . . .' She stopped and blushed.

Thomas helped her out without apparent embarrassment. 'You mean once you're married, your husband will cease to pay you enough attention?' Elizabeth nodded. 'Maybe,' said Thomas. 'But it seems you should have no difficulty in finding a better life than this.' Almost any life would be better, he thought, but did not wish to humiliate her by saying so.

There was a silence between them for a moment. 'You see, sir. . .' said Elizabeth suddenly, stumbling over the words. 'At least now I am free.'

'Free?' said Thomas in genuine astonishment. 'You call this freedom?'

Elizabeth stared at him, her eyes bright with anger. 'It may not seem much to you but at least I have a roof over my head and food in my belly, and I am answerable to no man.'

'What about your father?'

She waved a hand of dismissal in the general direction of the bar. 'He's drunk all the time, I can put up with him.'

'And your mother?'

'Some days she is well, but mostly she's not quite right in the head.'

'Your father tells me you can read and write – is this so?'

'Oh, yes, sir, yes I can. My mother made me learn. She says it is the way to have a better life than she has, though I do not see how.' Elizabeth's pretty face crumpled into a frown. 'I like reading. No, I love it, but I cannot see what good it will do me – I will be here until I rot, I know it.'

'And I am equally sure you shall not,' said Thomas. 'But it grieves me that your life is so hard and has little sense of purpose, particularly when you are skilled at learning.'

'What does it matter to you?' Elizabeth answered rudely. His pity angered her.

Thomas hesitated. The wind had got up again and was rattling the windows so loud it was necessary to raise his voice above the din. 'It's my duty to care about how ordinary people live. I should be more caring, more involved in the troubles of everyday folk.' What the hell was he saying, he asked himself, talking to this child as though she could understand his problems? 'Do you know who I am?' he asked, suddenly.

'Why, of course,' said Elizabeth. 'You are Thomas Chadbrook, Earl of Clare, and you are married to the Lady Eleanor. You are a good man, everyone says so, although you have a fine temper on you. You are kind to your tenants but the estate is very run-down. Your father gambled away most of his money.' She bit her lip, suddenly aware of her boldness. 'I'm sorry,' she stammered, but looking at Thomas she saw he was laughing and she laughed too. 'It is just what people say.'

'Do they now, young Elizabeth, do they?'

Elizabeth hesitated. 'But I know you, not because of what people say of you . . . I have met you before.' Her voice was proud.

'And when was that, pray?' said Thomas, still laughing.

'When I was six, on Boxing Day. You took your hounds up to the green as usual and then headed towards Kentwell. I . . . I opened a gate for you.'

61

'That was good of you. Thank you.' Thomas leaned forward with a mock bow.

'And you gave me a penny,' Elizabeth said.

'A penny, how generous!' Thomas's voice was still mocking.

'I have it here, look.' She put a hand on the bodice of her dress and pulled out a penny through which a hole had been drilled, so that it could be hung from the leather thong around her neck.

Thomas sobered in an instant. 'You were six when I gave you this?' Elizabeth nodded. 'Then why did you not spend it in the market, on sweetmeats or a rag doll perhaps?'

'Because then it would have been gone,' said Elizabeth. 'The blacksmith made this hole for me and I have kept it with me always. You see . . .' she hesitated '. . . it is the first, the only money I have ever had of my own.'

'Come here, and let me look at your penny.' Thomas's voice was soft and gentle. An experienced woman would have recognized the danger signals, but Elizabeth felt only a warm glow at his kindness.

She went to him and he rose, a huge man towering over her despite her own height. He held the penny carefully, then gently pulled it towards him so that she was forced closer. The kiss was so unexpected that for a moment Elizabeth was too shocked to react. His arms were about her, his hands fumbling with the buttons on her dress. Warmth flooded through her body and she returned his kiss, but as the bodice of her dress began to slip from her shoulders, reality returned. She struggled to free herself but he held her tight. In desperation, she drew back her hand and struck him hard across the face.

The blow caught him just below the eye and he reeled away from her, momentarily losing his balance. 'What the hell did you do that for?' he shouted at her.

'You may be the Earl of Clare and I may be only poor Elizabeth Monson, but you cannot have me just because you want me,' Elizabeth spat out. 'You have a wife and in the morning you can go home and bed her – not me.'

'I thought it was what you wanted, too,' said Thomas, stunned by the venom in her voice.

'Then you were wrong,' said Elizabeth, and turning, she ran from the room.

Thomas watched her go and with a sigh returned to the chair. He threw another log on the fire and poured himself more brandy. Lying back, staring into the fire, he tried to think of the duties he needed to perform in the morning but his mind was instead full of Elizabeth

Monson. What an extraordinary child. How could such a beautiful creature have been born in these surroundings, and have acquired such freedom of spirit and ability to express herself? He supposed that from infancy she had been used to meeting strangers, but it did not explain her pride, her poise, her natural grace, nor her desire to better herself with learning. He laughed aloud. He could not remember ever having been rejected by a woman before, of any class. Perhaps he was losing his touch, getting too old. No, it was not that, for he knew that just for a moment he had lit a fire in Elizabeth which she had needed all her willpower to extinguish. He touched his cheek and winced. She had dealt him quite a blow, he would have a bruise in the morning.

Elizabeth was shaken roughly awake the following morning. It was one of Mary's good days, her eyes were clear. 'Get that kitchen fire going, Lizzie. The blacksmith is already at work and the Earl will need his breakfast.' Elizabeth staggered out of bed, threw some ice-cold water into her face and went downstairs.

Peeping into the bar, she saw the Earl was still asleep. She tiptoed across the room and put fresh logs on the dying embers of the fire. Glancing nervously at him, she saw there was a big blue stain below his right eye. Far from feeling guilty, the fact that she had left her mark on him made her feel oddly elated.

'Tell me what he looks like,' Mary asked, as the two women set to work in the kitchen.

'Go and see for yourself,' said Elizabeth. 'He is still sleeping.'

'No,' Mary said, 'I do not want him to see me prying – go on, tell me about him.'

'Well, he is handsome right enough,' said Elizabeth, not wanting to be drawn.

'What else?' Mary persisted. 'Tell me what he is wearing?'

'A shirt with much fancy lace upon it, a waistcoat with gold embroidery, black breeches and top boots.'

'What of his coat?' Mary persisted.

'Oh, enough, Mother,' said Elizabeth wearily. 'You will think less of the Earl, I wager, when I tell you he tried to have his way with me last night.'

Her mother looked sharply at her. 'And you let him?'

'No, I fetched him a slap across the face.' Elizabeth laughed.

Jem came stumbling into the kitchen.

'Lizzie says she struck the Earl last night, Jem.' Mary addressed her husband nervously.

'You did what?'

'I had to,' said Elizabeth defiantly. 'He put his hand into my shift.'

'That is the way of the gentry,' said Jem. 'Why, you stupid wench, you should not have struck him. We are here to do his bidding, whatever it be, and he will not regard us so handsomely now, I shouldn't wonder.'

Elizabeth turned on her father. 'So you would rather I lost my virtue than he not pay handsomely for his brandy?'

Jem was not impressed by his daughter's rage. She was head and shoulders taller than him so that now he rarely beat her, but nor would he stand by while she cheeked him. 'It would do us no harm if the Earl were to bestow his favours on you now and again.'

'I'll not give myself to a married man so that you can earn a few shillings.' Elizabeth turned from her father.

'Nor will she,' said Mary, suddenly bold. 'Elizabeth is keeping herself for her wedding night.'

'Keeping herself! For what? No man will ever marry her. The whole village knows she's bone lazy, and that there's madness in the family.' Jem spoke with relish, knowing just how cruel his words were.

'I am not mad, not mad,' Mary sobbed. 'It's you who have driven me to it, worn me down over the years. . .'

'Enough.' Jem raised an arm to strike his wife but she was already gone from him, running up the stairs to her room.

'Look what you've done,' Jem said, addressing Elizabeth. 'Go at once and apologize to the Earl for your bad behaviour last night.'

'I will do no such thing,' said Elizabeth.

'You will do as I say or I shall take a strap to you.'

'You shall not,' Elizabeth challenged.

'I will that.' Jem began unfastening his belt and Elizabeth could see from the gleam in his eye that he meant it. She pushed past him and reaching for her cloak, ran out of the kitchen.

It was just getting light. The snow was baked hard by the frost, like icing on a cake. She pulled her cloak tight around her for it was bitterly cold, and turning her back on the village began climbing the hill behind the inn, heading towards the sunrise. The sky was dark navy blue, it was going to be a beautiful day and she felt her spirits rise. By the time she reached the summit, the sun had risen, painting the countryside apricot. She turned into the spinney and slowing her pace looked around her in wonder. Every twig, every leaf was etched in snow and frost. It was magical.

She did not regret her rejection of Thomas Chadbrook the previous evening. Her reaction had been a spontaneous one but now she had time to think about it, she knew it had been right – if he had taken her then, he would have forgotten her by morning while she would never have forgotten him.

Warmed now from her climb, she sat down on a log and let out a sigh at the sight of the beauty around her. Long ago, perhaps when she was four or five, her father had been particularly drunk one night and had badly beaten both herself and her mother. As the woman and little girl lay crying, bloodied and bruised in a corner of the tap room, her mother had told her with fierce pride that Jem Monson was not her father. Elizabeth's father, Mary said, had been a passing nobleman, a member of the gentry who had made love to Mary while Jem was away at a fair. During all the years of hardship and some-times downright cruelty which followed, Elizabeth had hugged this knowledge to herself, but she had never asked her mother about it again and for the first time she wondered why. What if her mother knew the whereabouts of her true father? Perhaps she could go to him and he would help her. Yet even as she formed the thought, she rejected the idea and suddenly with a flash of clarity she understood her feelings. She would not risk asking her mother whether the story was true for fear that it was not, or in any case, for fear that her mother would deny it. Through all the years since that day she had hugged to herself the knowledge that she did not belong to the cruel, ignorant world into which she had been born, and she could not live without her 'secret' now. Certainly her looks tended to suggest the story was true. Not only was she much taller than either of her parents, her colouring was not theirs, nor her striking facial features. Somehow she did not feel that she belonged to them, nor indeed had she ever been able to make friends with the other children in the village. She felt in some way set apart. She could not bring herself to run the risk of being told that it was simply a freak of nature that had made her different and not the noble blood which ran in her veins. She would bide her time and find a way to escape.

The cold began seeping into her bones. She rose stiffly and started to walk back towards the inn. The sun was climbing higher now and as she broke out of the spinney and started down the hill, she saw the figure of a lone horseman ploughing resolutely through the snow, heading in the direction of Chadbrook. 'Adieu, Thomas,' she said, and as she spoke the words she knew, suddenly and without a shadow of doubt, that it was Thomas Chadbrook with whom her future lay.

CHAPTER EIGHT

Wearily, Thomas urged his horse through the great stone gates and headed up the long drive to Chadbrook. For once, he did not feel the usual lift of spirits at the sight of his home. Born and raised at Chadbrook, he knew every inch of it – loved it, cherished it and could never happily be away from it for long. After several weeks in London and a dangerous, tiring journey, arriving home should have been a joyful occasion, but not today. Chadbrook was in trouble – deep trouble. His purpose in going to London was to see his bankers. He had hoped that they would be able to help him survive the poor harvest of the previous summer. However, they had made it very clear that no further funds were available to him and their advice had been to sell, unless he could raise money from a patron. Begging did not come easily to Thomas but with his beloved home in jeopardy, he had sought help from every influential friend and acquaintance he knew. The search had proved fruitless. He calculated that what remaining money there was could be spent on one more planting, one more spring and summer, and if the harvest failed again, then Chadbrook would have to go.

As he approached the house, a groom intent on sweeping the snow away from the driveway abandoned his task and ran to his master. 'Welcome home, sir,' he said. 'Your journey must have been a hazardous one.'

'It was,' said Thomas, easing himself out of the saddle. He paused by his horse for a moment, stroking her neck which was wet with sweat. The going had been difficult from Long Melford. 'Look after her, Simon, she has served me well these past few days, this old mare. I would rather have Sorcha carry me than a hundred younger, stronger horses.'

'She would carry you 'til she dropped, sir,' Simon said.

'I know,' Thomas smiled at him, 'and nor do I undervalue her loyalty. It is rare to be the recipient of such love and devotion.' He turned and made for the front door. It opened as he approached.

66

Jack, the footman, bowed low. 'Welcome home, sir. I trust your stay in London was a successful one.'

'Not particularly, Jack, not particularly. Where is her Ladyship?'

'In the drawing room, sir. If you would care to join her, I will arrange for some refreshment to be brought to you there.'

'Not yet, Jack. What I most covet is a hot bath and a change of clothes. Will you bring plenty of hot water and stoke the fire well – it is a bitter cold day.'

'Yes, sir. Shall I tell her Ladyship that you have arrived?'

'As you wish.' Thomas could not disguise the bitterness in his voice.

The bath eased the grime and stiffness from his limbs. He relaxed, watching the steam swirl upwards. He must think positively, act decisively – if only he were not so tired. No, it was not physical tiredness from which he suffered – it was a weariness of spirit. He knew he owed it to the generations who had gone before him and the generations yet to come, to keep the family seat, but try as he might, he could summon no enthusiasm for the future. His wife, Eleanor, was a shrew. She cared for nothing save her position as the wife of an Earl, and seemed almost to derive pleasure from demonstrating how little he, the man, meant to her. She had been pretty once, in a pale, insipid way. Now, her always sharp features had become more finely drawn and her mouth was permanently dragged down, for she rarely smiled and never laughed. Then there were his children – Christopher, his firstborn, now seven and Amy, five. God knows, he had tried to love them, particularly the boy, but they were made so much in their mother's image.

It was his disappointment with Christopher which robbed Thomas's fight for Chadbrook of much of its lustre. He thought of the boy now – pale and thin, undersized for his age, with mousy hair and Eleanor's cold, grey eyes. Christopher, who liked nothing better than to sit by his mother as she read, sewed or played the spinet, who was frightened of horses and who complained of the cold on a brilliant frosty morning when a young boy's blood should be whipped up with the excitement and splendour of the day ahead. Thomas knew he frightened the boy and that grieved him, for much of that fear, he suspected, stemmed from Eleanor's coaching. He never had the opportunity to be alone with his son, nor was he given the chance to show him life outside the parlour.

His thoughts shifted to Amy. Sometimes he wondered whether the child was quite right in the head – her temper, her tantrums, her sulks were so violent, they suggested a derangement of mind. When she was in a temper, no one could reach her and her rages had not slackened now babyhood was over – if anything, they were worse. Eleanor was no more able to control her than he was. Only Amy's old nurse seemed to have the gift for calming her. Had he and Eleanor been close, they could have grieved together for their daughter's plight and perhaps planned some course of treatment for her. But they had never communicated well together and therefore chose to pretend that Amy's behaviour was normal. Theirs had been a marriage arranged by the old Earl to bring money to Chadbrook, and certainly, for a few years, Eleanor's dowry had helped. However, a loveless marriage had been a high price to pay for what had been less than ten years of respite from the crippling debts the estate had incurred in his father's time.

It seemed to Thomas that Chadbrook had never been in greater peril than it was now and the fact that the responsibility for maintaining it fell to him was a daunting one. Circumstances had conspired against him. His father had been a gentle, kind man whom Thomas had adored but Simon Chadbrook had been feckless and irresponsible with his inheritance. Without doubt he was obsessed with gambling and over the years had lost a fortune. Indeed the debts from his gambling days hung over Chadbrook still. Simon had by nature been an artistic man who loved fine paintings and objets d'art, and spent much of his time engaged in foreign travel and acquiring both. His wanderings in Europe not only took him away from Chadbrook and his responsibilities but always proved costly, for he never returned from one of his travels without a vast collection of mementos. His taste was excellent – his eye for a talented artist or craftsman was unquestionable but he spent money which the estate could ill-afford. At the time of his death, not only was Chadbrook heavily mortgaged but there was no capital left with which to run the estate. Even so, Thomas was newly married, and the benefit of Eleanor's dowry might well have changed the fortunes of Chadbrook had it not been for a series of different problems.

Thomas was a progressive farmer. On acquiring the estate, he had embarked on a programme of enclosing the land, with a view to intensifying his farming methods. In the long term, he knew that his policy would pay off but in the short term it was a very expensive business. He had needed labour for making hedges and ditches and he was greatly concerned with the wellbeing of the cottagers and small farmers on his estate, who no longer had the use of common land. Where possible, he had employed them on the estate to meet the needs of his more labour-intensive farming. This, of course, had resulted in a very high wage bill. He had begun experimenting with crops to ensure that none of his land had to lie fallow at any time, and here he had become the victim of his own success, inasmuch as both his farm buildings and equipment had needed to be renewed and modernized in order to cope with the greater capacity of his crops. His thinking was progressive but with each new step forward he seemed to create a whole lot of new problems which invariably proved expensive. At the moment his current worry was his sheep. He had introduced a new ram to the stock which he had been assured would improve both the quality and quantity of his flock. The reason he had returned in haste from London, in the teeth of such appalling weather conditions, had been because of a message received. It seemed that the ewes had begun slipping their lambs a week or so early. The lambs were almost all still-born and there was a very high proportion of twins amongst them. The message had been over a week old when he had received it and Thomas was almost afraid to ask what the outcome would be now.

Chadbrook's other problem was Eleanor. The daughter of a rich man, Eleanor had expensive tastes. She was always buying new furniture and furnishings. Her chairs had to be Sheraton, the wall-paper Chinese. She loved porcelain and refused to consider any flooring but rugs even in the children's bedrooms where rushes would have been more than adequate. In many respects, she was like her father-in-law – any objet d'art which took her fancy, she had to have. What applied to her home applied also to her person – her clothes had to be immaculate as did her children's. She had demanded and harassed him until he had provided her with her own carriage, complete with a matching pair of horses, and when she travelled abroad she insisted on being accompanied not only by the coachman but also by a footman, dressed of course in finest livery. It was not fair to blame Eleanor for Chadbrook's current parlous financial state, but certainly she had not helped. Tired and travel-worn as he was, it seemed to Thomas at that moment that there was no solution, no way ahead.

He sighed and eased himself from the bathtub. Jack had laid out clean clothes on the bed and then withdrawn. Thomas always pre-ferred to dress alone; he liked time to plan the day ahead. Today, though, he could raise no enthusiasm for anything. The snow would have thwarted all activity on the estate in any event and precluded callers. Besides which, it was his duty to spend time with his wife and children having been away for over a month. As he began dressing he cursed under his breath. While in London he had bought some silks for Eleanor and trinkets for the children but all the presents were on the pack horse he had left behind with his sick servant at Bishops Stortford. They would be expecting gifts from him and would be disappointed. Inevitably, it would prompt a tantrum from Amy, and sulking disapproval from Eleanor.

As soon as he could, he would escape to think things through yet again. He had a special place, not more than half a mile from the house – a stream, a tributary of the River Chad flowed past a clump of hawthorn bushes. It was nothing special, but even on the harshest winter day, he found it helped to sit there and consider his problems.

Unbidden, the memory of the red-haired girl at the inn came suddenly back to him. He had been disappointed not to see her before he left. By daylight her startling colouring must be all the more vivid. She was a strange creature, a little wild, certainly unusual. Thinking of her now, he realized that in their brief time together he had felt more alive, more vibrant, more in touch with the real world than he had felt in months, years perhaps. It was strange to feel so in the company of an ignorant serving wench, in a run-down, unwelcoming inn. He wondered, idly, whether he would ever see her again.

CHAPTER NINE

The day of the horse fair at Long Melford dawned bright and clear. It was cold for early April, with a strong wind blowing in from the north-east, sending fluffy white clouds high across an otherwise cloudless blue sky. But it was an exhilarating day – winter was over and summer just round the corner. Thomas travelled to the fair in his landau, accompanied by his wife and children. He would have preferred to have ridden over earlier on Sorcha but today he had in mind to buy his son a new pony and thus he wished to make a family occasion of it. Christopher sat next to his mother and stared sullenly out of the window.

'Have you a preference for how your new pony should look?' Thomas asked him.

'I told you, Father, I do not need a new pony nor do I desire one, thank you.'

'Rubbish, boy. That lazy, good-for-nothing pony of yours is not spirited enough for you any more,' Thomas insisted. 'You're nine now, you need something with more life to it. Godwin will go to Amy and we will find you a little horse who will put you out in the very front of the hunting field.'

'I hate hunting, you know that, Father.' Christopher met his father's eye defiantly. The boy needs a good hiding, Thomas thought.

'I really do not understand your need to pester Christopher so, Thomas. He is perfectly happy with Godwin. It is you who is always complaining how poor we are, so why spend money on a new horse when he is happy with the one he has?' Eleanor's face looked pinched and drawn in the early morning light. She tossed her head with exaggerated irritation.

'Because if he is ever to be a gentleman he has to learn to ride like one,' Thomas thundered. 'Now I'll hear no more argument. This is supposed to be a pleasurable day and you should think yourself lucky, boy, that you have a father prepared to buy you a new horse.'

The day was not a success. Eventually, without either Christopher's enthusiasm or co-operation, Thomas bid for a dappled grey

71

mare, named Marie, who seemed sound in wind and limb, and who had a gay and lively temperament. The pony cost more than Thomas had intended but the purchase seemed to hold no pleasure for Christopher who appeared more interested in listening to the strumming of a travelling minstrel than looking at the horses, or even playing with the other boys. It was a sorry business.

Leaving his family in the company of Lady Bowen and her children, he began walking across the green, intent on a mug of ale and a chat with local farmers to discuss the lambing. As far as he was aware, only his flocks had suffered still-births this season, but he wanted to make sure. The devil of it was finding the cause, and Thomas never underestimated the native wisdom of the local Suffolk farmers, however small their holding compared with the Chadbrook acres. His mind full of his problems, he strode along, acknowledging greetings from passers-by with a smile or a nod of the head. Suddenly, through the crowd, he saw the unmistakable back view of the girl from the inn – her long red hair was caught with a piece of old ribbon. It was like the taming of flame itself. She was walking fast, her head held high. He hurried his pace and caught up with her, searching his mind for her name as he did so. 'Elizabeth?'

She turned and seeing who it was, dropped a curtsy. 'Good day, sir,' she said, her eyes lowered.

'Good day, Elizabeth. Are you enjoying the fair?'

'Yes, sir.' She was very demure, very different from the girl who had so violently protected her virtue on that winter night, months ago. Her skin, he noticed, was almost translucent and pale but for a spot of colour on her high cheekbones. Her eyes he could not see for her lowered lashes, but her features were exquisite and she was both tall and slender.

'Walk with me awhile, Elizabeth. I am going in search of a glass of ale.'

'There is plenty for sale across the green there.' She pointed a finger.

'Then walk with me to the spot.'

They began to saunter in the direction of the temporary bar. Thomas was aware of the whisperings around them. Clearly they must have made an unusual sight – he, the Earl of Clare, she, a serving wench from the inn. He did not care what people thought and he was aware, too, that Elizabeth seemed unconcerned by the sensation they were causing. 'How is your book-learning progressing?' he asked.

72

She raised her eyes to him for the first time – emerald green, flecked with gold, he almost gasped at their beauty. 'Very well,' she said. 'I have worked hard since we met last. The monks say they have taught me everything they can – indeed they say that I should pass on my skills to children. I do have a way with children I believe, but, of course, I fear I have no chance of finding such a position.'

'Maybe if your skills are as good as they say, I could help you,' said Thomas.

'Oh, sir, could you?' The girl's face lit up.

He was awestruck by her beauty and simply could not look away. 'I am sure something could be arranged,' he said, hoarsely, at that moment having not the slightest idea what. They were nearing the bar – there was a growing press of men around them, drinking, swearing and no doubt passing comment on Elizabeth. He knew the feeling was irrational but his need to protect her from the rough uncouthness of these local men was very strong. 'We can't talk here,' he said. 'I think we should meet somewhere – somewhere quiet. In the meantime I will consider how I can help you and we can talk through your future – in peace.'

'When? Where?' She looked up at him. He could see in her face conflicting emotions – of suppressed excitement, of disbelief, of wariness, of joy.

'I will help you, Elizabeth, if I can,' he said, to reassure her. He thought quickly. 'Tomorrow, what of tomorrow? Can you meet me somewhere?'

She nodded. 'Oh yes.'

'At any time of the day?' Again, she nodded and he lowered his voice, pressing closer to her to avoid being overheard. 'Let us meet at noon, but where?'

Elizabeth did not hesitate. 'Behind the inn, up on the hill, there is a spinney. A path leads to it; it is easy to find. I could meet you there.' She blushed, suddenly aware of her boldness.

Thomas laughed delightedly. 'That will do very well. I shall see you on the morrow, Elizabeth.' He turned and began walking towards the bar. Because of his height and because everyone knew who he was, the crowd of men parted to let him through, doffing their caps as he passed. Elizabeth watched him, and as he moved through the press of bodies with such ease, it seemed to her as if his progress was somehow symbolic and that for her, too, through him, the way ahead would be clear and open to her at last.

The following morning, Elizabeth was unusually co-operative

73

around the inn. By sunrise she had made up the fires, had a fine piece of mutton roasting in the tap room, and was busy preparing pastry for pies. Jem became suspicious. 'What's happened to you, girl? Could it be that at last you recognize what a lazy slut you are?'

'I don't know what you mean,' Elizabeth said.

'You are working hard at your chores and singing as you go – what ails you?' His voice was heavy with sarcasm.

'It is a lovely morning and spring is here at last,' Elizabeth said, silently cursing herself for being so transparent.

'There must be more to it than that,' Jem grumbled.

Mary had not moved from her bed for the last three days and Jem wondered, briefly, what it would be like to have a wife with whom he could discuss things. The current mood of their child had to spell trouble but for the life of him he could not imagine what that might be.

Just before noon, two farmers came into the bar. They had bought horses from the fair the previous day which had needed the attention of the blacksmith, and now they had come to collect them. Jem became involved in conversation with them and while he did so Elizabeth slipped upstairs and changed into a clean shift, covered it with her best flannel petticoat and then tiptoed into her mother's room. Mary seemed to be asleep. Carefully, heart beating, Elizabeth removed the gown which hung in place of honour behind the door, and hurried back to her bedroom. The gown was made of moss-green silk which perfectly suited Elizabeth's colouring. It had been given to Mary by Lady Constance from Melford Place in return for some domestic services undertaken when her cook fell ill. It was Mary's prize possession but without a qualm Elizabeth slipped it on and the effect was magical. She felt instantly like a lady. She brushed her tangled hair and pinched colour into her cheeks. Then, running down the stairs as lightly as she could, she let herself out of the back door and began running up the path towards the spinney.

Even when she was out of sight of the inn, she did not slacken her pace. There was a great well of excitement building in her at the prospect of seeing the Earl again. As she neared the summit, she slowed down to a walk, aware, perhaps for the first time in her life, of the need to take stock of her appearance – she was panting hard, her hair whipped across her face by the wind. She leant against a tree for a moment and looked down at the gown. She was bitterly disappointed. In good light she could now see it was heavily stained, the fabric worn and there was mud around the hem. As she was so tall, the gown was too short for her and exposed the heavy, unattractive clogs she wore. It was too late now to do anything. He would have to accept her as she was. She sighed. Then, taking a deep breath, she straightened up and, holding her head high, walked with as much decorum as she could manage over the brow of the hill.

He was already waiting for her – she had not expected that. He was sitting on a fallen tree, his horse grazing nearby. When he saw her, he stood up and waved, his face boyish, eager, not at all intimidating. In that moment he might have been her equal and it was hard to resist the temptation to run to him. She waved back and hurried to the spot where he stood. 'I am so sorry,' she stammered. 'Have I delayed you?'

'No, not at all. It is such a fine day that I took my time riding over here – but also I did not wish to hurry Sorcha – she has not been fit since that journey home from London, when I first met you.'

Elizabeth looked at the horse. She was no expert but it was obvious that the mare was not in her first youth. Although impeccably groomed, her mane and tail were straggly and lacklustre. Her eyes, as she raised her head to the sound of her name, were clear but contemplative and rheumy with age. If asked, Elizabeth would have imagined Thomas Chadbrook to have chosen a fiery stallion as his mount. 'Why don't you have yourself a new horse?' she asked. 'That old mare looks well past her best.'

'Never,' said Thomas, seriously. 'Sorcha and I have been a long way together. No other horse could have brought me home from London so surely. She is as steady as a rock, as faithful an old friend as you could wish for. She will be right enough once the warm weather comes.' He smiled at Elizabeth. 'You are too young to value continuity in life. For you, when something new and different occurs it is exciting, while I, well, I crave permanence.'

Elizabeth remained silent, sensing that she had been rebuked. The feeling of being at one with the Earl had vanished. She became again an ignorant and immature girl of sixteen.

The Earl seemed to sense her disquiet. 'Come, sit beside me and I will tell you what I have arranged for you.' She did his bidding, sitting as demurely as she could on the log beside him. 'Have you ever heard of Lord and Lady Bowen?' Elizabeth shook her head. 'The Bowens live at Harkst, in a fine house called Sturbridge Hall. They are but three or four miles from Chadbrook, indeed they are our nearest neighbours. Lord Bowen and I have been friends since we were boys, and remain good friends now. His wife is some years

75

younger than he, and French. She has found living in England very difficult and lonely, complicated by the fact that she does not find it easy to master our tongue. She is a charming woman, but very shy.' He hesitated.

'Why are you telling me of Lady Bowen?' Elizabeth asked, boldly.

'Because I have secured you a position in her household.'

Elizabeth gasped. 'A position?'

'Yes. The Bowens have two children and a third is to be born in a month or so. They have a girl and a boy, aged, I believe, four years and two. They have a nurse, of course, but she is very old and Lady Bowen feels the children are in need of someone younger, though they are still too young for a governess. I have suggested that you should help look after the children – initially, to play with them and gradually, as they grow older, begin to teach them their letters, which is something their mother cannot do since her English is still so poor. It is an ideal arrangement – when they are old enough for a governess, they will already be blessed with a good knowledge of their letters, and in the meantime they will have had the benefit of your youthful company.'

'But I cannot!' Elizabeth cried, deeply distressed. 'I do not know how to behave, I have known no life but that at the inn. I have no clothes, no manners, I am nothing – a rough, ignorant girl. Oh, sir, it is kind of you to try to help me, but I cannot do this.' Her vehemence surprised not only Thomas but also herself. All her life she had dreamed of an opportunity such as this and now that it was presented to her she realized, suddenly, the enormous gulf that stood between her and the better life she had always craved.

Thomas smiled and took her hand. 'Do not worry about clothes, nor about your manners. I will arrange for you to have some of my wife's gowns and petticoats which she no longer uses. Normally they are passed to our maids but there is no reason why I cannot secure some for you. As for the question of etiquette, I will teach you myself.' He smiled, gently. 'After all, if you have an Earl to teach you your manners, surely your training could hardly be bettered.'

'But . . . why should you do this for me? Why should you be . . . so kind?' Elizabeth felt hot tears on her face. She felt desperate and way out of her depth.

Thomas started to speak, a platitude on his lips – then he stopped. 'The truth is, Elizabeth, I do not know.' He searched his mind for the right words. 'I see in you something special, a spark. I realize you are lowly born but you have so much courage, such a strong

76

desire to better yourself that I want to help, and I recognize that if I do not, it is possible that no one else ever will.'

'I am like Sorcha,' Elizabeth said, shrewdly, her tears abating.

Thomas glanced at his old mare and back at Elizabeth and then let out a roar of laughter. 'I can see very little similarity myself.'

Elizabeth blushed but attempted to justify herself. 'You are good to her when you do not need to be, as you are to me. The difference is that she can serve you, she can carry you safely about your business, while I can do nothing to repay you for your kindness.'

Thomas shifted uneasily. 'Perhaps you can, Elizabeth, perhaps you can, one day.'

Elizabeth frowned and stared into his face. Suddenly, she did not like what she saw there. 'There is a price then, for your help,' she said, her voice at once cold and hard. 'I must give myself to you, is that right? What are your terms, is it to be once or many times? It is surely not unreasonable of me to ask.'

Thomas was astounded by her words, by their boldness, by the proud way she held her head and met his eye. 'I . . . don't know what I want of you, Elizabeth,' he answered truthfully. 'I find you very beautiful and, yes, I desire you, but I will not force myself upon you, now or at any time in the future. You can have my assurance on that.'

His words made her feel ashamed. 'I am sorry,' she murmured. 'You are a gentleman and I am not used to dealing with gentlemen.'

Thomas smiled and squeezed the hand he still held. 'That is obvious, but if we are to secure you the position with the Bowens, we must turn you into a lady. No, it was correct and brave of you to ask me my intentions. Before accepting my help, you had a right to know what I expected in return and the answer is nothing except, perhaps, a kiss.' He leant forward and their lips met. This time it was very different from the cold, bleak night in the inn. The moment they touched, the fuse lit – in an instant they were straining to be close, their arms about one another, until in their efforts they toppled backwards off the log, down onto the mossy flooring of the spinney.

Thomas continued to kiss her, his hands running freely over her body, but made no attempt to undress her. All Elizabeth could do was cling to him, as the world spun about her. At last he drew away and his voice, when he spoke, was harsh and trembling. 'There now, my Elizabeth, perhaps you see why I wish to help you, but I will keep my word and will not dishonour you . . . not until you beg me to do so.' He stood up and holding out a hand to her, drew her to her feet. 'I must leave you now – we will meet again, soon.' He turned and strode towards his horse.

'When?' Elizabeth called after him, desperately. 'When will we meet again?'

Thomas climbed into the saddle before replying. 'Soon,' he said. 'You will hear from me, rest assured.' He swung his horse away from her and was off down the track and out of sight within seconds.

Elizabeth stood motionless, staring at the place where he had been. Her mouth felt bruised, her body was on fire. The longing she felt for him seemed to be tearing at her. She would see him again, he had said so, or was it all a dream? She stared about her, as if seeking reassurance from the trees, from the birds, from all the wild things which had been witness to their passion of moments before. She sat down on the tree trunk. Did he mean what he said about her position with Lord and Lady Bowen? A sense of terror swept over her – she would never manage it. How could she, Elizabeth Monson, ever take up such an appointment? Yet he had said he would help her and instinctively she knew that he meant it. He was not about to abandon her now, and most important of all, he believed in her. She smiled, suddenly. With Thomas Chadbrook at her side to guide her, to advise her and perhaps, perhaps . . . to love her, she could do anything, anything at all.

CHAPTER TEN

In fact it was nearly four weeks before Elizabeth heard from Thomas again – two weeks during which she experienced the most extreme of emotions from dizzy, unreal happiness to the depths of despair. At times she wondered whether she was actually going mad like her mother and had in fact dreamt the whole encounter – that such was her longing to escape, she had actually invented the meeting with Thomas. Her father was drinking even more heavily than usual, her mother was having one of her bad spells and so most afternoons Elizabeth found it possible to leave the inn without anyone seeming to notice. Indeed business at the inn was very slack and standards had never been lower. Jem no longer seemed to care whether the mugs and platters were clean or the floor left unswept. Elizabeth hated their slovenly ways but at least it gave her more freedom. She took to walking up to the spinney, partly to reassure herself of the reality of their meeting and partly, too, because she kept hoping that by some miracle Thomas would appear. There were so many unanswered questions. When would the Bowens want her to begin working for them? When would Thomas have time to teach her manners? What would happen when her father found out – would he accept losing his only daughter because the Earl had arranged her new position, or would he realize that he would be losing his unpaid slave and try to prevent her leaving? Then there was her mother. It was not true to say that Elizabeth loved her mother exactly, but she certainly pitied her. Mary Monson had allowed her circumstances to grind her down. Elizabeth could not understand this and did not recognize that it was easy to be strong when you were young and healthy. She could not remember a time when her mother had been normal. Sometimes Mary went for days on end not knowing who she was, not recognizing her own family, stumbling around the inn, appearing to have forgotten all the basic skills of living. Then, as though nothing had happened, she would suddenly rally, the dark days of her insanity seeming to have had no impact on her at all. What would become of her mother once she had left?

It was a subject that vexed Elizabeth, but she was aware that she could not let her mother's problems destroy her own chance of escape. Jem might beat his wife, might drink too much, might allow the inn to decline still further, but it was their life, their squalor, their misery and she had a right to make the best of whatever opportunities came her way.

One evening as the sun was setting, Elizabeth was just about to take the path down from the spinney where she had spent the afternoon, when from her vantage point she saw a horseman approaching the inn. The distance was too great to make out the detail of either man or horse but instinctively Elizabeth knew who it was. Her heart leapt with wild excitement. She started off down the path and then hesitated – he would know where to find her. She turned back and sat demurely on the fallen tree, waiting for him, her heart thudding, at once sure that he would seek her there and yet terrified that he would not, half believing she was mistaken and that it was someone else entirely. When he came into sight she stood up and in seconds he was out of the saddle and they were running towards one another. She fell into his arms, they kissed and this time there was no room for doubt, or hesitation. They clung together, murmuring endearments, touching, feeling, reassuring one another that they were indeed together again.

'Wait here.' Thomas's expression was suddenly dark and unreadable. He stepped away from Elizabeth and turned to Sorcha who stood patiently by.

'Don't leave me,' Elizabeth cried.

'I am not leaving you.' Thomas pulled a blanket roll from behind Sorcha's saddle and carefully unfolding it, he placed it on the ground. Then, holding Elizabeth's gaze, he walked towards her and began slowly to slip her shift from her shoulders. 'Tell me to stop and I shall,' he murmured.

'No, do not stop – please do not stop.'

He looked deep into her eyes for a moment. 'Are you sure, really sure?' Elizabeth nodded. 'Am I the first, my Elizabeth?'

'Yes,' she whispered. 'And it is right that you should be.'

'Not right, certainly not right, but destined, I fear,' Thomas said as his lips crushed onto hers.

At last Thomas raised himself on one elbow and looked down at Elizabeth. She lay naked, like some wild creature who belonged to the woods, her red hair fanning out across the ground, interwoven with traces of moss and leaves. 'I beg your forgiveness, Elizabeth, I

80

did not mean this to happen – at least, I did not mean this to happen so soon.' He ran a hand gently down her breast. 'It was my intention not to come and see you again. I knew I would be breaking my promise to you but I felt to pursue our relationship would be bad for us both. It seems I was right, yet I could not keep away.' His voice was full of remorse.

'You must not be sorry for what has happened.' Elizabeth clutched at his hand and pressed it to her lips. 'Nor can you say that this will harm us, not after. . .' She hesitated and then smiled, blushing slightly. 'I do not know what to call you. Lying like this together, "sir" does not seem right.'

Thomas threw back his head and laughed, his mood of the moment before gone. 'Thomas,' he said. 'Call me Thomas. Thomas and Elizabeth, that is who we are here. What is a title anyway? It is nothing, meaningless.'

'It means power and wealth,' Elizabeth said.

Thomas grimaced. 'Not much wealth, I fear.'

'Compared with me and my family, it means a great deal of wealth.'

Thomas felt instantly ashamed. 'You are right, of course. I have never known a day's poverty in my life, never needed to worry where the next meal would come from, whether there would be fuel for the fire, clothes to wear. I have never struggled to feed my children. You make me ashamed, Elizabeth, and rightly so.'

Elizabeth frowned. 'That is not what I wish – I desire only to please you and bring you a little happiness, perhaps.' She looked doubtful.

'Oh you do, you do,' said Thomas. 'How can I be anything but happy with you beside me? You are the most beautiful creature God ever created.' He leaned forward and kissed her again.

Their lovemaking this time was gentle and considerate, and Elizabeth, more confident, responded with a passion that shook them both. By the time they lay sated in one another's arms, it was almost dark. It was too early for the moon but lying back, wrapped in the rug for warmth, they counted the stars, laughing and talking together as lovers do. At last Thomas stood up and began dressing and then tenderly helped Elizabeth to do the same. 'I must take you home, your parents will be worried that something has befallen you.'

Elizabeth gave a hollow laugh. 'They will not care what has happened to me, only that I am not there to do their bidding.'

'Will they be very angry?'

'My father will most likely take a strap to me.'

The thought of anyone striking this lovely girl, injuring her perfect skin, was too much for Thomas. 'I will come to the inn with you and explain. I will not have your father beat you.'

'Explain what?' said Elizabeth, smiling.

'I'm not sure,' said Thomas, 'but I will find some story to tell.'

'My father has a loud mouth on him. He will know what we have been doing and by the end of the evening so will everyone who visits the inn.'

The logic of her argument could not be disputed and once again Thomas was struck by the girl's intelligence. Life had given her nothing and yet she seemed naturally to have so much, so many gifts. He kissed her tenderly. 'I have a busy week, but on Friday I will come to you and we will begin your tuition. Who knows, I may be able to turn you into a real lady.'

She saw the flash of white teeth in the dark, suggesting that he was laughing at her. 'Who knows, you might,' she said, angry and a little hurt that he should laugh at her.

They parted outside the inn. Elizabeth was lucky that night. There had been no custom – her mother was asleep upstairs and her father was dead drunk, sprawled before the kitchen fire.

Over the coming weeks, Thomas and Elizabeth developed a pattern to their relationship, and at least once a week they met in the spinney. Although at every leave-taking Thomas made promises to himself that on the next occasion he would end the affair, he found himself falling more and more under the spell of Elizabeth's charm and beauty. He found her youth so refreshing. Although only twenty-seven, there were days when he felt like an old man, weighed down as he was with the money problems at Chadbrook and locked into a loveless marriage. With Elizabeth he was young and carefree again and as her confidence grew, she teased him, made him laugh and loved him as no woman had ever done. On each occasion they met, they could think of nothing until they had made love, but then firmly, painstakingly, he began to teach her everything he could of how a great country house was run. He was a good teacher and certainly he had a quick and ready pupil. She listened intently, questioning him over anything she did not understand. He had arranged with the Bowens that she should start working for them immediately after harvest, so that she would be settled in in good time before the Christmas festivities began. However it was never to be, for on a

82

warm, early August evening something happened which changed the course of Elizabeth's life.

The moment she woke, Elizabeth sensed that something was wrong. The sun was already high in the sky, she could feel its warmth shining through the window directly above her bed. She had been dreaming of her new life and for several moments she lay in a state of confusion. Perhaps she had not dreamt of it, perhaps she was already living it for normally, even in summer, it was still dark when her father dragged her from her bed to fetch wood and water and begin the backbreaking chores of lighting the fires and heating water. Stretching languorously, she lay staring up at the rafters, thinking of Thomas. In daydreams, she put herself with him in so many different situations – dancing at a ball, the chandeliers sparkling, she would be dressed in a beautiful gown, whirling round and round; or she and Thomas in London, riding in a splendid chariot; or making love in a bed made with a feather mattress and linen sheets. . . There was something wrong. Her thoughts snapped back to the present and for a moment she could not think why she was so certain that all was not well. Then she realized it was the silence. There was no cursing and swearing as her father struggled with the barrels or shouted at her mother, there was no banging of doors or sound of chopping wood. The silence was oppressive and in seconds it had Elizabeth out of bed and reaching for her shift. She called out to her father as she climbed down the loft ladder, her limbs still clumsy with sleep. The kitchen was empty. She opened the back door and looked out into the yard. It was a beautiful early autumn day, sunny and crisp. For a moment she stopped and sniffed the air appreciatively, then the sense of unease returned. Perhaps he was still drunk from last night's excesses. She shivered, closed the door hurriedly and walked through into the tap room.

Nothing could have prepared her for the sight that met her eyes. There was blood everywhere. It was this she saw first and it reminded her instantly of the annual killing of the household pig – there was blood on the walls and the floor and on an upturned chair and table. Her eyes followed the trail to the hideously prone figure on the floor, beside which sat an old, grey-haired woman, whom Elizabeth did not at first recognize as her mother. Jem Monson lay with his head on his wife's lap. He had multiple stab wounds which in themselves could have proved fatal, but in addition, his head was almost severed from his body. His eyes were wide open, as if in shock, his mouth as in a scream. Yet because of the terrible wound, the head lay absurdly cocked on one shoulder, as if he was listening intently, and all the while Mary stroked his hair, singing a lullaby in a surprisingly sweet voice, her skirts drenched in her husband's blood.

For a moment Elizabeth was too stunned to move. Then she felt her stomach heave and taking a few short steps to the front door, she flung it open and ran outside. Her sickness left her weak and trembling, but steeling herself she went back inside. This time the scene looked even worse, for the light from the door showed the hideous reality of it.

'Mother?' Elizabeth said, softly. Mary did not appear to hear. 'Mother?' Elizabeth raised her voice. The singing continued. 'Mother, will you answer me,' she screamed. Mary looked up with glazed eyes. She stopped singing but continued to stroke her husband's hair – her hands were covered in blood. 'Mother, what has happened here?'

'Your father is tired, he is resting.'

'He's not tired, Mother, he's dead. Look at him, look at you. Come away, now.'

'Dead! He is not dead.' Mary clutched at the body.

Elizabeth had to look away. 'You'll leave him be and come with me, now.' Forcing herself to walk over to her mother, she seized her by the shoulder. Initially, Mary tried to resist but she was a small, frail woman and Elizabeth's strength soon got the better of her. Once Elizabeth had her mother on her feet, she marched her out of the tap room, through into the yard, to the pump. 'Bend down,' she ordered.

The freezing water flowing over Mary's frail body made her scream but Elizabeth held her firmly, watching grimly as the blood-stained water flowed away. She held her there relentlessly until every last vestige of blood had been removed, then taking the shivering, crying woman back into the kitchen, she sat her in her father's chair by the fire and helped her to undress. Tenderly she wrapped Mary in a horse blanket – the only thing near to hand – and seeing that she was already nearly asleep, she ran down to the cellar, fetched a bottle of brandy, and poured a tumbler each for them. 'Drink this, Mother.' She held her mother's hands round the cup as she drank. Mary choked a little, then seized the cup eagerly and drank it dry. The cup empty, she lay back in the chair with a sigh, her eyelids flickering.

'What happened, Mother? What happened to Father?'

Mary opened her eyes sleepily. 'He's resting.'

'He's not resting, he's dead. Someone killed him.'

Mary stared at her daughter with something close to hatred. 'What a dreadful girl you are to speak so of your father. Maybe you wish him dead – if so you are a wicked ungrateful daughter. He is a good man – it is my fault we are in this sorry state.'

Elizabeth fought to stay calm. 'You didn't kill him, did you, Mother?'

The face before hers suddenly crumbled and with the emotion came blessed sanity. 'No,' said Mary, tears beginning to flow down her face. 'No, no, I did not kill him.'

'Then who did?'

'Men, two men, travellers – they came late last night, they wanted ale and food, but they would not pay. Jem got angry. He was very drunk and there was a fight. I tried to stop them but they said they would kill me, too. There was nothing I could do to save him.' Her eyes suddenly clouded. 'It must be getting late. It's time I fetched your father his dinner. There's a fair this afternoon, up on the green. He wants his dinner early before he goes.'

The moment of sanity had passed. Fleetingly, Elizabeth wondered whether her mother would ever be sane again. The shock of seeing her husband killed was enough to send a sane woman mad, let alone one already so severely deranged.

'Come on, Mother, it's time you went to bed. I'll help you.' Together they made the tortuous journey up the loft ladder and Elizabeth tucked her mother into bed. She whimpered a little but was soon sound asleep.

By seven that evening, Elizabeth had removed most of the traces of Jem Monson's life and death from the inn. His body had been taken for burial. The vicar had visited her and arranged the funeral for the following day. Surprisingly, the villagers had been kinder than she had expected. There had been offers of help from almost every quarter but she had declined them all. She spent most of the day scrubbing out the tap room, removing all traces of the blood, cleaning the room as it had never been cleaned before, washing the mugs, scrubbing the platters, scraping from the floor filth and grime which had lain there for months. She laid down clean sweet-smelling rushes and stoked the fire into a good blaze, using the logs she cut herself. By evening, the room was ready for any visitors who cared to call, but for the problem of the ale – she could not lift the heavy barrels alone and there was only half a barrel on the racks ready to serve.

She was standing back admiring her work when she heard heavy footsteps approaching through the kitchen. For a moment she was terrified – the men who had killed her father, whoever they were, had perhaps returned. The door was flung open and standing there was, of all people on earth, the person she wanted most to see. 'Thomas!' She ran into his arms and he held her tightly.

'My poor darling. Did they harm you, these people who killed your father?'

Elizabeth suddenly felt very tired and weak, and all but fainted in Thomas's arms. Sensing her distress, Thomas bent down, picked her up and carried her over to the fireplace, seating them both in the chair where months before he had first encountered her. She began to cry, great gulping sobs. He simply held her on his lap, rocking her to and fro, as if she was a child. At last she stopped. 'Oh no, I have made your coat all wet.' She sat up. 'It is a beautiful coat – Thomas, forgive me, I was so glad to see you.' A thought occurred to her, suddenly. 'How is it you know what happened, and how much I needed you?'

Thomas smiled. 'I was not very clever, I fear. You have forgotten, but we were due to meet tonight, up at the spinney. I was there as usual at five o'clock. When you did not come I rode down into the village. I went for a mug of ale at The Lion and it was there I heard what had befallen your family. As you can imagine, I drank my ale with all haste and presented myself here. Now, what's to be done? What can I do to help you?'

'Nothing. I think I have attended to everything that needs to be done at the moment. My father is to be buried tomorrow.'

'Have you enough money for the funeral?'

Elizabeth nodded. 'He kept his money in a chest in the cellar. There is more than I expected, and after paying for the funeral I will have enough to repair and improve the inn a little.'

Thomas frowned. 'But why spend money on the inn when you will shortly be leaving it? If there is money to spare then you and your mother should share it between you after which you should move to the Bowens with all speed. In the circumstances, the sooner you leave the inn, the better. I am sure I can arrange for you to go to Lord and Lady Bowen immediately after the funeral, if that is what you wish.'

'No,' said Elizabeth. 'It is not what I wish.' She stood up and straightened her gown, tossing her head in the defiant gesture he had come to love.

'I beg your pardon, my lady,' he said, inclining his head in a mock bow. 'What is it then that you wish?'

Elizabeth did not respond to his humour. 'I cannot leave my mother,' she said. 'I have thought of little else all day, but my decision is made and there is nothing that you or anyone else can do to change my mind. As you know my mother is mad. She has suffered from bouts of insanity for many years and since bearing witness to her husband's murder, I doubt she will ever be sane again.'

'Then surely. . .' Thomas began.

'I will not see her go to an asylum,' Elizabeth shouted. 'She is a gentle woman – a good, gentle woman who means no harm to anyone. She deserved a better life than the one she has had, and now my father is dead I will try to make sure that her remaining years are as happy and as tranquil as possible.'

The girl never failed to astonish him and he loved her for it. Her fierce loyalty to the woman who had borne her but had done precious little else to make her life easy was not just touching, it was noble. In that instant Thomas vowed to do everything he could to help her to achieve her goal. 'So what is your plan?' he asked.

Sensing that Thomas both understood and accepted her decision, Elizabeth continued more calmly. 'I intend to run the inn myself. I will need someone to help me lift the barrels but I know just the man in the village to do that. With the money I have I will improve the property and with luck will be able to attract some of the coach trade which at the moment goes only to The Lion. I know what ladies and gentlemen want – good hot food, a clean and tidy inn, and proper stabling for their horses. If I work hard I feel sure I shall be able to support myself and my mother. I will succeed, Thomas, I know I will.' Her voice trailed away – shock and weariness showed themselves on her lovely face.

'I too am certain that you will succeed,' said Thomas gently. 'Despite your tender years, you have a good head on your shoulders. You are a clever girl and a very beautiful one.' He stood up and kissed her tenderly, but she was in no mood for love. Her mind was racing with plans for her own and her mother's survival. 'I have a proposal to make to you,' Thomas said. Elizabeth looked up at him distractedly. 'I want you to allow me to go into partnership with you.'

'Partnership?' Elizabeth looked confused.

'Not the partnership of marriage, I am afraid, for as you know, I have a wife already, but a business partnership. The money your father has left you should keep safely for your use in the event of any ill-fortune which might befall you or your mother. I will provide you with sufficient resources to repair and improve the property. You are right about what you need to do to attract customers, but the inn needs much alteration and repair. You must have bedrooms and one or two private dining rooms for the wealthy travellers. I have workers on my estate – good carpenters and glaziers – who could transform this old inn into a place of beauty. There is much of the building which is sound and good.' He looked around him, suddenly enthusiastic about the idea.

'I cannot take your charity,' said Elizabeth.

'I am not asking you to take my charity – give me a little credit for knowing the kind of person you are,' said Thomas. 'My proposal is this. From the profits you make on the business, you shall keep two thirds and I one third.'

'Would not an equal share be better?' Elizabeth asked.

Thomas shook his head. 'All I have to do is to provide you with money and labour from time to time. It is you who must work from dawn until sunset. It is a hard life, Elizabeth, running an inn.'

'I do know,' said Elizabeth, with a faint, ironic smile.

'Of course you do, but with a little money, we can perhaps make life easier for you. You are right, Long Melford is well placed. Newmarket races are gaining in popularity and with Sudbury becoming ever more prosperous, there are many wealthy merchants who use this road to travel to Bury. These are the customers who will pay handsomely to rest at a well-kept inn, and who have little liking for mixing with the stage coach travellers at The Lion. It is these people you must woo, Elizabeth.' He smiled at her and put his hands on her shoulders. 'Tell me, does this inn of yours have a name?'

Elizabeth shook her head. 'Not that I know. It has always been known just as Monsons since we have been here.'

'Then it must have a name and a fine sign to go with it.'

'Yes,' said Elizabeth. 'Yes, it must, but what name shall we give it?'

Thomas considered for a moment and then he smiled delightedly. 'We shall call it The Lady in Waiting.'

Elizabeth frowned. 'A strange name – waiting for what?'

Thomas smiled. 'Who knows? You are the lady now, so you tell me – for what are you waiting, fair Elizabeth? Are you perhaps waiting for prosperity, for fame, for beautiful clothes, for many admirers?' He smiled. 'Or perhaps, if I may dare presume it . . . for me?'

CHAPTER ELEVEN
Long Melford – Christmas 1781

The Boxing Day meet was better attended than usual, which was, thought Thomas, perhaps a reflection of the comparative prosperity with which Suffolk had been blessed the previous autumn. The harvest had been good, indeed it had been a record year. Not only had it been of benefit to Chadbrook, it had also saved many a smallholder and cottager from another winter in which starvation threatened. Sitting astride his faithful Sorcha, his hounds milling around him, he looked on the scene with pleasure. There was something special about a hunt – class and rank were not relevant, everyone was there for good sport, and with this shared aim, nobleman rubbed shoulders with peasant with none of the normal formality and awkwardness. In many ways a man ahead of his time, Thomas sensed that this was right, and during the Christmas period particularly, the sense of community he felt about him now pleased him greatly. He searched the sea of faces, beyond the milling horses and hounds. It was not difficult to pick out Elizabeth – her hair was like a beacon and, unlike the other women, no shawl covered it. In the emerald gown and cloak which he had bought her on his last visit to London, she was set apart from everyone – from her own kind and from his.

Elizabeth had matured a great deal in the last few months. The responsibility of running the inn, plus the confidence she had gained from Thomas's help and support, had brought a new calmness of spirit. Her life was no longer one of drudgery – it was now one of purpose and achievement and her appearance reflected this. Six months ago, Thomas would have been too discreet to seek her out but now he no longer cared. Relations between himself and his wife, Eleanor, were at an all-time low. For months she had refused to let him come to her bed and she actively avoided his company on every possible occasion. In these circumstances, if a man chose to seek solace elsewhere, Thomas reasoned, he was so entitled. Besides which, he was proud of Elizabeth now, of how she looked, of the person she was becoming. He raised an arm in greeting and urged Sorcha through the crowds, towards her.

'Will you be opening the gate for me, today?' he asked, his eyes alight with love and humour. 'There will be a penny in it for you.'

'If it please you, sir,' Elizabeth dropped a curtsy and bowed her head, 'then most certainly I shall.'

Thomas leant forward in the saddle. 'And you more than anyone should know what pleases me,' he whispered.

Most women would have blushed but not Elizabeth. She met his eye. 'I think you may be right in that, sir,' she said. 'Have a good day but be careful, the ground is hard and treacherous.' For a moment her eyes clouded with anxiety.

It pleased him to see how much she cared. 'Oh, I will be careful, but then I have Sorcha to see me safely home.'

Elizabeth put her hand on his horse's flank for a moment. 'Yes, dear beast. I never thought much of horses until I met her.' She glanced around her. There were many interested eyes upon them but they kept a respectful distance. 'She brings you safely to me, again and again, and for that she will always have a special place in my heart.'

Thomas smiled. 'The gown becomes you.' He bent low over the horse's mane again. 'I shall hope to see you tonight – do not turn away good custom but send everyone home to their beds by ten o'clock if you can, so we can be alone.'

'I shall,' said Elizabeth.

An air of excitement and tension mounted. The huntsman blew his horn, the whippers-in rounded up the hounds and the field began to move off. With one last glance over his shoulder to where Elizabeth stood, Thomas followed. Ahead of him he could see the slim, black figure of his wife. For a moment he was tempted to ride on and catch up with her but he could not face the sour look she would give him, the angry rebuke at his having forced her to join the hunt this day. Boxing Day, every year, caused problems within the Chadbrook family. Thomas felt it essential that his whole family should be represented on the hunting field, but Eleanor was a poor, nervous horsewoman. Christopher, it appeared, was plain terrified. Normally, Thomas gave in to family pressure but this year he had been determined that at least Christopher should accompany him. When Eleanor had said that she would not allow it because the boy was not strong enough, Thomas had issued an ultimatum – either she had to be at his side or Christopher. In the event, it was Eleanor who had opted to come, rather than let her precious boy run the risk of becoming damp or cold. Momentarily admiring her sacrifice – for

Thomas knew how much she hated hunting – he had bought her a new riding habit, with a hat of the latest fashion, and it became her very well. He had not been so lucky with her horse. He had bought the beast the previous year as a failed racehorse. He knew it to be an unreliable jumper but he consoled himself with the fact that Eleanor rarely jumped anyway. In an effort to rid himself of his misgivings, he turned his thoughts to Elizabeth.

Elizabeth was making a considerable success of The Lady in Waiting. Already she was attracting a fair proportion of the passing coach trade and with a little help and guidance, she had transformed the inn into a homely, hospitable place such as any traveller would welcome. She now employed a full-time cellarman and a local woman from the village provided excellent food. The building was large and in a surprisingly good state of repair. The next stage had to be to provide overnight accommodation, more stabling and a wider selection of food and drink. Any investment he made along these lines would result in greater profits, Thomas had no doubt. Elizabeth had already proved that she had a good head on her shoulders when it came to the business of running an inn, and the increasing flow of traffic through Suffolk provided ready-made custom. It was a question of timing. To invest in the inn now, ready for the spring, might be good for business but it would deplete his capital just at a time when he was beginning to make inroads into Chadbrook's debts. There again, the income he would gain from the increase in business at the inn would be useful for ploughing back into Chadbrook. It was a difficult decision.

Just past Lineag Wood the hounds got a scent and were off. Soon the hunt was in full cry, many riders streaming ahead of him. The land here was open and flat, with just the occasional hedge and ditch – it was perfect hunting country. In the distance ahead of him the horn sounded and he felt a surge of excitement. It was a dull day, dank and cold, but it did not worry Thomas. Elizabeth had rejuvenated him, he felt younger and fitter than he had in years. Suddenly, there was a commotion ahead of him, a shout and then a scream, a riderless horse running out of the field. There were several riders pursuing the horse and the incident was of no interest to Thomas until he saw Simon, his stable lad, urging his weatherbeaten old pony against the stream of riders. 'Sir, it's her Ladyship. She's taken a fall. It looks bad.'

'Where is she?' Thomas reined in his horse beside the white-faced boy.

'She's over there, sir.' The boy pointed to the horse, which Thomas could now make out to be Eleanor's dapple grey, still being pursued, as maddened with fear it dashed hither and thither across the wide expanse of field.

'Not the horse, damn it, man, my wife!'

'She's, she's still with the horse, sir. Her foot is caught in the stirrup.'

'Oh my God, come, Simon.' He wheeled Sorcha and dug his spurs deep into her flank. She responded to the urgency, stretching out her long neck, her mane flying.

They cut off the path of the terrified horse. As Thomas drew near he saw that the body of his wife was still being dragged along the grass. He urged Sorcha on and on until they were beside the runaway mare. Then leaning forward, he grasped at the reins. At first the horse fought him but feeling Thomas's strong grip, her pace began to slacken. Thomas hurled himself from Sorcha and ran to his wife's body. He eased the twisted and misshapen foot from the stirrup, releasing the body fully onto the ground. Then he turned her onto her back. She was unrecognizable, her head and face beaten to a bloody pulp. She was quite dead.

Elizabeth attempted to collect the discarded mugs and platters. Her movements were nervous and awkward and her heart was not in the job. From the moment she had heard that Eleanor was dead she had been fighting a battle of warring emotions. The implications of Thomas's being a widower thrilled and excited her, she could not deny it. She knew it was wicked even to think of such a thing. A woman in her prime had been alive, hale and hearty this morning, and now lay dead, leaving behind her two young children. Yet Eleanor had never made him happy, quite the contrary, and was he not always saying that she, Elizabeth, was the only woman who could fulfil him. Eleanor had been a poor wife, and now, some might say, conveniently, she was no more. Somewhere in the recesses of her mind, something told Elizabeth that things could not be as simple as that. The fact that his wife was now dead did not automatically mean that Thomas would marry her and yet. . . She continued clearing and stacking and when the bar was at last clean and tidy, she threw more logs on the fire and replaced several of the candles as they burned low. Of one thing Elizabeth was sure: if Thomas came to her that night, maybe, just maybe their future lay together.

She was almost asleep by the time the door opened and his tall figure shuffled in. He looked terrible, exhausted and somehow bowed down. She ran to him without a word and threw her arms about him. He held her tight. 'You've heard then?'

'Yes,' Elizabeth murmured into his jacket. 'I am so sorry.'

'It was terrible, a hideous thing to happen.'

'Come to the fire,' Elizabeth urged. 'I will fetch you brandy.'

'Yes, by God,' said Thomas. 'Yes, that is what I need.'

Elizabeth poured him a large mug of brandy and watched him while he swallowed it down eagerly. Instinct told her that she must take her lead from him. It was vital that he should not see that she had no regrets at Eleanor's death. She did not speak until she judged he was ready to talk. 'Tell me about it,' she said, at last.

His face was expressionless. 'I suppose it was a freak accident, though in truth, Elizabeth, I fear it was my fault. Eleanor was not a good horsewoman, yet I forced her out today and now she is dead.'

'But surely,' said Elizabeth, 'it was her duty to be beside you today.'

'Maybe,' said Thomas. 'But then I should have taken more care with her mount. I bought the horse for a small sum last year. She was unreliable – I knew that and yet I let Eleanor ride her this morning.'

'You have so many calls on your time,' Elizabeth suggested.

'No, do not excuse me, it was not that. It happened because I did not really care, or rather did not care enough. I did not think she would attempt to take a jump.'

'And did she?' Elizabeth asked.

'No,' said Thomas, heavily. 'I do not think it was her intention but the hounds had the scent, the hunt was off and I suspect she was out of control of the horse. He took the hedge like everyone else but Eleanor lost her seat. That in itself need not have been serious but her foot remained caught in the stirrup.'

Elizabeth winced. 'She was dragged then?' she enquired, gently.

'I'm afraid so,' said Thomas. 'It was some quarter of a mile before I caught her. I pray to God that the fall itself may have stunned her so that she did not suffer much. I have had the horse shot, of course, but that cannot absolve my sense of guilt. I should have taken more care, Elizabeth, I should have.'

Elizabeth went to put her arms around him but he pushed her away. She had not expected this reaction. She had expected him to be shocked and sorry but not this appalling sense of doubt and guilt.

93

She did not know how to cope with it. 'How are the children?' she asked, to hide her hurt.

'That is why I am so late. I have just left them. My son is inconsolable, and I do not know what to say or do for I barely know the boy. He was very much his mother's pet. I wish to help him in his distress but what can I say? His mother has been taken cruelly from him. Nothing and no one can bring her back.' He hesitated.

'Please,' said Elizabeth. 'Speak of it, it will help you ease the pain.'

'I should not, must not speak ill of Eleanor.' Thomas looked deep into Elizabeth's eyes. 'Particularly in the circumstances and particularly to you, yet there is no one else in whom I can confide. Eleanor drove a deep wedge between myself and my son. For some reason she did not want him to be like me. Perhaps she was right, who knows. He has never been a strong child but he did not need the pampering she subjected him to. I never had proof but I am sure she had been poisoning him against me since birth.'

'Surely not,' said Elizabeth.

'I think so. We were . . . not the happiest of couples. Maybe it was her way of punishing me for not being a better husband.' He helped himself to some more brandy. 'In any event, Christopher seems frightened and wary of me, as if I am some unknown and not particularly welcome stranger.'

'Every tragedy, every sadness in life, has a good side,' Elizabeth said. 'The death of your wife will at least provide you with the opportunity to get to know your son.'

'If it is not too late,' said Thomas.

'And your daughter, how is she?'

'She's upset, but too young to realize the implications. She will mend,' said Thomas.

Elizabeth hesitated, picking her words carefully. 'I have always imagined that your marriage was not a happy one or you would not have needed me. I suppose once, though, you loved your wife and for that reason alone it must be a great sadness to you that she is dead.'

Thomas sighed. 'I am sorry that she is dead,' he said, 'for she was but a young woman with years of life ahead of her. I am sorry for her sake that she will not see her children grow up. For my own part, though I feel responsible for her death, I cannot pretend our marriage was happy. We did not marry for love but because our families wished it so. Still, we might have found friendship and warmth but we did not. Eleanor was a cold, hard woman who was not prepared to give anything of herself – at least not to me. She liked the position I could offer her, the title, the lands, the privileges, but she cared little for the man who provided her with these things.'

'Then she was a very foolish woman,' said Elizabeth, crossing herself as she spoke.

Thomas smiled down at her, sadly. 'Whereas you, I suppose, think you are a wise one to care for me so. Somehow, I doubt it.'

'I do not, nor shall I ever,' said Elizabeth, vehemently.

Thomas stood up. 'As usual you ease the troubles I bear. Come, Elizabeth, and show me just how much you love me, for I have a great need for you tonight.'

CHAPTER TWELVE
Brundon Hall – August 1782

Surprise completely silenced him. He could not before remember an occasion on which anybody had asked him to wait. Thomas, Earl of Clare, was a punctual man by nature, but his position afforded him the view that his convenience should be given priority over that of almost anyone, save the King. He stared in frank amazement at the ostentatiously dressed butler, now standing before him. Mr. Naylor, he had been informed, would be with him as soon as possible – he was currently engaged with his bankers. Thomas pulled his watch from his waistcoat. 'My appointment with Mr. Naylor was for eleven o'clock and it is past that now by some ten minutes. I, too, am a busy man. Would you kindly inform your master that the Earl of Clare wishes to see him and wishes to see him now.'

The butler appeared unimpressed. 'If you would come this way, sir, I shall show you to the drawing room. Would you care for a glass of Madeira?'

The man's manner irritated Thomas but he was too weary to pursue the matter. Certainly, his heart was not in this meeting, but there was really no alternative. The butler showed him to an uncomfortable upright chair placed before an agreeable fire and withdrew, leaving Thomas to his thoughts. He stared gloomily around the room, a riot of silks, satins and gilt – hideous in the extreme. What was he doing here – he felt like a traveller in a foreign land. That he should be forced to go to these lengths appalled him. He shook his head as if trying to rid his mind of the reality before him.

His thoughts turned painfully to Elizabeth – she would have to be told, and soon. Women were given to strange fancies at times and of late it seemed to him that now he was without a wife, and Elizabeth with child, it was almost as if she was expecting that they should marry. It was out of the question of course – ludicrous. Even if he had not so desperately needed substantial funding for Chadbrook, there was the question of social standing. Beatrice Naylor was not from a family of breeding, but at least she would be able to conduct herself properly at Court, whereas Elizabeth . . . Fleetingly, he wondered whether time and careful tuition could have changed Elizabeth sufficiently. She had beauty, wit, intelligence, she held herself well . . . he fought off the thought and was mercifully interrupted by the arrival of the glass of Madeira and George Naylor's wife, Mary.

Mary was not a handsome woman but it was possible to see that once she must have been attractive in a rather overblown way. Her dark hair was swept up into a lavish arrangement of curls, her face unfashionably rosy-cheeked and her ample figure forced into an elaborate gown which was far too small for her. She curtsied. 'Sir, it is a great honour to welcome you to Brundon.'

He stood up and inclined his head. 'Thank you, madam. You have a fine house.'

'Oh, do you think so?' Mary was clearly flustered. She sat down quickly, in the chair opposite him. 'You would not easily imagine how it was when we found it, George has spent a fortune restoring it. Then there were the furnishings – the silks for those curtains I bought in Bond Street. They cost. . .'

Thomas smiled politely and switched off as Mary began a monologue as to where the contents of the house had been purchased and for what price. Newly rich people could never stop talking about money, Thomas thought sourly. He controlled his temper for as long as he could but finally the dam burst. 'Madam, I am sorry not to show more interest in the purchase of your furnishings but I am an extremely busy man. Would you please tell your husband that I wish to see him at once. He knows the purpose of my visit, but I shall be leaving forthwith unless he has the courtesy to receive me, now.'

'Oh, sir, I do beg your forgiveness,' said Mary Naylor, jumping to her feet. 'I shall go to him directly.'

Moments later, Thomas was escorted by Mary to the door of George Naylor's study, which he entered with a considerable degree of ill-grace. George Naylor was a little man, nearly bald, with a pale, plain face and a large, bulbous nose. His best feature was his eyes, which were small, grey and very shrewd. 'I am pleased to meet you, sir.' He came from behind the desk. 'And I apologize for keeping you waiting but business must always come first.'

'I, too, am here on business,' Thomas remarked, tersely.

'Yes, of course.' George indicated a chair and they both sat down. Thomas was about to speak, when George began. . . 'I am a plain man, sir, I have worked hard all my life, and have been blessed with the good fortune to possess a handsome wife and two handsome daughters. I have also been blessed with not inconsiderable wealth.

I understand you wish to marry my elder daughter, Beatrice, and I also understand that you are in some financial embarrassment with regard to the Chadbrook estate.' Thomas was astounded by the way in which the man addressed him, by his outspoken, forthright manner. The surprise must have shown. 'I do not apologize for my manner of speech,' George said. 'It is my way, when there is business to be done. You want my daughter and the dowry that will come with her. I would like to see her married and I will admit it gives me pleasure to imagine her the wife of an Earl. So . . . with my daughter, sir, will come twenty thousand pounds, which you will receive by banker's draft on the day of the wedding. I have to admit to having undertaken some investigations of my own into the extent of your debts, and it would seem to me that this sum will clear them. Am I right?'

'Yes, yes indeed,' said Thomas. The man was extraordinary.

'Furthermore, I will settle on my daughter the annual income of ten thousand pounds. This sum will continue to be paid after my death, only while Beatrice remains married to you and living as your wife. If there should be any major breakdown in the relationship, or, of course, if she should die, then the income will cease. I will further settle five thousand pounds by way of annual income on any children of the marriage. I propose that I shall make the first payment on, shall we say, the 1st October, assuming by that date you and Beatrice are wed. I see no merit in delaying matters, since Beatrice is getting no younger and presumably you would like more children. Do you find the arrangements satisfactory?'

It was extremely satisfactory, a great deal better than Thomas had dared hope. George Naylor was right, twenty thousand pounds would almost exactly clear Chadbrook's debts and ten thousand pounds a year would keep him and Beatrice very comfortably indeed, together with the profits from the estate which from henceforth would be unencumbered by debt. 'I find your offer perfectly acceptable,' he said, awkwardly – he did not like feeling beholden to this man but the generosity of the dowry made it impossible to feel otherwise.

'There is one other matter,' George said. He hesitated and Thomas sensed a change in him. He should have recognized the offer could not be as straightforward as it appeared. He waited, aware with some pleasure of the other man's discomfiture.

'I feel that my role in society and the contribution I have made to the local community, in particular, have been much overlooked and under-appreciated,' George said at last. 'I do a great deal of charity

98

work, I have been responsible for creating much local employment, I am one of the founder members of a new coach company which is making Suffolk and Norfolk more accessible to London.'

'Yes, yes,' said Thomas, impatient and anxious – Chadbrook's future depended on this meeting. 'What is it that you want?'

'A knighthood,' said George. For the first time there was genuine embarrassment and he did not meet Thomas's eye. Thomas could not help himself, he threw back his head and laughed. As he did so, he regretted it, George was clearly hurt and angry. 'I cannot see, sir, why you consider it to be a laughing matter. It would mean a great deal to me and my wife – a public acknowledgement of the work we have done.'

'Yes, I apologize,' said Thomas. 'But a title, you know, is really of so very little consequence. Still, if it is what you wish, I will speak to the Lord Lieutenant. I am sure something can be arranged.'

George beamed with delight. 'Then I think, sir, our business is concluded. Can I offer you another glass of Madeira and then we shall go and join the ladies.'

A quarter of an hour later, her parents having discreetly withdrawn, Thomas found himself alone with Beatrice Naylor. He had first noticed her at a hunt ball, a year before, and had then met her subsequently at several local houses, at soirées and dinner parties. She was not exactly pretty, but she was handsome and carried well her twenty-six years. She had dark hair like her mother, drawn back severely from her face, but it suited her. Her large brown almond-shaped eyes were her main feature and her hairstyle complemented them well. 'You must know why I am here?' Thomas said.

'I believe I do,' said Beatrice. There was not even a hint of coquettishness about her – she was straightforward like her father, which Thomas found rather refreshing. 'Then allow me, Miss Naylor, to ask you if you will do me the honour of becoming my wife.'

She was silent for a long moment and briefly he wondered if she might refuse him. It was something that had never occurred to him until that moment. Then she smiled. 'I do not really have a choice, do I? The business transaction is complete, I simply have to comply.'

These Naylors never ceased to surprise him – there was no blushing, no simpering ways. She just stated the facts as she saw them. 'Of course you have a choice. If you do not find me . . . if I am not to your liking, you must say so and the marriage will not proceed.'

'My father is set on it, and everyone tells me you are the most sought-after bachelor in England and I am very lucky.'

'And what do you think?' Thomas asked, amused.

Beatrice regarded him. 'I do not love you,' she said, carefully. 'But then how could I, I barely know you. I am not a young woman, I am plain, my father is wealthy but has little in terms of taste and style. If I were to refuse you, not only would I be unlikely to find a better husband, I would be unlikely to find a husband at all. The thought of growing to old age with no purpose in life but to look after my ageing parents is not an attractive prospect, and so, of course, I must accept.'

Her words chilled Thomas to the bone. She spoke them pleasantly enough, with a little smile playing on her lips, but they suggested cold emptiness. He felt compelled to bring some kind of warmth and emotion to the conversation. 'I, too, cannot speak confidently of my love for you but I know I will come to love you and that I will always cherish and honour you – you can be confident of that.'

'I am grateful, sir,' she replied formally.

He bent forward, took her hand and kissed it. It was a strong, capable hand, cool to the touch. It sat unresponsive in his. Helplessly, his thoughts returned once more to Elizabeth, to her warmth, to her generosity, to her wild, helpless, hopeless passion for him, and his for her. He was betraying her and their love but it had to be done. He had no choice. . .

The pain ripped through her, making her gasp aloud. She turned her head away so that they would not see her cry and tried to concentrate on the view from her open window. High above her she could see the spinney, the leaves already turning gold and red. At this moment she wished that it had never happened, that Thomas had not chanced by the inn that night, not returned to see her again and again . . . another pain came – this time she screamed aloud.

Dr. Morgan took her hand. 'Steady, Elizabeth, steady. You have a long way to go yet, my dear. Do not tire yourself.'

A long way to go . . . why had no one told her that childbirth would be like this? Why had she not been warned? She could not cope with it – not for another moment, and as she tried to gather her strength together to withstand the next onslaught of pain, all she could think of was that she hated Thomas for doing this to her.

The months immediately after Christmas had been busy for both Thomas and Elizabeth. For Thomas, the aftermath of his wife's death had presented him with domestic responsibilities which he had not dreamed existed, and then there were the children. Christopher had become a recluse, while Amy. . . Amy's problems could now no longer be ignored. What little control she seemed to have had over herself had vanished completely with her mother's death and as well as her behaviour problems, she had now started having convulsions. An endless round of doctors in London had helped not at all and against this background of domestic trouble, the weather was poor, the sowing had been late, the corn was slow to ripen and the harvest seemed doomed.

Elizabeth had been equally preoccupied but in a more positive way. The inn was going from strength to strength and she now no longer served behind the bar at all, employing two pretty girls from the village instead. For her part, Elizabeth mingled among the customers, making sure that they had everything they needed. It had become common knowledge that the inn was owned by a woman and, strangely, it seemed to work to Elizabeth's advantage. People came to see her out of curiosity, but not to take advantage. Far from behaving badly, travellers showed an unexpected respect, so that the inn quickly gained a reputation for being a suitable place to bring both women and children travelling on the coaches from London. As Thomas had predicted, she was starting to attract the prosperous travellers, who mainly travelled by post-chaise. It was perhaps for this reason that Elizabeth did not realize for nearly two months after that Boxing Day night that she was pregnant. Her dresses seemed a little tighter and some mornings she did not feel too well, but the baby growing inside her was nearly twelve weeks old before, finally, she acknowledged what must have happened. Initially she was horrified but a trip to the spinney and a few hours of quiet reflection made her realize that the baby she carried could only be of advantage to her. She loved Thomas, loved him passionately, but she saw him so infrequently, particularly now he was so preoccupied both with the problems of his estate and family life. With his wife dead and the need for discretion therefore less relevant, Elizabeth had assumed he would become a more frequent visitor and the fact that he had not troubled her greatly. However, now she was to bear his child, she was confident he would be more attentive. She was sure, absolutely sure, the baby was a boy and in these circumstances, since now he was free, Elizabeth began seriously to think of marriage. Of one thing she was certain – Thomas needed a son in his own image. Christopher seemed unlikely to live beyond childhood and Amy, from the brief references Thomas made, seemed not to be right in the head. A strong young son – her son – was what Thomas needed to give back his zest for life. And so she daydreamed during the long, warm spring nights, seeing herself and Thomas in a state of wedded bliss, surrounded by their happy, healthy children.

She chose an evening in April to tell him her news. He arrived tired and preoccupied, though he made love to her with a passion which suggested that there had been no woman in his life since last they had met. 'I am sorry to have been away so long,' he said. 'Every day I have wanted to visit you, every single day, but there is so little time.'

'It is of no matter,' Elizabeth had murmured sleepily against his shoulder. 'You are here now and I have something to tell you.'

Thomas had greeted the news of her pregnancy with less enthusiasm than she had imagined. In her mind, she had conjured up a scene in which he would instantly ask him to marry her. The fact that he seemed both surprised and alarmed had angered and hurt her. He fussed over her, of course, insisted she would have a good doctor to attend her when the time came. As to her future and the baby's, however, he made no reference.

During the summer months that followed, he visited her only four times and on each occasion, briefly. On the last occasion they had met in late August, Elizabeth, by this time heavily pregnant, had seized her courage in both hands. 'Could the baby and I not come and live with you at Chadbrook, after he is born?' she had asked.

'No, you could not,' Thomas had replied shortly. Elizabeth, worn out with pregnancy and the running of the inn, had uncharacteristically burst into tears. 'I'm sorry, my darling,' Thomas had said, 'only I do not even know if I shall be living at Chadbrook by the time the baby is born. I am so close to ruin, it seems I shall be forced to sell before the year is out.'

'Sell Chadbrook?' Elizabeth was astounded. 'But you cannot, it is your home, it has been your family home for generations.'

'I am well aware of that,' said Thomas wearily. 'If I could find another way I would, but as things stand I face bankruptcy any day. My London home has already gone and I am afraid it is just a matter of time before Chadbrook follows. At least you and the baby have the inn. I thank God that you will both have a secure home, and obviously, once the boy is born, I shall not ask for my share of the profits – you must keep them for him.'

So Elizabeth had to be satisfied with staying where she was, at least consoling herself with the fact that Thomas was so preoccupied with his financial problems, it was understandable that he could give no thought to love and their future.

True to his word, two weeks before the baby was due, a nursery nurse had arrived from Sudbury and it was she who had sent for Dr. Morgan when Elizabeth's pains began. Already considered an oddity from childhood in the village, Elizabeth had become something of a legend – firstly, by her ability to run her father's inn single-handed and make such a success of it, and secondly with the carrying of a child, Thomas Chadbrook's child. For despite Elizabeth and Thomas's attempts at discretion, since Eleanor's death their affair had become common knowledge.

The arrival of a doctor at the inn was the final straw. No one before in Long Melford had been born attended by the ministrations of a doctor. Mrs. Jenkins, the local handywoman, whose mother and grandmother before her had carried on the same profession, was responsible for birth, as she was for death and much of the sickness in the village. In many respects she was a skilled woman. She had saved many a mother and child in difficult circumstances, though cleanliness and hygiene were generally unknown to her, and she had a drink problem. A case of child-bed fever had broken out in the village three years earlier and Mrs. Jenkins had lost seven young mothers in the space of three weeks. What she did not and could not know was that she herself had caused the infection by moving from woman to woman without any thought of personal cleanliness. Still, she was the accepted authority and the arrival of Dr. Morgan in the village caused a frenzy of gossip.

By early evening Elizabeth could cope no more. The pains were as sharp and as frequent as ever but the baby seemed no nearer to making an appearance. Unable to contain her curiosity, Mrs. Jenkins came to see what was happening and within moments was arguing fiercely with Dr. Morgan as to the best course of action. 'If you leave me be to mix up one of my herb potions, I will have that baby born within the hour,' Mrs. Jenkins assured him.

'No, thank you,' said Dr. Morgan, firmly. 'I acknowledge the baby must be born soon but I will use forceps if necessary, to hurry the birth.'

'Forceps! What are forceps?' Mrs. Jenkins said, suspiciously.

Dr. Morgan sighed with impatience. 'They are instruments which I use for extraction of the baby. They clamp round the baby's head and help ease it out when the mother is exhausted and cannot push hard enough.'

Mrs. Jenkins let out a shriek. 'Instruments round the head! You'll kill the baby that way and the mother, too, I wouldn't reckon. Either that or the head will be born separately from the body. You'll tear the child in half.'

'Rubbish,' said Dr. Morgan, heatedly, 'and I would thank you to leave at once.'

'Leave at once! Leave at once, he says,' said Mrs. Jenkins, clearly enjoying the scene. 'I've known this girl all her life. Indeed, I attended her poor mother at her birth. I'm not prepared to stand here and watch you rip her baby apart.'

'Madam, you go too far. You were not invited here and. . .'

'Stop it, stop it,' Elizabeth cried from the bed. 'For pity's sake, if you must argue go somewhere else so that I do not have to listen to you.'

'I'm sorry, my dear. You are right, of course.'

'If only Thomas was here,' Elizabeth moaned, half to herself.

'Your precious Earl will not be coming this night,' said Mrs. Jenkins, a light of triumph in her eyes.

'Why not?' As she spoke, Elizabeth regretted the question for she did not want to discuss Thomas with this woman who, instinctively, she neither liked nor trusted.

'Didn't you know,' said Mrs. Jenkins, obviously enjoying herself, 'today was his wedding day? He has married Miss Beatrice Naylor – a fine, rich young lady, whose father owns much of Sudbury, I understand.'

'Married?' Elizabeth frowned. The pain was making her hallucinate. What was the woman talking about?

'Aye, that's right, miss, your Thomas married today and I should think he will have other things on his mind this night than attending the birth of one of his bastards.'

The scream was so loud that afterwards they said you could hear it the length and breadth of Long Melford. When she stopped at last, Elizabeth was unconscious.

'You stupid woman,' shouted Dr. Morgan. 'Get out, get out of here.' He all but pushed Mrs. Jenkins through the door, slammed it behind her and, turning to his bag, reached for the forceps.

It was daylight when Elizabeth woke. So used was she to the scene from her bedroom window that for a moment she was unaware of the events of the previous day and simply lay, tranquil and relaxed, enjoying the early morning scents that flowed through her window. Then she remembered the baby – she felt her stomach, it was slack, there was no longer a baby there. What had happened, it must be dead? She sat up in a panic, but there beside her bed was a cradle. She leaned forward, full of apprehension about what she would find there.

The child lay on its side, facing her, deeply asleep. Its hair was very dark, the tiny perfect features instantly recognizable, even to the dimple on one cheek. With trembling fingers, Elizabeth parted the clothes that covered the child – a boy, as she had known he would be and in every respect the mirror image of his father. The child stirred, she quickly covered him again and lay back on the pillows. She felt tired but clear-headed and it was obvious that there was nothing wrong with the child. They had survived the ordeal of his birth, the two of them . . . but what now?

The sudden thought of Thomas's marriage caused Elizabeth to let out a groan of pain and she began to turn this way and that as if to ward off her fears and misery. Why had he not told her what he intended to do? That she should hear it from the village gossip was unforgivable. She had understood, or thought she understood, his infrequent visits of late. Occasionally, she had wondered whether he sought comfort from other women but whenever the thought had crossed her mind, she had dismissed it, believing there could be no serious contender for the love he professed to feel for her. Chadbrook stood between them, but once he had sold the estate she felt sure that she, he and their son would be together. Now it was not to be. Who was this Beatrice Naylor and why had Thomas married her? The handywoman's words came back to her – her father owned much of Sudbury. So it was money that had prompted Thomas to marry in order to save his estate. The thought brought her a momentary crumb of comfort, until she considered how the new Earl's wife would feel about Elizabeth Monson and her illegitimate son. Eleanor, by all accounts, had cared so little for Thomas she had not been worried by his affair. A new wife would be more zealous, and perhaps it was his intention never to see her again.

The door opened and her mother entered. Elizabeth made an effort to dry her eyes and sit up. Her mother, it seemed, was having a good day. 'You're awake, lovey,' she said. 'Have you seen your baby son? Isn't he beautiful?'

'He looks healthy enough,' said Elizabeth.

'He is, you both are, thanks to that doctor – you should have died, you know. Look, he stirs.' Mary went to the crib and lifted up the baby. 'He needs his milk, let me help you.'

Elizabeth studied the tiny face of her son as he sucked greedily at her breast. She felt nothing for him as yet, though his urgent dependence touched her.

'What will you call him?' Mary asked, sitting down on the side of the bed.

'Guy,' said Elizabeth, without hesitation.

'A fine name,' said Mary, 'but why Guy?'

'It is his father's second name,' Elizabeth said, quietly. Her mother nodded and Elizabeth wondered whether Mary, too, knew that the Earl had remarried. Probably not. Her ability to remember anything was limited – she was probably not even aware of the identity of her grandson's father.

The child finished his feed and drifted off to sleep against her breast. Awkward, clumsy still, Elizabeth placed him back in his crib. She was suddenly very tired. 'Would you leave me now, Mother, please,' she said. Mary got up without a word and shambled towards the door. Her moments of sanity were becoming shorter and shorter, Elizabeth thought wearily, as the door closed behind her.

She must have slept a long time for the sun was high in the sky when she woke again to find the doctor bending over her. 'How are you feeling?' he asked.

'Tired.'

'I'm not surprised. It was something of an ordeal. I would like to examine you but before I do, the Earl wishes to see you. He is downstairs waiting.'

Instantly Elizabeth was wide awake. She sat up in bed. 'No, I will not see him.'

The doctor hesitated, clearly unsure as to how to handle the situation. 'I think perhaps you should.' He glanced towards the crib. 'The boy, as I understand it, is his son.'

'The boy is mine,' said Elizabeth. 'He gave up all rights to the child yesterday, when he married another woman. Tell the Earl to leave the inn and leave directly. I have no wish to see him ever again.'

'I shall tell him what you say,' the doctor said, reluctantly, and left the room.

Elizabeth lay in the bed, her heart beating loudly, straining to hear the sounds of voices below. The temptation to see Thomas, to have his arms around her, was enormous. Suddenly she felt very vulnerable – an eighteen-year-old girl with a new-born baby, an inn to run and a mother mad for most of the time and certainly more of a hindrance than a help.

'Elizabeth, Elizabeth!' His voice drifted up to her through the open window from the stableyard below.

Just to see him once more, there could be no harm in it. She clambered cautiously out of bed and leaned over the sill. He stood in the cobbled yard – a fine, dashing figure, the sun shining on his dark hair, so like her new-born son's.

'I came as soon as I heard. Please let me see you, and the child.'

Elizabeth fought her feelings. 'No,' she answered.

'Please, Elizabeth, I want to help you.'

'You have done enough,' said Elizabeth. 'Besides, how can you help now? You have a new wife – no doubt she will give you fine sons and you can forget all about me and this child.'

'I can never do that,' said Thomas. He looked about him, as if to see whether they were being overheard. 'I love you,' he said, 'I will always love you.'

'You should have thought of that before you married another woman. It was I who was bearing your child – it is I you should have honoured.'

A look of surprise and then sudden understanding crossed Thomas's face. 'You thought I would marry you?'

Elizabeth suddenly felt very young and naive. 'Was it such a silly notion?' she asked.

'Let me come up,' said Thomas. 'We must talk.'

'No,' Elizabeth shouted.

'But how can we talk of such intimate matters like this?'

'We talk like this or not at all,' said Elizabeth.

'Then surely, my love, you must see why I could not marry you? A man in my position must marry into a respectable family. In my case I had to marry into a family where there was wealth enough to save Chadbrook and Chadbrook has indeed been saved.' He looked about him and smiled. 'The income from your old inn could not have saved my home.'

'And love, what of love?' said Elizabeth.

'It has its place,' said Thomas, his voice deadly serious, 'but rarely in marriage.'

'Then go back to your loveless marriage,' said Elizabeth, 'and leave me alone.'

'I cannot,' said Thomas. 'This is not the end for us. I shall come upstairs and we shall talk.'

Elizabeth looked wildly around. Then, on impulse, she seized the baby from his crib and thrust him through the window, holding him dangling over the cobbled courtyard below. The baby woke with a start, his tiny fists clawed frantically at the air. 'Unless you leave, and leave now, Thomas Chadbrook, I will drop this child of yours to its certain death.'

'Are you insane, Elizabeth?' Thomas shouted. 'Put the child down, I am coming up.'

'One step nearer and I will drop him, I swear to God I will.'

Thomas looked at the girl – her red hair streaming down her shoulders, her face pale and taut, her eyes blazing – and at the tiny figure of his son, frantic with fear, struggling in the arms of his mother. Thomas met Elizabeth's eyes and he stared up at her in silence for a moment. There was no room for doubt – he knew, with a terrible cold certainty, that she meant exactly what she said. 'I will take my leave,' he said, 'I will go now, you have my word on it, but for pity's sake, save the child and treat him well.' Elizabeth hesitated and then lifted the baby onto her shoulder. His screams subsided to shaking sobs. 'What is his name, if I may ask?' Thomas asked.

'Guy,' Elizabeth replied.

'Then Godspeed to you and Guy. I shall not trouble you again but I will think of you, often.' He turned away abruptly lest she should see the tears in his eyes and in moments he was gone.

Trembling, Elizabeth returned to bed and parting her nightgown, put her son to her breast. He sucked desperately a moment or two, his tiny body still quivering. Then gradually he began to relax, his head becoming heavy on her arm. She stroked his downy head. 'I am so sorry, little one,' she whispered. 'I did not mean to frighten you, but it had to be done. You will be safe with me now, I promise. I will take good care of you – you will want for nothing.'

The baby stopped his sucking. Bright blue eyes stared up at his mother as they regarded one another in silence, and at that moment, for Elizabeth, a new love was born.

CHAPTER THIRTEEN
Antibes, South of France – April 1981

Charles Chadbrook sighed heavily and threw down his pencil. He stood up, stretching long legs, and leaned forward over the edge of the balcony to watch the activity in the street below. Mercifully, it was too early in the season for serious tourists. Antibes still belonged to the French and that was how he loved it best. He had been living in France for ten years now and in most respects it felt like home. Yet sometimes . . . he shook his head as if to clear his mind. There had been too much woolly thinking of late. For years his life had been straightforward. He had lived here in this comfortable flat, with his pretty French wife, Evette, confident in the knowledge that as his father declined in health, so James, his elder brother, was gradually taking over the reins of Chadbrook, building it into a prosperous and successful estate . . . but not any more. Everything had changed in the last year and there could be no more ducking issues.

James had died, on Christmas Eve 1979, piloting a helicopter. He had been in London for a few days and was flying home to Chadbrook for Christmas with some friends. Two women and another man had also died. The papers at the time had suggested that perhaps James had been drinking, but the bodies had been so badly burnt that it had been impossible to pinpoint this as the cause of the crash.

Charles had gone home to Chadbrook for the funeral, of course, but he and his father, the Earl of Clare, still had nothing in common – it had been an awkward stay. The death of his beloved elder son seemed to break the Earl's spirit and now, just over a year later, he too was dead. It had meant another melancholy trip home for Charles, this time to inherit both the Earldom and Chadbrook – neither of which he wanted, nor felt he deserved. Daunted by his new responsibilities, he had returned as quickly as possible to Antibes and to yet another bombshell. Evette was leaving him. She felt they had no future together and was not prepared for what was now the inevitable – his return to England to take up his position as the Earl of Clare. 'I thought the French were rather keen on the English aristocracy,' he had reasoned, in an attempt to display sophisticated calm.

It was then that Evette explained she had been having an affair with a colleague at work for some years. She had recognized that at some point she had to make a choice between the two men in her life and this was clearly the right moment. She had been so calm about it, so matter-of-fact, that Charles had been quite unable to summon up any real show of grief. Indeed after she had left, he began to wonder whether he had ever truly loved her or whether he had used her just as much as it now seemed she had been using him.

Charles Chadbrook's childhood had not been a happy one. As the Earl of Clare's second son his life should have been more carefree than his brother's, since he was not to be burdened by inheritance. This, however, did not prove to be the case. Life for James seemed so easy – he rose to every occasion, enjoyed every challenge, was happy at school, had plenty of friends, revelled in the country pursuits on the estate, and most important of all . . . had an excellent relationship with his father. Charles, it always seemed, was somehow swimming upstream. He was not as strong or athletic as James and was also hampered by acute shyness. As a small child, he was constantly plagued by tonsillitis which left him with a temporarily delicate constitution and very few friends, since he was hardly ever at school. He was not a good horseman and found hunting and shooting unspeakably cruel. His only real pleasure at Chadbrook was to creep into the library when his father was not at home, and read – read endlessly, voraciously – everything he could lay his hands upon. In particular his forebears fascinated him and he was soon an expert on the previous Earls of Clare, for his was a family which could be traced back in detail to the fourteenth century.

Life at home was not entirely friendless in that he was without doubt his mother, Julia's, favourite. This in itself, however, produced problems. Clearly, his parents' marriage was not a happy one and Charles was still quite young when he realized that he was the chief weapon they used with which to berate one another. His father believed that he was a soft and sickly child because he had been pampered by his mother. His mother believed that his father was too hard on him and showed too much favouritism towards James. Therefore up to a point, Julia's concern and sympathy was not entirely welcome, for inevitably it created tension between his parents and provoked his father's apparent contempt.

At Eton, things were no better. While James was head of his house, captain of cricket and rowed for his school, Charles was bullied to the point where at one stage he even ran away – only, of course, to be sent back. But at Eton, with the help and encouragement of an English master who recognized the boy's talents, he discovered his ability to write. So with encouragement at last, Charles worked hard and won a place to read English at Oxford. There, for the first time, he felt at home, among people of like minds, and when his university career was over, he decided that for his own survival he must keep away from Chadbrook, from the inevitable comparisons with his brother and from his mother's pity.

Following the ghost of Graham Greene, Charles had gone to Antibes and had felt instantly at ease there. Within weeks, he had met Evette, a young French student on vacation. She was orphaned, an unhappy girl with no roots. In this respect they had much in common and for neither was an affair enough – they both needed more permanence and security in their lives and so they had married within a few months of meeting. Now it was over. Charles had not the least idea of how or why things had gone wrong, except that what had happened was inevitable. He always seemed to fail at everything he tried to do, sooner or later. Rejection was part of his life . . . even his writing was mediocre. He blamed no one for this situation, nor indeed did he have any real sense of self-pity. He just accepted his lot – it was as much a part of himself as the nose on his face. It did mean, however, that he viewed the future with an enormous amount of apprehension for it seemed inevitable that he would fail in his responsibilities towards Chadbrook, as with everything else.

'Charles, Charles!' The patron of the cafe opposite waved to him. 'Your newspaper has arrived. Do you wish me to send it up or are you coming down?'

Charles glanced at his watch. It was too early for an apéritif, but what the hell, work was not flowing today nor any day, come to that. The novel had not progressed at all since Evette's departure. 'I'll come down, Henri,' he shouted. He was drinking too much, he knew, but since Evette had left, there seemed nothing much else to do. As he walked through the flat to the front door, he tried to shut his mind to the chaos around him. Normally a fastidious man, he found the state of the flat very distressing but somehow could not summon up the energy to do anything about it. Evette had been gone for over three months and during that time the place had become a pig sty.

He rarely ate in now – it was easier simply to go across the street to the cafe, which had become more of a home than the empty flat. He sat down at his usual table and found his paper and a glass of kir already waiting for him. He drank his kir quickly and ordered another one.

He was about to pick up his paper when he heard a familiar voice, and felt a light touch on his shoulder. 'Charles.' He turned to see Evette standing beside him.

The shock was considerable. She had told him she was moving to Paris and certainly the girl standing beside him was every inch a Parisienne. She wore a beautifully cut navy suit. Her hair, normally long and wavy, was caught up in a tight chignon. She wore high heels which made her appear unusually tall and slender. Used to seeing her barefoot, in bikini and T-shirts in the summer and sandals and jeans in winter, he was stunned by the change in her. He had always considered her pretty; now she was beautiful. 'Evette!' he croaked, standing up awkwardly. She waved him back to his chair and sat down beside him. 'A drink?' he asked.

'No, just a coffee. I was on my way up to the flat when I saw you here. How are you, Charles, you look tired?'

Charles felt awkward. He was aware he had not shaved that day, that his clothes were crumpled and none too clean. 'You should have told me you were coming,' he said, accusingly.

'I am sorry. It was a spur-of-the-moment decision.' Charles waved to the patron and ordered coffee. His second kir arrived, he drank it hurriedly, it made him feel better. 'You're drinking too much,' said Evette. 'You always do when things do not go well for you.'

'I am perhaps a little,' Charles admitted.

'Don't let yourself go to seed. You have so much to offer if only you could recognize it.'

'That's rich, coming from you,' said Charles, with mounting irritation. She looked so damned good and so damned unapproachable. She was his wife, wasn't she? Yet strangely at that moment he felt he did not even know her.

'I mean it,' said Evette. 'If only you could just develop a little confidence in yourself and your talents, you'd be fine, Charles.'

'But not fine enough for you apparently.'

'We were going nowhere, I had to make a change. I'm sorry if I hurt you.'

'I'm not sure whether you did,' said Charles, honestly. 'My pride was hurt, but since you've been away, I've found my feelings confused – I'm not sure how I feel.'

'Exactly,' said Evette. 'The trouble is, you've never made a commitment to anything or anyone in your life which is why you felt no pain at our parting.'

'No commitment!' said Charles. 'I was married to you for eight years, that's commitment enough, surely? And during that period, I swear to God I never looked at another woman – you know that, anyway.'

'Yes, I know that,' said Evette, wearily. 'But nor did you try to advance our relationship either. No relationship can stand still – you have to work on it.'

'In what way?' said Charles. 'You were happy enough, or so I thought.'

'Yes, but we needed to progress – we could have had children, for example.'

'You never said you wanted a baby.' Charles suddenly looked and felt old beyond his years, weary and confused, completely out of his depth.

'I didn't,' said Evette. 'Because I knew you weren't ready for the commitment.'

'How could you know, when you never even asked me?'

Her coffee arrived and she sipped it in silence for a moment. 'Look, I didn't come here to get into an argument with you. Our marriage is over, as you know, and it's about that I've come. My lawyer keeps writing to you and you don't reply. Claude and I want to get married, and soon.' She bit her lip and looked down at her coffee.

Charles had a sudden flash of inspiration. 'You're pregnant?'

Evette nodded. 'Are you angry?' She glanced up at him from under long, dark lashes.

'Angry? No, I don't suppose so.' He was stunned, trying to come to terms with the fact that his wife was pregnant by another man. 'How soon is the baby due?'

'Not for six months, but I would like us to be married when the child is born. I'm sure you understand that, Charles.'

'Yes, I do, of course.' He had switched onto auto-pilot, he felt nothing at all. 'Well, what do you want me to do?' he asked, with forced heartiness.

'Somewhere in the flat there are some forms to sign. Have you opened your post recently?'

113

Charles grimaced. 'I only open letters which look interesting, the rest, I'm afraid, stays in a pile.'

'Come on then, drink up. We'll go and look.'

Charles remembered the state of the flat. 'I'd rather you didn't come up, I'll go and look. Why don't we have some lunch here? You stay and order and I'll join you in a minute.'

'I know the place will be in a mess,' said Evette. 'Don't worry, I shan't be at all critical, in fact I imagine I'll be rather flattered.'

Reluctantly, Charles followed his wife up the shabby stairs to their flat, aware of how often they had walked up them together and how this would be the last time. At the top of the stairs Evette paused and took out the key from her handbag. She opened the door and then held the key out to Charles. 'I'm sorry, I should have returned this to you before.'

He did not take it. 'There's no need. Keep it. Who knows, maybe you'll need it one day.' He pushed past her, uncharacteristically rude, and headed towards his study. He could not stand her pity, and suddenly he wanted this meeting to be over and over quickly.

Evette followed him into the flat, leaving the spare key on the hall table. The place looked worse than she had expected – there were empty cups, glasses and over-full ash trays all over the sitting room. She would not risk looking in the kitchen, she decided. Although she felt completely detached from Charles and the life they had shared, her instincts to help him were very strong. To begin clearing up, however, was a gesture which would humiliate him, she knew.

'Make yourself at home, I won't be a moment,' Charles called, his voice heavy with irony.

'Let me come and help. I know what I'm looking for.' His office was in an even worse state. Evette looked around her with distaste. 'You haven't been working for weeks, have you, Charles?'

He ignored her. 'I can't find the damn letter. Can't your lawyer send me a copy?'

'No, he can't. Here, let me look.' She sat down at his desk and began sorting through the papers, her fingers quick and efficient – long and slender like the rest of her. It was hard to imagine that her body would soon be swollen with pregnancy and with someone else's child. 'Here it is,' she said, triumphantly, waving a large brown envelope at him. 'Do you want to open it?'

He shook his head. 'You open it. Just tell me where to sign.'

She tore open the envelope, too eagerly, and extracted a large

114

document. She scanned through each page. 'You need to sign twice, here and here, and then initial each page.'

'Pass me a pen,' said Charles.

'Don't you want to read it first?'

He shook his head. He signed the papers hurriedly, handling the pages as if he were in danger of becoming contaminated by them. 'Here you are,' he said, handing them back to Evette and avoiding her eye.

'Thank you,' she said, awkwardly. 'Well, I suppose I'd better be going . . . or shall we have some lunch?'

Charles shook his head. 'No, in the circumstances I. . .' His voice trailed off.

'Charles. . .' Evette studied his face. 'Oh hell, it doesn't matter.'

Charles looked at her. 'What were you going to say, that you are sorry, or some other damn silly platitude?'

'No,' said Evette. 'Because I'm not sorry. I've done what is the right thing for us both. We were in a rut, we needed to start again. I just wanted to say. . .' She hesitated. Charles turned away impatiently, staring sightlessly out of the window, and Evette suddenly found she could speak with his back turned. 'You have . . . so much to offer, Charles. You're good-looking, clever, amusing, and now it seems you will also be very rich and titled. If only you could stop playing at life.'

Charles swung round at her words. 'What do you mean?' His voice was angry but as usual his face showed none of the emotions he must be feeling.

Evette shrugged her shoulders. 'I don't know why it is exactly, but you. . .' She struggled for words. 'You seem so reluctant to take life seriously.'

'Is it a matter to be taken seriously?' Charles asked. 'I've always viewed life as one long practical joke. From the moment we're born we deteriorate until we die. Laughing at the situation seems to be the best way of handling it, given all the circumstances.'

'Listen to me, please,' said Evette. 'Just for once.' He was silent. 'I think it may be the fault of your father. By your own admission, he was always disappointed in you and as a result I think you undervalue yourself. You could be a very talented writer but you skim the surface. Your books are so clever – the ideas, the plots so original, yet you never really get to grips with any of the situations you explore.'

'Oh, so it's my writing you want to criticize, not me?'

'I don't want to criticize you at all. I'm just trying to say that me leaving you is giving you a fresh start, that and the fact you have inherited from your father. Grab at life, take hold of this new beginning and don't run away from yourself any more, Charles. You're like Peter Pan. I grant you it's attractive to be the boy who has never grown up in some respects but after a while, for the rest of us who are trapped in an adult world, it palls a little.' She stretched out a hand and touched his arm to soften her words. 'You're such a good, kind person – so honest, so trustworthy – but you're hard on yourself and everyone else because of your refusal to confront real issues. You are always running away.'

Charles sighed. 'So if it had been me who had made you pregnant, rather than this . . . this Claude, would you have taken me seriously, is that what you're saying? Damn it, Evette, I loved you, perhaps I still do, I don't know. If you'd told me you wanted a baby, we'd have had one, but you seemed so involved in your career. I suppose you thought I was too immature to be a father, is that right?'

There was a bitterness in his voice which Evette had never heard before. Perhaps she had gone too far. The last thing she wanted to do was to hurt him – she only wanted to help. She was well aware that she had come to know Charles Chadbrook better than anyone else in the world had ever done. She must not abuse her position. 'Perhaps I'd better go,' she said, 'I seem to be making rather a mess of this. Thank you for signing the papers.' She turned and headed towards the door.

A sudden panic sent Charles after her. 'Are you sure you have to go now? Why don't you stay to lunch? I promise not to talk about anything controversial.'

Evette studied his face for a moment. 'No, I don't think either of us would enjoy ourselves very much. It's better we part now and quickly.' She hesitated. 'I shall miss you, Charles.'

'Then why. . . ?' She silenced him by reaching up and kissing him briefly on the lips. Then she was through the door and down the stairs so quickly that there was no time for protest. For a moment Charles hesitated, then he turned and hurried through his office and out onto the balcony. Moments later she emerged from the front door below him. Instinctively she looked up and waved. He waved back, she smiled and turned away, hurrying down the street. At the corner she did not hesitate but simply turned left and disappeared out of sight, out of his life . . . his wife.

Charles felt tears prick at the back of his eyes. He brushed a hand across his face angrily, went back into his office and taking a bottle of wine from the rack, he opened it and poured himself a generous tumbler. He drank deeply, sitting down in the chair by his desk and surveying the room miserably. She was right in everything she had said, of course, that was what really hurt. If he could have written her off as a silly bitch, everything would have been all right but she had wanted to help him by making him face up to the reality of his situation. He drained the glass and, standing up, went down the stairs and across the street into the cafe. His newspaper and empty glass were still on the table.

The patron saw him. 'Is Madame Chadbrook not joining you for lunch?'

Charles shook his head. 'I'll have a plate of pasta and a carafe of red wine, please, Henri.' The pasta was good, hot and rich and he ate it hungrily. I can't be suffering from a broken heart, he told himself cheerfully, not with this appetite. The wine relaxed him – he felt mellow and at peace with the world. The meal finished, he sat drinking wine and coffee and picked up the paper once more. Leafing through it, he stopped short at the photograph of a pretty, fair girl who, for some reason, seemed at once familiar. The words 'Long Melford, Suffolk', jumped out of the print at him and he read the article accompanying the photograph. It was an editorial piece on the reopening of an old coaching inn, with the curious name of The Lady in Waiting. He knew it, of course, he had passed it many times, and he remembered it as a depressing, down-at-heel place. This girl had apparently refurbished it with the help of a backer, and it was being reopened as a luxury hotel and restaurant. The reporter was fulsome in his praise. Charles studied the girl's face. She was looking directly at the camera, at him it seemed, and somehow it appeared as if she was trying to tell him something. He clearly had drunk a great deal too much wine.

'Can I join you, Charles?' Henri drew up a chair and placing a glass on the table, helped himself to Charles's carafe. 'Madame, she has gone?' His face was full of sympathy.

'Yes,' said Charles. 'She is living with another man now. In fact, she is expecting his child. I'm happy for her, Henri, I really am.'

Henri tipped his head back and took a hearty swig of wine, then he thumped the table with considerable anger. 'Happy for her, happy for her! Why aren't you fighting for her? She is a beautiful woman, Charles, beautiful, talented and she loves you. Why do you let her go to another man? Where is the spirit in you?'

For the second time that day Charles felt deflated by criticism, yet the wine made him feel able to try to justify himself. 'There's no point, Henri. She's committed to this new man. I can't deprive her baby of a father.'

Henri shook his head despairingly. 'So, what will you do without your wife, apart from drink too much and make me a rich man?'

Charles glanced at the newspaper; it was still folded open to display the photograph of the girl. 'I think it's time to go home,' Charles said, quietly.

CHAPTER FOURTEEN
Long Melford – November 1981

'Prue, it looks great. Shit, is that really the time? I have to go or I'll miss my flight.'

Prue straightened up wearily from bending over the plans spread out on the desk in front of her. It had been over a year since she and Jonathan had begun conversion work on The Lady in Waiting. Although all the detailed planning had been hers, Prue still felt she needed Jonathan's approbation on every decision made. It was, after all, his money. 'You've hardly even glanced at these,' she said, accusingly. 'There's a great deal of money involved in this project, Jonathan – your money. Don't you think you should take the time to see what I'm actually proposing?'

'Why – I trust your judgement completely,' said Jonathan. 'You're a genius, hell, look what you've done to the main building. Besides, we've agreed it's a great idea to convert the stable block. As you say, more bedrooms will cost very little extra in the way of overheads but will provide a reliable trade for the restaurant. Prue, go for it, I'm right behind you, but right now, I have to leave.'

'I just can't understand why you have to go back to New York at such a critical stage in our development plans.' Prue despised the whining note she could hear in her own voice, but could do nothing about it.

'I've told you,' said Jonathan with studied patience. 'It's a business matter to do with the bank.'

'But you have nothing more to do with the bank now, I just don't understand.'

'Prue, you're crowding me.' He was smiling but his eyes were suddenly hard.

She stood up. 'I'm sorry. How long did you say you will be away?'

'I've told you over and over – a week, ten days maybe, but no more.'

'I know I'm making a fuss but I wish you could have waited until we could have a holiday together. I just hate being here alone.'

'Alone!' Jonathan laughed. 'With half a dozen resident staff, not to mention the guests, you could hardly find any situation that's less like being alone.'

'All right, all right,' Prue relied, testily. 'Supposing I say I'm going to miss you, is that better? After all we've been together for well over a year – living and working so closely. It's going to feel very strange without you.'

'I'll miss you too, you know.' Jonathan leaned forward and took her in his arms.

Prue, pressing her face into the cool cotton of his shirt, was suddenly seized with panic. 'You will come back, won't you?'

'Of course I'll come back, you nut,' he murmured into her hair. 'What on earth gave you the notion I wouldn't?'

'I don't know. The last few weeks you've seemed . . . well, restless. I can't understand it – it's so exciting seeing all our hard work come to fruition.' She drew away from him and looked into his face, as if searching for something. 'It's been fun, hasn't it, you've enjoyed it?'

'Yes, of course.' His reply seemed too pat, too careless, but she was in a mood to believe him. He tried again, sensing her mounting unease. 'Prue, don't worry. This is no big deal – I just have some insurance policies which need fixing. I'll be back in no time. Trust me, will you?'

'Yes, of course, sorry – you go and pack.'

Alone in the office, Prue suddenly felt very tired. She sat down in her chair and gazed out of the window across the stableyard to where work would shortly begin. Not for the first time she wondered why she could not tell Jonathan of her true fears. He professed to love her, they were sharing a life together which was as close and intimate as any married couple, yet she could not confide in him and therefore in no one. Strangely enough, the place she felt safest was in this little office they had built out from the kitchen and which they used as their headquarters to plan the conversion and refurbishment of the inn. Why was that? Prue wondered. Was it because it was so personal, with all her paraphernalia around her – her books, her ornaments, her furniture – or was it because the office was the only modern room in the house? The rest of the building dated back to the early seventeenth century, with the most recent extension – the modern east wing, as Jonathan liked to call it – being late eighteenth century. What caused her reluctance to confide in him? Was she afraid that he would laugh at her? Yes, that certainly, but there was also the problem of how to explain something which had no tangible form. To say that the inn frightened her, no, occasionally terrified her, was so difficult to express when the fears themselves were nameless. At times, it was as if the whole building seemed to close in around her, holding her in an iron grip of terror – yet there were no bumps in the night, no apparitions, no clanking chains . . . indeed no sensations at all except those mind-boggling, all-encompassing bouts of fear that could come on her at any time of the day or night, but nearly always when she was alone. It was not difficult, of course, to make sure that she was never alone. By day, there were the builders to supervise and as the inn took shape, staff to recruit, and now, customers to serve. It was only at night, as she turned out the lights before coming to bed, or made a last cup of coffee in the kitchen, or waited up for a guest who had forgotten his key, that the fears won the battle to take over her consciousness. Sometimes she had physically to run from them, clawing her way up the stairs to Jonathan, to lie in his arms and wait for the sensations to pass. When she was in the midst of a crowd and free of them, she was able to tell herself that the fears were imaginary. When she was in the grips of an attack, she knew that they were not. She seesawed wildly from feelings of despair to elation. She was proud of what she and Jonathan were achieving, more especially since she knew that The Lady in Waiting was hers rather than his creation. Yet against the background of this solid sense of achievement, there was a feeling of growing unease. Was she going mad? Everyone told her that she worked too hard – was she perhaps having some kind of breakdown? Yet instinct told her that the fears did not come from within herself and certainly she had never felt any sense of unease on the rare occasions she left the inn. It was baffling, worrying, but up until now she had been able to keep her feelings at bay. However, with Jonathan going to New York and the prospect of long nights alone, she was very frightened indeed.

Terry Derbyshire stood behind the bar, polishing a glass distract-edly as he watched Jonathan and Prue saying goodbye beside the waiting taxi. They made a good-looking couple, he had to admit. The girl, if she took a little more care with her appearance and dressed up a bit, would be a real corker, but she always looked so tired and strained and then there was that sharp tongue of hers. He sighed and placing the glass on the rack, took another. He would have to be very careful while Jonathan Lindstrom was away for he knew that Prue would not hesitate to relieve him of his job if the opportunity presented itself. Someone up there had been looking after Terry the day he had been interviewed for this job because Prue had been out and the interview had been conducted by Jonathan alone.

Although no great student of human nature, Terry could see immediately that the American was homesick. Having quickly established that Jonathan was from New York, Terry was able to reminisce at some length about his years working as a barman in Manhattan, carefully neglecting to mention the fact that he had worked in a sleazy strip joint, doubling as barman, bouncer and occasional pimp.

Terry's childhood had been tough. He had never known his father and his mother had been a drunk. A spell in a borstal when he was fifteen was sufficient to put him off penitentiary establishments and his childhood in the East End of London had left him with a strong desire to escape his background. A chance job shifting beer barrels for a brewery introduced him to the world of bars, and by nineteen he was an accomplished barman. His work had been his passport to travel all over the world but now, fifteen years on, he was tired of the seamy side of life and on a whim had decided to return to Britain, and seek a job outside London. This job was perfect – not too demanding and well paid. However he recognized what Jonathan clearly did not, that he was not right for The Lady in Waiting – he was far too much of a rough diamond. As for Prue, his appointment had clearly infuriated her, but until he put a foot wrong, there was nothing she could do about it. What the hell, it was a doddle – he had a nice little flat on the premises, he would stay for the rest of the summer and then take stock.

'You'll be missing him then,' he called out to Prue, as she came into the bar.

Prue shot him a ferocious look. 'He's only gone for ten days,' she said, brusquely.

'I can't understand what he sees in Suffolk – he must find it a real drag compared with New York. If you ask me, you should have gone with him just to make sure he comes back.' Terry winked at her.

Prue eyed the barman with distaste. In his way he was a good-looking man, with his straight, dark hair and rosy complexion. He was small but thickset and tough. You felt on meeting him that a quarrel with Terry Derbyshire was not something to be entered into lightly. 'Someone has to run this place,' she replied, aware that his words were too near her own thoughts for comfort.

In the kitchen, Martha the cook was in full flood and Jeff, her sixteen-year-old sous chef, was the recipient of her venom. The boy stood by the chopping board, his head hanging miserably while Martha called him every name under the sun. 'What's going on here?' Prue asked.

122

Martha stopped in mid-sentence. 'I don't know why you saddled me with this boy, Prue, he's hopeless. He knows nothing. Do you know what he's been trying to do – pod mange tout! Pod mange tout – can you believe it?' Even as she spoke the anger left her and she began to laugh, her mirth sending great ripples through her mountains of surplus flesh. Curiously, despite her vast size, Martha was not a repulsive figure. From the tip of her snow-white curls to the somewhat eccentric electric-pink trainers she wore, she was always clean and well scrubbed. Her big, round face was normally friendly and amused and her eyes unexpectedly shrewd. She stopped laughing at last and wiped away a tear. Jeff looked greatly relieved. He was a scrawny youth who always gave the appearance of being severely undernourished – he and Martha provided a fine contrast for one another. Martha waddled to the shopping basket hanging on the back of the kitchen door and after a search, threw a battered old leather purse at Jeff. 'Go and fetch me a Guinness, boy, and take your time.'

Prue waited until Jeff was out of earshot. 'A little early in the day, isn't it, Martha?' she said, cautiously.

'Have I ever let you down?' Martha replied, her eyes suddenly steely.

'No,' admitted Prue.

'And I won't today, but I'm not in the best of humours and as you know it's only the Guinness that can sort me out.'

'That I do know,' said Prue, with a smile.

Martha's love affair with Guinness was a well-established local tradition in Long Melford. Martha had cooked on and off at The Lady in Waiting since she was no older than Jeff, and she was now nearly sixty. The fortunes of the inn had fluctuated along with the abilities or otherwise of the landlords that had come and gone. But the reason the inn had never been short of a customer, however bad the current landlord, had been because of Martha's cooking. She made no concessions to the French, nor indeed to any other nationality – she was simply a brilliant, plain English cook, and visitors and locals alike loved her for it. Jonathan and Prue had discovered this wonderful natural resource the day after Jonathan purchased the inn. They had agonized about Martha a great deal. While her cooking was splendid, the fact that she was an alcoholic stood heavily against her and their initial feeling was that perhaps she should be replaced. If they were to turn The Lady in Waiting into a top-class hotel, there certainly could be no room for error. Yet again they very quickly realized that if they replaced Martha they would alienate themselves from the local people of Suffolk. Custom from miles around came to The Lady in Waiting purely to sample Martha's fare, and they could not afford to turn their back on this trade. So Martha had stayed and while there had been a few nasty moments when the Guinness threatened to get the better of her, as she so rightly said, she had not failed them yet. With the increase in trade, it was obvious she needed help but it had taken some persuasion to talk her into taking on a boy assistant. Wisely, Prue had left the choice of assistant to Martha and her decision had surprised them – Jeff was a local boy from the village, from a very deprived home, one of nine children, his father in and out of prison. It was a compassionate choice but also a shrewd one. Jeff idolized Martha and worked tirelessly for her.

Now Martha looked at Prue searchingly. 'How are you?'

'Fine,' said Prue, feigning surprise at the question.

'You'll miss him, of course, but perhaps being apart from each other for a while will be no bad thing in the long run.'

'Why?' Prue asked, despising herself for falling into the trap. Martha had become Prue's self-appointed confidante on the subject of Jonathan. Martha considered Prue to be 'a nice girl' who was being taken advantage of and never failed to make her feelings known on the subject.

'Well, it's obvious, isn't it? Hopefully he'll miss you enough that he'll do the right thing by you on his return.'

'Oh really Martha, not that again.' Prue was exasperated. 'Anyway, who says I want to marry him?'

'You'd marry him all right and a lucky man he'd be if only he realized it. Still, you know my views on the subject well enough.'

'Martha, please. . .' Mercifully, their conversation was interrupted by Jeff's return.

'Terry said you'd better start with a half, seeing how early it is,' Jeff said nervously.

'Oh he did, did he? Well you can take that straight back to Terry and get the bugger to pour me a pint. No, on second thoughts, I'll come and tell him myself.' Martha seized the glass from Jeff's hand and headed for the bar. Prue raised her eyes to heaven – it had all the hallmarks of being one of those days.

At seven-thirty, the restaurant was ready for the first guest to appear and, as always, Prue felt as if they were waiting for the curtain to rise on a stage play. Everything was ready – the silver shone, the glasses sparkled and Edward in his measured, sombre voice was briefing his staff. He glanced up as Prue came into the room, and came over at once to join her. 'You look charming tonight, Miss Mansell,' he said.

'Thank you, Edward,' said Prue, with a smile.

Edward Devereaux had spent thirty years working as butler to the late Earl of Clare. The new Earl no longer required his services and Edward had decided that he did not wish to become involved with a new family nor leave Suffolk which had been his home for so many years. The old Earl's death had coincided with the need to hire a head waiter at The Lady in Waiting and Prue reckoned they could not have been more fortunate in finding Edward. His manner was deferential but firm – dining under Edward's careful eye, the guest felt completely relaxed and yet confident that his every need would be catered for, and in most cases, anticipated.

'I'm glad of the opportunity to have a word with you, Edward. I'm a little concerned about Martha tonight, she is unusually. . .' She hesitated, it was somehow not possible to say 'pissed' to Edward.

'So early in the evening?' Edward said, saving her the trouble of finding a suitable word. 'We have a very full restaurant tonight, including the Earl of Clare so I understand.'

'The Earl of Clare? I thought – oh, I see, this must be the son of the man you worked for.'

Edward inclined his head. 'Yes, the younger son, Charles. The elder son, James, died in a helicopter crash just over a year before his father – his heir dying like that undoubtedly hastened his own end.'

'That's very sad,' said Prue.

'Yes, indeed. I know very little about Charles Chadbrook since he grew up, other than the fact that he no longer wished for my services. However I imagine his view of our newly opened restaurant will be of considerable influence in the county and it would not be good if something were to go wrong tonight.'

'Will you need any extra help in here this evening, Edward?'

'I don't think so,' Edward replied. 'In fact, I feel sure we can manage – the bookings are nicely spaced.'

'In which case,' said Prue, 'I shall go upstairs, take off my glad rags and be prepared to spend an evening in the kitchen.'

Everything that could go wrong went wrong that evening and Prue had little time to think of anything other than the task in hand. When she did think of Jonathan, hovering somewhere over the Atlantic and well away from the crises going on around her, she could not help feeling more than a twinge of resentment.

Judge Browning was very particular about his Bloody Marys. Normally Jonathan made them for him, American style, but Jonathan was not there and when the judge complained to Terry about the standard of his drink, Terry told him to come and make it himself. There was a scene in the bar and it took all Prue's persuasive charm to stop the judge and his wife storming out and taking their dinner guests with them. The incident seemed to set the trend for the evening – even the impeccable Edward served the incorrect wine to a particularly querulous group of diners. The kitchen was a shambles – Martha was very, very drunk but did not know it and did not want to be helped, especially not by Prue. She became angry and increasingly uncooperative, and the crosser she became, the more she drank. Jeff rose to the occasion magnificently and somehow, despite Martha, Prue managed to get the meals out more or less on time and to a satisfactory standard, but it was a real struggle.

It was after midnight by the time the last guest was served. Martha was in excellent spirits by then and began singing bawdy songs taught to her by her father, who had been a merchant seaman. 'Be quiet, Martha,' Prue urged. 'They'll hear you in the restaurant.'

On cue, Edward burst through the door. 'I'm sorry, Miss Mansell, but can't you stop her – you can hear her all over the inn.'

'I wish I could, Edward – are there many guests left?'

'Only the party from Chadbrook,' said Edward.

'Chadbrook, who are they?'

'The Earl of Clare and his party,' said Edward, stiffly.

'Oh, I see.' Prue had forgotten about them entirely. She studied Edward's wooden expression for a moment. 'What's wrong, they're not being rude to you, are they?'

'Oh no, it's nothing like that.' He hesitated. 'They are just such an odd group of people – artists and writers I believe. Their dress is hardly appropriate and even the Earl isn't wearing a jacket.'

Prue tried unsuccessfully to suppress a smile. 'So they're not quite the cream of the county you expected the Earl to be entertaining?'

'I suppose I have to admit to being surprised by his choice of friends.'

'Well, let's face it,' said Prue, 'the man can't have a great deal of taste or he'd never have let you go, would he?'

A ghost of a smile crossed Edward's face. 'You certainly have a way with you, Miss Mansell. I remember. . .'

At that moment there was a piercing scream from across the kitchen, by the hob. Martha had picked up a large casserole, clearly red hot, and then dropped it. As she tried to side-step to avoid the spilling contents, she tripped and her large frame crashed onto the kitchen floor. There was a sickening thud as her head hit the ground.

'Oh my God!' In the moment's silence which followed the fall, Prue and Edward stood rooted to the spot. The kitchen door swung open abruptly. A tall figure filled the doorway. 'What's happened, is anyone hurt?'

Prue was at last galvanized into action and ran to Martha's side. She was lying on the floor, her eyes closed, her breathing shallow. 'Oh, Martha – is she badly hurt?'

The man who had followed her crouched down beside Martha's recumbent form, lifted her eyelids and then felt her pulse. 'Hurt no, drunk very, I should say.'

'But she hit her head really hard, I heard it.'

'She'll probably have a sore head in the morning, for a variety of reasons, but there's no serious damage done, in my view.' He sounded amused.

'What about her hands? She picked up a hot pan just before she fell?' Prue turned over the palms and examined Martha's podgy fingers. Apart from a little redness there was no sign of an injury.

There was a groan and Martha opened her eyes. 'Ah Prue,' she said. 'Can you fetch a pint of Guinness, I've such a thirst on me.' Her eyelids flickered and closed again and she began to snore softly.

'What did I tell you? She's fine. I assume this good lady was the one serenading us from the kitchen. We were greatly enjoying her ballads.'

Prue looked up at the man kneeling beside her for the first time. He was dark and tanned, with warm brown eyes, a marked dimple on one cheek and a large, lop-sided mouth now arranged in a broad grin. Not strictly speaking a good-looking man but undeniably attractive. 'Thank you for your understanding. I just wish I could be sure she was all right.'

'I'm sure,' said the man, confidently. 'I've spent the last ten years in the South of France so there's very little I don't know about the various stages of drink.' He stood up. 'Well, we'd better get her shifted – you can't leave her here all night.'

'Do you think I should call a doctor?' said Prue.

'Probably as well to have her checked over in the morning but what she needs now is rest. Does she live here?'

'No,' said Prue. 'She lives in the village.'

'Alone?' Prue nodded. 'Well, my suggestion is that we get her to a bed in the inn for the night. Have you a spare guest room?'

'Yes, several,' said Prue. 'But they are all on the first floor, I'm afraid.'

The man turned to Edward, who was hovering a fair distance away, clearly finding the whole scene extremely distasteful. 'Come on, Devereaux, there's a good chap. Between us we should be able to get this old girl upstairs.'

'If you say so, sir,' Edward said, reluctantly.

Prue regarded the man with new eyes. So *this* was the Earl of Clare. As Edward had implied he certainly did not look like an Earl. He was dressed in faded denims and an old guernsey sweater, his hair over-long and his manner easy-going and casual. No wonder Edward did not approve, but Prue was intrigued. She had expected something quite different from a man in his position. There was a gentleness about him – he seemed slightly unworldly – which would have charmed her in any event. The fact that she now knew he was the owner of one of the country's oldest titles and largest estates made his diffidence even more attractive.

Prue followed the two men on their tortuous journey upstairs, half carrying Martha who protested vehemently, in between snatches of song. Once in the bedroom they deposited her on a large double bed and Prue did her best to tuck her up for the night.

'I hope you and your party will have a drink on us to say thank you for all your efforts,' Prue said, as they went downstairs.

The Earl turned and smiled at her. 'That would be very kind.'

'Will you arrange it, Edward?' Prue asked. Edward nodded curtly.

'So you're the proprietor?' the Earl said to Prue, as they hovered in the hall.

'Joint proprietor – my partner Jonathan is away at present.'

'My name's Charles Chadbrook,' the Earl said.

'Prue Mansell.' They shook hands, formally.

'I must say I am very impressed with what you've done to The Lady in Waiting. It can't have been a very easy renovation job but you've converted it very sympathetically and the food tonight was excellent.'

'I'm afraid you caught us on a bad night,' said Prue.

'Well if this is a bad night, I'd like to see the place on a good one. I've been meaning to come here for weeks. While I was still in France I saw your write-up in the *Telegraph*.'

'In which case, I hope this will be first of many visits,' said Prue, with relief.

'Oh it will,' said Charles, with a smile which lit his face. 'You can be sure of that.'

It was nearly two by the time Edward and Prue had cleared up and even then Prue lingered. Edward seemed to sense her mood and suggested they made some coffee. They sat either side of the old fireplace in the bar – it was good to relax; after the rigours of the evening they were both too tense to sleep immediately.

'Don't you dare tell me Martha will have to go,' Prue said after a lengthy silence.

'I wouldn't dream of it,' said Edward. 'She'll be better tomorrow. Today was a very difficult day for her.'

'What makes you say that?' Prue asked.

'Today is the second anniversary of her husband's death. He was rather a splendid old chap and she clearly misses him a great deal. It's such a shame that none of her children live around here, then she wouldn't be so lonely.'

Prue looked at Edward with a new respect. 'Edward, how awful that you should know about this while I knew nothing. You make me feel totally inadequate.'

'I have to admit to having a slight advantage over you. I knew old George Hewitt slightly. He was a signalman on the Melford to Sudbury line for many years. There wasn't a thing he didn't know about railways and being rather a train buff myself, I used to chat to him – he had some fascinating tales to tell. It was very sad actually. He was killed on the railway, though some would say it was fitting.'

'How?' Prue asked.

'Trying to save a dog. Some children were playing near the railway and they had a puppy. Old George was trying to keep the children off the line and rescue the puppy at the same time. He didn't hear the train coming until it was on him. Martha has always enjoyed her Guinness but nothing to the extent she does now.'

'You're a strange man,' said Prue, 'but very nice. Do you have any family?'

'Absolutely not,' said Edward. The shutters clamped down and Prue knew better than to press him further.

Edward had a cottage just outside Long Melford, which he had bought with his savings some years before. As he let himself out of the front door of the inn, he paused and studied Prue in silence for

129

a moment. 'Would you rather I stayed here while Mr. Lindstrom is away. I can easily, if you would like me to.'

'Oh no,' said Prue, hurriedly. 'I'm perfectly all right. There's Terry after all.'

'Yes, I suppose there is,' said Edward dismissively. 'Well, think about it tonight. I'd be very pleased to do so from tomorrow if you'd like me to.'

'Thank you, Edward, goodnight.'

Prue shut the bar door and drew across the big bolt. She kept her mind firmly on the tasks at hand – setting the burglar alarm, turning out the lights, putting up the fireguard . . . but gradually, insidiously, the fear began to mount so that by the time she had finished her jobs, she could not stop herself running up the stairs in an effort to escape. In her bedroom, she turned on all the lights and on an impulse locked the door. She undressed hurriedly, and not bothering to wash or brush her hair, climbed into bed. She lay very still listening to . . . she knew not what. In an effort to keep her mind active, she thought through the events of the evening but she could not concentrate. She was cold although she knew the room was warm and, as the fear gathered within her, she recognized she had lost the battle to fend it off. She bunched herself up into a tight ball and pulled a pillow over her head, but still they would not go away – those feelings of fear, of misery, of despair. At last exhaustion won and she slipped into an uneasy, fitful sleep, but when she woke in the morning, the feelings were still there, as sharp and clear as ever, to greet her.

CHAPTER FIFTEEN
New York – November 1981

Jonathan shifted uncomfortably in the plush leather upholstery. It was typical of Jo to keep him waiting.

'Jo Lindstrom, Publicity, how may I help you?' the spectacularly good-looking receptionist breathed into the telephone mouthpiece. She sounded wonderful.

Jonathan waited until she had finished. 'You can help me, if you like,' he said. 'You can tell Mrs. Lindstrom that I'm a busy man, that I don't have time to spare and that she's currently running thirteen minutes late. For a professional woman, I consider that very unprofessional.'

The girl looked at him stony-faced – a hard bitch, just like her boss, Jonathan thought sourly. 'I'll let Mrs. Lindstrom know your views, if you'll excuse me.' She rose and minced her way out of the room.

Jonathan sighed. He knew Jo was keeping him waiting for a purpose – to try to exercise a sense of superiority, to score a point in the stupid power struggle on which their relationship had been based for a long time now – perhaps always. She would never change. If anything, as the years passed she became more devious, more calculating, more infuriating. . .

The receptionist returned with an amused grin. 'Mrs. Lindstrom will see you now – I'll show you the way.'

'I know the way,' said Jonathan and headed off down the corridor.

Jo Lindstrom was smart and successful and it showed. She had style, too. Even Jonathan, who believed he had tired of her charms years ago, was momentarily struck by her appearance as he entered her office. She wore a neat little cream suit, with a bright orange shirt which only a very few woman could wear successfully. Her blonde hair was styled into a close-fitting cap which should have looked terrible but with Jo's high cheekbones and slanting almond eyes, it only served to emphasize her good looks. She smiled at him, the sleek self-satisfied smile of a cat who knows for certain that she has cornered the mouse.

Pull yourself together, Jonathan thought, this woman means nothing to you now – it's just a question of formalities. 'I'm sorry to keep you waiting, Jonathan,' she said. 'But you know how it is, business always has to come first.' She raised an eyebrow. 'Though I guess that's not the case for you any more, now you're out of a job.'

'I'm no such thing,' said Jonathan, instantly rising to the bait. 'In fact I'm working my butt off. I've bought an old coaching inn in the UK and believe me, running that place is a round-the-clock job.' Why had he said that, why did the bitch always wind him up so? Surely it did not matter a damn what she thought of him any longer?

'Oh yes,' said Jo, 'I know all about The Lady in Waiting and your little partner Prue Mansell.'

'How the hell. . . ?' Jonathan began.

'Oh come now, Jonathan, a private dick, how else?'

'Why?' said Jonathan, instantly alarmed. A private investigator operating in the UK cost money. Jo never wasted money.

'I'm coming to that, but let's deal with why you've come to see me first. Won't you sit down?' Reluctantly, Jonathan took a seat on the sofa at the far end of her office. 'On second thoughts,' Jo said with obvious relish, 'I think I can save you the trouble of telling me why you're here. You want a divorce, don't you? You've fallen in love with little Prue and have decided that she should be your next wife or, should I say, victim. Well, before you say any more, Jonathan, I'd like to put you in the picture right away. My answer is no deal.'

Jonathan was astounded. Firstly by the fact that Jo seemed to have anticipated precisely the reason for his visit, and secondly because of her immediate refusal to co-operate. What did she want? 'That's crazy!' he said. 'You don't want me around any more, you've made that quite clear. So, we made a mistake, we should never have married, but that's no reason why we shouldn't each get on with our own lives.'

'You could make a case for saying that it's my duty not to unleash you on the unsuspecting female population. Let's face it, Jonathan, I'll be performing a considerable community service by keeping you unavailable. I have to say, though, I'm not that philanthropic – I have other reasons.'

Jonathan made an effort to pull his thoughts together. 'Don't you think you're letting your sense of power run away with you, Jo? You can't stop me divorcing you, or have you conveniently forgotten that?

132

We've been separated long enough, so I guess it doesn't matter much what you think. You're right in one respect – I want to marry Prue but I'm going ahead, with or without your co-operation. I just thought I'd tell you as a matter of courtesy. I see I was wasting my time.' He stood up, ready to leave.

'I do have the power to stop you, Jonathan.' Jo's voice was deadly serious and it stopped him in his tracks. 'You have a choice – either you take my word for it, or I can give you the reason why. If I were you I'd plump for the former.'

'Like hell I will,' said Jonathan, increasingly agitated. 'What's wrong with you, Jo, what do you want from me? Our relationship's finished, over. OK, so I was unfaithful to you but we never discuss our love life, do we? It takes two to make a marriage fail.'

'Would you like a drink?' Jo asked, conversationally.

'No, I would not,' said Jonathan, 'I don't want to prolong this meeting any longer than we have to.'

'I reckon you should have a drink before I tell you what I have to – believe me, you're going to need one.'

'To hell with your threats – can you say whatever it is you have to say. I don't want to stay here a second longer than necessary.' He sat down again, tense and anxious now.

'All right,' said Jo. She sat down on a chair opposite the sofa and took her time to light a cigarette. As she did so, Jonathan noticed her hands shook slightly. He felt a quickening of apprehension – Jo had her faults, plenty of them, but she did not bullshit. If she said she had something unpleasant to say, she would not be exaggerating. 'Are we ever going to get started?' he asked, testily.

'I have evidence,' Jo began at last, 'to prove conclusively that neither you nor your mother are entitled to run Lindstrom's Bank, nor indeed to own any of the shares.'

'I don't own any shares,' said Jonathan.

'But you will, when your mother dies.'

'I very much doubt it,' said Jonathan, 'I imagine she will take great delight in cutting me off without a penny.'

'She won't,' said Jo. 'Because she can't.'

'Can't?'

'As I thought, she's never told you the full details of John Lindstrom's will, because I imagine she likes to maintain the whip hand. The fact is, Jonathan, she only holds the bank shares in trust – for you.'

'I don't know where you got your information from, Jo, but I'm certain you're wrong.'

'I'm not wrong. I've been seeing a good deal of your mother over recent months since you've been in the UK, and she has told me all about John's will. He left all his bank shares to his sole surviving children, to be administered in the form of a trust fund by your mother, until such time as she felt it was right to hand over the reins. A rather unusual arrangement – normally the procedure is to hand over an inheritance on a given birthday. However, in this instance, Harriet can pick her time although the shares have never been hers. The shares have always been yours, Jonathan, she's just chosen not to tell you so.'

'Well, I'll be damned,' said Jonathan. 'The bitch.'

'Thinking about it,' said Jo, 'I suppose it is quite a sensible arrangement. As a TB sufferer, John knew he could die at any time. Equally he could have lived for another twenty years. He had no idea how many children they would have nor how they would turn out, so he took what he imagined to be a practical course of action. He left it to your mother's judgement to hand over the reins to whichever of his children she felt most appropriate. Parents are often forced into the situation of bestowing their inheritance on the eldest child, which is not necessarily the best solution. It is a very clever will, given all the circumstances.'

'OK,' said Jonathan. 'So let's suppose you're right. I don't see what the hell this has to do with our divorce.'

'Then I'll tell you,' said Jo. 'When you inherit from your mother – which if you don't before, you will do on her death – you will be a very wealthy man, and a powerful one. I have spent eight years putting up with your philandering ways and I think I deserve a little something for my trouble. The figure I have in mind is ten million dollars, which I consider to be quite modest, bearing in mind what you will be worth overall.'

Jonathan exploded with rage. 'Ten million dollars? You have to be joking! Let's just assume for a moment you're right and I do inherit the bank on my mother's death, there's no way I'd hand over that sort of money to you, or any money come to that. You have your business, you have the apartment which was once ours, you're young and strong and too damned sharp by half. You paddle your own canoe from now on, Jo – you've had enough from me.'

'I thought that's what you would say,' said Jo, with a self-satisfied smile. 'Which is why you have left me no alternative but to spill the beans.'

'What do you mean, spill the beans?' said Jonathan. 'Shit, you make me angry, Jo.'

'Before I go any further,' she said, apparently unruffled, 'I want you to think very carefully. What I have to tell you will come as a great shock and in my view it would be better if you were never made aware of the information I hold. The price for peace of mind is ten million bucks. I'm not asking for it now, only when you inherit.'

'You can threaten me all you like,' said Jonathan. 'But I'm not changing my mind. Quite apart from the fact that I owe you nothing, inheriting the bank doesn't mean I'll suddenly have access to that sort of money.'

'Oh rubbish,' said Jo. 'You could sell a few shares and raise sufficient to pay me off within a few hours of your mother's death, if you so wished.'

'I don't wish,' said Jonathan.

'OK,' said Jo. 'Just don't forget I gave you the option not to hear what I have to say next, and I did advise you very strongly to accept my terms.' She looked up and met his eye, silent for a long moment. 'John Lindstrom was not your father, Jonathan.' Her voice trembled slightly as she spoke.

Jonathan visibly blanched and jumped to his feet. 'Oh come on,' he said, 'you'll have to do a lot better than that.'

'Lindstrom was not your father and I can prove it.'

Jonathan studied her face in silence for a moment. She was not lying. She was cold and calculating and clearly gaining some satisfaction from the scene, but she was telling the truth, he could see it in her eyes. 'Go on,' he said, sitting down again, because suddenly he felt he could no longer stand.

'This is the part you're not going to like,' she said. 'Your father is Edward Deckman – you're the result of an affair between your mother and Edward.'

'Edward Deckman!' Jonathan threw back his head and laughed. 'Oh Jesus, Jo, that's rich, it really is – there's no way Edward's my father – we've hated one another all our lives. What will you dream up next – that creep – what a joke!'

'I'm sorry, Jonathan, but it's the truth. God help me, I wouldn't lie to you over something like this.' There was silence in the room for a moment, as Jonathan tried to grapple with what she had said.

'We don't even look alike – he's about a quarter of my size.'

135

'If you recall, Harriet has always maintained that you favoured her side of the family, which is true. She's small, I'll grant you, but her father was a big man.'

'I can't believe it's right to encourage you,' said Jonathan, at last. 'But I have to see what kind of evidence you think you've dreamed up.'

'Do you remember how we met?' Jo asked.

Jonathan nodded. He felt disorientated and strangely light-headed, he didn't believe her and yet. . . 'Of course – it was a party at the Deckmans.'

'You were there because you were the boss's son. I was there because I am Sylvia Deckman's god-daughter.'

Jonathan felt a sinking sensation in the pit of his stomach. Of course, he had forgotten the association between Jo and the Deckmans – it somehow made the story more likely, though why, he wasn't sure. 'Yeh, I remember now,' he said, as casually as he could.

'As you must be aware,' said Jo, 'Sylvia and Edward were unable to have children because Sylvia had some irreversible gynaecological problem. It has ruined her life, there's no doubt about it, and as her god-daughter, I guess, I've always been favourite in her mind as the child she never had.' Jo paused, in order to light another cigarette. 'Sylvia's dying of cancer,' she added, through a haze of smoke.

'Really,' said Jonathan, sarcastically. 'You do surprise me – she looked perfectly OK when I had dinner with her and Edward in London a while back.'

'She's putting on a brave face – she's a brave woman. The fact is she has only months to live. Anyway, back to you – at the time of your birth, the affair between your mother and Edward was hushed up and the Deckmans were bought off, which is why Edward Deckman has always held such a powerful position within the bank. Sylvia agreed to keep silent although she was obviously very hurt by the affair, particularly since she subsequently discovered she could not have any children of her own – you were to be Edward's only child. Nonetheless, everything would have been watertight but for the fact that your mother, in the full flush of maternal pride, made one classic error – she wrote a letter to Edward, from her hospital bed just after you were born, telling him all about his son, and Edward compounded that error by keeping what was obviously for him a precious letter. Sylvia came across it one day and copied it. She has now passed it to me and I have it here. Do you want to see it?'

Jonathan felt a sense of rising panic. He searched his mind for some reason to delay sight of the letter. The whole story was moving too fast for him. 'Why should Sylvia Deckman give the letter to you?' he asked.

'It is her legacy,' said Jo. 'It's simple really. She knows that the secret of your birth will die with her, for neither Edward nor Harriet will ever disclose the truth. She considers both she and I have suffered at the hands of the Lindstroms. She has always played second fiddle to your mother. The affair ended with your birth in order to protect you, but Sylvia had to live with the knowledge that Harriet was her husband's first love. Once you grew up and left home, Sylvia believes the affair began again and the move to London was nothing more than a clumsy attempt on Harriet and Edward's part to stay away from one another while she is so ill.' Jonathan said nothing. 'Aware as she is of your unfaithfulness to me, Sylvia felt somehow it was fitting that the knowledge should be passed on to me, to use if I felt it appropriate. I guess I think it's appropriate right now.' She got up and walked over to her desk. 'Are you ready to see the letter?' she asked.

Jonathan nodded. There was no mistaking it. The letter was written in his mother's hand, the notepaper that of the Parkland Hospital, New York – his birthplace. It was a lover's letter to a man he despised, yet he was aware as his eyes blurred over the words on the page that he would have been touched by the way in which Harriet had described her baby in such loving terms had it not been for the circumstances. He laid down the letter at last and stared blankly into space, his mind trying to reel away from the truth. Edward Deckman was without doubt his father so why had there been so much animosity between them over the years – was it Edward over-reacting in order to hide the truth, or was nature playing tricks, creating him in anything but his father's image? 'Why the hell did she have an affair with him of all people?' he said, half to himself.

'I think that was fairly obvious,' said Jo. 'Your father was a sick man and Harriet was a young, active woman. I should think their sex life was pretty non-existent. Edward is actually very attractive from a woman's point of view.'

'Is he?' Jonathan said, weakly. Jo nodded. 'Good God.' There was silence again.

'Anyway,' Jo said, 'it only remains for me to sum up.'

'Sum up!' Jonathan frowned. 'What do you mean?'

'I expect in all this you've forgotten the original objective,' said Jo, with a note of impatience. 'I want ten million bucks and if you're not prepared to give it to me, then I'll tell all. Think about it for a moment, Jonathan. Your father's will is quite clear – I've checked and double-checked by questioning your mother carefully over recent months. John left the bank to his surviving children. In the event of no children surviving his death, then the money passes to his cousin Billy Lindstrom.'

'So,' said Jonathan, 'you tell all and I don't inherit. So what? I wasn't expecting to anyway.'

'It's not as simple as that,' said Jo. 'Your mother will almost certainly be sent for trial because she's committed fraud by allowing you to inherit. It will appear that she used her illegitimate child to get her hands on the Lindstrom millions. You'll destroy her utterly, Jonathan. Her whole life and her reputation as a hard-headed, clever banker will be finished. I respect your mother a lot – she's the sort of woman I would like to be, perhaps I shall be in time – but that bank and her position in Wall Street mean everything to her. She could not live with the consequences of her deceit being made public knowledge.' Jo shrugged. 'Still, what the heck, maybe this is what you want, maybe this could be your opportunity for revenge.'

'No,' said Jonathan, with surprising force. 'I don't want revenge, certainly not on that scale. If my father was not John Lindstrom then I'd rather she'd chosen any man on earth than Edward Deckman, but I don't hate her enough to destroy her in the way you describe. I couldn't live with myself if I did that.'

'Then you'll have to pay up,' said Jo, quietly.

Jonathan looked up at his wife. 'You're really enjoying this, aren't you?'

'As a matter of fact, you're wrong,' said Jo. 'I'm not, but I'm not hating it so much that I'm making any kind of hollow gesture. Believe me, Jonathan, I'll tell all if you don't co-operate.'

Jonathan put his head in his hands and rubbed his tired eyes. He was still jet-lagged. Prue, Suffolk and The Lady in Waiting seemed a lifetime away. 'I still don't get it. I still don't see why you can't agree to our divorce.'

'Ah,' said Jo. 'I wondered when you'd remember that. I guess I'm offering a kind of incentive to speed things up.'

'How come?' said Jonathan.

'Your mother's as strong as an ox, she could live for another twenty-five years and I don't want to wait for my money that long. If you badly want a divorce all you have to do is spring me ten million dollars. I'll hand over this letter and guarantee to keep quiet

138

the moment I have my money. However, if you try to divorce me or fail to give me the money when you are in a position to do so, then I'll sing like a canary. In other words, Jonathan, put it like this – if you want to marry Little Miss Mansell, you'll have to negotiate the release of the money from Lindstrom's Bank, to pay me off. How you handle it is up to you. You can tell Harriet everything I've said to you today or you can pretend it's all part of a regular divorce settlement. Either way, until I have my money we stay married. Now, can I get you that drink?'

Jonathan staggered to his feet. 'It would choke me,' he said, and without another word he stumbled from the room, his whole world folding in around him.

CHAPTER SIXTEEN
Long Melford – November 1981

Prue had kept her troubles to herself as much from force of habit as inclination. However, when Jonathan telephoned on the second morning following his departure, ironically she felt a strong urge to confide in him. She resisted the temptation – for one thing a transatlantic telephone call was not the ideal medium for trying to explain her complex feelings and besides, he sounded rather distracted and was obviously in a hurry. The call left her restless and unhappy, despite his promise that he would be back in Suffolk within a week.

Three days later, the cumulative effects of lack of sleep, the additional work involved in not having Jonathan to help and a building sense of stress, made Prue feel not only desperately tired but also oddly light-headed. She knew she could not cope much longer alone without talking to someone. It was her normal habit to have coffee with Martha in the kitchen around ten o'clock to discuss the day's menus. Martha had been very contrite since Saturday night and her Guinness consumption had dropped considerably. On Thursday morning, she poured a mug of coffee for Prue as usual and they sat down at the kitchen table.

'You look awful,' said Martha, without preamble. 'What's wrong, dear?'

'Nothing,' said Prue. 'I'm fine.'

'You're not fine. I suppose you're missing that man of yours?'

Prue looked about her expecting to find Jeff listening with interest but he was nowhere to be seen. Clearly, Martha had arranged for him to be absent, which meant it was an official interrogation. 'No, it's nothing to do with Jonathan, I'm all right, honestly,' Prue said, hurriedly. 'Now about today's menus. . .'

'You don't go home to see your family often enough and you never seem to have friends come and visit you. With Mr. Lindstrom away, you must be leading a very lonely life. Something's wrong, I know it, I've been around too long. I'm not prying, dear, it's your life but something's troubling you so why not tell old Martha – it'll go no further, you can be sure of that.'

There was a lengthy silence. 'It's these awful feelings. . .' Prue suddenly burst out, surprising them both. She had not been aware she had been going to speak.

'What sort of feelings?' Martha encouraged, her big round face wrinkled with concern.

'Well, that's just it,' said Prue. 'I-I don't really know. It sounds so silly when I put it into words but when I'm on my own here in the inn, I get these terrible waves of fear and despair – it's terrifying, Martha. I can't begin to describe how awful it is.'

'Have you seen a doctor?' Martha asked.

'No,' said Prue, surprised. She tried again. 'You see it's not something that comes from within me, it's . . . well, an outside influence.'

Martha stared at her. 'You mean . . . you're saying the feelings are in the inn and you're picking them up. They're someone else's feelings – a spirit, maybe?'

'I know it sounds crazy,' said Prue.

'Not crazy, but are you sure the feelings aren't yours? You're working ever so hard and with Mr. Lindstrom away and the inn to see to and all – maybe it's not a very easy time in your life.'

Prue shook her head vehemently. 'It's not that, Martha, honestly. You see it's happened before. When I told my parents I was coming to live and work here, they were a little strange about it. Eventually I pressed them to know why, and they said that I had been frightened by something in the inn when I was a child. Apparently as soon as I walked through the bar door I went wild, ran out of the bar screaming and was nearly killed on the road outside. I don't remember the incident at all, I must have blotted it out, but when they told me about it, the story was instantly familiar. At the time they thought I was upset about seeing my old nanny dying but I know now that wasn't the reason – it was these same fears I'm experiencing now.'

'Perhaps because of the story, you're imagining things,' Martha suggested.

'No,' said Prue. 'It's definitely not that. My parents only told me about the childhood incident a couple of months ago, yet I've been feeling this sense of fear since the day I arrived, from the very first night in fact. Honestly, Martha, I'm not exaggerating when I say that the emotions I experience are so extreme, so vivid, I sometimes don't think I can bear it any longer.'

'And it only happens when you're on your own?' Prue nodded. 'In any particular rooms in the inn, dear, or all of them?'

'I'm always all right in my office,' said Prue. 'But everywhere else is fair game if I happen to be alone, even for a minute or two. You think I'm mad, don't you, Martha?'

'No, dear, I don't. I believe what you're telling and I believe in things happening which we can't explain. I suppose it stands to reason you feel all right in the office – it's the only new piece of the building isn't it? The inn has been here a long time – it wouldn't surprise me at all if you were picking up some emotions from an earlier age.'

'Obviously I've thought of that,' said Prue. 'In fact, in a strange way, that's one of my problems. While on the one hand I sometimes feel that I can't stand it any more, I can't help being fascinated too. I think if I simply admitted defeat and was scared away, I'd always regret not knowing why I feel as I do. It's a sort of love-hate relationship I suppose.'

'That's not doing you any good by the look of it.' Martha studied Prue's face. She was very pale, there were blue-grey smudges under her eyes and she looked drawn and strained around the mouth. She was still a startlingly pretty girl but compared with the Prue Martha had met back in the summer, she was a totally altered person. 'You've changed,' Martha said, putting her thoughts into words. 'You're much more serious and you've lost your sparkle. It's all very well you saying these feelings are interesting but they don't seem to be making you very happy.'

'I'm certainly taking life more seriously than I did,' Prue admitted. 'But that's because I have such a responsible job – it's nothing to do with how I feel.'

'I'm trying to think back,' said Martha, frowning with concentration. 'The landlord who was here before Mr. Lindstrom, Gerry Jackson, he did a fair bit of research into the history of the inn way back – before he took to drink. His idea was that he would write up some sort of historical record to go in the bar to interest the customers. He was a lazy devil and he never completed the job, but I remember him saying the inn gets its name from someone who actually lived. I'm trying to think what her name was . . . wait a moment, it'll come to me.' Martha took a sip of her coffee. 'Elizabeth,' she said triumphantly. 'That was it. She carried on with a member of the local gentry. Apparently, in return he helped her build up the inn, as I understand it. He was married, no doubt, and because she was always waiting for him to visit her, the inn took its name from their relationship. I'm afraid I can't tell you any more than that but she

142

was a woman who must have had problems – perhaps it's the lady in waiting who's giving you these nightmares.'

The name Elizabeth echoed around Prue's mind – Elizabeth, of course, Elizabeth – she had always known . . . terror and excitement stood side by side. 'Have you any idea what sort of period you're talking about?' she said, managing to sound normal despite the sudden desperate need to know more about this Elizabeth.

'Not really,' said Martha. 'But I suppose the builders might help you. Her lover paid for a lot of work to be done, by all accounts. I'm afraid history isn't my strong point, dear – it's a very long time since I went to school.'

'The main extension was built in the late eighteenth century,' said Prue excitedly. 'So if you're right about Elizabeth it must have been very unusual for a woman to run an inn at the time. The woman's place in those days was in the home, having endless children. She must have been a very special sort of person.'

'Like you,' said Martha, quietly.

'Not like me,' Prue replied brusquely. Martha's words were dangerously close to her own thoughts – there were, it seemed, suddenly comparisons to be made.

'The trouble with you, dear,' Martha continued, happily oblivious of the turmoil she had caused, 'you always talk yourself down. You need to be married to a kind man who realizes how lucky he is and tells you so every day.'

'You're starting to sound like my mother,' Prue said.

'Maybe I do, but it's my view if that Mr. Lindstrom doesn't recognize his good fortune, you ought to find someone else – like the young Earl who was here the other night – now he was a nice gentleman.'

'Martha!' said Prue, laughing. 'I don't know how you can say that. You've no idea what he was like, you were pissed out of your mind.'

'I know more than you think,' said Martha, smiling. 'He carried me upstairs, didn't he?'

'Yes, he did and no doubt he's still getting over the experience.'

'Yes,' said Martha, ruefully. 'You're probably right at that.' She studied Prue for a moment, her blue eyes full of compassion. 'So it's really these feelings which have been bothering you, dear?' Prue nodded. 'You know what I'd do if I were you? I'd do a bit of research myself into the history of the inn. You're a bright girl, you'll do a lot better than Terry and it will keep your mind occupied.'

'Research? No, not me, I wouldn't know where to start.'

'Terry looked up the Parish Records, I know. You could start there. Why not talk to the vicar?'

'Yes, I could, I suppose,' said Prue. 'And my father has a lot of records. He has an amazing library, it would be worthwhile asking him.'

'There you go then,' said Martha. 'Don't tell me Martha can't solve your problems.'

'And create a few of her own as well,' said Prue, with feeling.

Martha was right, Prue thought as she organized the inn for the day ahead. If something from the inn's past was frightening her then the best possible solution had to be to find out what it was. Her fear stemmed largely from the fact that the feelings she experienced were unknown, their source unidentified. Recognizing them for what they were had to be a major step forward and for some reason she could not explain, she knew she had to begin with Elizabeth.

It was not until Friday afternoon that Prue had a chance to take a few hours off. Long Melford Parish Church stood up on the green, a fine building, large and imposing. Although it was a cold November day, the air was crisp and the sun was shining, so she walked the mile to the church, having telephoned the vicar first for permission to study the Parish Records around the 1780s. Earlier she had telephoned the builder who had undertaken the refurbishment on the inn, and he had confirmed the most 'recent' extension had been built in the late eighteenth century. As Martha had suggested, it was therefore reasonable to assume that Elizabeth and her lover had been responsible for the building.

It took Prue only half an hour to find all that she was looking for. The records showed that Elizabeth Monson had been born at the inn at Long Melford on 15th May 1764, to Jem and Mary Monson. Twenty-four years later, the records showed a christening. A son for Elizabeth, named Guy. The father's name was not mentioned but this time the inn was referred to as The Lady in Waiting, Long Melford. The strange part was that Guy's date of birth was recorded as being 7th September 1782, making the child almost six years old at the time of his christening. Prue's historical knowledge was not great but she had always believed that children of the period were christened soon after birth because of the high rate of infant mortality. There was no record of any marriage, nor indeed, apparently, other children. Working her way through the pages, yellow with age, there appeared to be no record of Elizabeth's death either, suggesting perhaps that she had moved away from the area. It was little enough to go on but Prue now knew that Elizabeth had really existed and that the inn had taken its name sometime between her birth and her son's christening. It all tied in with the story Martha had told. She sat looking at the entries for a long time, excited, but not surprised. It was almost as if she was confirming knowledge already held within her.

Later, walking back to the inn through the gathering gloom, Prue realized she felt better than she had done in some time. She knew she was drawn to this eighteenth-century woman who had run the inn single-handed, as she herself was doing, but whether this had any bearing on her feelings of terror she could not yet tell. Jonathan, of course, was the figurehead of the business, but on a day-to-day basis he did little enough, as Prue had become increasingly aware since his absence. Two women, joined in some way across the centuries, by the fact that they were doing the same job in the same place? It was plausible – perhaps too plausible.

The inn looked warm and inviting as Prue approached it. It was hard to believe it housed so many fears for her. She pushed open the door, her cheeks glowing from the cold air.

'Oh Prue,' Terry called from behind the bar. 'There are some friends of yours here to see you.'

A middle-aged couple stood by the bar, drinks in hand. Prue looked at them, bewildered. As far as she was aware, she had never seen them in her life before. The woman stepped forward, her hand extended. 'Prue, you haven't the least idea who we are, have you, and who can blame you? I'm Marian Gospack and this is my husband, David. We did meet you once, in London. Our daughter, Ann. . .'

'Say no more,' said Prue, laughing. 'The name Gospack is enough. Of course, you're Ann's parents, I'm so sorry not to have recognized you immediately. It's lovely to see you – what a coincidence.'

'No coincidence,' said David, a small rotund man with a jolly, friendly face, and a shock of white hair.

'We're here to see you,' Marian said. 'And we've booked to stay the night. We are on a very loose schedule. David has just retired and we thought it was time we saw a little of our own country. When the children were still holidaying with us, we always went abroad.'

'That's lovely,' said Prue. 'How is Ann?'

'And more to the point who is Ann?' Terry interrupted from behind the bar.

Prue was intensely irritated by his interruption but the Gospacks did not seem to mind. 'Prue and Ann used to share a flat together in London,' Marian explained. She turned to Prue. 'She's absolutely fine. You know she's living in New York now – in fact we were with her when she received your birthday card, telling her all about the inn. It's what made us decide to come and see you.'

'I'm so pleased,' said Prue. 'And how's Rob?' She turned to Terry. 'Rob's her husband, Terry, just to keep you fully in the picture.'

'OK,' said Terry, without rancour. 'I've got the message. I'll go and find something else to do.'

'Rob's fine,' said Marian. 'He's doing very well indeed, in fact so well Ann's given up her job and we're so excited, she's expecting a baby in March.'

'I am pleased,' said Prue a little wistfully. And so she was. Of all the people she had known in London, Ann was really her best friend, her closest confidante and she had missed her very much when she had married Rob Shield, an American, and moved to New York. Yet despite her feelings of warmth towards her friend, she felt a tinge of jealousy – Rob was such a nice, straightforward man who clearly loved Ann very much and now they were to have a baby. Everything had worked out for Ann while her future with Jonathan was anyone's guess. As she exchanged platitudes with the Gospacks, her mind went back to those early days in London when she and Ann had been teenagers. Their lives had seemed so full of promise then, an exciting future just there for the picking. Prue forced herself to concentrate. 'Will you be having dinner here tonight?' she asked.

'Oh yes of course,' said David.

'Then why don't I book a table for three and I can come and join you, unless of course you'd rather be on your own?'

'Of course not,' said Marian. 'It would be lovely to catch up on your news, if you can spare the time.'

The conversation during the meal consisted almost entirely of a trip down memory lane. Martha surpassed herself, and after a large meal and a considerable amount of wine, Prue felt very relaxed. She had worked hard over the last few days and felt she deserved an evening off so she accepted David Gospack's invitation for coffee and brandy in the bar afterwards. It was only then that the conversation came round to Prue and her current situation and she found herself telling the Gospacks about Jonathan – purely in his capacity as partner and backer, she was not ready to admit to anything more – their future seemed too uncertain.

'Is he here much of the time?' David asked.

'Yes, quite a lot,' Prue said carefully. 'But he's in New York at the moment – like Rob he is an American.'

'A New Yorker!' David said. 'Then how on earth did he become involved in a Suffolk inn?'

'It's rather a long story,' said Prue. 'He was in banking, a family business, but feelings ran rather high, and he left. On the spur of the moment while visiting my family he decided to put his money into this place.'

'A banker – which bank?' David asked, his interest quickening.

Prue had forgotten until that moment that David Gospack, too, had been a banker. 'Lindstrom's – I don't expect you will have heard of them, it's very. . .'

'Lindstrom's!' David said. 'Well of course we've heard of them. Young Lindstrom and his wife, Jo, are Ann's best friends. In fact Ann used to work for Jo up until a month or so ago, when she gave up because of the baby.'

'It must be a different branch of the family,' said Prue, confidently.

'No, no, I don't think so. Jonathan, you said your backer was called – Jonathan Lindstrom?'

'Yes, that's right,' said Prue.

'Oh well then, it's definitely the same one – in fact it all fits in. We had dinner with them both on the trip before last but this time we only saw Jo, because Jonathan was over here on business.'

David Gospack's voice suddenly seemed to be coming from a long way away. Prue's heart was thumping, she felt suddenly very short of breath. 'I don't think it can be the same person,' she said. 'I really don't. Our – our Jonathan isn't married.'

David Gospack frowned. 'Well this guy we met was certainly Jonathan Lindstrom of Lindstrom's Bank. He had a quarrel with his mother and quit the family business, oh, it must be a year ago now. She's quite a formidable lady, old Harriet. If that's your guy he's certainly married, in fact I think he and Jo have been married for some years, though Ann says the marriage is a bit rocky at times.' He glanced shrewdly at Prue. 'We haven't upset you in any way, have we?' he asked.

'Oh no,' said Prue, brightly. 'No, not at all. Jonathan's just a business colleague, and I really don't know him very well. It's just, I don't know why, I formed the impression he was single but obviously I was wrong.'

Somehow Prue managed to limp through the next half hour until at last the Gospacks decided it was time for bed. Hardly knowing what she was doing, she murmured something to Edward about having a bad headache, asked if he could lock up, and then mercifully escaped to the privacy of her room. When she reached it she expected to cry but at first no tears came, she simply sat on the bed she had shared with Jonathan – a married man – and stared at the blank wall in front of her.

Presumably this was why he had returned to New York, to see his wife. Did she, this Jo, know anything about her and The Lady in Waiting? Prue wondered. She sat for a long time thinking through the details of their life together, and now that she knew Jonathan was married, Prue suddenly realized that it should have been obvious to her long ago. Normally so full of himself, Jonathan was unusually reticent about his life in New York . . . and small wonder. She had forgotten to ask if there were children – the thought appalled her. Surely not, even if he had left his wife, he would not leave his children for a whole year – would he? None of it made sense. Why had he decided to settle in Suffolk? Clearly the marriage had to be extremely unconventional, and what really were his plans for the future? Her mind was reeling, and there was still the whole of tomorrow to get through before Jonathan's return in the evening. She prayed the Gospacks would go the following day and that nobody would tell them that Jonathan was due back, for no doubt if they knew of his arrival, they would wait to see him. The thought of attempting to put on some sort of brave face for the Gospacks' benefit was too appalling.

Prue stripped off her clothes and uncharacteristically threw them in a heap on the floor. In bed, she turned out the light and lay staring up at the ceiling, waiting. Sure enough, within a few moments the fear and misery began to creep over her, only tonight it was worse than ever. How could she be expected to cope with the burden of someone else's misery, when she had so much of her own at this moment? Her life was a mess – she would have to get away from The Lady in Waiting and more particularly from Jonathan, before he made an even bigger fool of her. She lay alone in the darkness, sobbing, her life seeming to have lost all its purpose. It was only then that Prue suddenly remembered Elizabeth. She had loved a married man, or at least a man who was unobtainable. Another similarity – a coincidence, nothing more, or was it? Lying in the dark, battling with her own misery and someone else's, it occurred to Prue that the description The Lady in Waiting was as applicable to herself as to Elizabeth Monson.

CHAPTER SEVENTEEN

Prue was in the kitchen when he arrived. She heard the sound of raised voices in the bar, as Jonathan greeted Terry.

'It sounds like your young man has returned,' Martha said. On receiving no response she tried again. 'Aren't you going out to say hello?'

'Yes, of course I am going to say hello,' Prue said, clearly irritated.

'Now mind you tell him about your problems,' Martha said, unrepentant.

She had forgotten how handsome he was. He was wearing a long navy overcoat with a fur collar which suited his dark, rather old-fashioned good looks. He let out a whoop of delight as he saw her, bounded across the bar and swept her into an embrace, kissing her soundly on the lips. In any circumstances Prue would have hated such a display in front of Terry, but as things were, she shrank from him. 'Hey, what's wrong? Don't tell me you haven't missed me?' Jonathan hugged her again, his strength overcoming her reluctance.

'Everyone's missed you,' Prue said. 'Did you have a good flight?'

'We sure did. We had a tail wind all the way back, that's why I'm early. So how's business been?' Jonathan looked from Prue to Terry.

'Great,' said Terry. 'We're picking up every day. The restaurant's been full most nights. We had trouble with Martha one evening when she got pissed, but that apart. . .' Prue cursed Terry under her breath; she had not intended to tell Jonathan about the incident with Martha.

'Did she now? Well, darling, you know I've always had my doubts about her.'

'Not now, Jonathan,' said Prue, tersely. 'Come upstairs – we need to talk.'

'Whatever you say, it can't be too soon for me either,' said Jonathan, tipping a wink at Terry.

Prue had to fight to control her fury. He followed her up into the bedroom and the moment the door was shut, Prue turned on him, speaking in a cold, bleak little voice. 'So you're married?'

'What?' said Jonathan, his face blank with shock.

'Don't try to deny it because it'll just make you look stupid and waste time. I'll tell you how I know – I used to share a flat in London with a girl called Ann Gospack and she married an American named Rob Shield.' Instantly Prue saw a flash of recognition cross Jonathan's face. Somewhere in the recesses of her mind, she had clung to the idea that perhaps the Gospacks had been wrong and that it was a different Jonathan Lindstrom whom they knew. Now, staring her in the face was confirmation that she had been deluding herself. She forced herself to continue. 'Rob and Ann, I understand, are friends of yours and of your wife, Jo. When Ann's parents were last over in New York visiting, she told them about this place since I had written to her with my news. They came and spent last night with us here, and left after lunch today. When I mentioned the name of my partner, and the fact that he was an American, it didn't take them long to realize that they knew you too. You had dinner with them once, apparently – you and Jo.'

Jonathan sat down heavily on the bed. 'Shit, if only you hadn't found out like this. I intended to tell you, I promise, and I'm sure you'll understand when I explain.'

'I can't see that there's anything to explain. You don't deny you're married, do you?' said Prue.

'No, I don't deny it. I am married, but in name only.'

'Oh come on, Jonathan, you can do better than that,' said Prue. 'Even a naive idiot like me deserves a more original line.'

'OK, but just hear me out, will you? Jo and I married eight years ago, we have no kids and we've always led very independent lives. About three years ago she came home unexpectedly from the office – she's a high-powered lady in PR – and I was caught, how shall we say, in somewhat compromising circumstances with my secretary. It was the fact I was being unfaithful to Jo in our bed that she didn't like – neither of us made any pretence of being faithful at the time. Anyway, there was a big scene and we parted. That's why when I split with the bank I no longer had a home in New York. I gave Jo our apartment when we split and my mother let me have use of the bank apartment – I just never got round to getting my own place.'

'So, if your marriage has broken up, why aren't you divorced and why, when you met the Gospacks last year, were you together?'

'We still meet, Jo and I, or rather we did,' Jonathan said. 'She does a lot of work for the bank, handles all our, sorry, *their* publicity. I do remember that evening. Jo had spent a day at the bank and mentioned Ann's folks were in town and so we all went out to dinner.'

'I'm sorry,' said Prue. 'I want to believe you, but I just can't get to grips with the fact that you've deceived me all this time.'

Jonathan let out a sigh and sank down on the bed. The last thing he had expected was to arrive back in Suffolk and face yet another scene. Ever since leaving Jo's office, he had been in a daze, trying to come to terms with the fact that he was not the person he had believed himself to be for all of his life – even his name was a sham. What had kept him going had been the thought of coming back to Prue – to her warmth, her kindness and the safe, secure little world of village life in Suffolk, so different from New York. Yet he had walked through the door into a whole new set of emotional demands and suddenly he knew he could not cope – his own feelings were too out of control, there was no way he could take on board anyone else's problems even if he had created them. It seemed to him at that moment that everybody was making demands on him, yet nobody really cared about him. He had thought this girl was different and yet here she was, like everyone else, full of condemnation, ready to put the boot in at the first opportunity. Such was his state of mind that he could not see how Prue had been hurt, only that like everyone else she seemed to be against him.

'I can't handle this right now, Prue,' he said wearily. 'You must make your own decision as to whether or not you choose to believe what I tell you. I didn't have a very easy time in New York and I . . .'

'Didn't have a very easy time!' Prue burst out. 'What about me, do you think I had an easy time finding out you were married from the lips of a comparative stranger? It was such a shock, Jonathan.'

'I am sure it must have been,' Jonathan said.

'You're so cool about it, sitting there. It's as if you don't care at all.' Prue's voice was shaking with emotion and she was clenching and unclenching her hands as she spoke.

'I care,' said Jonathan, raising his eyes to look at her, 'but as I said, I just can't cope with any more scenes at the moment. Look, I don't know whether this will help or not but I went out to New York for a quite specific reason – to see Jo and ask her for a divorce. My reason for doing that was because I want to marry you.'

'And what did she say?' Prue asked, momentarily stunned by his words.

'She wasn't over-keen on the idea. Not that she wants me,' Jonathan added hastily. 'Just that . . . oh, hell it's kind of complicated.'

'Complicated, or is it just that you aren't prepared to tell me?'

151

On the plane back Jonathan had made the decision to tell Prue everything that had happened and to seek her advice as to what to do next – whether to approach his mother and give in to Jo's blackmail or whether to stand firm. There were so many possible options open to him but he had been confident that Prue would help unravel his thinking. Now, he just wanted her to go away and leave him in peace – she was starting to sound terrifyingly like Jo.

'I want to tell you about it,' said Jonathan, 'but not now. I'm very tired and I can't think straight. I need some time.'

His evasiveness strengthened Prue's resolve. 'Time is something I'm afraid you don't have,' she said. 'I'm leaving, my bags are packed and the taxi is on its way.'

Whatever he had been expecting it was not this. 'Prue, this is crazy. Look, I know I have a hell of a lot of explaining to do but you're badly over-reacting.'

'I am not over-reacting,' Prue shouted. 'I know I'm not a particularly good person but I do believe in honesty and truthfulness. We've lived together for the best part of a year and I just don't know how you felt able to go on from day to day without telling me you were married.'

'I kept meaning to tell you,' said Jonathan, 'but you know how it is, I kept putting it off and then it got to the point where I felt I had left it too late. I wanted to organize the divorce before explaining the situation.'

'I don't believe you,' said Prue. 'I don't believe you ever intended to tell me. I don't know what you had planned for our future but I assume you imagined you could keep a woman either side of the Atlantic and no one would be the wiser.'

'No,' said Jonathan. 'That's not what I wanted.'

Prue opened the door. 'I've left everything organized for the rest of the day – menus and staff – so you can take time to get over your jet-lag.'

'Don't leave me, Prue,' said Jonathan. 'I need you.'

Just for a split second she hesitated. The look on his face was close to desperation and in a moment of intuition Prue sensed something awful must have happened in New York for him to look so totally vulnerable. The moment passed – she had already done her soul-searching, there was no going back. 'You don't need me,' she said. 'After all, you have a wife.'

Terry met her at the bottom of the stairs. 'There's a taxi here for you, at least that's what he says. Is it for you or did you order it for one of the guests?' He suddenly saw the suitcases. 'What's happening, Prue? Are these yours?'

'Ask Jonathan,' said Prue. 'And, yes, the taxi is for me. Goodbye, Terry.' She pushed past him, staggering under the weight of the suitcases.

'Here, let me,' Terry said. He opened the door for her and wrested the suitcases from her hands. The sudden act of kindness from someone she did not even like brought easy tears to Prue's eyes. She tried to brush them away without Terry seeing, but he did not miss them. 'So you two have had a bust-up?'

'Mind your own business, Terry,' Prue said, rudely.

'OK, but please don't leave us, Prue, we can't manage without you. Jonathan's a great guy but he can't run this place on his own, you know that.'

'He's just going to have to try,' said Prue.

Outside a storm was blowing up and it was already wet and windy. Terry stowed her suitcases in the back of the taxi while Prue clambered inside. He tapped on the window and she wound it down. 'Please think about what I've said. Let's face it, you *are* the Lady in Waiting.' He laughed, embarrassed at the play on words. 'Sorry, I didn't mean it like that.'

'It's OK and more appropriate than you know. I'll see you some-time, Terry.'

As the taxi driver drove down the main street of Long Melford, Prue rubbed the condensation away from the back window so that she could peer through. She watched the inn until it was out of sight, aware, suddenly, that the pain of leaving was not just all about losing Jonathan but leaving the inn as well.

Robert and Margery Mansell did their best to be understanding parents but in the few days following Prue's return home, their patience was stretched to the limits. Initially, she would not even explain why she had arrived so unexpectedly, halfway through what otherwise had promised to be a tranquil winter evening. She had been monosyllabic, argumentative, totally self-absorbed and apparently in no rush to shift the black mood which was upon her.

'It feels like a throwback to the teenage years,' Robert suggested to Margery, on the first night following Prue's return, when sleep eluded them both.

In the end, after several days of Prue refusing to respond to Margery's gentle probing, Robert formally invited his daughter to join him for drinks in the study before dinner and demanded, rather than requested, an explanation, both for her unexpected arrival and her ill-humour.

'I'm sorry,' said Prue, immediately. 'I have no right to take this out on you and Mum. It's just a very difficult time for me.'

'I assume,' said Robert, 'that you've had some sort of disagreement with Jonathan Lindstrom.'

'You could say that,' said Prue.

'Are you going to tell me about it?'

She hesitated. 'He's married,' she said, bleakly.

'I'm not at all surprised,' said Robert. 'As you well know, I never liked the fellow, nor trusted him. So, you've only just found out?' Prue nodded. 'And you were serious about him?'

'Yes, I suppose I was. We never talked about a permanent future together but I suppose I assumed we would marry one day. Now, of course, I understand why he was always so vague about the future.'

The pain in her eyes and the hesitant manner with which she spoke made Robert realize the depth of her feelings and his need to tread carefully. For once he exercised commendable sensitivity and tact. 'There are a host of questions I'd like to ask you, some because they are relevant, some purely out of vulgar curiosity I suspect, but can I take it that you probably would rather not talk about it at all – for the time being, at any rate?'

'There's nothing much more to tell,' said Prue. 'But yes, you're right, I don't want to talk about it just yet.'

'And your job at The Lady in Waiting . . . I suppose you've thrown that up?'

'Yes, I have, and you know, Dad, in a strange way I almost miss the inn more than Jonathan.'

Robert laughed and refilled her sherry glass. 'That I can under-stand. You've put a great deal of hard work into that place, Prue, and you should feel very pleased with yourself. We never go anywhere these days, your mother and I, without being told what a fabulous job you've made of that old inn. I'm very proud of you, we both are, it's just such a damned shame you can't sit back and enjoy the success that you've created. The man's a bastard.'

More to divert Robert's thinking away from Jonathan than any-thing else, Prue found herself saying, 'I have the strangest kind of relationship with the inn, a sort of love-hate. In some ways it repels me, in others it seems to draw me to it.'

Robert sat down in his chair and stared at Prue in silence for a minute. 'You remember my telling you about that incident in your childhood?'

'Oh yes,' said Prue. 'I often think about that, and it still goes on now, though I suppose because I'm older, I can handle it better.'

'What goes on?' Robert asked.

'The feeling of fear. You're going to think I'm mad but I have the strangest sensations when I'm there alone as if I'm sharing the emotions of somebody else – someone perhaps who lived there long ago.'

'Describe the emotions, if you can,' Robert said, clearly intrigued.

'Fear, misery, nothing very cheerful, I'm afraid.'

'And you say you feel these sensations only when you're in the inn?'

'Oh yes – I'm really not falling apart, Dad, if that's what you're thinking. You see, I know what I'm feeling doesn't belong to me. Oh hell, I find it so difficult to explain . . . but it's as tangible as if I . . . well, as if I put on your coat instead of my own. Martha says that the inn was run once before by a woman, in the late 1700s, and I think I may have found her in the Parish Records. Her name was Elizabeth Monson. She was born at the inn and had a child there, named Guy. There is no indication from the records as to what happened to them but the moment I heard her name I recognized it and I feel instinctively that it's her emotions I'm feeling. I feel drawn to her somehow. Crazy, isn't it?'

Robert stared at Prue in silence for a moment. 'Monson, you say? Well, well – no, you're not crazy, in fact I think I might have something quite interesting to show you on the subject of your Elizabeth, but I need time to look out the documentation. Bear with me and we'll talk again tomorrow.'

'What sort of information?' Prue asked, amused by her father's immediate interest.

'Try to be patient. I have some work to do first. As you know I have a vast number of old documents here in the study, I need to sift through them.'

Prue smiled. Her father was always looking for an excuse to bury himself in the family archives. 'I could help,' she suggested.

'No, later perhaps, but I need a little time on my own first.'

While Prue appeared better for her talk with her father, Robert seemed unusually preoccupied. After supper he retired to the study and at breakfast the next morning Margery told her daughter that so far as she was aware, Robert had not even been to bed. Halfway

155

through the morning, he called Prue back to the study. 'I think what I have to tell you is going to come as rather a shock to you. I don't know what it means, if anything.'

Prue sat down. 'What is it, Dad? I think I've had enough shocks just recently!'

Seeing the alarm in her eyes, Robert smiled reassuringly. 'Don't worry, it's nothing awful, but what you told me last night was so intriguing, I just had to investigate further. You see our name, Mansell, was originally Monson.' Prue gasped. 'Yes, I guessed you wouldn't remember that – perhaps I've never even mentioned it to you. I know when I've had a few drinks, I become rather a bore on the subject of our first Baronet, who received his title for services to King and country in the Napoleonic Wars – a very brave man, by all accounts.'

'Yes, Dad,' said Prue, with a smile, having indeed heard the story many, many times.

'However, if you'd paid more attention to my ramblings, you would have remembered that his name was Guy, Sir Guy Monson.'

There was a stunned silence in the room. 'You mean . . . he's the same person as the baby born at the inn – Elizabeth's son?'

Robert did not reply for a moment. He got up and stood by the window, gazing out across the parkland. 'That's what I've been trying to prove, in fact I've spent all night trying to do so. The problem is that our family records are absolutely impeccable from the time Guy arrived here with his French wife, Marcelle, but not before. From Guy onwards, all births, deaths and marriages are recorded in the front of our Bible, as you know. Every child, even if it lived only for a few hours, has been noted down. However, there is no record as to where Sir Guy came from. All I do know about him is that he was under the patronage of the then Earl of Clare, Thomas by name. Guy travelled to France and then Belgium with Thomas and they fought beside one another at Waterloo, which is where Guy distinguished himself. He was thirty-three and by then a very experienced soldier, having fought under Wellington in the Peninsular Campaign. When they returned to England, Thomas gifted Guy this house and farmlands, which at the time belonged to the Chadbrook estate. However, it would appear that they must have had some kind of argument for although they both lived for some years after Waterloo, there is no mention of Thomas in Guy's records. Still stranger is the fact that although he had three sons, none bore the name Thomas – in fact the eldest was named Robert, like myself.

156

Under the circumstances, it seems unthinkable that Guy should not have named his firstborn after his benefactor.'

'Surely,' said Prue, 'you can't assume there was a rift between them just because there's nothing to indicate that the two men remained friends.'

'Yes, you're right, of course,' said Robert. 'It's just a hunch. Guy was a great correspondent and he seems to have kept all the letters he ever received, most meticulously, yet there are none from Thomas nor is there any reference to him.'

'They lived close enough to make letter writing unnecessary perhaps,' Prue suggested.

'Possibly. Anyway I made a major discovery in the early hours. There is a letter Guy received from his mother-in-law after the birth of his first son. His mother-in-law, incidentally, was the Comtesse Marie-Claire de Villefranche and Guy appears to have been very fond of her. In the letter she says how sad she is that his poor, dear dead mother, Elizabeth, did not live to see her grandson, as she herself had done.'

'Elizabeth!'

'Exactly,' said Robert, triumphantly.

Prue stared at him. 'Then we have to be talking about the same people.'

'I don't disagree,' said Robert, 'and there is one way we can double-check. You said you had made a note of your Guy's date of birth?'

'Yes,' said Prue. 'I'll fetch my notes, they're upstairs.' She was back in moments. 'He was born on September 7th 1782.'

'1782 to 1815. There we have the final proof, beyond doubt, I'd say.'

Prue frowned. 'How do you mean?'

'Remember I told you that Guy was thirty-three at Waterloo. Your baby Guy from The Lady in Waiting would have been thirty-three in 1815.'

Father and daughter did not speak for several moments. It was Robert who eventually broke the silence. 'So, Prue, if you're having strange feelings at The Lady in Waiting and if you believe instinctively those feelings relate specifically to Elizabeth Monson, perhaps it is hardly surprising, since it appears there is little doubt that she is your great-great-great-great-great-grandmother.'

It was Prue's turn now to burn the midnight oil. She read and re-

157

read her family documents until she felt she knew them by heart. As he had indicated, there was nothing further which Robert's library could reveal in terms of hard evidence as to Guy's origins, but Prue began to feel she knew the man. He was clearly very conscientious and hard-working. The estate prospered under his care as the accounts revealed, and he appeared to have great concern for his tenants. In 1820, he began keeping a journal which according to Robert was unusual, as normally it was kept by the wife. However, as Guy's wife was French, it probably explained why the task fell to him. The journal was most revealing about Suffolk life in the early 1800s but it was almost entirely concerned with farming matters. Socially, it appeared that the life of Sir Guy and his wife, Marcelle, was something of a desert. He frequently referred to a quiet Christmas with the family and there was no mention of journeys to London or social gatherings with other local families. Guy seemed happiest with his workers and tenants for he gave graphic descriptions of harvest suppers and Christmas parties for them. It was easy to understand, Prue supposed, that being a new Baronet and the son of an innkeeper, Guy might not have the social graces of the other landed folk around, and having a French wife, if she spoke little English, could also have been a distinct social disadvantage. Prue formed the impression of a rather disappointed man, who had somehow not fulfilled his early promise. He clearly loved his children and his wife, but he seemed to be in a kind of backwater which did not really suit him. Instinctively she liked him, yet also felt sorry for him. She discussed her feelings with Robert.

'You may well be right,' he said. 'There are plenty of men around today for whom life has been downhill ever since the Second World War. Guy was clearly a man of action and the life of a Suffolk farmer – which, after all, was what he became – can hardly have compared with the life of a soldier on active service.'

'I wonder why he was under the Earl's patronage in the first place.'

'I don't know,' said Robert. 'It was not unusual for the rich and influential to take someone less fortunate under their wing, but there is perhaps a more obvious explanation.'

'What's that?' Prue asked.

'Perhaps Guy was his son, his illegitimate son.'

'You mean. . . Elizabeth and Thomas?'

'Possibly,' said Robert. 'You say there was no evidence of Elizabeth entering into a marriage and Martha mentioned a relationship with the gentry.'

'That's right.'

'Well, there you go – taking an active interest in one's bastards was not at all unusual.'

'It's strange,' said Prue. 'The current Earl of Clare was in the restaurant the other night. He seemed a nice man and he helped me with Martha, who'd had too much to drink. It's weird, isn't it? There was I, apparently Elizabeth's direct descendant, and Charles, who undoubtedly is Thomas's, meeting under the same roof two hundred years after Thomas and Elizabeth.'

'And you have the gall to wonder why you have strange feelings about the place,' said Robert, with a laugh.

Jonathan arrived at the Mansells' family home the week before Christmas. Whether she would have refused to see him, Prue was never to know for, as it happened, she opened the door to him and so there was no escape. He looked very tired and considerably thinner and Prue realized immediately that she could not send him away. They made coffee and sat in the kitchen, much to Robert and Margery's disapproval. They eyed one another warily, their conversation initially stilted.

'How are things at the inn?' Prue asked.

'Not good. The staff miss you, the customers miss you and hell, Prue, I miss you most of all. Nothing works without you being there, the place doesn't gel. You have to come back.'

'I'm not coming back,' said Prue. 'There's no point, Jonathan. We have no future together, you must see that. What you need now is a hotel manager.'

'No, I don't see that,' said Jonathan. 'When I arrived back from New York I'm afraid I just couldn't cope with your outburst. It was foolish of me but I didn't feel able to explain to you what had been happening to me. I needed time to try to clear my head. I intended to explain everything to you but then I walked into that scene and. . .'

'It's no good trying to make it sound as though it's my fault,' said Prue.

'I'm not, I'm not,' said Jonathan. 'Will you please listen for once and then maybe you'll understand.'

'OK,' said Prue.

'I married Jo too early. I wasn't ready for marriage, I was a fairly wild young man, but my mother was very keen to see me settle down and Jo was a bright and attractive girl, and a strong person, too, which my mother insisted I needed. She was probably right. The

159

first few years were OK – not great, we fought a lot – but OK. Jo didn't want kids, at least not initially. She had her own publicity business and gradually it began to absorb more and more of her time and I suppose I felt shut out.' He looked at Prue seeking understanding and the expression on his face made her heart twist – he seemed so uncertain and unlike his normal self. 'You see, I guess I've never rated myself very highly.' Prue started to protest. 'OK, I know I go in for a lot of bullshit but deep down I have always known I only had my job at Lindstrom's because I was the boss's son. My car, my apartment . . . everything was provided for me, not because I'd worked like hell to achieve it but because someone else had. I guess I was jealous of Jo's success and the more it absorbed her and the more successful she became, the more I resented it. Not very noble, I'll admit, but perhaps not totally surprising.' He looked to Prue for confirmation and saw the compassion he needed to continue. 'Anyway, here's where I started to behave badly. I had one affair, then another. She got pregnant and my mother had to bale me out by paying for an abortion. Things started to get fairly messy. Jo knew about it, of course, but chose to ignore it. In a way, that only made things worse. I felt that because my affairs didn't matter to her, I had to go on and on until I did get some sort of reaction, hence the business of taking a girl home. Looking back on it, I think I almost wanted to be caught – pathetic, isn't it?'

'Go on,' said Prue.

'Anyway, that was it, our marriage folded. Mother let me use the bank apartment and Jo and I drifted along, meeting occasionally. She never suggested a divorce, I think, initially, because she'd found the Lindstrom name very useful. I didn't want a divorce particularly because I didn't want to admit defeat and, in any case, I couldn't imagine meeting another girl I'd want to marry. There was no need – we had no kids and no financial problems. Then I fell in love with you, so I went back to New York to fix up the details of our divorce – not to ask her blessing, you understand – we've been separated long enough to qualify for a divorce – but just as a matter of courtesy to tell her what I was doing and why. As it turned out she already knew all about us – she's had a private detective keeping tabs on me over here.'

Prue gasped. 'But why?'

'Well, hold onto your seat,' said Jonathan, 'and I'll tell you.'

It took him nearly quarter of an hour to explain to Prue what Jo wanted and why, and what she was prepared to do if he failed to comply. When he had finished, there was a lengthy silence.

'I'm sorry, Jonathan. It must be terrible for you. I'm trying to put myself in your position – it must be so disorientating to think you are one person and then find out you are someone else entirely – even . . . even your name's not right.'

'Yes,' said Jonathan, heavily. 'You see, Prue, I just don't know what to do. If you'd have me, I really do want to marry you, yet if I go ahead with the divorce, Jo won't hesitate to pull the rug out from under my mother. Perhaps the obvious thing is to confront Mother, but I don't know where to start – our whole relationship has been built on a false premise. The third alternative, I guess, is to go and see Edward Deckman but I can't bear to do that. I really dislike the man and he, me. Any interview which involved exposing our true relationship has to be a disaster. Then there's the moral dilemma – should I go to the cops and admit the fraud although it means destroying my mother? It's one hell of a situation but perhaps now you understand why I didn't behave better when you told me about the Gospacks. There is still no excuse for not telling you I was married straight away but I didn't feel married, I haven't done for years, and, as I say, it's never been relevant before. By the time I realized I was serious about you, I was in so deep I didn't know how to explain. I thought if I went and squared things with Jo, I could at least come back and in the same breath ask you to marry me and explain I was getting divorced. I don't know what else to say, Prue, except please come back. Don't leave me. In this increasingly uncertain world you are the only person I believe I can rely on.'

As a plea it was irresistible. In moments Prue was in his arms, promising to take care of him, to help him sort out his future, to marry him if that's what he wished . . . all her resolve, all her certainties that their relationship was over were tossed to the wind.

At last they drew apart. 'I'd better go and break it to my parents that I'm going back with you. I have to say, they won't be pleased.'

'We'll face them together,' said Jonathan. 'I don't want to tell them all about my problems, if that's OK, but I'll do my best to reassure them that my intentions towards you are at least honourable – it's just a question of obtaining a divorce.'

'Thanks,' said Prue. 'It might help.'

Jonathan smiled at her. 'Not that I'm sure I should be asking you to marry me at all. I don't know whether you should be Mrs Lindstrom or Mrs Deckman and I don't know how you feel about marrying a bastard.' He was joking but there was an edge to his voice.

'Ah well,' said Prue, with a smile, anxious to reassure him and at the same time lighten the moment. 'Our family has its dark secrets, too. I'm a direct descendant of an illegitimate child, so you're in good company.'

It was then that Prue told Jonathan about Guy and his mother, Elizabeth, the first Lady in Waiting.

'So it's been a kind of revealing time for both of us,' Jonathan said when she had finished. He drew her close. 'Thank you for telling me about your family. It just goes to prove that my situation certainly isn't a new one, and hell, it's not the past that matters – it's you and I and the future that really count.'

CHAPTER EIGHTEEN
September 1786 – Long Melford

'Guy, you will have a terrible pain in your belly if you eat any more of those brambles.'

'More, Mother, please more – they are very good.' Guy smiled up at his mother; his mouth and teeth were stained with blackberry juice but the grin was irresistible.

'Just you remember then, boy, there will be no sympathy from me if you are ill and I expect you to eat all your dinner.'

'I will.' He ran off through the spinney, darting this way and that.

Elizabeth stood in a patch of sunlight, her eyes trying to follow the dark green of his jacket. He was a big, strong boy for four and his adventurous spirit was always getting him into trouble. It was one scrape after another and she knew that the years ahead promised more of the same. Still, she would have him no other way, her son. She still could not come to terms with how much he meant to her. She who had never wanted a child, seeing motherhood only as a burden, increasing the life of drudgery which was the lot of most women of her acquaintance. Yet now, the thought of anything befalling him brought terror to her heart, she loved him so much. Suddenly, in the distance, she heard the sound of hooves beating loudly on the ground still dry from a perfect summer. Anxiously she looked around for Guy. Very few travellers ever passed through the spinney for it led nowhere. Recently there had been a highwayman plaguing the life out of the coaches as they left Long Melford on their way to Bury St. Edmunds, waylaying travellers as they negotiated the steep hill past Kentwell. Stories abounded as to the way he abused women passengers. Could this be his hiding place? It had a lot to offer a man who did not wish to be seen by day. Fear clutched at her – should she call for Guy or not? She stood rooted to the spot, her mind clouded with indecision as the sound grew louder and louder.

In the same instant the man and his horse came into sight, Guy erupted from a nearby bush, running to his mother, not for comfort or reassurance but to stand proudly and defiantly in front of her. Even in this moment of fear, Elizabeth felt a rush of maternal pride.

The rider, seeing the boy's gesture, threw back his head and laughed. 'Do not be afeared, young sir, I shall not hurt you or your. . .' The words died on his lips and in the same moment Elizabeth knew why. The man reined in his horse in front of mother and child and stared down at them. 'Good day to you, Elizabeth,' he said, quietly. Elizabeth was for once robbed of speech as she stared up into the eyes of Thomas, Earl of Clare. It was the first time she had seen him in the four years since the day she had threatened to dash their child onto the cobbles if he did not leave her. For a moment, neither could look away. At last it was Thomas who turned his attention to Guy. 'And you, young sir, so properly ready to defend your mother from strangers, what is your name?'

'My name is Guy Monson, sir, and I am four years old.'

'Are you indeed – only four, you say? Then you're a fine boy; you look nearer six or seven to me.' Guy visibly swelled with pride. 'May I walk with you awhile?' Thomas dismounted before Elizabeth could answer.

'We were just going home.' She stumbled over the words. 'Guy is about to make himself very ill from eating too many brambles.'

'It's not possible to eat too many brambles when you are four, is it, Guy?'

For a moment Thomas laid his hand on his son's shoulder and the boy, encouraged by such a gesture, began to exercise his insatiable curiosity. 'What is the name of your horse, sir? He is very grand. You must be a very important gentleman to have such a horse.'

'Guy, hold your tongue,' Elizabeth snapped.

'Let the lad ask all the questions he wishes,' said Thomas. 'It is his right, after all,' he added, softly. 'My name is Thomas, Earl of Clare, Guy, and this fine horse is named Trumpet.' Thomas turned to look full at Elizabeth, his expression sad, his eyes clouded with memories. 'Sorcha died two years back. No horse will ever compare with her . . . for so many reasons.'

Guy's eyes were round, like saucers. He had heard of the Earl of Clare. He knew little of titles or what made a gentleman, but he knew this man must be important. He brushed a lock of dark hair back from his forehead and as he did so, Thomas gasped. Guy was startled. 'What ails you, sir?'

'Nothing, boy, nothing. You go and look for brambles while I talk to your mother.' Guy hesitated, looking to Elizabeth for confirmation, but he found his mother curiously unresponsive – she seemed to be in a daze. In the circumstances, it seemed best to do as he was told.

164

'He's a credit to you, our son,' Thomas said, when the boy was safely out of earshot.

'My son,' Elizabeth corrected.

'How can you say that, when every time you look at him you see me? The same face, the same hair, he will be tall like me, too, and the gestures. . . It is alarming to see one's mirror image so faithfully reproduced. At Chadbrook there is a likeness of me painted by Thomas Gainsborough when I was six. It could be of Guy in every detail, Elizabeth, in every detail.'

Elizabeth turned on him. 'You married another woman on the day my son was born. When you did that you forfeited your right both to him and me.'

'And I have not troubled you since, have I? I respected your wishes but it has not made me stop loving you. Never a day goes by when I do not wonder how you fare and how goes things for our son.'

'I expect by now you have other sons, a house full of sons.'

Thomas shook his head. 'No, I do not. Beatrice has carried but one child, a daughter, still-born. Since then it would appear she is barren. Christopher lives but is a poor, weak creature and his sister is dead, drowned in the pond during one of her fits. It seems my children are blighted, all save Guy.'

The bleak expression on his face for a moment softened Elizabeth, then, fighting her own weakness, she said, 'I want you to leave us now, Thomas. I know well we did not meet here by accident, that you must have been seeking us. So you have seen Guy now and you can ride on knowing he is well and I, too. I doubt our paths shall meet again but, if it is what you wish, should anything befall Guy, I shall acquaint you of it. No news from me means that he prospers. It is the most I can offer you.'

Thomas touched Elizabeth's arm. 'I am grateful for that,' he said, hoarsely. 'I love you still, and I would wish to love our child, but I suppose I must continue to respect your wishes. Adieu, Elizabeth, think of me sometimes.' Without another word he left her, mounted his horse and was gone.

Elizabeth watched the disappearing cloud of dust that followed in Thomas's wake. Nothing had changed – as he rode away it felt as though he tore the heart right from her body. Did he really think she had failed to notice how much Guy was made in his own image? Every day it pained her and yet in a perverse way it gave her pleasure to see her son grow to be so like his father.

165

'Mother, Mother, where has he gone, the . . . Earl?' Guy stumbled over the word.

'He had to leave, little one, he is an important man, with many demands on his time.'

'I like him, he is very grand but very kind to me.'

'Yes, he was. Come now, it is time to go home.'

'Have we met the Earl before?' Guy asked, as they walked along, hand in hand.

'No,' Elizabeth replied, surprised at the question.

'Then why do I think I have seen him before today?'

Because you have seen your own reflection in the pond at the bottom of the garden, in the pewter mugs in the bar, in your grandmother's old looking glass, Elizabeth thought. Instead she said, 'I can't imagine.'

A long, dreary evening stretched ahead for Elizabeth. Trade was not brisk. The inn earned sufficient to keep herself, her mother and Guy all the year round but on many an evening few travellers passed The Lady in Waiting and fewer still stopped. It was the inn at the other end of the village which took most of the coach trade and there was no way she could compete. Weary travellers stopping at The Lion were provided with a good meal, a bed, even hot water to wash in. In the early days after her father's death, when Thomas had still been with her, the inn had begun to prosper and grow in popularity. However, the problems of caring for a tiny baby and running the inn had taken their toll. Trade had dropped off and never recovered. Now it seemed that her life was going nowhere, ebbing away with no hope for the future. Guy was a strong, healthy boy and as each month passed his need for her grew less. There had been no serious man in her life since Thomas. Once or twice a passing traveller had fleetingly appealed to her and she had taken him to her bed, but no lovemaking could compare with Thomas's and the experience invariably left her more dissatisfied than ever.

The meeting with Thomas had unsettled her. She went through the motions of feeding her son and seeing him to bed, of fetching more logs and lighting the candles. Then she settled herself in the fireplace to wait for the odd customer. Staring into the fire, she thought back to the night which seemed so long ago, to when she had first met Thomas – a sixteen-year-old girl, so full of hope for a better life. Now it seemed that this would always elude her. It was true she was no longer subject to the tyranny of her father, but her need to support herself, her son and her mother – now quite mad but apparently still strong in body – meant that she would ever be tied to The Lady in Waiting. A log shifted in the fire and she glanced up at the clock on the wall. It was after nine, no one would be coming now, she would bolt the door and retire for the night. She rose a little stiffly, having been sitting for so long, and she was about to cross the room when the door burst open.

As once before, he stood tall and broad in the doorway. His voice was strained as he tried to catch his breath. 'Elizabeth, I know I should not have come but I could not stay away. Seeing you today set me on fire. I love you, I love you still, I always have. . .' His voice died away.

She stood her ground and tried to concentrate her mind on something, anything, to keep herself from running into his arms. He was dressed carelessly, his clothes mud-splattered. He looked tired and far less imposing than he had appeared earlier in the day. 'You should not have come,' she said. 'You promised to leave us be.'

'I know I promised but I need you back in my life.'

'Need me, or my body, or perhaps my son?' Elizabeth said.

He edged nearer and she shrank back towards the fireplace. 'I am a man with faults like any other, grievous faults some of them, but I have never lied to a woman and told her that I loved her when I did not. Yes, I wish to acquaint myself of our son, I would like to share in his childhood, but that is not why I am here tonight.'

'So, Thomas, you wish to bed a woman and your wife will not give you what you want,' Elizabeth said. Her heart was beating unnaturally fast and she was trembling from head to foot. She knew she had to find some method of sending him away or she would be lost.

'Damn your impertinence, how dare you speak to me like this! Do you forget who I am?'

'I know who you are and what you are and it is of no consequence to me. If you want a woman, I have no doubts one of your servants will oblige. I am sorry you have had a wasted journey.'

He stepped forward and struck her across the face. She was not expecting it and stumbling backwards she tripped over the chair and collapsed on the ground. In an instant he was on his knees beside her. 'Elizabeth, I am sorry, I did not mean to hurt you. Oh my darling girl.' He drew her into his arms and kissed her. She clung to him and in moments they were making love there on the floor in front of the fire, oblivious to everything around them, such was their need for one another.

Within a matter of weeks the affair of Thomas, Earl of Clare, and his Lady in Waiting, was the talk of Suffolk. Thomas was so in love that this time he made no secret of his frequent visits to the inn, and this time there was a different quality to their relationship. Elizabeth had grown up, she was no longer the child who had first attracted him. Although the gap in their social standing was still vast, it had closed a little and under Thomas's influence Elizabeth began to blossom. He bought her new clothes, she learnt to dress her hair, she began taking lessons on a spinet and read voraciously every book that Thomas brought her from the library at Chadbrook. For their son, Thomas engaged a governess, but made a wise choice – a young woman, plain and unsophisticated, who did not look down on Elizabeth. For his fifth birthday, Thomas presented Guy with a pony and Elizabeth with a fine young mare. Over the weeks and months that followed, the people of Long Melford became used to seeing the three of them out riding together, like any normal family. Indeed, they travelled abroad a great deal. They visited The Rose & Crown in Sudbury on one occasion to see the caged birds and to Market Hill to see jugglers and performing bears. Father and son were much entertained by their antics while Elizabeth took pleasure in exploring the new shops Sudbury had to offer. On another occasion, Thomas's groom, Simon, took Guy to watch his father race his horses between Shrimpling Church and Hawkedon. The boy's pleasure in horse racing stood out in stark contrast to Christopher's indifference.

It was a golden period which, searching his soul, Thomas knew could not last, but as if by mutual consent, they never discussed the future. Thomas helped Elizabeth with further conversion of the inn. He went to see the coach owners personally and soon coaches began to stop at The Lady in Waiting, in preference to The Lion. The inn prospered and while Elizabeth no longer served the travellers who stopped by, a woman's touch to the hospitality gave the inn a warmth and friendliness that was lacking in most of the houses along the roads of England. There were cots for babies and children, good-quality bedding for women and well-cooked food and drink available twenty-four hours a day.

Shortly after her father's death, Elizabeth had learnt her first and major lesson in the art of innkeeping. When a drunken brawl broke out in her father's time, he simply left his customers to fight it out – there was nothing much to damage, he reasoned, so why become involved? Her father had only been dead three days when Hewitt, the blacksmith, a kindly but regular drunk, became involved in an argument with a local farmer who maintained that Hewitt had badly shod his horse. Everyone in the tap room took sides and soon a fierce brawl was underway. Elizabeth calmly went to the pump in the stableyard and filled a pale of ice-cold water. She returned to the tap room, aimed carefully and threw it over the chief offenders. In the shocked silence that followed her actions she told her guests in no uncertain terms that this was her inn now, that it was the height of ill manners to treat a woman's home in such a manner and that from now on she would keep an orderly house and any offenders would be horsewhipped off the premises – by her personally. The effect of her fine temper, her extreme good looks and brave words humbled the assembled company. She never had any trouble again, which greatly added to the inn's reputation.

In addition, undoubtedly, another attraction which brought people from far and wide was the opportunity to catch sight of the Earl's red-haired woman and her bastard son, but such notoriety did not trouble Elizabeth – she was too happy, too busy, too much in love.

Increasingly, Thomas spent more of his time in Long Melford. His wife's money ensured that Chadbrook was now out of danger and the estate ran itself for much of the time. In recent years he had spent at least half a year in London. Now he chose to stay part of the time at Long Melford, taking as much pleasure in the prosperity and increasing popularity of the inn as he did in his own estate. Carefully and tactfully, Thomas and Elizabeth chose their moment to tell Guy the truth of his parentage. Blissfully ignorant of the implications of illegitimacy, the news realized all his boyhood dreams. To have not only a father at last but such a father! After much lively debate with the vicar of Long Melford church, Guy was finally christened there on 13th May 1788. While the short service, attended by the whole parish, could not make Guy legitimate, it did at least make him a Christian, and in the eyes of both Elizabeth and Thomas, the ceremony seemed to represent a blessing to their union. It was a situation which could not and did not last.

CHAPTER NINETEEN
Long Melford – March 1789

Harry Naylor was not an impressive man in either looks or stature. His dress, however, was impeccable – foppish perhaps but not without a certain style, and from the tip of his immaculate maroon leather shoes, to his startling cream and maroon stock, his attire smacked of prosperity. Elizabeth did not like him, long before she knew who he was or the purpose of his visit. His fashionable clothes and stylish wig could not hide the fact that his eyes were mean and calculating, his chin weak, his complexion pallid and unhealthy. 'You wish to speak to me,' she said, having been summoned to the bar by a breathless serving girl, who said there was a very grand gentleman to see her.

Harry Naylor looked around the bar. 'Is there somewhere more private where we can retire to talk?'

Instinctively Elizabeth sensed it unwise to conduct an interview with this man alone. 'We can sit by the fire, if you wish.'

They moved to the fireplace. Elizabeth sat down and motioned Harry to take the other chair. He declined, standing instead with his back to the fire. The moment Elizabeth was seated she regretted it, for she felt instantly at a disadvantage.

'I assume my name means nothing to you?' Harry said.

Elizabeth took time and pleasure over her reply. 'I have to admit, sir, that I have never heard of you in my life.'

'Surely you are acquainted with the Naylors of Brundon,' he said, pompously. 'From our mill, we supply the county with its corn and grain, and in addition we control most of the coach travel in eastern England. Indeed, I am a partner in the company whose coaches frequent this very inn on such a regular basis.' There was menace in his voice and suddenly he had Elizabeth's full attention. This man was a threat, she could sense it, and if what he said was true, he was in a position of considerable power.

Elizabeth summoned her not inconsiderable charm and smiled at him demurely. 'I must apologize, sir, for not recognizing your name immediately. My . . .' She hesitated over the word, 'my sponsor deals with the business side of the inn, which is why I did not know you.'

'Your sponsor – by such a description I assume you are referring to the Earl of Clare?'

'I have that honour,' said Elizabeth, with due humility.

'It is about this dubious honour that I wish to speak to you.' He smiled slightly, curling his lip. 'You should perhaps also be aware that I am a kinsman of your Earl, your Thomas.'

Elizabeth could not hide her surprise. 'You are kinsman to the Earl of Clare?'

'My sister, Beatrice, is his wife. I assume you knew he had a wife?' The sarcasm was only too obvious.

'Yes, of course.' So now she had it. Already, her mind was whirling as she began to wonder at the purpose of Harry Naylor's visit.

'My sister is becoming a little tired of you, madam, but my father, Sir George Naylor, is more than tired, he is extremely angry. Your . . . liaison with Thomas was tiresome enough while its existence was known only to local people. Now, however, I am sure you will be flattered to hear, it has reached London. In the drawing rooms of London, they talk of it in length and, so I am told, the matter has even been discussed at Court. I should imagine this pleases you a great deal.'

'I do not know to what you refer,' said Elizabeth. 'The Earl of Clare is my benefactor. He helped me establish this inn because I was left destitute when my father was killed in a brawl. There is no harm in this act of charity, surely.'

'Do not waste my time, madam,' said Harry Naylor. 'There is no point in denying your liaison with Thomas, nor the fact that you have borne him a bastard son. You can bluff all you will, but you and I know the truth, as does the rest of England, by all accounts. For this reason I shall go straight to the purpose of my visit here today. I mean to stop this relationship, and I mean to stop it at once.'

Elizabeth felt sick and faint with panic but it was vital that he did not see how much he was frightening her. 'And how do you propose to do that?' she asked, pertly.

'Money,' said Harry Naylor, bluntly. 'Firstly, I can kill the trade here at your inn within a day. I can see to it that no coach ever comes here again – neither my coaches nor those belonging to other companies. Your livelihood, madam, will cease and you will no longer

171

have the means to support yourself, your son and, I understand, your lunatic mother.'

'We have other trade besides that which the coaches bring us,' Elizabeth said.

'Barely enough to scrape a living, if that. You are no longer used to poverty and I have no doubt you would find it very hard to go back to your former life. Still, I have not yet finished and I must insist you have the courtesy to hear me out. We, my father and I, have within our power the ability to destroy Chadbrook and ensure that Thomas is forced to sell the estate – to see it pass out of the Chadbrook family for good.'

'I don't believe you,' said Elizabeth.

'Then you had better let me explain how this is possible. As a family we have no illusions and neither does my sister – Thomas married Beatrice for her money. It is Beatrice who has provided the income to maintain the Chadbrook estate, and perhaps equally relevant to this conversation, it is she who has financed the rebuilding here at the inn and your improved lifestyle. Yes, your bastard son's governess, your fashionable clothes . . . everything has been paid for with Naylor money.'

'No, it is Thomas's money,' Elizabeth protested.

'I'm afraid you have been misled if that is what you believe. At the time Beatrice married Thomas he had nothing, nothing at all. He could not have helped rebuild your inn nor anything else. He was destitute with Chadbrook like an albatross round his neck. My sister changed all that.'

Elizabeth rallied. 'But under the terms of a marriage settlement, a husband may do with his wife's money as he wishes.'

'True, but in Beatrice's case, her money comes by way of an annual income gifted by my father. Currently, he has a mind to withdraw his support for he has no wish to see his money being squandered on a harlot, nor will he have the Naylor name made a laughing stock.'

Elizabeth gasped. 'You go too far, sir.'

'I think not, given the circumstances.' There was a tense silence between them until Harry continued. 'Let me put to you my proposition – you were over-hasty in arguing the case. My father requires you to undertake never to see Thomas again. In return, I will ensure that the coaches continue to come by your inn, indeed, if you wish, we will put more trade to you. I will grant this is an exceptionally well-run establishment and we are after all businessmen. As to Chadbrook, the estate will be allowed to prosper, with the benefit of Beatrice's income. However, if you do not comply with our wishes, you and Thomas are finished – you will both be destitute within weeks.'

'Get out of my home, get out of it now,' Elizabeth hissed, rising to her feet with as much dignity as she could muster. She was taller than Harry Naylor and for a moment the benefit of her stature gave her confidence. 'I will speak of your visit to the Earl of Clare and tell him of your allegations and your filthy blackmail. I am sure that he will see to it that you never raise your head in society again.'

'You are wrong,' said Harry Naylor. 'Society is changing, though in your position you know nothing of it nor cannot be expected to understand. My father began life with nothing yet he has risen to be one of the wealthiest men in England, through his own hard work and that of his sons. Money is as powerful as breeding these days, and my father is not about to see the fruits of his labour squandered on a whore, albeit an Earl's whore.'

Elizabeth lost control. She lunged at him wildly, her fingernails ripping at his face. He was surprisingly strong. In seconds he held her by the wrists, pinning her back against the wall. 'Do not underestimate me, madam, nor the power of my family which is far greater than that of the Chadbrooks. You may believe that Thomas loves you but even you must recognize that faced with a choice between you and Chadbrook, he would not hesitate to put the estate first.'

'Get out, get out.' Elizabeth twisted this way and that, unable to escape from the grip. In desperation she spat directly into Harry Naylor's face.

Disgusted, he let go of her hands and stepped away from her, taking a handkerchief from his pocket and wiping his face fastidiously. 'As I suspected, you're nothing but an animal,' he said. 'What a strange bedfellow the Earl chooses when he could have any woman in the country and will, again, no doubt when he is free from whatever spell you weave. I trust you understand my proposal – what you decide will affect not only your future but that of your benefactor. If you do not send him away next time he visits you, then you can be sure that you have sealed not only your fate but also his. Good day to you, madam.' He turned and strode from the bar.

For the first time Elizabeth realized that the serving girls and local customers were staring at her. She had been oblivious of their presence until now. She muttered excuses under her breath, left the bar and climbed the stairs to her bedroom, her head thumping, her face flushed, while the rest of her body was ice-cold and trembling. She flung herself on her bed and, rolling over, stared up at the rafters dry-eyed. As she lay there she felt a movement deep within her. For a moment she was bewildered, then she recognized it for what it was – the first sign of the quickening of the child within her. She had not told Thomas that she was to bear him another child. He had been tired and preoccupied of late, and she sensed in a way she could not put into words that the bearing of a second bastard child would change their relationship, and it was this that she feared. Part of the charm she knew she held for Thomas was that when he was with her, he was young and carefree again. The added responsibility of another child threatened to destroy this. She put her hand on her stomach and only then did she begin to cry, great racking sobs.

What was to become of her, of Guy, of the child she carried? The position was impossible. Harry Naylor was clearly not a man to be ignored and she did not for one moment doubt the sincerity of his threats. To force Thomas to choose between herself and Chadbrook was unthinkable, unbearable for, as Harry Naylor had rightly indicated, undoubtedly Thomas would choose Chadbrook. After all, it would not be the first time – he had done so once before – on the day Guy was born, and she knew she could not cope with another rejection. Again, she felt the fluttering in her womb, the child's kick seeming as weak and futile as her own inability to influence the course of her life.

CHAPTER TWENTY
Chadbrook – February 1982

Away in the distance, Charles heard the peal of the front door bell and resisted, with difficulty, the urge to go and answer it himself. Since he had dispensed with Devereaux's services, Mrs. Plum, the housekeeper at Chadbrook for many years, insisted on receiving callers. So upset was she by the concept of Charles answering his own front door that in the end he had acceded to her request. The door bell presumably heralded the arrival of the girl from The Lady in Waiting. He had been intrigued by her call, particularly since after careful cross-examination, it appeared she did not want to see him on a matter which in any way was connected with charity work. So far as Charles could see, one of the chief occupations of his new-found status was to answer an endless stream of begging letters, which in the estate's predicament could hardly be less appropriate.

Charles had spent a dull few weeks wrestling with the estate accounts, and as far as he could see there was no way he was going to be able to pay the Inheritance Tax due. Yes, the estate was run profitably but not to the extent to be able to cope with the crippling burden of taxes he now faced. The premature death of James was something that, naturally enough, nobody had anticipated and the consequences were dire. He felt so helpless. James had modernized the farm considerably in recent years and after lengthy talks with the farm manager – a sensible, intelligent man named Peter Graham – it seemed unlikely that there was much more which could be done to increase the income. Indeed, as Graham had said himself, they were very lucky at Chadbrook that they made a profit at all – many large estates could not make their farming activities pay.

There was a discreet knock on the door of the study and Charles made a determined effort to push aside his own problems. 'Miss Prue Mansell is in the morning room,' Mrs. Plum announced, suspiciously. 'She says she has an appointment.'

'She does indeed, Mrs. Plum,' said Charles, rising to his feet. 'Please do show her in.' Mrs. Plum's new-found role was starting to go to her head. The nature of her introduction clearly indicated her personal view on each of Charles's visitors. Prue Mansell obviously was viewed somewhat dubiously.

Prue was duly ushered in and the very sight of her swept Charles's worries away. Her red-gold hair was caught up in a French plait. She was dressed simply in a cream polo-neck sweater and jeans, her green eyes sparkled and her skin glowed with health and vigour. She seemed slightly out of breath. 'It was such a lovely morning and I was a little early, so I've been for a walk. I hope you don't mind, it was trespassing.'

'Of course I don't mind,' said Charles. 'The sight of you does me good – you look so . . . healthy.'

'Oh Lord,' said Prue. 'That sounds awful – I instantly feel buxom and red-faced.'

'You're certainly neither. Come and sit down.' Mrs. Plum had stood hovering by the door during this exchange. 'Would you like some coffee?' Charles asked Prue.

'Oh yes, please.'

'Two coffees then please, Mrs. Plum.' Mrs. Plum retreated without a word.

'What have I done to offend her?' Prue asked anxiously. 'She's absolutely terrifying.'

'Nothing, I'm sure,' said Charles. 'But she is becoming frightfully pompous, I'm afraid, ever since she took over the duties of butler.' He looked at her, sudden realization dawning. 'Of course you know all about my dispensing with Devereaux's services. You probably think I'm an absolute sod.'

'It does seem rather extraordinary,' said Prue. 'He is so efficient, loyal and hard-working – and after all those years with your family.'

'I know, I know,' said Charles. 'It's just that I . . .' He hesitated, an excuse at the ready, but suddenly he felt the need to explain honestly, to seek understanding from this girl. 'Devereaux had been my father's butler for many years and was intensely loyal to him. I've always lived in my father's shadow and somehow I felt Devereaux would always be looking over my shoulder and comparing me unfavourably with my father. I'm ashamed of being so, so spineless but that's the truth of it.' He smiled suddenly. 'In any case, a butler isn't quite my style.'

Prue laughed and surveyed Charles with interest. He was dressed like her – casually in jeans, his dark hair untidy and boyish, his navy sweater heavily darned. 'I suppose if I'm honest,' she admitted, 'you don't really look the part . . . am I offending you?'

'Certainly not,' said Charles. 'In fact I think you've just paid me a compliment.' His face was suddenly serious. 'I was never cut out for this job. My elder brother, James, was groomed for the Earldom and was absolutely perfect for the role.'

'I heard about his death,' said Prue. 'I'm sorry.'

'Yes, thank you.'

The coffee arrived and Mrs. Plum made much of pouring it and handing round the biscuits. 'So,' said Charles, when at last she had run out of reasons to stay. 'What is it I can do for you? You said you needed my help, which I found most intriguing.'

'It's an odd tale,' said Prue, 'but it seems possible that you and I may be distantly related.'

'Really!' said Charles. 'Mansell – Mansell, the name doesn't mean a thing to me, I have to admit. Is there some glorious scandal that I've missed?'

'There is a scandal, I think, but it's not a very recent one. I'm talking about the late eighteenth century.'

'Good grief,' said Charles. 'What's prompted this interest?'

'I'd better start at the beginning,' said Prue. She spent some time explaining the background of her research into Elizabeth Monson and carefully avoided mentioning her feelings of foreboding. It was not right to confide in a stranger, it was too personal. 'The trouble is,' she said, when she had explained the position, 'the trail's gone cold and I do so very much want to know more. That Elizabeth had a son who was our first baronet, is not in dispute. That young Guy was taken under the patronage of Thomas, the then Earl of Clare, is also not in dispute. What I want to find out is why Thomas took an interest in the boy. You see I have a theory, or rather it is my father's idea, that Guy may well have been Thomas Chadbrook's illegitimate son, and what I am wondering is whether there is any possibility that you may have records of the period which might confirm this one way or the other.'

'Thomas Chadbrook you say?' said Charles. 'He's the poor devil who inherited his father's gambling debts?'

'Oh, so you do know something of your family's history?'

'Yes, I may be a hopeless Earl as we've both agreed but I've taken a great deal more interest in the history of the family than I think either my father or brother. Let me tell you what I do know about Thomas, without reference to any records. He was born in 1753, I'm fairly sure, and he had two wives – Eleanor, who was killed in a hunting accident, and then Beatrice. In both cases, it appears he married for money.'

'Really!' said Prue. 'That's interesting. An unhappy marriage would seem to be a good reason to have a mistress.'

'Yes, I suppose so. Thomas's father, Simon, I'm afraid was not unlike me – he was a thinker rather than a doer and a man who patronized the arts very heavily. Many of the lovely paintings and furnishings we have here in Chadbrook today are the result of Simon's interest in the arts. He travelled extensively and showed exquisite taste but the problem was he had a darker side. He was an obsessive gambler and by the time he died he left poor old Thomas with one hell of a job – crippling debts and a very run-down estate.'

'Still, he obviously succeeded in putting things right,' said Prue.

'Well yes, and no. He certainly saved the estate but at the expense of personal happiness, I would imagine.'

'Is there likely to be any more information on Thomas?'

'There may be, I'll have to do some digging about.'

'I don't want to put you to too much trouble,' said Prue.

'It's no trouble at all, I can't think of being set a nicer task. Tell me, what is your interest in these people? Is it just idle curiosity?'

'Yes . . .' said Prue, with little conviction.

Charles eyed her shrewdly. 'But that's not the whole reason, is it?'

'Well no,' Prue admitted. 'Since I've been living at The Lady in Waiting, I've been sort of haunted, I suppose is the only way to describe it.'

'Really,' said Charles. 'How fascinating! People walking round with heads under their arms, that sort of thing?'

'No, not that sort of thing,' said Prue, immediately regretting her decision to confide her feelings.

'I'm sorry to be flippant, go on,' said Charles, sensing her mood.

'It's a difficult thing to describe,' said Prue, after a moment. 'I get these terrible feelings of fear and foreboding when I'm on my own, even just for a few seconds. It's as if someone is using my mind, my emotions if you like, to express their own feelings. I was in the cellar on my own the other day when this terrible feeling of misery and despair hit me so hard, I literally cried out. It was as tangible as a physical pain, and no, before you say anything, I'm not going mad and I'm not imagining it.' Prue hesitated. 'To make things even more improbable I am convinced these forebodings are connected with Elizabeth. There seem to be a number of similarities between us, too. I am her direct descendant but it's not just that. It appears she probably ran the inn single-handed as I'm doing, more or less, and I think there are some parallels in our personal lives, too.' Prue's voice trailed away.

The obvious comparisons which could be made between her position to that of Elizabeth was what had obsessed Prue recently. It was three months since her return to The Lady in Waiting, and during that period Jonathan seemed to have slipped into a state of inertia, hardly helping at all with the running of the inn and seemingly unable to decide how to handle his wife's ultimatum. They had been very busy over the Christmas and New Year period and it had been easy for Prue to let the whole matter slide. Increasingly now, however, she was becoming impatient for him to make some sort of decision. She was shamelessly jealous of Jo and the knowledge that Jonathan was married undermined her self-confidence. If Guy was Thomas Chadbrook's son then these were many of the emotions which Elizabeth herself must have experienced, or so Prue imagined.

She forced her mind back to the present, to find Charles watching her. She could not read his expression but she was surprised by the intensity of his gaze. 'I'm sorry,' she said. 'You must think I'm a complete nut-case.'

He stood up and walked over to the window, staring out into the parkland. 'No, I don't think you're a nut-case at all. From the way you describe it, I understand completely. It must be terrifying.'

'It is,' said Prue, absurdly grateful for his immediate understanding.

There was silence in the room for a moment. Charles continued to stare out through the window, trying to make sense of the strangeness of his own feelings. The moment Prue had described her experiences at The Lady in Waiting, they had at once been familiar and accompanied by a great sadness he could not understand. He had only met Prue once before and her story about them being related was, to say the least, far-fetched. It did not make any sense that he should react so intensely. He forced himself to concentrate on the moment. 'I tell you what I'll do,' he said. 'I'll have a thorough search through our records and see what I can find. I'm not promising anything, mind, but this library is very comprehensive. Leave it with me for a few days and I'll see what we have for you.'

'It's very kind of you,' said Prue. 'I would offer to do the searching myself but I imagine you wouldn't want me poking through your family archives.'

'It's not that,' said Charles. 'It's just a question of knowing where

179

to look. Anyway, I probably have more time on my hands than you – running the inn must be a very full-time job.'

'It certainly has been busy in the last few months but we're slacking off at the moment. February is always quiet in the trade,' said Prue. 'In fact today's my day off, the first I've had in weeks. Well, the first ever, really.'

Charles glanced at his watch. 'If that's the case, why don't I take you out to lunch?'

'Oh no,' said Prue, hastily. 'You've been kind enough as it is.'

'To be honest,' said Charles, 'you would be doing me a favour. I could do with a break. Please do say yes.'

They had lunch in a French restaurant in Sudbury. The food was excellent and they were soon into their second bottle of wine. 'It's wonderful,' said Prue, 'to be sitting here, not worrying about what's going on in the kitchen and fretting over the quality of the service. This is a real treat and I really am most grateful.'

'It's the least I can do,' said Charles. 'After all, it's not often one comes across a long-lost relative.'

'We don't know we're related yet,' Prue reminded him. 'With any luck that's what you're going to be able to tell us.'

As the meal progressed, Prue, relaxed by the wine and a sense of release at being away from the inn, began to question Charles about his life. She sensed without being able to pinpoint the reason that he was something of a lost soul. Indeed, by his own admission he had been forced by circumstances into a role which did not really suit him. 'Do you see yourself ultimately enjoying being Earl of Clare and running Chadbrook?' she asked, over coffee.

'I don't know,' Charles answered. His smile was lop-sided and very appealing. He was an attractive man, particularly now when he looked somewhat vulnerable at being questioned about himself. 'I'm a failed writer and frankly that isn't the best of qualifications for running a large estate. My business experience is nil.'

'When you say *failed*, have you ever been published?' Prue asked.

'Well yes, I've had eight or nine novels published, but as my former wife pointed out, none of them have been wildly successful.'

Prue was surprised at the reference to a wife. In a way Charles seemed strangely untouched by life – it was not easy to imagine him married. 'I didn't realize you'd been married.'

'Yes, married and divorced. I was married to a French girl for eight years, until she found a better alternative. I can't say I blame her.'

'You're very defeatist about yourself,' Prue suggested.

'Not without cause,' said Charles. His voice was bitter and Prue found it oddly shocking.

'I don't know how you can say that, with eight novels published. Have you tried writing since you returned to Chadbrook?'

'No,' said Charles. 'And to be honest, I don't see myself going back to it in a serious way. For one thing I haven't the time and for another I have no inclination. It was a phase, an enjoyable one, but it's over. In a way it was like playing at life – we had a flat in Antibes, I spent the winter commuting between my desk and the cafe across the road, and in the summer commuting between the cafe across the road and the beach.'

'A far cry from life at Chadbrook,' said Prue, thoughtfully.

'Yes, indeed.' Charles pushed back the hair from his eyes and took another swig of his wine. 'Would you like a brandy?'

'No thanks,' said Prue. 'I've had more than enough.'

'I think I will.' He summoned the waiter and gave his order, and Prue realized suddenly he was already fairly drunk. 'You see, Prue, in addition to everything else that's wrong, I've come back to one hell of a mess.'

His need to talk was obvious. 'In what way?' Prue asked, encouragingly.

'The estate is facing a very difficult, if not insurmountable financial future. It's running profitably enough but shortly I will have to pay a double set of Inheritance Tax. Of course my father had never assumed for one moment that he would outlive James, so over the years he passed to James as much of the estate as it was tax-effective to do. When James died, the estate reverted to my father and attracted the first slice of Inheritance Tax. When he died within eighteen months, the estate came on to me and attracted Inheritance Tax all over again. The result is the most enormous bill.'

'Could you talk to the tax people and try to negotiate payment in stages?' asked Prue.

'My accountant has already done the best he can do on that score and is enormously pessimistic about our being able to cope with the deal he has struck.'

'Then you're just going to have to do something to get more money out of the estate.'

'That's the problem,' said Charles. 'There isn't really any more money to be had. James, I must say, did an excellent job in the last few years of his life. It is being run as efficiently as it can be.'

'You could open it to the public,' said Prue.

'Oh, don't,' said Charles. 'I can just see it – a fairground in the park, a mini-railway, a burger bar . . .'

'Well, why not?' said Prue, patiently, 'if it's going to save Chadbrook.'

'The whole thought appals me and to be honest, I don't think I've got either the energy or the ability to carry off such a scheme, even if I had the inclination.'

'You're being very defeatist,' said Prue. She smiled suddenly. 'Think about Thomas and his financial troubles.'

'What about him?' said Charles, morosely.

'He had to marry twice for money rather than love – surely the odd burger bar would be better than that. After all, you owe it to the past generations and to the future ones to keep Chadbrook going.'

'That's another thing,' said Charles. 'There are unlikely to be any more Chadbrooks. I'm the last of the line, I've had my fill of marriage and I don't anticipate marrying again.' The brandy arrived and Charles downed it in one.

Prue was exasperated by his negative attitude. 'So you're drinking too much in order to escape from reality.' The words slipped out before she could stop herself.

Charles looked at her sharply. 'Considering we've only just met, you're being very free with your opinions.'

'I'm sorry,' said Prue, not at all contrite. 'It's just such a waste. You're young, you have a lovely home, a title and your whole life ahead of you and you're being so dreary about it all.'

Charles shifted uncomfortably in his seat. The words were an echo, an echo of Evette's. Two women, very different – one knowing him better than anyone else in the world, one knowing him hardly at all. He frustrated them both with his inability to make any kind of commitment to the future. What was wrong with him? It was easy to blame his father, but wrong – the fault lay within him. All his life he seemed to have been marking time, waiting for something to happen, searching for something he could never find. He managed a small smile. 'You are right in everything you say, of course, but let's stop talking about me. You've given me a fairly hard time, so it's only fair I reciprocate. At Chadbrook, this morning, you said there were personal as well as professional parallels between you and Elizabeth, and then you hastily changed the subject. Are you going to tell me about those similarities?'

Feeling slightly guilty about her outburst, it did not seem right to be evasive. 'My partner, Jonathan Lindstrom, who owns The Lady in Waiting is, well . . .'

'The current man in your life?' Charles suggested, helpfully.

'That sort of thing,' said Prue, with a smile. 'But the problem is he's married. The marriage is over, you understand. His wife's an American. She doesn't want a divorce and is making things rather difficult for Jonathan. I admit this is a real flight of fancy but it occurs to me that the situation must have been much the same for Elizabeth and Thomas. It worries me that the feelings I have when I am at the inn are increasingly less alien these days. I have become used to them of course, but although they are horrible, frightening too sometimes, I find I can identify with them more and more.'

'It's not surprising you've become used to them,' Charles said. 'When you first arrived at the inn, it must have been a dreadful shock to have your thoughts and emotions invaded by this outside influence, but presumably it's almost like part of the furniture now. How long have you been at the inn?'

'Nearly two years.'

'Well, there you are. You had to learn to live with them or you wouldn't have been able to stay.'

'I've done more than learn to live with it,' said Prue, thoughtfully. 'I think I would find it very difficult to leave now. I must see it through.'

'See what through?' said Charles. 'This is fascinating, what do you mean?'

'I – I don't know,' said Prue. 'I feel so silly trying to describe it. I have to know what causes the feelings and try, if possible, to put an end to them.'

'What does Jonathan think?'

'We don't talk about it much.'

'Well perhaps you should,' Charles suggested, frowning.

'He really isn't very interested. In fact he thinks I'm talking a lot of nonsense and imagining the whole thing, but I'm not, I'm truly not.'

'I believe you,' said Charles. 'You're just not the type of person to be neurotic. You've certainly convinced me that what you're feeling is real enough.'

At his words sudden tears came into Prue's eyes. 'Oh I'm sorry,' she said. 'Excuse me.' She got up and bolted for the ladies. Mercifully it was empty. She took time drying her eyes and reapplying some make-up, staring at herself all the while in the mirror. How extraordinary it was that she had found herself confiding in Charles Chadbrook in a way she could not to Jonathan. She wished she had not made such a fool of herself.

When she returned, Charles had paid the bill. 'We seem to have touched one another's raw nerve, I'm sorry,' he said, putting his hand on her arm to guide her from the restaurant.

'No . . . it's all right – it's such a relief that someone believes me so readily.'

'Of course I believe you,' said Charles. 'And believe me when I say I'll do everything I can to help you unravel the past.'

On the journey back to Chadbrook, Prue leant back in the seat as Charles drove his Landrover through the country lanes. She felt suddenly very relaxed and at ease with life and the February sun warmed her through the windscreen as they drove. As they came to the village of Shrimpling, the nearest to the Chadbrook estate, Charles slowed the car. 'Would you mind if I just popped into the vicarage and collected the lesson for Sunday? I've been talked into reading it and I hate reading aloud. I thought I'd better practise.'

'Of course not,' said Prue. 'I'll wait in the car.'

Charles parked the car and crossed the road to the vicarage. Prue looked around her with interest – it was a delightful sleepy little village. To the left of where she sat in the car, there was a grassy track, flanked either side by an avenue of limes. On impulse, she got out of the car and began walking down the lane. The track seemed well used, though not by cars, and as she neared its end she could see its destination was a little church. After the warmth of the car, she was suddenly cold and more for protection from the wind than anything else, she opened the door of the church and went inside. The interior was tiny and very friendly. She sat down on the edge of a pew and looked around her. There was no mention of the Chadbrooks, which puzzled her at first. Then she supposed that the existence of a family chapel would account for why the Earls of Clare were not buried at Shrimpling. She leant back in the pew and tried to imagine what would have been different about the church in Thomas and Elizabeth's time. Her mind drifted away and she was startled suddenly by the opening of the church door.

'There you are,' said Charles. 'I've been looking for you everywhere. I thought you'd run off and left me.'

'I'm so sorry,' said Prue, dazed. 'I just lost track of time.' She jumped up, suddenly self-conscious. 'Did you collect your lesson?'

'Yes. It's very long with all sorts of difficult words.'

'Do you want to read it to me for practice?'

He shook his head. 'No, I'd be too embarrassed. Come on, let's go. It's very cold in here.' He took her arm as they began walking back up the path towards the car.

'This is a wonderful setting for a church.'

'Yes, it is,' said Charles, 'I've always loved it here.'

'I can understand that.' As she spoke, unbidden into her mind came the thought that perhaps Thomas and Elizabeth had walked up this same path together, as she and Charles were doing now. It was a strange thought but as she considered it Prue knew, suddenly, with utter conviction, that they had.

CHAPTER TWENTY-ONE
Shrimpling – Easter – 1789

Shrimpling Parish Church was packed for the Easter Sunday service – in fact so well attended was it that a group of parishioners had to gather outside the open door, as there was no room to stand, let alone sit in the church. It was a joyful service, the sun shone and the graveyard outside was a mass of daffodils and primroses. The second lesson was read, as was tradition, by Thomas, Earl of Clare, and as he recounted the familiar story of the resurrection no one considered there to be any significance in his stumbling over the words at the end of the lesson, as he raised his head to survey the congregation.

Only one person knew why he had faltered – Elizabeth, sitting in the back row, with a very restless Guy, caught his eye as he finished the lesson. She knew she was taking a risk in breaking the unspoken code between them. He travelled freely from his world into hers, but she knew she must never trespass upon his. She would not have come if she had not been desperate. It was eight weeks since she had seen him and three had passed since the visit from Harry Naylor – she knew she could not go on for another day in this state of limbo. If Harry Naylor had made an approach to Thomas, too, then this could be the reason for his absence, or was it that Thomas no longer loved her, or had a new love or perhaps had even achieved some form of reconciliation with his wife?

As they rose for the final hymn, Elizabeth craned her neck for a sight of Beatrice in the family pew. Beside Thomas stood the slender, stooped figure of an adolescent boy, whom Elizabeth took to be Christopher, and on the other side of Christopher stood a short, dark-haired woman, exquisitely dressed in a deep blue robe. Elizabeth could not see her face but fancied her to be the Lady Beatrice.

The service ended, the congregation held back while the Earl and his family left the church.

'There's Father!' said Guy, excitedly. 'Can we not go and talk to him?'

'Hush, Guy, not now,' Elizabeth whispered nervously. 'He knows we're here, he'll come and speak to us when he can.'

'But I want to talk to him now. I want to tell him about . . .'

'Guy, quiet,' Elizabeth hissed.

Several of the congregation turned to stare at the strange, red-haired woman and her loud, unruly child and Guy, intimidated by their curiosity, was mercifully silent. Once outside the church, Elizabeth looked around her. There was no sign of Thomas or his family but this did not surprise her – the sooner he left the church, the sooner he could return.

'What do we do now?' Guy asked.

'We wait,' said Elizabeth.

'Will Father come back to see us?'

'Yes,' said Elizabeth, with more conviction than she felt.

Gradually the congregation dispersed, families going back to their homes to celebrate the Easter day. Elizabeth felt a keen sense of envy as she watched – mothers, fathers and their children – all to her eyes seeming happy and settled together, while she and Guy . . .

The curious stares persisted until all of the congregation had gone. As they stood, awkwardly, by the door of the church the vicar approached them. 'Good day to you, madam, you have a fine boy there.'

'Thank you, sir,' said Elizabeth.

'Can I be of assistance, in any way? You seem to be waiting for someone and you are not from these parts, I know.'

'No, thank you,' said Elizabeth. 'We come from Long Melford and I have brought Guy to Shrimpling today because a distant relative of ours used to worship here. We have our pony and trap waiting at the top of the lane and after the long journey we are not in a hurry to return home.' The excuse sounded ridiculous even to her own ears.

'Then will you do me the honour of joining myself and my family for luncheon before you make your return to Long Melford?'

Elizabeth had to think quickly. 'It is most kind of you, sir, but we have brought refreshment with us. I do very much appreciate your hospitality, we both do.' Guy, who had the normal healthy appetite of a six-year-old, grimaced at her.

'Then if you will excuse me, good day to you.' The vicar, much to Elizabeth's relief, began walking off up the track.

'Why could we not have luncheon with him, Mother? I am very hungry.'

'We have some bread and cheese in the trap, Guy, and we will have it directly, just as soon as we have seen your father.'

The wait seemed interminable, made worse by the fact that Guy plagued her with endless questions. The sun rose higher in the sky and beat down strongly for so early in the year. Elizabeth had slept little recently, the combination of the pregnancy and looking after the inn was starting to wear her out. She longed to lie down, to rest her weary head on Thomas's shoulder, to have him take from her the responsibilities of her day-to-day life, even for a moment.

The time dragged by and at last it was Guy who said, in a subdued voice, 'I do not think Father will be coming today. I think our journey has been wasted. Can we go home now?'

Elizabeth, who had been sitting on a tombstone, put out a hand for Guy to pull her up. 'I think you are right, Guy. I expect he is too busy, but do not fear, he will come and see us soon.'

'It has been such a long time since his last visit,' said Guy, wistfully.

'I know,' said Elizabeth.

They walked across the churchyard together, hand in hand, and as they did so a figure appeared out of the shadows of the pathway.

'Thomas!'

'Father!'

Mother and son ran to him, clamouring to be in his arms, and for a moment Thomas held them both. Elizabeth's face was wet with tears and she clung to him desperately. At last he drew away. 'You should not have come,' he said to Elizabeth.

'I had to.'

Thomas saw immediately the desperation on her face and sensed that some crisis had befallen her. He turned his attention to Guy. 'How are you, Guy? It seems to me you have grown some more. Are you looking after your mother well?'

'Yes, sir,' said Guy.

'And young Nemus, your pony, how goes she?'

'Well, sir, very well.'

'Good, good,' said Thomas. 'Now, I must talk to your mother alone, just for a few moments. Go and attend to the trap – I saw it at the top of the lane.'

'I wish to talk to you, too, sir.'

'Another time, Guy. Please do as you are told.'

Reluctantly Guy shuffled off, and caught up as she was with her own worries, Elizabeth felt a pang of sorrow for him. He loved his father so much and saw him so infrequently. Now, within seconds of seeing him for the first time in two months, he was dismissed from his company. 'You were too abrupt with the boy,' Elizabeth said.

'I had to be,' said Thomas. 'I can only be a few minutes but I assume that you have something important to tell me or you would not have come here.'

'Are you very angry?' Elizabeth asked.

'I am angry,' said Thomas. 'Your presence here is already the talk of the village. It will not be long before my wife hears of it, if she has not done so already.'

'I'm sorry,' Elizabeth cried. 'But I had to see you.' She began to sob in earnest and for a moment Thomas's harsh expression softened.

'Do not cry, my love. Tell me what ails you?'

'I received a visit from Harry Naylor,' said Elizabeth.

Thomas blanched. 'When was this?'

'Three weeks since. He threatened me, Thomas, threatened us both.'

'In what way?' said Thomas. 'Tell me exactly what he said.'

'He said that unless you and I ceased to meet, he would ruin us both.'

'How?' said Thomas.

'In my case,' said Elizabeth, bitterly, 'it is simple. As you may know, his family own many of the coaches which travel this way. He said he had the power to make sure that coaches no longer frequented The Lady in Waiting. It would mean, of course, that the inn would go back to what it was in my father's day and we could no longer live on that.'

'And how does he propose to ruin me?' Thomas asked.

'He was speaking on behalf of his father,' said Elizabeth. 'I understand that your wife receives an annual income from her father. It is her father's intention to stop further payments unless you agree never to see me again.' Elizabeth began to cry again. 'And Thomas, Thomas, I am with child.'

'With child?'

Elizabeth nodded. 'The baby will be born before the summer is out, at harvest time.'

'Come,' said Thomas. 'We must talk.' He slipped an arm round Elizabeth's shoulder and drew her back to the porch, where they sat on the low wall which surrounded the church doorway. 'I should have come to see you before this. I am sorry I have been so absent from your life. There is much to do at Chadbrook at the moment.'

'It is of no consequence, we are together now. What shall we do, Thomas? What shall we do?' Elizabeth's voice shook as she spoke. She had never felt so nervous, so unsure of herself in her life, and the pregnancy had sapped her of energy, of her usual fighting spirit.

189

She just wanted somebody else to take control for once. She was tired of fighting for everything.

'I think it is best,' said Thomas, carefully, 'that we do not meet for the time being, for a while at least.'

She had half expected it, but as he spoke the words, she uttered a cry – an animal cry of pain – and began to sob again. 'No, I cannot be without you, I cannot.' She was hysterical.

'You must be strong,' said Thomas. 'You have been on so many occasions before, and our parting will not be for ever.'

'But for how long?' Elizabeth wailed.

Thomas shrugged his shoulders. 'A few years, not many I shouldn't think.'

'A few years!' Elizabeth said. 'So I am to bear your second child alone and bring it up, fatherless, as I did Guy?'

'We have no choice, Elizabeth,' Thomas thundered.

'We have a choice,' said Elizabeth. 'We can refuse Harry Naylor's demands and tell him that we love each other, that he can do as he wishes, that it will make no difference.'

'I cannot do that,' said Thomas. 'A man in my position.'

'You can do whatever you like, in your position,' said Elizabeth, scornfully. 'The one thing your position gives you is power.'

'Not on this occasion,' said Thomas. 'Chadbrook cannot survive without Beatrice's money. That is a fact, Elizabeth.'

'So once again, you choose between me and Chadbrook and once again your estate comes first – before me, before me and your children. How is it that we mean so little to you, Thomas?' She stood up.

'Elizabeth, try to understand,' said Thomas. 'Chadbrook is only on loan to me, as it is to all the other members of my family – those past and those in the future. It is the duty of each one of us to do our best to maintain the house and estate in order to pass it on – I cannot simply throw it away. It would not be right for me or for Christopher.'

'Christopher!' Elizabeth spat out. 'And what about Guy? You profess not to love Christopher, you said he was like his mother, that you would never make a man of him. You have a fine, strong young son in Guy – what of him, why can you not consider his future?'

'Christopher is my heir,' said Thomas, quietly. 'I must put him first.'

The words seemed to create a tight band round Elizabeth's chest and suddenly she found breathing difficult. For a moment she thought

190

she was going to faint and Thomas, too, must have thought so, for he put out his hands to steady her. She fought free of his grip. 'Leave me be,' she said. 'Do not touch me.'

'Elizabeth, you are overwrought and not thinking sensibly. In a day or so, when you have had time to consider my decision, you will see that it is the right one. You, Guy and the new baby need a home and an income. The Lady in Waiting will provide that. I have my duty to Chadbrook which I cannot shirk – the only way ahead is for us to part.'

'You don't love me any more, do you?' said Elizabeth. 'Is there a new love in your life?'

'There is no new love in my life,' said Thomas. 'The circumstances require that I put duty before love. There is nothing you can say, Elizabeth, to change my mind because I know the course of action I am proposing is the right one.'

'So, are we never to meet again?' Elizabeth said.

'I am sure we shall,' said Thomas. 'I know where you are and it will be my duty to make sure that I receive reports on your well-being and that of our children.'

'How shall I manage without you?' Elizabeth said, half to herself.

'You will manage very well,' said Thomas. 'Remember how it was when Guy was born?'

'That was different,' Elizabeth said. 'Then I was secure in your love. I only sent you away because I was angry. Now I know you have tired of me, you have broken my spirit.'

'Come,' said Thomas. 'It is time I was gone. I will walk with you to the trap, for a last word with Guy.'

'What shall I tell Guy?' Elizabeth suddenly burst out in panic. 'He worships you, he needs you, just as much as I.'

'Guy will have to learn to be strong, to grow to be a man without my help. You have a son to be proud of, Elizabeth – he will not let you down.'

Guy was waiting at the trap. He looked anxiously from one parent to the other. 'What ails you, Mother?'

'Your father will tell you,' said Elizabeth, and accepting Thomas's arm in support, she climbed up into the trap.

'Come here to me, boy.' Thomas called his son out of earshot of Elizabeth. He hesitated. 'I shall not be coming to see you and your mother for some long time, if ever. Do you understand me?'

Colour suffused Guy's face and then drained away. 'I understand you, sir,' he managed in a croaked little voice.

191

'The reasons are difficult to explain, as you are only a child, but I am relying on you to be strong, for yourself and for your mother, and I charge you with the duty of looking after her and your brother or sister, when the child is born.'

Guy frowned. 'My . . . my mother is with child?'

'Y-yes,' said Thomas, momentarily shocked. It had not occurred to him that Guy did not know of the child. 'Now can I rely on you?'

The boy met his eye bravely and for a moment Thomas felt a terrible, all-encompassing sense of love for the child – terrible because at that moment he was severing the relationship for ever – for despite what he had said to Elizabeth, he knew that the parting must be final and irrevocable. 'You can rely on me, sir, to do my duty,' said Guy, stiffly, but as he spoke his lip trembled and his eyes clouded with tears. He flung his arms round his father's waist. 'Don't leave us, Father, I love you,' he burst out.

Thomas felt the tears in his own eyes. For a moment he relented and caught the boy to him, holding him tight. Over the top of his son's head he could see Elizabeth sitting in the trap. She was not looking at them but staring blankly ahead. Her expression worried him but there was nothing he could do for her now. At last he prised the trembling little boy from him. 'Guy,' he said. 'Remember that I love you and that I always will. Maybe some day . . .' The words died on his lips. There was no point in making the boy promises – promises he would be unable to keep. 'Be strong, for me,' he begged.

Guy made a desperate effort to control his tears, rubbing at his face with the back of his hand. 'Now, can you drive the trap?' Thomas asked.

'Yes, sir,' said Guy.

'Then take your mother home, carefully now.'

The boy nodded and, turning without a backward glance, climbed into the trap beside his mother. He flicked the reins of the pony and as the trap moved off, he turned suddenly and raised an arm in a farewell salute to his father.

The gesture, so brave and proud, brought fresh tears flooding down Thomas's cheeks, tears he had not shed since he, too, was a child. He stood his ground until the pony and trap were out of sight, round the bend in the lane. At no time did Elizabeth turn around, nor did Guy. Thomas simply stood powerless, watching the stout little pony bear away the only woman he had ever loved, and the finest son a man could wish for.

CHAPTER TWENTY-TWO
Long Melford – March, 1982

Prue's lunch with Charles Chadbrook had been good for her. It was clear he had enjoyed her company and had taken seriously her research into their mutual families' background, and her reasons for needing to know more about Elizabeth. He had also indicated that he hoped they would be friends in the future. His interest could not have come at a better time, for her ego was at an all-time low and Charles had done much to raise her flagging spirits. Like everyone, Prue had experienced periods in her life when she had lacked confidence but now at twenty-four, having successfully launched what everyone agreed was an excellent hotel, she knew she should be feeling relatively buoyant about life. In fact nothing could be further from the truth and as she lay in a deep, hot bath on the evening following her lunch with Charles Chadbrook, she tried to analyse why this was so.

Martha had been right – her research into the past had done much to relieve her fear. She certainly did not enjoy the alien emotions which assailed her but she had become quite cunning at coping with them. Now was a case in point. Lying in the bath with the radio playing in the background, she forced her mind to relax and allowed her thoughts to drift from topic to topic. The feelings were there in the background but she was managing to keep them at bay. Even when they did overwhelm her, they were at least now familiar and her concern was almost entirely directed at the poor soul whose spirit did not seem to be at peace, rather than for herself. No, The Lady in Waiting was not responsible for her lack of confidence – it was Jonathan. Prue leaned forward and turned on the hot tap. It had been a long time since she had relaxed like this and she vowed that in the future she would ensure she had more days off and, more important, make sure she had a little personal space for herself. She still loved Jonathan, there was no doubt about that. Since he had discovered he was Edward Deckman's son there was a new vulnerability about him which actually enhanced his appeal for her. He was less brash, less sure of himself and he seemed to need her more.

She turned off the tap and lay back, watching the steam curling up towards the ceiling. That was the up side of their relationship, but there was also a down side. Because he had no friends in Suffolk, Jonathan's reliance upon her was almost suffocating. He had a tendency to hang around her, like a child waiting to be entertained, and he seemed completely to have lost interest in the day-to-day running of the inn – in fact he was no help at all. Even the major decisions no longer seemed to concern him. He continued to stress what an excellent job she was doing, but he did not seem to want to be involved, which in turn made her feel increasingly isolated. Often, Prue wondered how on earth he could bear to spend his days as he did – rising late, chatting to customers at the bar before lunch and again in the evening, and spending the rest of the day walking in the town or reading the newspapers. It was a fine life for a man in his seventies but not in his thirties, and Prue could not help feeling that he was simply marking time, because he did not know what to do next.

On several occasions, Prue had tried to discuss Jo's proposal with Jonathan but on each occasion he had shied away from any detailed discussion. She could understand his difficulties. As well as the practical problem of what to do next, he was also faced with a moral dilemma. If he were to go along with Jo's scheme and pretend he was unaware of his true parentage, one day he would receive an inheritance which was not by rights his. Coming from a totally different culture from her own, it was difficult for Prue to assess how much this would affect Jonathan. However, she sensed that while he was self-indulgent, he was nonetheless a basically honest man who would find it difficult to enjoy somebody else's money. On bad days she felt that Jonathan was testing her in some way, making comparisons in his mind between his life in New York and life with her in Suffolk. The day-to-day life of the inn was repetitive – it had to be in order to ensure a smooth-running operation. She felt certain the monotony bored Jonathan and feared that she, too, probably fell into the same category. The whole situation of indecision was debilitating for them both, and lying in the bath, she suddenly realized that as with every other aspect of their life together, it would be up to her, ultimately, to make the decision, not only about her own future but about Jonathan's.

Prue chose her evening carefully. Two days later, Jonathan spent most of the day in Clare at an antiques sale, buying odd pieces of furniture for the new bedrooms in the stable block. This was the sort of thing he very much enjoyed, pitting his wits against the auctioneer. He returned in high spirits in the early evening, confident that he had picked up several bargains. 'Let's go out to dinner,' Prue suggested, as they were changing before the evening session.

'Can we?' said Jonathan, surprised. 'Is it really possible for you to take the evening off?'

'I've already arranged it,' said Prue. 'I've even booked a table at The Bear in Lavenham. They've just opened a restaurant and I'd like to try it.'

She waited until their meal and wine were served. It was not difficult, Jonathan was full of his day's activities – the people he had met, the fools who had bought over-priced goods and his own skilful buying. 'You've enjoyed today, haven't you?' Prue said, at last.

'Yes, I have. Why shouldn't I?' He was instantly defensive.

'No reason, but have you considered why you've enjoyed it?' Prue asked.

Jonathan shrugged. 'I guess I felt I was doing something useful for a change.'

'Precisely,' said Prue.

'What are you saying, that I'm not helping you enough around the inn?'

'Not exactly,' said Prue. 'I appreciate that now we have the place up and running, you've more or less lost interest in it.' He started to protest but she silenced him. 'Oh come on, Jonathan, be honest, it's true, and not at all surprising. After all, it's the reason we went into partnership. Running a place like The Lady in Waiting is what I've been trained to do. You're a banker – seeing to the financing and the launching of the project is what you've been trained to do, but the job's over now so far as you're concerned.'

'So what are you saying?' said Jonathan, carefully.

'I'm saying that if we could plan the future we could decide what you should do next. Maybe we could open another inn somewhere else; maybe we could sell The Lady in Waiting and move on; maybe, just maybe, we could go mad and raise a big lump of capital and open a chain. I don't know . . . you're the boss. But we can't do any of these things without some kind of future and at the moment, Jonathan, we have none, do we?'

'I guess not,' said Jonathan.

'Look,' said Prue, 'I know you don't like talking about Jo and Edward Deckman and all your troubles but we have to do it sometime.' She leant across and took his hand. She expected him to pull away but he did not and it encouraged her to continue. 'You have a clear choice – either you have to call Jo's bluff, which means a degree of co-operation between yourself, your mother and Edward Deckman, or else you're going to have to bring the whole thing out in the open and get it over and done with. What you can't do is to go on living in this sort of half life.'

'What do you mean, calling Jo's bluff?' Jonathan asked.

'I don't know exactly,' said Prue. 'But presumably if your mother and Edward Deckman are prepared to swear blind that you are John Lindstrom's son, the whole situation could be dismissed as nothing more than a malicious rumour.'

'You've forgotten the letter,' said Jonathan. 'Sylvia Deckman still has the original, remember. She is very ill with cancer, and who knows, she may be high on drugs and very bitter about life, in which case she could do anything.'

'Couldn't your mother say the letter was a forgery?' Prue suggested.

'I doubt it. The letter was written in my mother's hand, I have no doubt about that. I've thought it through again and again, Prue, and there is no easy solution. All I know is that I don't see how I can allow the bank to be destroyed and my mother with it. My great-grandfather built the business from nothing and so many people have put a lot of hard work into it along the way. Then there are the shareholders to consider – they could really lose out.'

'Your great-grandfather,' said Prue, gently. 'You still see yourself as a Lindstrom, don't you?'

Jonathan blanched. 'OK, so maybe he wasn't my grandfather but even though I'm not a Lindstrom, I was raised as one.'

'I know,' said Prue. 'I do understand how you feel.'

'You don't, no one can,' said Jonathan, 'not unless it happened to them.'

'All right, maybe not,' said Prue, anxious to take the heat out of the moment. 'You know in my view, there is only one thing you can do and you must do it right away.'

'What's that?' Jonathan asked.

'Go and see your father and talk the whole thing through with him.'

'My father. . .' Jonathan began. 'There's no point in speaking to that guy, we have nothing in common, we actively dislike each other.'

'But then you've never confronted one another before as father and son, have you?' said Prue.

'He must always have known I'm his son.'

'Yes, but he's had to go to enormous lengths to pretend otherwise. Maybe that's what has made him so aggressive towards you. Either way, he's been with the bank a long time and he's obviously very close to your mother. It would seem to me that the only sensible thing to do is to ask his view. After all, it's time he had a few sleepless nights because you could say this whole mess is his damn fault.'

Jonathan smiled and squeezed her hand. 'I guess you're right.'

Edward Deckman suggested the venue, taking the initiative from Jonathan when he least expected it. He had telephoned Lindstrom's London office with the intention of speaking to Edward's secretary to make an appointment. Instead, maybe because he mentioned who he was, he was put through to Edward direct. Such was his surprise, that to his fury he found himself sounding nervous and ill at ease. 'I need to discuss an urgent bank matter with you,' he had said faltering. 'I can come into London any day this week. When would you be free?'

'Tomorrow,' Edward had replied, without hesitation. 'You won't want to come here – unhappy memories, I should imagine. How about the Wig and Pen Club in the Strand, say twelve o'clock? It's quiet that early.'

So here he was, at five to twelve, waiting for Edward in the bar. Despite his apprehension, he was attracted to the atmosphere of the club which he had never visited before. The place where lawyer and scribe meet was at the end of Fleet Street, and clearly the building was several hundred years old, the atmosphere steeped in tradition. He felt an outsider, a foreigner, but then, of course, he was.

'Ah Jonathan! I'm sorry, I hope I didn't keep you waiting. Am I late?' Edward, small and dapper as ever. His suit was expensive but dark and conventional, the shirt white, the tie restrained. He looked more English than American, Jonathan thought. This man, his father – it seemed impossible. 'What can I get you to drink?'

Jonathan looked at his empty glass. 'This was a gin and tonic, I guess I'll have another.'

'I won't be a moment and I'll bring some menus.'

Over the drinks in the bar they chatted amiably enough about The Lady in Waiting. "It sounds an interesting project,' said Edward, seeming genuine enough. 'Have you considered expanding?'

'Prue – she's my partner – and I were talking about it the other day,' Jonathan said. 'I think Prue would be quite keen to open another one. It's finding the right property though, and at the right price. The Lady in Waiting is quite unique.'

'A fascinating name,' said Edward. 'Do you know anything about the history of the place?'

'Prue's the one who knows all about that,' said Jonathan. 'I believe a woman ran it single-handed in the 1700s and the inn took its name from her. She had an influential lover for whom she was always hanging around waiting, hence the name.'

'Poor soul,' said Edward. He seemed more relaxed and easier to talk to than usual, Jonathan was finding, which was crazy since he had expected to feel even more anger and animosity towards him. They ordered. 'Shall we go upstairs to the table?' Edward said. 'If you want to talk about bank business it would be a good idea to do so before the place starts filling up, don't you think?'

As promised, they were shown to a little room three floors up, where they were entirely alone. Sitting by the window, it felt as if they were going to fall out onto the street below. 'This is a typical Tudor building,' Edward said. 'It has a tendency to lean, I hope you don't mind heights.'

'No,' said Jonathan.

The wine was delivered. Edward poured a glass for them both. 'Do we have a toast?' he asked Jonathan.

'To fathers and sons!' Jonathan suggested quietly.

Edward froze. 'What do you mean by that?' he asked.

'I know you're my father, my natural father,' Jonathan said, surprised at how calm he sounded.

Edward hesitated. 'What makes you think I am?'

'My wife, Jo, told me,' Jonathan said. 'She learnt of it from your wife, who in turn learnt it from a letter my mother wrote at the time of my birth. You rather carelessly left it lying around.'

All colour drained from Edward's face. 'Jesus!' he said. 'I'm real sorry, Jonathan, that must have been one hell of a way to find out.'

Whatever reaction Jonathan had been expecting it was not this. Edward's instant concern for his feelings in turn compelled him to reassure. 'It's OK,' he said. 'You can imagine it came as quite a shock initially but I'm kind of getting used to the idea now. I've known about it for a couple of months, you see.'

Edward reached for his glass and drank deeply. 'I'm sorry,' he said. 'I guess I just have to collect my thoughts for a moment here. Does your mother know that you have found out?' Jonathan shook his head. 'How do you feel?' Edward asked. 'Don't pull any punches, tell me the truth.'

'At first I couldn't believe it,' said Jonathan. 'We've never exactly got along, you and I, have we? I've been brought up to believe I was a Lindstrom. I feel like a Lindstrom. I guess it's kind of disorientating – it seems to change everything yet I suppose I'm the same person inside?' It was almost a question.

'Of course you are,' said Edward. 'I just don't know what to say, to reassure you. Shall I try to explain what happened?'

'I think before you do that I should perhaps tell you why I know,' said Jonathan. 'Jo didn't tell me about my true identity just for the hell of it, she has a reason which I guess you could call blackmail.' Quickly and as efficiently as he could, he ran through the details of the various options Jo had outlined to him. The telling of it was an enormous relief and there was a long silence when he had finished.

'I suppose I've really been expecting it all these years,' said Edward. 'It was just a matter of time.'

'No one need have known,' Jonathan said, suddenly angry, 'if you'd just thrown that goddamn letter away. Why the hell did you keep it?'

'I love your mother, you were the only child I've ever had, it was a precious letter. Obviously now I wish I hadn't kept it.'

'And I wish to hell I'd never known the truth,' Jonathan said, bitterly.

Edward looked up at him quickly. There was hurt in his voice. 'I can understand that.'

Their meal arrived. They had both ordered steak and kidney pie and they were each delivered a monstrous helping. The sight of so much food made Jonathan feel slightly sick.

'Are you hungry?' Edward asked. Jonathan shook his head. 'I'm sorry,' he said to the waiter, 'can you take this lot away and bring us some coffee.'

'Is anything wrong, sir?'

'No. We just need some good coffee and plenty of it.' He waited until the waiter had withdrawn. 'This Prue you mention, she's more than a partner I presume – do you love her?' Jonathan nodded. 'And she reciprocates your feelings?'

'I guess so.'

'Tell me, Jonathan, can you see yourself making a life here in England, running this inn and maybe a few more?'

It was a question Jonathan had asked himself many times. 'I'm not sure.'

'That sounds kind of negative to me,' said Edward. 'I have to say that I can't see it. You're a New Yorker, born and bred, and you've been trained as a banker. Standing behind the bar in a country pub doesn't really seem to me to be your style.'

'Trained as a banker maybe, but not much of one, according to you,' Jonathan said, unable to resist the jibe.

'I'll come to that,' said Edward. 'Jo still loves you, you know.'

Jonathan gave a hollow laugh. 'You have to be joking! What makes you suggest such a crazy idea, anyway?'

'Because Jo confides in Sylvia and Sylvia confides in me. She's a tough lady, your wife, and she's not about to show you how much you've hurt her over the years, but she'd be back in your life in a second if she thought you really wanted her.'

'I reckon that's pure fantasy,' said Jonathan.

'No,' said Edward, 'it's not. It is a factor that perhaps you might like to consider, since I imagine it's something she's gone to great pains to ensure you know nothing of.'

'We're losing the thread here,' Jonathan said. 'I didn't come to talk about my relationship with Jo. It seems to me that everyone's in a mess, everyone's got something to lose or gain, and ultimately it's me who has to make the decision as to what to do next.'

'Certainly that's true,' said Edward. 'Have you made a decision?'

'No.'

'Good,' said Edward. 'I don't expect you to take advice from me kindly, but you wouldn't be here if you weren't at least curious about my views. I am sure you should take whatever steps are necessary to suppress the truth about your birth. Not only would your mother go to prison but the bank would be finished, at any rate for the time being, which would mean both the employees and the shareholders would suffer. Billy Lindstrom is far too old to take over the bank even if he had the ability, which he hasn't, and his two girls are safely and comfortably married to farmers like their father. Inheriting Lindstrom's Bank would ruin their lives. As for you, you've been brought up to think of yourself as Jonathan Lindstrom and I don't think you would be doing yourself any good by changing your identity.'

For some reason he couldn't quite understand, Jonathan was hurt by Edward's words. He hadn't expected any show of emotion from the man but he did not like the easy way in which he suggested that

Jonathan should ignore his true parentage, 'And what about you, haven't you got an axe to grind?' he asked, aggressively. 'Presumably, you've acted fraudulently as well as my mother – it wouldn't be in your interests for the truth to come out.'

'I suppose that's right,' said Edward. 'But my future is of no concern to me. My duty is to care for Sylvia during these last few months of her life, and then do whatever I can to help you and your mother.'

'Duty! That's something which hasn't figured much in your life so far,' said Jonathan. 'At least not to the man who employed you, the man I called father.'

'I can't expect your understanding,' Edward said, quietly.

'Tell me, why was it necessary to be so unpleasant to me all those years, bearing in mind that I am your son?' Jonathan continued the pressure, goaded by Edward's reluctance to rise to any bait he offered.

'It began when you were little,' Edward said, after a pause. 'Your mother and I could never see eye to eye as to how you should be brought up. We both agreed that you must never know that I was your father but the fact that you were fatherless, I felt, put you at an enormous disadvantage and this was made worse by your mother's obsession with her work.'

'Go on,' said Jonathan.

'From the moment your father died and your mother inherited the bank, she became obsessional about it. I suppose because she knew she had inherited on a false premise, she felt it necessary to work even harder, to prove herself even more than if the bank had been hers by right. She could not fail you see, Jonathan. Her only justification for doing what she did was to ensure the bank was an enormous success, a far greater success than it could ever have been under anyone else's direction. She put everything into it, worked round the clock and considering she'd had absolutely no commercial experience whatsoever, her success has been phenomenal – but at a price.'

'What price?' Jonathan asked.

'Your childhood. She'd work late say three or four nights in a row, coming home after your bedtime. So what would she do – she'd send a secretary out at lunchtime to buy you a toy. I'd say, "Forget the toy, go home and spend an hour with him, half an hour even, that will do him more good." "There's no need," she'd say, "his nurse is looking after him." "Give the nurse the afternoon off," I'd say, but she wouldn't, she couldn't. She was driven by guilt, by the need to succeed. Don't think I'm criticizing her, Jonathan, I think the world

201

of your mother. She couldn't help herself you see, but it made things very difficult.'

'For whom?' Jonathan said, sarcastically. 'Not you, surely?'

'In a way, yes. As you came out of babyhood, I started to see more of you. I'd meet you and the nurse in the park most evenings and spend an hour with you on the way home.' Jonathan stared at him incredulously, it was so hard to imagine. 'I became more and more involved with you. The more I saw of you, the more I realized that you were entirely in the care of the nurse and your mother was nothing but a figurehead. I started to interfere, your mother and I argued about it and in the end she said it was better I stopped seeing you. She was right – I knew, I either had to acknowledge you as my son, which I couldn't do, or keep well away. You'd be about two and a half by then. I'll never forget the last afternoon we spent together. It was winter, just after Christmas. We went for a walk in Central Park, made a snowman, drank hot chocolate, you had a good time . . .' His voice broke as he spoke the words and Jonathan looked away embarrassed. 'I didn't see you again for nearly a year. Then one evening, I had to go to your mother's house to collect some papers and you wouldn't talk to me, you turned away. You remembered me OK, but I guess I'd let you down by just walking out of your life. You've disliked me ever since and I can't say I blame you.'

There was a lengthy silence between the two men. 'And then to add insult to injury I became a lousy banker, right?' said Jonathan.

'I don't know how to make you understand what I did and why I did it,' said Edward. He ran a hand through his hair. 'By the time you were a teenager, you were a spoilt brat, through no fault of your own. Every time you wanted anything your mother gave it to you, just to keep you quiet so she could get on with her work. You have a good brain, your grades at school proved that, but no sense of purpose. How could you have? Everything you ever wanted was handed to you on a plate. You never had to struggle for anything. No, you're not a particularly lousy banker, Jonathan, you just had no chance of being very good at anything.'

'That's terrific,' said Jonathan.

'Listen to me, please,' said Edward. 'It was I who begged your mother to let you come to London. I thought, perhaps, that getting you away from her I could try to do something to help. It was a mistake, of course. You resented me enormously and I acted heavy-handedly – the whole situation was doomed from the beginning. I was at my wits' end that morning Mail Sale crashed, and then suddenly it occurred to me that perhaps the one thing I could do for you was to set you free from Lindstrom's. OK, it was a cock-eyed idea but I was fresh out of bright ideas at the time.'

'So you sacked me,' said Jonathan.

'I sacked you.'

'And Mother backed you.'

'She had to. She wasn't best pleased, as you can imagine, but she had no alternative.'

'She could have sacked you and kept me.'

'Yes,' said Edward. 'But she needs me. She's a very talented woman but she needs someone with both feet on the ground, to stop her from going too far, that and the fact that deep down she knew I was right – you needed some space.'

'And now?' said Jonathan, with ill-disguised irony in his voice. 'What do you think I need now?'

'I think it's time you went home,' said Edward, quietly.

'Home, where's home? I don't even know who the hell I am, let alone where home is.'

'You can be whoever you want,' said Edward. 'If you decide to acknowledge I'm your father, I will give you every support and backing in what is going to be a very difficult road ahead. If you decide to stay Jonathan Lindstrom, I'll do likewise.'

'You mean you'd back me against my mother if I decided to shop her?' Jonathan said.

'It's about time someone came out on your side, Jonathan.'

The fight went out of Jonathan, the anger, too – just sadness remained. 'I'll have to think about it,' he said.

'Of course you will. My advice would be to go to New York and talk the whole thing through with both your mother and with Jo. I may be wrong to advise you to perpetrate a fraud, but however I examine my conscience I cannot see what anyone can possibly gain from the disclosure of your true parentage. There would be an awful lot of losers, however.'

'I don't know how you've got the gall to suggest I could run Lindstrom's after all you've said about me in the past.'

'You've changed,' said Edward. 'I do believe you can do it if you set your mind to it – after all, one way or another banking's in your blood.'

'But who will inherit after me? I suppose maybe that's one way I could put things right – leave the bank shares to Billy Lindstrom's kids, or grandchildren by then, I guess.'

'What about your own children?' said Edward.

'If I marry Prue and stay in England then I'll have kids, she's that sort of woman, but then I won't have the bank. If I go to New York and patch things up with Jo, then I'll have the bank and no kids – she's never wanted them.'

'She might change,' said Edward. 'A lot of women do as they get older. Maybe you can fix things so that you can take Prue to New York.'

'No,' said Jonathan. 'She wouldn't fit in, she'd hate it.'

'Then that's another decision you alone can make. You're a young man yet, there's plenty of time for children.'

'I guess you're right,' said Jonathan.'You know I never expected it, but it's helped talking things through with you.'

'And do you know something?' said Edward. 'What you've just said is the best thing that's happened to me since that snowy day in Central Park.'

CHAPTER TWENTY-THREE
Long Melford – August 1789

In the weeks that followed her parting from Thomas, Elizabeth became increasingly desperate. She could not believe that he had truly abandoned her and their children and found it impossible to contemplate a life without him. Guy, with the resilience of extreme youth, seemed less desolated than she had expected. He was sadder and quieter than he had been formerly but clearly he was able to pick up the pieces of his life and carry on much as before. Trade was excellent and since there were no further visits from Harry Naylor, Elizabeth assumed that he intended to keep his part of the bargain. All the success in the world, though, could not compensate her for the loss of Thomas – the hurt seemed to be eating into her very soul, destroying her by degrees.

By contrast, the baby inside her was growing apace – a harvest baby was predicted, yet there was no love within Elizabeth for her unborn child, indeed she blamed it entirely for Thomas's departure. Had she not been pregnant, she reasoned, he would not have abandoned them. It was the prospect of another child, yet more responsibility and the inevitable speculation and interest that the birth would arouse, which had driven him away. She grew to hate the child in her womb, willing it to be born early and dead. She saw it as a cancer growing inside her rather than a new life, full of hope and joy. She had imagined that Guy would be raised a gentleman. While she knew her rough ways and lack of breeding could never be extinguished, she had hoped that Thomas's influence on Guy, at so tender an age, would equip her son for a very different sort of life from her own. Now it seemed there was no hope for his future and in recognition of this, she had dispensed with the services of the governess Thomas had employed for Guy. He had no further need of learning now. The son of a prosperous innkeeper was not such a bad start in life, she recognized in moments of clarity, but she had wanted more for him, much more. If Christopher died, and by all reports he was a sickly boy, would it not be possible for Thomas to make Guy his heir? She had planned and plotted so much over the years, that it was now difficult for her to distinguish possible goals from impossible dreams. Now she knew the fairy tales were over and she could not bear the reality which was left behind.

As August approached an idea came to Elizabeth and conveniently she pushed Harry Naylor's threats to the back of her mind. It seemed to her that by now Thomas would be bound to be missing her and regretting his decision. The time had come to woo him back. The moment the idea was formed, it changed her from the dull, lethargic person she had become – she was at once more vivacious, excited, her eyes over-bright, her cheeks pink. She had an old gown altered to fit becomingly over her lost waistline and she set about plotting and scheming ways in which she could meet Thomas, as if by chance. As it happened an opportunity fell into her lap. A horse fair on the green was due to take place during the second weekend in August and Elizabeth was sure Thomas would be there. His growing interest in racing was well known – he would never miss an opportunity to look at new stock.

On the morning of the fair, Elizabeth took great pains with her appearance and was well satisfied with the altered gown, although the baby was still clearly visible. She dressed a protesting Guy in new breeches and a well-cut, double-breasted jacket. If anything he had grown even more like his father. He looked every inch a young gentleman. Elizabeth was very proud of him and confident that Thomas would not be able to resist the pair of them.

'Why are we going to meet Father, Mother?' Guy asked. 'He said we could not see him for a long time. Should we not follow his wishes?'

Elizabeth shook her head vehemently. 'Your father will be ready to see us by now – I am sure he, too, has been waiting for this opportunity.'

Guy looked at her doubtfully, but said no more. He was as anxious as his mother for a sight of Thomas. He had missed his father sorely in the intervening months, not least because his mother had been such poor company.

The day was brilliant, not a cloud in the sky but the air fresh and invigorating with the hint of autumn, which all contributed to Elizabeth's feeling of happy exhilaration. There was a large crowd at the fair, with many fine horses for sale. Guy and Elizabeth joined the throng but Elizabeth had eyes for nothing or no one but Thomas. It was Guy who spotted him first. He was examining the legs of a young chestnut mare. A group of men stood watching as Thomas ran an expert hand over the horse's flanks, totally absorbed in what he was doing. For a moment Elizabeth did not move but stood watching him, her heart pounding at the joy of seeing him again. She clutched at Guy's hand, more for support than to give him comfort, and strode forward. 'Good day, sir,' she said. 'That is a fine horse.'

Thomas looked up, startled, and for a moment said nothing. He simply stared at her, his expression unreadable. The men around him did not move. 'Good day, madam,' said Thomas, steadily. He nodded briefly to Guy and then, without a word, turned and resumed his examination of the horse.

Elizabeth could not believe he had so deliberately snubbed her. She had lived this scene many times in her imagination – Thomas leading her away to some secluded spot to tell her that he loved her, that he could not live without her, and that they would face even financial ruin to be together with their children. She looked now at his deliberately turned back, and the temper, which was never far below the surface, rose, almost choking her. 'How dare you turn away from me, Thomas Chadbrook? Am I not a lady enough for you that you should treat me so?' There was a stunned silence among the group of men. Thomas continued to keep his back to her but he had stopped examining the horse. 'Why will you not answer me?' she spat at him. 'I am good enough to lie with you and bear your children yet there you stand, your back towards me, refusing to acknowledge either myself or our son. Look at him, Thomas, look at him. Is he not made in your image?'

A crowd was gathering. Guy shifted uneasily beside his mother. 'Mother, please,' he said, faintly. Elizabeth did not even hear him.

Slowly, Thomas turned and the expression on his face for a moment silenced Elizabeth – it was dark with fury. 'I would be grateful, madam, if you would hold your vile tongue – this is not the tap room of your inn. I am engaged in other business and I would be obliged if you would take your son and leave me be.'

'Leave you be, leave you be! Look at me – you should have thought of that before you came to my bed and gave me your bastard, not one but two. You may think you can turn your back on us, Thomas Chadbrook, but you cannot. Your duty lies here –' She placed a hand on her womb – the baby churned around inside her, no doubt troubled by her agitation.

Thomas's voice was icy with contempt. 'I insist you leave, madam. My groom will escort you home. This is no place for you . . . clearly.'

'How dare you order me from the fair, just because it does not suit you to have me here. I have as much right to be here as you . . . more, this is my village, not yours. Take your hands off me.' The groom had detached himself from the crowd and went to take her arm. She struck him away and he hesitated, looking to Thomas for further instruction.

'I have every right to ask you to leave, madam. You have no control over yourself – I can only assume you have been drinking.'

All around her a sea of hostile faces seemed to be pressing in. It was better sport than any horse fair to watch the Earl deal with one of his discarded mistresses. 'Whore,' hissed somebody from the crowd. The cry was taken up, 'Whore, whore.'

'Mother,' pleaded Guy.

Tears began streaming down her face. She looked from the cruel, jeering faces of the crowd to the harsh features of the man she had once believed to be her own. Blinded by her tears and hampered by her bulk, she allowed her son to lead her gently away.

The afternoon's events had a profound effect on Guy. Although he had known that his mother and father were not married, he had never really considered it to be a dishonourable state. However the venom and disrespect the crowd had showered on his mother made him realize for the first time that his position was far from enviable. He helped his mother home and upon arrival she took to her bed. There was noting more he could do for her – every time he tried to speak to her she turned away, her body racked with sobs.

He found his own position rather strange – while he felt sorry for his mother, he understood perfectly his father's anger and embarrassment at the scene she had created. If she had wished to talk to him further she should have gone to his house and seen him in private, Guy thought. He often wondered about his father's house. He knew it to be very grand. His mother often spoke of it, although on questioning her, it was clear she had not seen it either. Chadbrook . . . he let the word run through his mind, it had a good ring to it.

The inn was busy that night with trade from the horse fair. With Elizabeth still in her bed, the serving girls were finding it difficult to keep up with custom and Guy was pressed into service to fetch and carry and refill endless mugs of ale. By the time the last customer had left, he was too exhausted to consider further the problems of his parents and it took all his strength to climb the ladder to his bed, where he fell into a dreamless, exhausted sleep.

When he woke in the morning, however, his first thought was of his mother and how she fared. He climbed out of bed and tiptoed into her room so as not to wake her. The bed was empty – that was a good sign, she must be up and about her work. Clearly, she was getting over the troubles of yesterday. He felt cheerful as he climbed downstairs and went out into the stableyard. One of the grooms was saddling a horse, they exchanged a greeting and Guy put his head under the pump and dashed cold water over his face. He remembered promising his father that he would look after his mother and this he must surely do, for clearly Thomas would not be coming back to them. He thought of the new baby and the idea of there being another child gave him pleasure. He would be the man of the house, he would work hard to see that his mother and the child wanted for nothing, he would become someone of whom his father would be proud – that was Guy's dearest wish.

Back in the inn he could find no sign of his mother. He searched the rooms calling for her. In the kitchen, Betsy, who was permanently employed cooking for guests, was busy preparing the day's meat pies.

'Have you seen Mother?' Guy asked.

'No, boy, I have not,' said Betsy. 'I expect she's still in her bed, after the trouble at the fair yesterday.'

Guy did not like the tone in her voice, it was mocking. 'She's not in her bed, nor has been for a while. She must have gone out.'

'Perhaps,' said Betsy. 'But I have been here since dawn and I have not seen anyone come down from the rooms above. Perhaps she's gone for a walk, to clear her mind, poor soul.' She smirked.

'She does not need to clear her mind,' Guy said. 'It's people like you, Betsy, who need to do that.'

'I'm sorry, sir, to be sure. I do not wish to offend you nor the noble blood which runs in your veins.' She gave a mock curtsy.

Guy wanted to strike her but instead he turned and fled from the kitchen before he said or did something he would regret. Outside, he shaded his eyes and stared up the street, looking for a sign of his mother. There were few people about for it was still early but Guy trudged up the full length of the street calling in every shop or open doorway, to ask if anyone had seen Elizabeth. No one had. As he returned to the inn, for the first time he felt a sense of real disquiet. It was not like her to go out and not tell him where she was going – he could never remember it happening before. If Betsy had not seen her, what time had she left? He remembered, with a jolt of fear,

209

that he had not checked on her the previous evening – once trade became brisk, there had been no time.

Back at the inn, many of the guests were breakfasting in the tap room. The friendly chatter eased Guy's mind a little. He went and sat in a corner of the fireplace, silent and waiting – a small, hunched figure, unnoticed by most of the passing trade.

Darkness, despair, misery, fear – Elizabeth stared up into the rafters above her head, panic rising and falling within her like relentless waves on the seashore. The noise in the tap room beneath her had quietened. She could still hear one or two revellers taking their time over leaving but the inn's business for the evening was finished. They had been very busy, she could tell, but whether they had managed without her was of no interest – always conscientious she recognized that this lack of concern, this apathy was out of character. The truth was that the inn and its trade no longer mattered to her – indeed nothing mattered for she had failed, utterly, both herself and her son. What troubled her most was not Thomas's anger nor even the jeering of the crowd – it was the expression on Guy's face as she had ranted at Thomas which now tore her apart, as she lay alone in the dark. Guy had been ashamed of her, ashamed of her outburst, ashamed perhaps of what she stood for – the discarded mistress who had neither the good sense nor the courage to accept her rejection. Guy was not a gentleman – not yet – but the influence of his father and the governess Thomas had found for the boy had already placed him in a different class from her own. With a sinking heart, Elizabeth became aware that she was already an embarrassment to him and as the gap widened between them, greater would be his discomfiture in her presence. Her days with her son were over. In his early baby years he had belonged to her exclusively, but they were gone for good. She rolled over in the bed and moaned to herself as if in pain. What was to become of them now? When Harry Naylor heard of the scene at the horse fair, would he consider that she had broken her part of the bargain and divert his coaches elsewhere – it seemed likely. And Thomas, ah Thomas, he would never come to her again for he could not, would not forgive her for today, she knew that. Any hope she might have had of rekindling their relationship was over and the loss was not only hers, but Guy's. Her actions today had effectively alienated Thomas from his son as well as herself. How could she have been such a fool?

The baby within her womb stirred and began to kick strongly.

210

Elizabeth cursed it under her breath. It was this child who was to blame – the pregnancy had addled her mind as surely as it had swelled her body. This child had driven Thomas away and destroyed its brother's future. But for the pregnancy, Elizabeth could have been strong in Thomas's rejection, as she had been once before at the time of Guy's birth. Then she had been able to pick up the threads of her life and turn her back on him. This time the cursed baby had weakened her resolve. It was impossible to imagine her ever loving the child when it was born – she hated it and blamed it for everything that had befallen her. She did not want it to live, she wanted it torn from her body, lifeless.

She tried to see the way ahead, tried to imagine some sort of future for the three of them but Harry Naylor's threats kept surfacing in her mind. For all that he was a gentleman, Elizabeth recognized that he was not a man who could be appealed to on any level. She suspected that he would actually enjoy destroying her and her business and that he only needed an excuse, like the scene at the horse fair, to take his revenge. Without the coach traffic, the inn would fail. All the luxuries which Guy had come to enjoy – his pony, good food and fine clothes, would have to go. They would be forced back into the mindless, grinding poverty of her own youth, with another mouth to feed and no hope, no future. She cared not at all for herself, it was Guy's future on which all her thoughts were centred. She had betrayed him and somehow she had to make things right for him. There seemed only one solution – somehow she had to see to it that he came under the custody of his father. Her tired mind searched for how this could be achieved, but all her abilities to plot and scheme seemed to have left her. Only one idea made any sense . . . if she abandoned Guy, left him with no word as to whether she would ever return, whether she was dead or alive, then surely Thomas would take him in, and raise him. She thought of Beatrice Naylor – by all accounts she was not a pleasant woman, harsh with her step-son, a shrew to her husband, so local gossip would have it. How would she treat Thomas's bastard son? Would she even let him into Chadbrook?

As she lay in the darkness, her mind in a turmoil of anxiety and misery, a series of pictures came back to her – little scenes which had contributed towards the building of a relationship between Thomas and their son. Thomas loved the boy. With a sudden, growing certainty she recognized that. He did not love his wife, nor Christopher, his heir, nor, she recognized with a stab of pain, herself any longer. But he loved Guy, and Guy loved him. He would not

211

abandon the boy, whatever his wife said, whatever his critics said. Her confidence having deserted her, having been sure of nothing, she was suddenly utterly sure of this . . . and it galvanized her into action.

Clumsily, Elizabeth got out of bed, wincing as she straightened her back, the baby heavy within her. She put on an old shift and crept quietly out of her room. She hesitated at the door to Guy's room. To look at him carried a double risk – of waking him or softening her resolve. Carefully she tiptoed past his room and climbed down the ladder into the kitchen, holding her candle high. For a moment she hesitated. This was the kernel of the house, the room where she had spent most of her life. She shut her eyes for a moment . . . she was doing this for Guy, she must be strong. Her eyes snapped open, she squared her shoulders, made her way to the kitchen door, drew back the bolt and crept outside. It was a clear, cold night, the moon full and low, the sky a mass of stars. She walked as soundlessly as she could across the stableyard. Her horse, Megan, heard her footsteps and whinnied.

Feeling a slight lifting of spirits, Elizabeth hurried to the open stable door. 'Megan,' she whispered. The horse lowered its head, rubbing her nose against Elizabeth's palm. 'We have a long way to go tonight, little one.' She hesitated. Megan had been a gift from Thomas on her last birthday. She loved the little mare but suddenly she knew she could not take her. It was pride, partly, not wishing to be beholden to Thomas for anything, but also with her future so uncertain, she did not want anything to befall the little horse. She murmured endearments against the horse's cheek, and pulled her ears. Tears were close but she must not cry, not now. She turned away and hurried across the stableyard, out into the main street.

A few steps took her to the Hewitts' house. She hesitated and then rapped firmly on the knocker. Fifteen minutes later, after angry and protracted negotiations, Jamie Hewitt finally helped her into the saddle of a flea-bitten, dapple-grey gelding, which looked more dead than alive. As she turned the horse's head, she noted the look of relief in Jamie's eyes. She had frightened him, she realized, with her anger and her demands for a horse. The knowledge surprised her and she tried to soften their parting. 'Thank you, Jamie, I will not forget your help.'

He murmured something under his breath and surreptitiously made the sign of the cross before turning away. So, he thought she was a witch. She almost laughed aloud and the ludicrousness of his notion buoyed up her spirits long enough to see her out of Long

Melford and heading down the road to Bury. As the last cottages slipped out of sight behind her, the first grey streaks of dawn lightened the sky ahead.

It was Betsy who found Guy there, several hours later. He had fallen asleep, one cheek resting on his hunched-up knees. As he slept, the arrogance she had encountered during the day was gone. He looked very much the child, a baby almost, and she regretted her teasing – he had been right to defend his mother. Betsy, too, was becoming alarmed. Her family, the Griffiths, had lived in Long Melford for many years. She had known Elizabeth since they were both children, younger than Guy, and old Jem and his poor, mad wife, Mary. While Betsy and her family did not approve of Elizabeth's strange ways nor her relationship with the Earl, in times of trouble the villagers stood together and Betsy could smell trouble – something was wrong. She tiptoed away from the boy and walked briskly the few doors down the street to her home. Her father sat in front of the fire. An old man now, he dozed contentedly. Her mother was preparing a meal, and her two young brothers, the last of Margaret Griffiths' eleven children, romped around on the floor.

'Father, Father.' Betsy shook her father awake.

'What is it, girl?' he said, his eyes heavy with sleep.

'I'm worried about Mistress Monson, up at the inn. She seems to have disappeared and that boy of hers has looked everywhere for her. I am afraid of what she might have done, Father, after her meeting with the Earl yesterday, at the fair.'

'It is none of our business, Betsy. There is nothing we can do.'

'I feel for the boy, he is worried about his mother. I wondered whether you would take our lads and go and look for her.'

'Look for her where?' She had her father's full attention now, he was rubbing the sleep from his eyes.

'I don't know, around the village. She cannot have strayed far in her condition. Perhaps she went for a walk and took bad. She may be lying somewhere with her new babe – she cannot be far off her time now.'

'You are a good-hearted girl, Betsy,' said her father, 'even if you do disturb an old man from his slumbers. I will go and look for your Elizabeth, but only until sundown, mind.'

'Thank you, Father.'

Back at the inn, Guy was wandering aimlessly about. 'Have you seen Mother yet?' he asked, as Betsy came in.

'No, but don't you fret,' she said. 'I have sent my father and two of our boys to look for her. I am sure they will find her soon.'

'I can go and help,' said Guy, obviously eager to be doing something.

'No,' said Betsy. 'You stay here with me. If you go out looking for your mother and she comes back and finds you gone, you will worry the poor woman.'

'Perhaps she's fallen somewhere. Perhaps she's started having the baby,' Guy said.

'I expect she just needed a little time on her own after the problems of yesterday.' Guy looked at Betsy sharply but there was no longer any mockery in her words. He nodded in agreement. 'I will fetch you something to eat, Guy. Go and sit back by the fire – some pie and a glass of beer will raise your spirits.' Tears pricked at the back of Guy's eyelids at her kindness but he did as she asked and found to his surprise that he was very hungry.

The hours dragged by. Once it was dark Betsy became concerned for her father, he had promised to come and tell her the outcome of his search and it was strange that he had not. Betsy kept the boy busy with errands, although it was a quiet night at the inn. More than once she tried to send him to bed but he would not go and in the end she tucked him into the big rocking-chair by the fire, covering him with a rug, promising to wake him as soon as there was any news.

Guy had been asleep for only a short while when Martin Griffiths arrived, his face grave. 'I hope I have done right, lass,' he said, wearily.

'Why, what's happened? Have you found her?' asked Betsy.

'No, no I have not found her but I have sent for the Earl. Dickon should be on his way back with him now, that is if he is staying at Chadbrook presently.'

Betsy frowned. 'You have sent for the Earl?' She was clearly over-awed. 'Why, Father?'

'The poor lady has gone.'

Betsy stared at him. 'Gone . . . you mean she's dead?'

'Who knows, she may be by now. I searched the village, down by the river, all over, but there was no sign of her. I began asking around but no one had seen her. Then me and the boys stopped by The Lion.' Martin carefully avoided his daughter's eye for his relationship with the gin bottle was well established.

'Oh, so you thought you might find her there then, did you?' said Betsy, sarcastically.

'Enough of your cheek, girl – we were tired and thirsty. As events turned out, Jamie Hewitt was there, the blacksmith's lad. Apparently your mistress arrived at the Hewitts' before dawn this morning, demanding a horse.'

'But she has a horse of her own! In any case, she should not be riding in her condition.'

'True enough,' said Martin. 'Jamie Hewitt tried to stop her but then she offered him ten pounds for the horse, a miserable beast by all accounts, and he let her take it. She got him to saddle up and then rode off down the street.'

'Alone?' said Betsy, aghast.

'Quite alone.'

'Jamie Hewitt had no place letting her go. How could he do that?' Betsy said, angrily.

'Greed, and, in his favour, it seems she frightened him. He said she was half mad, like her mother, raving, screaming with temper. He thinks she is a witch and he feared she would put a curse on him. He was glad to see her go.'

'And no one knows where she has gone?' Martin shook his head. Betsy's practical mind suddenly remembered the Earl. 'We had best get this place tidied up if the Earl is coming. I hope you did the right thing sending for him – he disowned the boy at the fair yesterday.'

Martin glanced over his shoulder to where Guy slumbered by the fire. 'Look at him, girl. The Earl cannot disown that lad – he is the mirror image of his father. He will take the boy, raise him at Chadbrook and turn him into a gentleman, you mark my words.'

Betsy stared at her father. 'So you think Mistress Monson will not be returning?'

Martin Griffiths shrugged his broad shoulders. 'Who knows, but I can see nothing but disaster before her. She is a woman travelling unaccompanied, a prey to every passing villain. She is with child and, by all accounts, mad.' He glanced at Guy and lowered his voice almost to a whisper. 'I do not believe we will see Elizabeth Monson in Long Melford again.'

CHAPTER TWENTY-FOUR

Dickon Griffiths trembled with fear. Always an imposing man, the Earl, standing before him now in a richly embroidered dressing-gown, seemed almost not of this world – a King, an Emperor. 'What is it, boy, that you raise me from my bed at this hour? The reason had better be a good one.'

'It is . . . there's trouble with Mistress Elizabeth, from The Lady in Waiting.' He saw the Earl's eyes harden and his heart sank.

'What has happened?' the Earl barked. 'Is the baby born?'

'No, no,' said Dickon. The ride to Chadbrook had made him cold, his teeth were chattering so hard he could barely speak.

'Then what is it?' the Earl shouted impatiently.

'She . . . she's gone, she's left the village. M-my father thought you should know the boy, Guy, is alone.'

'Gone? What do you mean, gone?' the Earl asked.

'She bought a horse from the blacksmith early this morning, before dawn. She rode out of the village. Jamie Hewitt said she was mad, raving. She was alone and . . .' he hesitated, 'in her condition. . . .'

'The devil take her,' the Earl burst out. 'Is there no end to the woman's stupidity? Did anyone see which way she headed?'

'I-I don't think so,' said Dickon. 'Jamie may know more.'

'And Guy, where is Guy now?'

'He's still at the inn,' said Dickon. At the mention of Guy's name he sensed some of the Earl's anger was subsiding and it made him a little bolder. 'My father thought it best he should know nothing about his mother leaving Long Melford. We thought we should wait to see what you wished to do.'

'Your father is a wise man,' said Thomas. 'Wait here. I will dress, ride back with you to Long Melford, see what's to be done with the boy and organize a search for his mother.' He started out of the room and then hesitated. 'You did well, boy. It's a cold night, I'll arrange for you to have some food and wine while you wait for me.'

'Thank you, sir,' Dickon managed, weak with relief.

Thomas dressed hurriedly, cursing under his breath. He should

216

have foreseen that Elizabeth would do something like this. It was the wildness in her nature that had always appealed to him but he recognized that it was dangerous. Never far below the surface, there was an uncontrollable streak in her nature – perhaps her mother's madness. He was angry and disappointed in her behaviour of the previous day. Yet the thought that she could be the victim of any passing traveller, that she could be travelling alone on a night such as this, that the baby could be born at any moment, filled him with terror. In that moment he realized that denying his love for Elizabeth Monson was not a simple matter. Although all the social and civil laws of the land made it impossible for them ever to share their lives together, nonetheless they were bound by a thread that although intangible was strong – so strong that it would last a lifetime.

Once dressed, he glanced at the door of the adjoining chamber which was his wife's. All his instincts encouraged him to leave quietly, without disturbing her. The servants could bear the brunt of her anger when she found out his mission. Yet still he hesitated. If Elizabeth Monson was missing, then he could not simply leave Guy alone at the inn. The boy was too young, and in any event loved his mother so much he could not be left alone to mourn her departure. There was no alternative – he would have to be brought back to Chadbrook. If Beatrice was not forewarned, then the scene she would create in front of the boy would be truly terrible. He could not take that risk.

In sleep, the harshness of her features were softened a little, but not much. The dark hair which fanned out on the pillow was coarse and although the kindly light of the candle beside her bed flattered her, the harsh lines between nose and mouth were still much in evidence, an indication of her constant discontent.

'Beatrice,' he shook her. 'Beatrice.'

Her eyes snapped open. 'Thomas, what is it, what has happened?' She sat up in bed, pulling the sheets about her.

'I have to go, I must ride to Long Melford. I need to explain why before I go.'

'You need to ride to Long Melford?' said Beatrice, her mind still stupid with sleep. 'What time is it? It is not yet dawn.'

'No, it is not.'

'Then what is wrong, what is happening?'

Thomas took a deep breath. 'Elizabeth Monson has disappeared, abandoning her son.' Thomas met Beatrice's eye. 'If I cannot find her, then I will be bringing the boy back here to Chadbrook.'

217

Beatrice's mind was suddenly crystal clear. 'I will not have your bastards under this roof.'

'And I, madam, will not have you refer to my son in that manner, and I would remind you that this is my house and I will have under my roof whom I wish.'

'Your house, your house!' Beatrice said. 'Without my family's money Chadbrook would be in ruins today.'

'And without my hand in marriage,' Thomas said crisply, 'you would be a dried-up old spinster, not Lady Beatrice of Chadbrook.'

For a moment this retort silenced her. 'There is no need for the boy to be brought here,' she said, in slightly more reasonable tones. 'You could arrange for a nurse to care for him in a cottage on the estate – a governess, too, if he has any brains, which I doubt bearing in mind his mother.'

'The boy comes here,' said Thomas, 'to share equal status with Christopher and any children whom you may yet bear.'

'I will not have it,' said Beatrice. 'I will not share my home with . . . that woman's child.'

'Then you must leave Chadbrook,' said Thomas, his voice deadly serious.

Beatrice gave a short, sharp laugh. 'You are bluffing,' she said. 'You know the terms of my father's marriage gift – you will only receive the annual income while we have a marriage. If you force me to leave your home, then our marriage is over and so, too, is my father's income. Chadbrook is not strong enough financially to stand alone, as you well know.'

'If I have to choose between my son and Chadbrook, I will choose my son.' Thomas spoke the words calmly, confidently and in that instant Beatrice knew that he meant exactly what he said.

Chadbrook was a bigger, more marvellous building than Guy could ever have dreamt of in his wildest imaginings. He sat, open-mouthed, in the carriage beside Thomas, staring up at the great white pillars, his eyes like saucers. Thomas saw his expression and smiled, thinly – the first smile Guy had seen on his father's face since his extraordinary appearance at the inn in the early hours of the morning. There had been no explanations. Thomas had simply told Guy that he was to come with him and that he was taking him to Chadbrook. When Guy had enquired about his mother, Thomas had replied that they would talk of the matter later.

The carriage drew up outside a massive front door. A footman was

218

in place before the horses had hardly come to a stamping halt. The door was opened, steps folded down. 'Good morning, sir,' the footman said, eyeing Guy with interest.

'Good morning, Peter – come, Guy,' said Thomas.

Guy hurried through the door after his father and in the hallway stopped in wonderment. A huge flight of stairs led up to a galleried landing above. The hall was enormous, bigger than any room he had ever seen. He was overwhelmed. 'Come,' said Thomas, gently. 'This way.'

He followed his father through double doors to another enormous room. In this one there were rugs on the floor, and chairs, beautifully upholstered. A fire blazed in the grate, beside which two people stood – a tall, pale youth with fair hair and a woman, short and broad with dark hair scraped back from her face, in an unbecoming style. Guy did not much like the look of either of them.

'Guy, this is my elder son, Christopher.' The half brothers eyed one another in silence with instant animosity. Christopher could see only the son for whom he knew his father had always longed – indeed who was everything that he himself was not. Guy noted a small, mean mouth, the malevolent eye and instinctively felt the older boy's hostility. 'And this is the Lady Beatrice, my wife.' Guy bowed as he had been taught. The woman said nothing, no friendly greeting, she simply stared at him. 'My wife will be looking after your needs and I hope that you and Christopher will become firm friends,' said Thomas.

Even to Guy's childish ears his father's voice was full of false heartiness. 'How long will I be staying here?' he asked.

'For ever, if needs be,' said Thomas, firmly.

'But what of my mother? What will become of her? Will she be living here, too?'

Beatrice snorted. 'This is too much, Thomas. If you have not explained the position to the boy, it is about time you did, or is he too stupid to understand?'

Guy looked from one to the other, a sense of terrible dread rising within him. 'What has happened to my mother, what has happened? Tell me, tell me.' His voice was shrill, already heading towards hysteria.

Thomas crouched down so that his face was level with Guy's. He put his hands on his son's shoulders. 'Guy, I do not know what has become of your mother, but I will do my best to find her and bring her back to you.'

219

'W-where has she gone?' Guy managed.

'If I knew that then all our problems would be over,' said Thomas, gently. 'All I know is that she bought a horse from the Hewitts yesterday morning, while it was still dark, but I do not know where she went or why.'

'She would not leave me,' Guy said, in a small voice, staring into his father's face, willing his words to be true. 'She has never left me.'

'That is why I do not think she has gone very far,' said Thomas. He hesitated, there was no point in giving the boy false hopes. 'It would be wrong of me not to tell you the dangers, Guy. As far as we know, she left Long Melford alone, unaccompanied. As you know, she is soon to have a child. It is very important we find her before anything should befall her.'

'Can I help, can I help look for her?' Guy said.

'No, it is man's work, you must stay here. Trust me, I will do everything I can.'

Guy nodded. 'I know you will, Father.'

'If I must have this boy under my roof, I will not have him call you "Father". I will not be made a laughing stock in front of the whole neighbourhood. Do you hear me, boy? You are to call the Earl "sir" at all times.'

Thomas was about to protest and then checked himself. Beatrice was right. She might be a shrew of a woman but he knew he was expecting a lot of her. It would be the strength of character that made her such a difficult woman to live with, Thomas recognized, that would enable her to cope with this situation, which many a woman could not. 'My wife is right, Guy,' he said. Guy blanched but said nothing.

'And another thing,' Beatrice continued, 'I will not have the boy's mother mentioned in my presence again, is that understood? The name of Elizabeth Monson is never to be mentioned in this house.'

Guy looked up in horror at Beatrice's face. She met his gaze, her expression uncompromising, hard and bitter. In desperation he turned to his father and was rewarded with a smile of encouragement and understanding. 'Christopher will show you to your room, now,' Thomas said. 'You must be weary and you will need a little time on your own. You will be summoned for dinner.'

Numb with shock, Guy stumbled after the older boy up the splendid marble staircase, and then to smaller, steeper stairs until finally they reached a large, attic room, with a sunny aspect looking out over the parklands. 'This is your room,' the boy said, and without another word turned and shut the door behind him.

Guy looked around him. There was a small four-poster bed in the corner. On the floor, rather than rushes to which he was accustomed there were rag rugs and a wash-stand near the window. He walked over to the window and threw it open. The air smelt fresh and sweet and the view of the rolling acres of parkland was a sight which would please him for many years to come. The silence, too, was extraordinary. After the constant noise of the inn, the peace was very soothing. But at that moment, it all meant very little to him. All he could think of was that his precious mother was missing, in danger, perhaps even dead, and in that moment it suddenly came to him that he had failed her. If he had woken earlier or been to see her before going to bed, he could have dissuaded her from riding off to goodness knows where. Or if she insisted, he could have accompanied her, not left her to ride away alone, out of his life. Tears pricked at his eyes. He tried to brush them away but they were coming thick and fast. At last he went and lay down on the bed. It felt suddenly as though he were being crushed under a terrible burden. The burden was guilt and it was to remain with him for the rest of his life.

CHAPTER TWENTY-FIVE
Long Melford – March 1982

'Prue, is that you? It's Charles Chadbrook.'

'Hello, Charles,' said Prue, unexpectedly pleased to hear his voice. 'How's the research going?'

'Quite well, in a way, although I think I'm coming up with even more of a confusing picture than the one you presented to me. I was wondering whether we could meet and perhaps indulge in a spot of grave-watching.'

'Grave-watching – why?' Prue asked.

'No particular reason except that it makes the story more real somehow – I presume you know where Guy is buried?'

'Yes, I think so,' said Prue. 'All the Mansells are buried in Hawkedon churchyard. I assume Guy is as well – in fact I'm sure he is, when I think about it, my father's shown me the grave.'

'Good,' said Charles. 'Thomas is here, of course, in the chapel. Why don't you come over one morning and we'll look at Thomas first and then go and see Guy, perhaps have a pub lunch *en route*. I need to talk to you anyway about what I've found out. What do you say?'

'I'd love to,' said Prue. 'But Jonathan's away at the moment so I'm not sure I can spare the time.'

'Oh, come on,' said Charles. 'You can't be running the inn properly if you're so indispensable you can't even take a few hours off.'

They met the following day and immediately Prue sensed a change in Charles – he was more positive, more enthusiastic about life and seemed to be genuinely fascinated by the connection between their two families. Immediately upon her arrival, he took her to the chapel. It was built onto the east side of Chadbrook House so that the early morning sun shone through the stained-glass windows. Designed by Hawksmoor as an addition to the main house, it really was quite exquisite. Prue gazed in silence for some time at the beautifully illuminated ceiling, the delicately carved pews and the strange quality of light produced by the early morning sun.

'It is special, isn't it?' said Charles. 'I have to admit that I'm not really a religious man but since I was quite small, I've found great comfort in coming here just to sit and think, even though normally it's perishing cold. Come on. Thomas is over here.'

A simple plaque was set into the side of the chapel, to commemorate the life and death of Thomas, the seventh Earl of Chadbrook. Beside him was buried his wife Beatrice and slightly to one side his first wife Eleanor, and their daughter Amy, who appeared to have died at the early age of seven, just a year after her mother.

'It could have been anything in those days – smallpox, typhoid, even a minor childhood illness often had fatal complications.'

'So did Thomas have no son? Surely he must have for the title to carry on?'

'Oh yes, Christopher. He's over there.' Charles pointed directly into the sunlight, squinting. 'He married a woman named Anne Martin and they had a great many children – seven, no eight, I think. He, too, was Eleanor's child – Thomas and Beatrice had no children.'

'So I presume you found no mention of Elizabeth in your records – you would never have lasted this long without telling me?' Prue said with a grin.

'Not of Elizabeth, no,' said Charles, with a smile of ill-disguised triumph. 'But I have found a reference to Guy. Come, let's go back to the house, I want to show you Thomas's portraits.'

'The childhood one, first,' he said. 'Do you mind if I lead the way?' They crossed the hall and entered a huge drawing room, with windows on two sides looking out over the parkland.

'This is a beautiful room, Charles,' said Prue, noting the faded but charming William Morris curtains, the easy chairs and wonderful old fireplace.

'I suppose so,' said Charles. 'But next to the library, this is my favourite room.' He opened double doors into a much smaller room, with splendid parquet flooring, the main feature of which was a magnificent grand piano. 'This, needless to say, is the music room and here is young Thomas, aged six, I believe.'

The portrait was a small one, and it hung on the wall opposite the window. Prue went and stood before it. She felt strange – the child's features, his dark hair, the dimple on one cheek, the half smile were instantly familiar. Yet it was not this boy she recognized, but someone like him. She shook her head as if to clear her mind.

'Are you feeling all right?' Charles asked, anxiously.

'Yes, fine – it's a lovely portrait.' She was not ready to discuss the

223

very strange feelings she experienced at the sight of the child. The shock was too great and yet the sensations too indistinct to speak of with any clarity.

'It's Gainsborough, of course,' said Charles. 'Now come and see Thomas the man.'

The first thing she noticed was the similarity to Charles. It had not been so obvious in the boy's face, but Thomas astride his horse had a definite look of Charles. She told him so.

'Yes, you're not the first to say that, though I can't really see it myself. What fascinates me though is the horse – just look at it!'

Prue was no expert on horses but even she could see it was an ungainly beast. Too small a mount for Thomas really, with a big head, a distinctly Roman nose and rather an unattractive dull bay in colour. 'It's probably the artist's fault,' she suggested.

'Possibly,' said Charles. 'Certainly Gainsborough didn't paint this portrait – the artist is unknown and he may not have been good at horses. I favour my pet theory, however.'

'What's that?' Prue asked, amused. They were standing half-way up the marble staircase which led from the hall to a galleried landing above. It was hard to believe this pleasant, easy-going man could own all this splendour and remain so unaffected.

'I think it was a favourite mount of Thomas's – not a beauty certainly, but a good, reliable friend. He wanted a record of it, warts and all, because he was so fond of the beast.'

Prue studied the portrait in silence for a moment. Certainly, the face was of a man without a speck of arrogance or pride – an attractive, sensual face, oddly modern. Instinctively she felt drawn to him. 'I think you're right,' she said, almost to herself.

Back in Charles's study, Prue was suddenly mad with impatience. 'Tell me all about the reference to Guy you mentioned,' she begged.

'Wait,' said Charles, laughing at her. 'Sit down, we'll have some coffee and I'll explain exactly what happened.'

Mrs Plum delivered the coffee and had to be virtually ordered out of the room before Charles could begin. 'I started by looking through all Thomas's papers, of which there were quite a number, but I found absolutely no reference to The Lady in Waiting, to Elizabeth or to Guy.'

'Oh damn,' said Prue, looking crestfallen.

'Wait, patience, patience,' said Charles, with a smile. 'It became clear that Thomas had his fair share of financial problems in his youth, but everything seems to have been solved by his marriage to

224

Beatrice. The Naylors were very rich – indeed they still are – and her income seems to have saved the day for Chadbrook.'

'I know all that,' said Prue. 'We've discussed it.'

'Yes, but bear with me, I'm just giving you the background,' said Charles, exasperated. 'My breakthrough came when I found Beatrice's diary.'

'Her diary!'

'Yes, but don't get too excited. Most women kept journals or diaries during that particular period of history but they were normally just a record of housekeeping – nothing juicy or scandalous. I'm not underestimating their importance – they make fascinating reading – but the contents usually reveal how much fruit was bottled or when the cider was pressed, that sort of detail. In Beatrice's case, the diary, which I have here, is very money orientated. She meticulously notes the cost of everything – clearly she was a woman who had a very real sense of money which was unusual for the period. Perhaps she was particularly frugal because she knew it was her father's money being spent.' He paused and drew from the drawer a leather-bound book, faded and stained.

Prue watched, fascinated, as Charles carefully turned the pages to where he had placed a bookmark. 'Is that really her diary? How amazing. May I have a closer look?'

'Of course,' said Charles.

Prue came round and leant over his shoulder. Her thick curtain of red-gold hair brushed against his cheek and momentarily caused Charles to catch his breath. There had been no woman in his life since Evette and without doubt Prue was his sort of girl – tall, slender, fair. He forced himself to remember that she was already involved in a serious relationship. 'Here's the place,' he said, hurriedly. 'Beatrice is reporting on the crop of elderberries – how abundant it had been and how they had made much wine and preserves – and then suddenly she breaks off. Look, here is the sentence – "the boy arrived today and he was everything I feared. It is an insult to expect me to have him in my household. While we dined, he called my Lord, the Earl, 'Father' by name in the hearing of the servants. I have seen to it that this will not occur again."

'You see,' said Charles, triumphantly. He raised his head to look at Prue, their faces were very close together. She smelt of summer lawns and he wanted badly to kiss her.

'No, I don't see at all,' said Prue, drawing away hurriedly as if sensing his feelings.

225

'You're not thinking straight,' said Charles, critically. 'There's more but let's look at what we have here, first. A boy has come to join the household, a boy who has to be stopped from calling Thomas "Father". Clearly the boy is Thomas's son, but Beatrice does not approve of the relationship.'

'It could be Christopher,' Prue suggested.

'No, Christopher would never have left the household – besides, why on earth would Beatrice object to Christopher calling Thomas "Father"? No, it has to be another son, an illegitimate son.'

'You said there's more,' said Prue.

'There is.' Charles eagerly flipped over several more pages. 'Here we are.' He read on. ' "There must be a way to remove the boy from the household." ' Charles paused to give his words impact. ' "To have him living here is quite unacceptable. I grant he is a personable youth but people will keep asking about him. How can it be that my Lord, the Earl ignores my wishes in this matter. Papa says that the boy should stay with his nurse and not join the family – he says I must be mistress in my own house, but he does not have to face the Earl's wrath. My Lord will keep the boy, Guy, beside him and will not be moved on the subject." '

'The boy, Guy,' Prue whispered.

'Yes,' said Charles. 'From the dates you gave me it would appear that your Guy would have been nearly seven at the time this diary was written. It was a fairly popular name at the time but bearing in mind what we know already, it seems to me that we've made our connection.'

'But why?' said Prue, sitting down opposite Charles. 'Why did Guy come into Thomas's household? Why didn't he stay with his mother at the inn?'

'I've been struggling with that one, too,' said Charles. 'Maybe Thomas and Elizabeth wanted the boy to better himself, but it seems unlikely that he would have been sent to his father in the circumstances. If they wanted to educate him then it could easily have been arranged without the need to inflict Guy on Beatrice. I have to admit that having read her diaries, I don't much like the woman – very hard and calculating – nonetheless, I can see her point of view. It was pretty unreasonable, being expected to look after her husband's bastard.'

'Maybe Elizabeth died,' said Prue.

'I thought of that,' said Charles. 'I've been right through all the Parish Records at Long Melford again in case you'd missed anything, and tramped round several churchyards, but all to no avail. She seems to have disappeared off the face of the earth, so it remains a complete mystery as to what happened to her.'

'She wouldn't have easily given up her son, she loved him so much,' said Prue.

'How do you know?' Charles asked, startled. Prue stared at him blankly for a moment, a strangely confused, almost disorientated look in her eyes. He tried again. 'Prue, you've just said she wouldn't have easily given up her son because she loved him so much.'

Prue frowned. 'Yes, I know, I'm sorry. I don't know what made me say that.'

'You feel very close to Elizabeth, don't you?' Prue nodded. 'And these miserable feelings at the inn, you're sure now they belong to her, aren't you?'

'Yes,' said Prue.

'When you consider how many people must have lived at and/or visited the inn over the centuries, how can you be sure that it's this one particular person whose feelings you share?'

Prue considered the question. 'I don't know. Put like that there's absolutely no logical explanation.' She looked at Charles and smiled slightly. 'You must think I'm mad, but honestly, Charles, nothing like this has ever happened to me before. I'm not in the habit of pretending to be fey, or striking poses.'

'I know that,' said Charles, gently. 'I don't know you very well, not yet anyway, but as I said to you the other day, I know there's no way you'd be making up how you're feeling.'

Prue ran a hand through her hair. 'Thanks, I'm a little hypersensitive on the subject, I'm afraid.'

'I'm not surprised,' said Charles. 'Come on, let's go to Hawkedon. We'll look at Guy's headstone and then we'll have some lunch.'

On the drive to Hawkedon, Prue was very quiet and, sensing her mood, Charles said little, besides which, he had thoughts of his own to consider. He knew now he could seriously make a fool of himself over this girl and he recognized the importance of treading warily from her point of view as well as his own. She had not mentioned Jonathan today and Charles wondered whether Jonathan knew where she was and whether he even minded. She had said he was away but not where, and it was taking all Charles's strength of character not to press her on the subject. He would have to bide his time, he knew that, but he sensed she was not really happy and if that was the case, well, maybe this Jonathan was not right for her.

'Next turning left,' Prue broke into his thoughts. 'The church is just over here.'

The village of Hawkedon was sparsely populated and the majority of gravestones belonged to the Mansells – indeed some of the family seemed to have been completely carried away with the need for great monuments. One particularly lavish affair from the Victorian era sported an enormous angel with spread wings. 'Sorry,' said Prue. 'Not very tasteful, I'm afraid.'

'Oh I don't know,' said Charles. 'If you've got to go, there's something to be said for making a big thing of it.'

They searched for some time before they found Guy's grave. It was a small stone, close to the vestry door, carved in the form of an open bible. 'Here lies Guy Monson, 1st Baronet, died December 24th 1859, and his wife, Marcelle, formerly de Villefranche, died April 15th 1863.'

'De Villefranche, de Villefranche, I don't believe it!' Charles said, excitedly.

Prue looked at him, amused. The strong wind had whipped colour into his usually pale cheeks and his eyes were bright with excitement. He looked like a small boy, jumping up and down with the discovery of the moment. He really is a very nice man, Prue thought briefly, before curiosity at his reaction took over. 'What on earth's all the fuss, Charles?' she asked.

'There are some love letters among Thomas's belongings from a Comtesse Marie-Claire de Villefranche, who lived in a chateau just outside Brussels. Clearly they knew one another during the War.' Prue looked blank. 'The Napoleonic War, stupid,' said Charles, taking her arm to soften the words. 'The Battle of Waterloo – heard of it, vaguely?'

'Beast,' said Prue.

'The letters span quite a long period,' said Charles, 'from pre-Waterloo days and for some years after the battle. Thomas kept many of them, it's rather touching.'

'Why didn't you mention them before?' Prue asked.

'I didn't like to,' said Charles. 'I thought you'd think it would tend to prove that there had been no relationship between Thomas and Elizabeth. I don't actually think it proves anything of the sort. Men of all ranks in all the wars through history have become involved with women in the country in which they are fighting. Assuming Thomas married Beatrice for money rather than love, it's not surprising he became involved elsewhere – both with your Elizabeth and

228

the Comtesse. Anyway, that's not the point – the point is that here is Guy, married to someone of the same name as Thomas's mistress. It has to be more than coincidence. Isn't it strange how as we delve deeper, so the strands seem to pull tighter together.'

'So, you're saying that Marcelle was perhaps a daughter or a sister of Thomas's Comtesse?'

'Exactly. We know that Guy fought alongside Thomas at Waterloo – it all fits together.'

'I don't see it really proves anything, interesting though it is,' said Prue.

'It proves that they spent time together socially, surely,' said Charles. 'Oh look, it's freezing out here, let's go to the pub.'

They continued talking over lunch. 'Put yourself in Thomas's position,' said Charles, waving a fork in the air. 'He has a mistress, from a fairly high-born family like his own, with whom he stays from time to time. It is extremely unlikely that he would invite a junior officer into the home of his mistress, if that's all Guy was to him. However, if Guy was his son, then it suddenly becomes a lot less strange. Guy joins his father at the de Villefranche home, falls in love with the daughter, or younger sister, cousin, or whatever and there we have it.'

It was late afternoon by the time they returned to Long Melford and Prue felt as though she had been away for days. 'I've had a lovely time, Charles – it is good to get out of the place sometimes, for all sorts of reasons.'

'Then we must do it more often,' said Charles. He studied the pebbles on the drive as he spoke. 'Is Jonathan away for long?'

'I don't know,' said Prue. 'He's in New York. He has some family problems to sort out – he could be home tomorrow or it could take a fortnight. I expect he'll ring tonight though and I'll have a clearer idea.'

'It must be lonely for you without him.'

'Oh, it can never be lonely at The Lady in Waiting,' said Prue, with a laugh, 'especially for me.'

Charles telephoned Prue just after ten, the same evening. 'Have you an up-to-date passport?' he asked.

'Yes, why?' said Prue.

'Good, because we're flying to Brussels first thing tomorrow morning.'

229

'You have to be joking,' said Prue. 'I can't possibly – anyway why should we?'

'I decided there couldn't possibly be many Comtesses de Villefranche living near Brussels and with the help of a very kind telephone operator, I tracked down the current Count – his name is André. He was fascinated to hear about our research and has asked us to come and stay for a couple of days. He feels confident he will be able to throw some light on the relationship between Marie-Claire and Thomas because he has a younger brother who has done a lot of research into the family history and is being summoned, especially for our benefit.'

'You are incorrigible, Charles. I never would have started this whole thing if I'd known you were going to make such a fuss.'

'It's not a fuss,' said Charles. 'There's no point in doing anything unless you do it properly. You wanted to know about Elizabeth and I'm only doing my best to help you.'

'But the trail's gone cold on Elizabeth. This is all about Guy and Thomas and Marie-Claire.'

'OK, so it is, but just remember who Guy and Thomas were. Guy was Elizabeth's son, Thomas, the boy's father – the more we find out about those two, the closer we get to Elizabeth. Look, I don't know what it is you want to do, but I presume it is to lay your ghost in some way. Clearly we can only do that if we know the full story.'

'I understand what you're saying and I'm deeply grateful but I still can't come, Charles. With Jonathan away, somebody has to look after the inn.'

'I'll just have to go alone then,' said Charles, with ill-disguised disappointment.

That night, the sensations which invaded Prue's mind were worse than ever before – indeed so powerful were they that they broke into her dreams, waking her again and again with the intensity of misery, heartache and yes, uncertainty. It was as if the person could not see the way ahead and was as confused and undecided as Prue herself. At one point during the night she wondered whether she was going mad, so mixed up did her own feelings seem to be now with those foisted upon her. She dreamed of death and decay, of faceless enemies clawing at her – there was no peace to be had that night. In the end she rose soon after five and began busying herself around the inn to try to gain some control over her mind. By seven she was utterly exhausted by the strain, and as she dialled Charles's number, it did not really seem as if she had made the decision – it was as if it had been made for her. 'I'll come,' she said, 'if it's not too late to change my mind.'

'Of course it's not too late,' said Charles. 'I'll be over to collect you right away. The flight's not until eleven-thirty, we've plenty of time. I'm so pleased, Prue.'

'Charles, I . . .' Prue began.

'It's all right. Look, this isn't some pathetic attempt to drag you away for a dirty weekend. Tell me to mind my own business but it seems that you're not terribly happy and settled with life at the moment. In many respects I could say the same, so our mutual quest to find out about Thomas and Elizabeth is a good escape for us both. It can do us no harm, in fact it can do us nothing but good.'

'You're a very nice person, Charles,' said Prue.

'Oh God – nice, the kiss of death,' said Charles. 'Don't you ever dare say that to me again.'

'OK, promise,' said Prue. 'So, Brussels, here we come.'

'I'm on my way,' said Charles.

CHAPTER TWENTY-SIX
Brussels – March 1982

It was a good flight, fast and smooth. Charles had booked Club class and they drank champagne all the way. The wine on her empty stomach so early in the morning only served to heighten Prue's sense of disorientation. What was she doing flying to Brussels with a man she hardly knew? What on earth would Jonathan think, and did it matter? Jonathan had not been in touch with her since he left for New York, which was four days ago. Following his meeting with Edward Deckman, he had telephoned Prue from the airport to say he was on his way to New York finally to settle everything. He seemed happy with the outcome of his meeting, and initially Prue had been pleased that at last something was happening. Now she was not so sure. Why had he been so long in contacting her? Presumably if anything had gone disastrously wrong, or indeed right, he would have let her know, yet putting herself in his position, she could not imagine not wanting to make contact. It was increasingly demoralizing waiting for him to call and it was for this reason, as well as the terrible night she had spent, which had finally prompted Prue to accept Charles's invitation.

Sitting beside him now as the plane circled over Brussels airport she glanced up at him and returned his smile. It seemed impossible that she had known Charles for such a short time. She would never have imagined that she could feel so relaxed with someone so quickly. As a character, he was in such stark contrast to Jonathan in every respect except one – like Jonathan, Prue sensed in Charles a restlessness and the same lack of direction in his life. It seemed ludicrous with Chadbrook expecting a lifetime's care and service from him. Perhaps that was it. Perhaps because he was trapped and his destiny could be no longer of his own making, he was finding it difficult to take up the yoke of his responsibilities. Prue was determined that over the next three days together, she would try to find out a little more about what made Charles Chadbrook tick and if possible help him. He seemed to have done so much to help her, she felt it was time she started paying her debts.

Their passage through the airport was swift. The immigration official looked at Charles's passport and smiled. 'Welcome to Brussels, sir. It is a great honour to have you here.'

'Oh, thank you very much,' said Charles, with easy grace.

Prue followed in his wake, with a puzzled expression. 'Why the VIP treatment?' she asked.

'It's being an Earl, I suppose,' said Charles. 'The Belgiums are very keen on titles – everybody's a count, or a prince, or something.'

'It's extraordinary,' said Prue, 'but I keep forgetting about your title – dreadful, isn't it?'

'Not at all,' said Charles. 'I forget about it myself most of the time.'

It was not false modesty that prompted such a statement, Prue realized. His title, his wealth, his position in society were all unimportant to Charles. But what was important to him – she was not sure. He was charming, courteous, friendly and concerned for everyone he met. There seemed to be no darker side to his character. It was impossible to imagine him being unkind or rude, nor yet was it possible to imagine him caring passionately for anything – a strange man in many ways, very insular, oddly naive.

Outside the airport complex Charles ordered a taxi. 'The Count's house is on the south side of the city, but then it would be,' said he, smugly, as they settled down in the taxi.

'You're trying to expose my ignorance again,' said Prue. 'I presume that Waterloo is to the south of the city?'

'Yes,' said Charles. 'The suburbs now reach almost to the battle-field – strange, isn't it?'

'You don't think we ought to book into a hotel, just in case?' said Prue.

'In case of what?' said Charles.

'In case they're ghastly and we can't stand the thought of staying there. We could always make an excuse then that we're visiting friends in the city, or something.'

'I can't imagine it'll be necessary,' said Charles. 'The Count sounded extremely charming over the phone.'

'I don't know why it should be,' said Prue, 'but every time you mention him, I can only think of Count Dracula.'

Charles laughed and made a hideous face. 'Well, you never know,' he said. 'Did you remember to pack the garlic and crucifix?'

'Don't,' said Prue. 'I've been spooked enough in recent months to last me a lifetime.'

'Sorry,' said Charles. 'I was being tactless. I'm sure they're a perfectly delightful family.'

The Count's house proved to be a charming, old-world, French-style chateau in a quiet sunny street in the suburbs of the city. It was possible to see as they drove up towards the house that the chateau had been there long before the street itself – indeed, it looked somewhat isolated and withdrawn from the surrounding community because of the way in which it stood back from the rest of the street and still possessed a substantial garden.

'Sorry it's not a castle,' Charles whispered, as they climbed out.

'Shut up,' said Prue.

The door was opened by the Count himself – an enormous man, six foot five or six and very broad of beam. He was obviously quite young, younger than either Prue or Charles had imagined, but the enormous amount of surplus fat he carried tended to make him look decidedly middle-aged. Only his hair – sleek and black – looked like that of a young man. He extended a podgy hand to Prue. 'Welcome, my dear, welcome to Brussels. This is a great pleasure, a great pleasure.' He turned. 'And you must be the Earl of Clare. What an honour it is, sir, to have a member of your distinguished family under our roof once more.'

'Thank you,' said Charles. 'My name is Charles and my travelling companion is Prue Mansell.'

'Then call me André. Come in, you must be tired from the journey. Luncheon is almost ready. Perhaps you'd like to wash first.'

The inside of the chateau was ostentatious to a point of extreme vulgarity – indeed everything about the Count seemed to be generally larger than life. Prue and Charles were shown up to adjoining bedrooms and having washed and changed they met outside on the landing.

'It's unbelievable,' said Prue.

'It is rather quaint, isn't it – all the furniture has frills.'

'And I have brocade curtains,' said Prue. 'Gold and pink, can you believe!'

They hurried downstairs to find André waiting for them in the hall. 'Come into the drawing room and we will drink champagne to celebrate.'

The drawing room was a riot – satins, silk, marble, gilt – all warring with one another for supremacy. 'Shades of Liberace,' Charles whispered as André opened the champagne.

He solemnly poured three glasses and handed them round. 'This

234

is a very special occasion,' he said, turning to Prue. 'Your friend Charles has explained to me about your research and the reason for it. Is it not strange to think that we three stand here now, linked by blood and by a common past, yet it has taken all these years to bring our families together again?'

'Yes, it is,' said Charles, obviously moved. 'Then, André, let me propose a toast – to the Comtesse Marie-Claire de Villefranche, her daughter Marcelle, who was your great-great-great-great-grand-mother, Prue, to Thomas, Earl of Chadbrook and to his son, Guy.' Prue noticed that Elizabeth had been omitted from Charles's toast and felt absurdly hurt on her behalf.

'They must all have stood together here in his very room,' said André, 'on many an occasion, I shouldn't wonder.' They drank in silence for a moment, the past seeming to overwhelm the present. 'And,' said André, breaking the silence at last, 'we must not forget why they were all gathered here – to play their part in one of the most momentous dramas in history – the ending of an empire, the defeat of Napoleon.'

'Do you know much about the period, as it affected your own family?' Prue asked.

'Yes, but only from secondhand. Is that the right word?'

'Yes, it is,' said Charles. 'Your English is excellent.'

'For which I am very grateful,' said Prue. 'For while Charles speaks fluent French, mine is terrible.'

'Thank you,' said André. 'It is my brother who is the historian in the family, indeed he runs one of the major museums in the city. He is coming to dinner tonight, to tell you everything he knows about our family during that period. If you are not too tired, I have planned the rest of the day to maximize your time with us. After luncheon I thought I would escort you to the battlefield. It is something of a tourist attraction now, as I am sure you will appreciate, but not unpleasantly so. It will give you a feel of what it must have been like.'

'I'd like that very much,' said Prue. 'Wouldn't you, Charles?'

'Absolutely, a splendid idea.'

'I thought then we could return here for a brief rest and be ready to listen to my brother's outpourings. He can be a little heavy on his subject but we will do our best to keep his mood light. Let me top up your glasses.' A second bottle of champagne was opened and quickly despatched. It was clear that the Count loved his drink as much as he must love his food.

Prue was increasingly curious about him. 'Do you live here alone, André?'

'Good heavens, no,' he said. 'My wife is in the kitchen preparing lunch, we can no longer afford servants, I am afraid.' He grinned a little sheepishly. 'And I have two children, both boys – they are away at boarding school.'

During the rest of the day Charles and Prue were assailed by a series of impressions. The strange marriage between André and his wife, Anya – he, flamboyant, larger than life, she dowdy, tiny, slender, clearly overworked and little appreciated by her husband; their gaudy house, nonetheless steeped in the atmosphere of a more elegant, bygone age; and then the battlefield itself. . .

They had a delicious lunch and afterwards Andre took them to Waterloo, as he had promised. It was not as eery as they had expected – the peaceful farmland on that sunny afternoon did not easily bring to mind the turmoil and bloodshed which must have taken place in the muddy rye fields on June 18th, 1815 – but the knowledge of what had happened did create a real sense of drama.

'It's not like Culloden,' Prue said. 'There you can actually feel a sense of mass death and bloodshed.'

'Just like the Normandy beaches,' said Charles. 'You get the same feeling there. Here it's strangely peaceful.'

They visited the Wellington Museum where the British general had set up his headquarters on the eve of the battle. 'Strange to think Thomas must have been here,' Charles said, as they wandered around, looking at battle plans and even the original furniture which had been in Wellington's bedroom.

Then they travelled south of the battlefield to a farm where Napoleon had made *his* headquarters and saw there the little man's camp bed, hat and utensils. They visited the souvenir shop where Prue bought some maps of the battlefield, not sure how they might be useful for their research but feeling they might help them to understand just what Thomas and Guy had been through.

'Do you realize,' said Charles, with amusement, 'there are a great many more busts of Napoleon for sale than there are of Wellington?'

'He was a more charismatic character,' said Prue, smiling. 'Certainly Josephine thought so.'

Charles returned her smile. 'Are women always attracted to rogues?'

It was a loaded question. Prue either did not realize it or chose to ignore it. 'Usually, yes,' she replied carefully.

236

'Perhaps that's why I so rarely have success with them,' said Charles. 'I'm just too boring.'

He left her side and wandered out of the shop. She watched him go – he stood staring out across the farmland, a lonely, forlorn figure. She wanted to follow, to tell him that there was no substitute for his kindness, for his generosity of spirit and his interest in people and their problems. She glanced around her, there were too many people about to make such a conversation possible – in any event she felt too shy to strike so intimate a note. Most of their conversations to date had been about their research into their mutual past. Of course she knew him better than when she had first met him but there was still a reticence about him which suddenly in a moment of clarity Prue recognized that she too possessed. Perhaps they would never know each other any better because neither would ever make a move towards closer intimacy. Still, that was the way it should be in all the circumstances. She forced herself to think of Jonathan, something she had not done all day – somehow he seemed totally irrelevant, a remote figure, almost someone from her past rather than the present. She fixed a smile on her face and went to join Charles.

They were all tired by the time they returned to the chateau. 'Shall we meet for drinks at seven o'clock in the drawing room?' André suggested.

'That would be fine, André, and thank you for showing us round, we appreciated it,' said Charles.

'It was a pleasure, a great pleasure.'

Prue and Charles wearily climbed the stairs. 'Come into my room for a moment,' said Charles. 'I'm dying to hear your impressions of the day.' They collapsed onto Charles's enormous four-poster bed and giggled over the eccentricities of André's household.

'Yet despite the horrors of André, it all seems so terribly real,' said Prue, suddenly serious.

'Waterloo, you mean?' Charles asked.

'Yes, but I was really thinking of Thomas and Guy and the Comtesse. We haven't heard anything about them yet but somehow I can see them here. Despite the awful decor that André has inflicted on the house, it does have a timelessness, a sort of elegance and dignity which even he can't extinguish.'

'Oh, Lord,' said Charles, 'you're not going to start having ghostly feelings here, too, are you?' He was only slightly joking.

'I hope not,' said Prue and smiled at him. 'Still, you're here so at least I won't have to face them alone.'

'Yes,' said Charles. 'Yes, I'm here and I'll protect you.' He leant forward suddenly and kissed her on the lips. The gesture was so unexpected that Prue found herself returning the kiss before she realized fully what had happened. They drew apart and regarded each other in silence for a moment. Extraordinarily, there was no embarrassment between them. 'I'm sorry,' said Charles. 'Hell, no I'm not. I've been wanting to do that for days.'

Prue smiled slightly. 'It's all right,' she said and meant it.

'Shall we try again then?' said Charles, smiling.

'No,' said Prue firmly, standing up. 'I think I'd better go to my room right now.' She started towards the door.

'Prue.' She looked back. Charles was still sitting on the bed. Again Prue was conscious of his vulnerability. He hesitated. 'I could fall seriously in love with you, Prue, I don't know whether you'd realized that.'

'No,' said Prue. 'I hadn't.'

'Just bear it in mind then, could you?'

Maximilian de Villefranche was not even slightly like his brother. He looked like an ageing student – careless of dress, his hair overlong and his pale blue eyes tired and strained.

The dinner was superb. A huge bowl of terrine was followed by a whole lobster each, which was delicious. Charles and Prue naturally assumed this was the main course but no, a chicken stew followed known as Water Zooi, which in turn was followed by a kind of cheesecake and fresh fruit. Charles caught Prue's eye several times during the meal and smiled in sympathy. It was agony to try to do justice to such a feast. They talked of trivial matters during the meal, since André was particularly unwilling to have the important business of eating interrupted. Only when at last they sat round the table drinking brandy and sipping coffee, did the focus shift to Max and what he had to say.

'I understand you are seeking information about your ancestor Thomas, and about his relationship with this family.' Max directed his comments to Charles.

'Yes,' said Charles. 'Prue and I have discovered that my family and hers were joined in what appears to have been an illicit relationship. Prue's ancestor, Elizabeth, is not really the subject of this visit other than the fact that she had an affair with Thomas and the outcome of their liaison was a son, Guy, who we understand married into this family.'

'That is correct,' said Max. 'Let me tell you what I know, both of the times and the circumstances of the last visit made here by the Earl of Clare.' He paused and took a sip from his glass. There was a sense of eager anticipation and concentration around the table – the candles flickered, adding to the atmosphere. 'It is virtually impossible to exaggerate when speaking of Waterloo,' he said. 'It was an extraordinary, unique battle for so many reasons. Wellington and Napoleon were already legends in their own lifetimes. There had been a sense of anti-climax in Europe once Napoleon was incarcerated on Elba – everyone relaxed. Then, suddenly, the whole of Europe was jolted back into war with Napoleon's escape. Strangely, though, there was almost a party atmosphere – war was back in fashion. For the officers of Wellington's army, the period leading up to the Battle of Waterloo was enormous fun. No doubt you will have heard of the Duchess of Richmond's Ball which was held on 15th June, three days before Waterloo. Believe me, that was not just one lone social occasion – there were parties, picnics and cricket matches and a young dragoon named Arthur Shakespeare even organized race meetings at Grammont. The British officers mixed freely with wealthy Belgian families and many brought their wives to join them. Wellington actually encouraged this frivolous atmosphere because he knew, for a variety of reasons, that his position was not entirely strong and he wanted to keep morale high. He even persuaded his niece, Emily Somerset, to remain in Brussels to have her first baby, to demonstrate confidence in her uncle's ability to beat Napoleon and hold the city.' Max looked directly at Prue for a moment. 'Can you imagine the contrast created between the hectic social round and what was to be arguably the bloodiest battle in Europe's history?'

'Yes, I can,' said Prue, quietly. 'It must have been very disorientating for the men.'

'Yes, it was,' said Max. 'Thomas, Earl of Clare, and his illegitimate son, Guy, arrived in Brussels separately but more or less at the same time. That would be about a month before the battle, sometime in early May. Wellington had already been in Belgium since the 4th April. He must have been very pleased to see Thomas for the two men had known each other for a long time. I don't know if you were aware but Thomas spent several years in the army as a young man and had been in India with Wellington when he was Governor General there. Of course the Duke was plain Arthur Wellesley then

239

– he did not acquire his title until 1804, and certainly he and Thomas would have considered themselves equals, despite Wellington's fame. Wellington was a great believer in the ability of the English upper classes to be natural officers and leaders of men. As well as his army training, Thomas would have had a natural sense of command, as a result of running an estate the size of Chadbrook. In addition he was an excellent horseman and a good shot.'

'Guy was thirty-three years old at the time of Waterloo and was an ideal recruit for Wellington. He had been in the army since he was seventeen and had served under Wellington in the Peninsular Campaign where, despite his extreme youth, he had distinguished himself. The army was the perfect life for Guy. It gave him an established social position, which as the illegitimate son of an Earl he would not otherwise have found easy to acquire. Forgive me,' he said, looking at Prue. 'I'm afraid I know nothing of Guy's mother. Was she of lowly birth?'

'Yes,' said Prue. 'Her father was an innkeeper, but for some reason, which we do not at the moment understand, Guy seems to have spent much of his life living with his father as opposed to his mother.'

'A difficult situation for everyone,' said Max. 'But the army was a great leveller, then as now.' He paused again and sipped his wine. 'I don't know how much you know about the way in which battles were fought in those days. The men slept on the line but the officers always retired to the local town at night, to be given accommodation by families in the area. In the case of Thomas and Guy, the choice of our family was no coincidence. Thomas and my great-great-great-grandmother, La Comtesse Marie-Claire de Villefranche, had been engaged in an affair for some years – certainly, I believe, since the turn of the century. Marie-Claire was widowed very young and had two children – a son, Henri, only a child in 1815 and a daughter who at the time of Waterloo was seventeen – her name was Marcelle. There was plenty of money around and it seems that Marie-Claire led a fairly exotic social life. She was . . . how shall I put it, a very up-market "lady of the town" in some respects, I fear. There was even a rumour that she found favour with Louis XVIII.' Max smiled. 'In any event, Thomas and Guy were billeted at this house for about eight weeks, during which time the four of them, mother and daughter, father and son, were inseparable, attending all the functions of the day and proving enormously popular and in demand.'

'How do you know all this?' Charles said, intrigued.

'Journals, letters, hearsay – our great-grandmother was still alive

240

when we were little and she had many stories to tell. It's really not so long ago, when you start talking to people about the past.'

'No, I suppose not,' said Prue.

'Then of course, I am a historian by trade.' Max smiled. 'I'm not boring you, I hope.'

'No,' said Charles and Prue, in unison.

'Something went wrong around the period of the battle, in terms of the relationship between the four of them. I cannot tell you what happened but I do know that Guy was in some sort of disgrace. Thomas wrote a letter to Marie-Claire on his return to England in which he apologized for his son's behaviour but assured her that he would make an excellent husband to Marcelle. There was a later letter, too, in which clearly Thomas tells Marie-Claire that Guy and he will never meet again. It is a very sad letter, I have it in my briefcase for you to study – but I digress.'

'That's extraordinary,' Prue said. 'My father formed the impression from Guy's letters and journals that he had quarrelled with Thomas. At the time, of course, we did not know they were father and son but we did know that Guy was very much under the patronage of the Earl and yet there was no reference to him once Guy settled back in England. Also, my father felt that in normal circumstances Guy would have named his first son after Thomas, but he did not.'

'Interesting,' said Max. 'Let me tell you what I know. There was some kind of trouble literally just prior to the Duchess of Richmond's Ball. Whatever happened, the direct consequences were that Marcelle and Guy were married on June 15th in the afternoon – the poor young things did not even spend the night together. They attended the Ball and Guy went from there straight to the line.'

'It sounds as though the two of them had been a little indiscreet,' suggested Charles. 'Perhaps Marcelle was pregnant and Guy responsible.'

Max laughed. 'I thought of that, too, but there wouldn't have been time for him to have had his wicked way with her and have a pregnancy confirmed. No, it has to be something else, though I've never been able to discover what. There are hints and innuendos but nothing is clear.' He sighed. '. . . And so to Waterloo. It was fought, you know, in an area of only three square miles and in that small space somewhere between forty and sixty thousand men lost their lives or were wounded. It was a victory for Wellington but the price was appallingly high. They say there were tears in his eyes as he rode back to Brussels, there was no rejoicing, the horror of it all was too stark. Picture if you will the contrast between the life they had been leading, as I've said, and the battlefield – the pelting rain, the mud, the air thick with smoke, the noise of cannons, of shot, screams of men and horses – but through it all came Thomas and Guy. Guy particularly distinguished himself during the French cavalry charge which took place at four o'clock on the afternoon of the battle. The British infantrymen formed themselves into squares. The squares were impregnable because the men in the front upturned their bayonets so that the horses could not pass through. Every time one of the men in the squares fell, he was instantly replaced by another, so that gradually the centre of the squares were filled with dead and dying. It must have been one of the most appalling parts of the battle but the British squares never faltered. Guy's square, which was nearest to La Haye Sainte – the farmhouse Napoleon was desperate to take – suffered worst, but he kept his men together, even reducing the size of his square to keep it impenetrable as his men fell about him – it was a splendid act of courage.' Max paused to allow them to digest what he had been saying. Then he continued. 'The aftermath of the battle must, in its own way, have been equally terrible. Normally, after a battle, the victorious pursue the defeated but in this particular instance, the Prussian troops pursued the enemy. The British were so shattered they had to stay on the battlefield and were forced to camp beside the dead and dying. It must have been ghastly.' There was silence around the table for a few moments. 'And so,' said Max, 'Thomas and Guy returned to England, Guy with his new bride Marcelle de Villefranche, and Thomas to spend what I understand was a lonely old age. Thomas was wounded in the battle and Marie-Claire nursed him back to health though as far as I am aware they never met again, although they did correspond.'

'Yes, I have her letters to him,' said Charles. 'I brought them with me.'

'Have you?' said Max. 'That's marvellous, wonderful! May I study them?'

'Of course,' said Charles. 'That's why I brought them, I thought you might like to keep them for a few months.'

'I am most grateful.' His round, blue eyes shone with enthusiasm. He was a very likeable man.

'So Guy wasn't wounded?' Prue asked.

'No,' said Max. 'Miraculously he escaped without a scratch. I do not have details of Thomas's injuries but he appears to have made a full recovery.'

242

'It's extraordinary,' said Charles. 'I knew Thomas was at Waterloo, of course, but the way you tell it, Max, brings the whole story to life. It makes a difference too, of course, knowing your own family were there.'

'So were many families,' said Max. 'It is so sad, our inability to pass on history to our children and grandchildren. I curse myself many times a day for not having listened to our older relatives' reminiscences, as a child. I loved them, of course, but I had to rely in later years so much on memory – I didn't write them down.'

'Max, as you will see, is the serious member of our family,' said André, with an indulgent smile. He had been surprisingly quiet while Max had been speaking – an odd mixture of a man, Prue thought. He was clearly proud of his brother's knowledge and quite happy for him to be in the limelight, at least for a while.

It was after one by the time the party finally broke up. Prue felt tired but strangely elated. Apart from her genuine interest in the past, she felt the trip to Brussels was doing her good. She had been in a rut, worn down by the daily grind of The Lady in Waiting and locked in her unsatisfactory relationship with Jonathan. And then there was Charles . . . During the whole evening, fascinated though she had been by what Max had to tell them, her thoughts kept returning to Charles's kiss before dinner. Was he truly falling in love with her, and if so, how did she feel? Flattered, yes, surprised, yes again, and elated – strangely elated. Yet her future lay with Jonathan, she was sure of that. Charles was a valued friend and so it was important, no, vital to keep things that way.

They said their goodnights and headed upstairs. At her bedroom door Charles kissed her carefully on the cheek. 'I've enjoyed today enormously,' he said. 'We've learnt a lot, of course, but it's being with you that's made it special. I'm sorry if that sounds a little trite but it's how I feel. I'm too tired and drunk to be subtle.'

'I've enjoyed today, too,' said Prue. 'Thank you for inviting me.' She opened her bedroom door and slipped inside. He did not try to stop her or follow her, just blew her a kiss and wandered off down the corridor towards his room.

Prue found her heart beating unnaturally fast as she shut the door behind her. What had she expected? Had she imagined he would stay and talk, kiss her again, perhaps . . . Her thoughts were in such turmoil, she could not make any sense of how she really felt. She undressed hurriedly, washed and climbed into bed but although she was tired she could not sleep. She had left the curtains open and the moon shone directly across her bedroom. In a desperate attempt to turn her thoughts from Charles she began thinking about Thomas and Guy. She felt particularly close to them in this house, in a way she did not in Suffolk. Perhaps one of them had slept in this very room, she thought. Once again she wondered what sort of family feud had caused the rift between them. It was so sad. And what of Elizabeth? She must have been terrified for them both – her son and her lover at Waterloo, but perhaps Thomas was no longer her lover by then.

There was a sudden noise from the doorway, the door opened slowly and a dark figure crept in. Prue was terrified. 'Who's there?' she cried out.

'It's all right,' Charles whispered. 'It's only me – no phantom, I promise.'

'That's a relief,' said Prue, sitting up in bed. 'I thought for a terrible moment it might be the monstrous André.'

Charles laughed. 'With an insatiable appetite for sex and violence as well as food and drink.'

'Something like that,' said Prue. 'What are you doing here?' She tried to ask the question casually as though a nocturnal visit from Charles was quite normal.

'I couldn't sleep,' said Charles. He came and sat on the edge of her bed. The moonlight cast a shadow across his face so that she could not see his expression.

'Do you want me to turn on the light and read you a bedtime story?' she asked, lightly.

'No,' said Charles. 'I just want to talk.'

'About the past?' said Prue, her mind still full of it.

'No,' said Charles, 'about the present, about the future, about us.'

Prue was instantly on her guard – she must keep Jonathan in the forefront of her mind – Charles was her friend, nothing more. She must not hurt him by letting him imagine anything different. 'There isn't an us, Charles,' she said, gently. 'We're good friends, even relations, but that's it.'

'That may be enough for you but it's not for me,' Charles burst out. 'I'm falling in love with you, Prue, or rather I have fallen in love with you. You're simply the most gorgeous, sweet, attractive, funny, wonderful woman I have ever met in my whole life.'

'It's the wine,' said Prue, still trying to lighten the moment.

'No, it's not the wine. I know you're heavily involved with Jonathan but I'm sure he's not right for you. Give me a chance, Prue, I could

244

love you so well and make you so happy. We're meant to be together, I know it. OK, so I'm a bit of a mess at the moment but with you beside me I could do anything – kill dragons, take on the world, whatever.'

'Oh Charles,' Prue sighed. 'What am I to do with you?'

'Love me a little,' said Charles. The desperation in his voice made her long to comfort him. She must keep talking.

'What do you mean – we're meant to be together?' she asked. Her voice sounded shaky even to her own ears.

Charles brushed the hair back from his forehead – a gesture which she had learnt meant he felt stressed. 'I can't explain it properly, even to you. It's just something that has been growing – a conviction that we must share our lives, be together always. I know it sounds crazy, but I feel so desperate when I think of you marrying Jonathan. It's not how the story is supposed to end, Prue.'

His words reverberated in her head. They were at once familiar as if an echo of her own hidden thoughts. He must have sensed her confusion for he leaned forward and in that moment his face was lit by the moonlight. 'I love you, Prue. I love you so much, please help me put things right – make amends for what I did to you before.' She saw the longing on his face, the desperate love. His words made no sense to her but it did not matter.

She came willingly into his arms, out of kindness and friendship and, despite his words, totally unprepared for the impact her closeness would have upon him. He kissed her, not tenderly as she had expected, but with a harsh hunger that knocked the breath from her body. He pushed her back onto the pillows, covering her body with his, and the sudden vulnerability of her position frightened her. She fought him, dragging her mouth from his, pushing at his chest, but he seemed unaware of her futile attempts to stop him.

He pulled her nightdress from her shoulders and began kissing her bare breasts. She heard a soft moan and realized with astonishment that the sound was her own. He was hampering her, weakening her resolve. No man had ever wanted and needed her like this. He kissed her again and suddenly her arms were about him, drawing him to her.

The sky was already lightening when they woke. They lay on their sides staring at one another for a long time, wordless, utterly content, caught up in a magical web of their own making. What they had done seemed so right, so inevitable that no doubts clouded their minds. They moved together again, familiar with one another now,

245

adding their lovemaking to the rich tapestry of the chateau, making their own contribution to the destiny of their families.

CHAPTER TWENTY-SEVEN

The magic lasted on the flight back to Heathrow, through Customs, into the air terminal and even during the hassle which accompanied trying to find Charles's old Landrover in the terminal car park. It was only as London slipped away, and they headed north-east on the M11 towards Suffolk, that reality started to return. Prue began thinking of the inn, wondering what crisis might have occurred in her absence, whether Jonathan had telephoned or worse . . . whether he had already returned. What she would do, what she would say to him, how did she feel . . .

They had hardly spoken at all in the car and it was Charles who at last raised the thoughts that were uppermost in both their minds. 'So where do we go from here?'

'I don't know,' said Prue.

'After last night . . . how do you feel about Jonathan?'

Prue glanced at Charles. He was apparently relaxed, concentrating on nothing more than the road ahead, but his knuckles were white where his hands were clenched on the steering wheel. Faced with such tension, she knew it was wrong to try to fob him off – she had to answer him truthfully, if only she knew what the truth was. 'Jonathan went to New York to try to start divorce proceedings so that he will be free to marry me,' she said, carefully.

'And if he returns, or indeed has already returned, with the news that he has been successful, will you accept his proposal?' Again Charles's voice sounded casual but Prue was not fooled.

'If you'd asked me that question twenty-four hours ago, I suppose I would have said yes. Now I'm not sure.'

'All right,' said Charles. 'Let's take it a stage further. *My* divorce is through and so I am already a free agent. If I asked you to marry me, would you accept?'

'That's an impossible question,' said Prue. 'For a start, you're not asking me to marry you – wisely because we've known each other such a very short time. So, how can I possibly say one way or the other? Please, Charles, I know this is very difficult for both of us but

247

you have to give me a little time. What happened is so disorientating. I know last night was important, at least to me, but I can't decide what should happen next without first slotting back into the real world in order to think things through.'

'The real world being Jonathan, I suppose,' said Charles.

'Up to a point, yes, but also my job, my normal way of life – don't you feel the same?'

'I don't have a normal way of life at the moment and that's the trouble,' said Charles. 'I'm marking time, trying to see the way ahead and not succeeding too well.'

'Tell me about it,' said Prue. 'I know so little about you really.'

'There's not much to know,' said Charles. 'In any case I think I've told you most of it.'

'No, you haven't,' said Prue. 'You haven't really told me anything about you. Please – who knows, maybe I can help.'

It was dark and there was very little traffic on the road. They were in a state of limbo, caught between their extraordinary few days in Brussels, and the return of reality. It was a good moment to talk.

'My mother and father were not happy,' said Charles. 'My father, in many respects, was a man to be greatly admired and he was tough as old boots. He made a first career out of the army and had a brilliant war. In 1951 he retired and took up responsibility for the estate, out of which he made a second highly successful career. He really transformed Chadbrook from the ramshackle run-down estate it had been in my grandfather's day, to a well-run highly profitable organization. My mother, by contrast, was a gentle, rather arty soul. Her idea of bliss was to sit in the garden in the summer, wearing a large panama hat, painting moderately good pictures of flora and fauna. It was a hobby which infuriated my father. Everything for him had to be action and he saw sitting still for five minutes as a waste of time. Goodness knows how they ever came to be married – two people less suited to one another, it is hard to imagine.' He paused for a moment and Prue did not interrupt him. 'The problem was compounded by the fact that their children were not a mixture of them both – James, my elder brother, was my father all over again, while I favoured my mother. In a divided marriage, each having a child made in their own image, divided the family still further. James and my father poured scorn on everything that didn't involve a great deal of energetic activity. My mother and I, bullied and hounded, just accepted the role of victim and did the best we could.'

'It doesn't sound like the blueprint for happy families,' said Prue.

'It wasn't,' Charles agreed. 'I was always a disappointment to my father. When I was very small I tried to be like James but by the time I reached the bolshy teens, I was damned if I was going to conform and I imagine I became fairly difficult. The main problem was that my father used my shortcomings as a weapon with which to beat my mother. My parents were always looking for ways to war with one another and I, of course, was the perfect subject. I was very unhappy at Eton, in fact I ran away on one occasion, but I did quite well academically and was offered a place at Trinity College, Oxford, to read English. I think that was the only time my father ever acknowledged that I'd done well – both he and James were very practical men but neither were terribly academic.'

'Did you enjoy university?' Prue asked.

'Very much. It was good for my ego. I had a splendid time socially and I did well academically. I spent most of my vacations in France. I love the French way of life and I already had the idea that I would be a novelist. I used to spend many happy and fruitless hours with a pen and empty notebook in hand, sitting in cafes watching the world go by, pretending I was studying life. I don't know, maybe I was. Anyway, university ended and that's when the trouble started. My father had a lot of contacts in the City and wanted me to go for a proper job. He suggested banking, insurance, you name it. I refused and said I was going to be a writer. We had an almighty row, he told me he would not support me any further and I told him that was fair enough and took the next ferry to France. My mother was very upset and I never saw her again – she died eighteen months later.'

'How sad – it was a brave thing to do, Charles,' Prue offered.

Charles shrugged his shoulders. 'Self-indulgent more like. I worked my way down to the South of France and spent the summer serving in bars and restaurants. By the winter I had a little money saved and found myself a permanent apartment in Antibes. I knew I could not survive the whole winter on the money I had earned but I set to and started to write my first book, thinking that something would come up before the money ran out, and it did.'

'What happened?' Prue asked.

'My grandmother died, my mother's mother, and for the first time my mother inherited some money of her own. Without telling my father, she sent me a cheque for five thousand pounds. Ten years ago that was a lot of money. God bless her, I don't know what I'd have done without her.'

249

'Did you have immediate success with your writing?'

'More or less, and that first winter when I was just twenty-two, I met a girl. I used to help out in the cafe opposite my apartment on busy evenings and she was there on her own one night – she had just broken up with her boyfriend. She knew the patron of the cafe and had come to drown her sorrows. We got talking, her name was Evette. She was training to be an accountant – a bright girl. She, too, was very broke and when she heard I was a writer, she asked whether she could type up my manuscript, to earn extra money. I was only too happy to let her. She was bilingual – her lover had been English. The whole thing worked very well. By the end of the winter I had a finished manuscript and found a publisher, and we had fallen in love and decided to marry.'

At his words, Prue felt a strange twisting in the gut. Was she jealous then of this former wife and if so what did it mean? 'So you married?' she said.

'Yes, in the spring, and our life took on a predictable pattern, perhaps with hindsight, too predictable. From then on Evette struggled with her exams, I wrote all winter and worked in bars all summer. It was a good life, it suited me though it was hardly the ideal training ground for the future Earl of Clare.'

'And you gave it up because your brother died.'

'Not entirely,' said Charles. There was a pause then for so long that Prue wondered whether she should break the silence. Eventually Charles spoke. 'Unknown to me, Evette had been having an affair with a man at work for some years. When my father died and I came back to Suffolk for the funeral, it gave Evette time to think. She was quite sure she wouldn't want to move to Suffolk with me, France was her home, so when I came back she told me of the affair and suggested we should split.'

'It must have come as an awful shock.'

'Yes, I suppose it did,' said Charles. 'Yet in a strange way I suppose her decision made things easier. I knew then there was no escape, I had to return to Chadbrook.'

'And you returned from France a stranger in your own home,' Prue said.

'That's it exactly. You see before James's death I never expected to come home. My life was in France with Evette and that's where I expected to end my days. Now, here I am, totally ill-equipped to do a job which should have been my brother's. In a strange way, it's not just the present I find intimidating, it's the past. Take Thomas

– from what we've learnt of him, it seems likely that he married, if not twice, at least once, purely to acquire sufficient money to keep Chadbrook going. Neither of us will know the extent to which he loved his Elizabeth and the Villefranche woman. Maybe he was just a wicked old womanizer but I don't think either of us believe it. He made sacrifices, Prue, sacrifices that meant that today I can call myself the Earl of Clare and Master of Chadbrook. I owe it to Thomas to succeed. The question is how, with the millstone of tax bills round my neck?'

'You'll just have to do it,' said Prue. 'You'll have to find a way, Charles.'

'There is no way. As I've told you before, I just cannot see how anything can be done to raise sufficient funds. The estate is being run very efficiently. My father was a good manager and gradually as James began to take over from him, he modernized and improved almost every aspect of the estate. That's the devil of it, you see, he spent a great deal of capital on modernization, capital which I desperately need now to pay the taxes. There isn't anything of significance that can be done to streamline or improve the running of the estate, believe me.'

'I understand that,' said Prue. 'But how about selling off part of the land, wouldn't that work?'

'Well, yes, but it would have to be most of the land rather than part of it. It's not a big estate, Chadbrook, only just over a thousand acres.' Prue whistled. 'I'm sorry, that was rather a blasé statement. I mean it's not big by big country house standards. If I sold off sufficient acreage to pay for the death duties, I'd be talking about seven or eight hundred acres. That would leave a farming concern so small that it would not be large enough to support the house, which as you can imagine needs a great deal of upkeep.'

'Then you're going to have to open it to the public,' said Prue.

'I've thought of that, too,' said Charles. 'But a few shillings every day from curious visitors is not going to solve the problem. We're talking big money, Prue.'

'Then you're going to have to raise big money. I don't just mean opening the house and grounds as they stand – you'll have to provide amenities, go commercial, really rake in the cash.'

'I wouldn't know where to start,' said Charles. 'I've had absolutely no experience of that type of thing.'

'Charles, you're being defeatist. I'm sure if we really put our minds

251

to it we could come up with a workable scheme that would bring in some real money.'

'We?'

'I could help you, I suppose,' Prue said, suddenly aware of what she had said. 'There is so much you could do . . . you have the lake which you could turn into a boating lake. You could build a restaurant on the banks – I could certainly help with that. You could consider turning part of the house into a hotel.' Charles winced. 'Maybe it isn't what you want to do, Charles, but if it's going to save Chadbrook then you must try.'

'I suppose so.' He sighed. 'You know, Prue, with you beside me, maybe I could. On my own, with no one to share it, the task seems impossible.'

'That is not a very fair thing to say,' said Prue. 'It's blackmail.'

'I'm sorry,' said Charles. 'But it's how I feel.'

Arriving back at The Lady in Waiting was something of an anti-climax. Naturally, Prue had told no one that Charles would be accompanying her on her trip to Brussels, simply that she had friends there whom she had been promising to visit for a long time, and had received a sudden invitation. There appeared to have been no major dramas in her absence, though clearly everybody was pleased to see her back. Only Martha was curious for details of her trip and Prue had some difficulty avoiding her questions.

Having changed and unpacked, Prue joined Terry in the bar. 'Has Jonathan rung while I've been away?' she asked, as casually as she could manage.

'Yes,' said Terry. 'I told him you were in Brussels and he seemed surprised.' He grinned. 'He said he hadn't expected us to be able to manage without you both, bloody cheek.'

'Does he want me to ring him?'

'He said he'd call you tonight.'

'That's fine then,' said Prue. 'Did he say when he was coming back?'

'No, he didn't. We had to have a fairly brief conversation because the bar was full and I was rushed off my feet.'

Terry had improved, Prue had to admit. His time at The Lady in Waiting had softened him, knocked off some of the rough edges. He was efficient, hard-working and nobody's fool. While she knew she could never really like him, Prue did admit a growing respect.

Her mind was so full of the trip to Brussels, her relationship with

252

Charles and the success or otherwise of Jonathan's mission, that her first evening back at the inn passed in a flash. It was only as she and Edward were locking up that she realized Jonathan had not telephoned, nor did she feel particularly heart-broken. As usual, Edward offered to stay the night but she declined his offer and bolted the bar doors behind her.

It was at that moment it hit her, almost before she could turn from the door – screaming, blinding misery and grief, so strong and all-encompassing that it made her gasp aloud as she met the emotion head-on. She was not up to this, she had problems of her own, she could not cope with another person's feelings – not these feelings anyway. 'Elizabeth,' she whispered. 'Please go away. Please leave me alone, I have problems, too.' She listened . . . there was a chilling silence broken by a log shifting in the fireplace which made her jump. It seemed suddenly as though someone was listening, the air grew chill, she could hear the wind whistling outside. A strange clattering noise began which was instantly familiar, and all at once, like a half-forgotten memory, her childhood visit to the inn flooded back into her mind, dug up from where she had filed it so many years before. The inn as it stood today disappeared before her eyes, only the fireplace remained. There were rushes on the floor, a piece of meat roasted in the hearth, all around her were the sounds of harsh voices but she could see no one. There was the stench of smoke and unwashed bodies, of horse dung . . . she had to get out. She ran from the room – not through the hall to the stairs, for the door was no longer there, but through the door which led into the kitchen. The moment she entered the kitchen it was over. The lights were still on and the room was as Martha had left it. There was no hint of another century, the noises faded from her ears. Her heart was beating like a drum, tears were running down her face and she was shaking uncontrollably.

She stood in the kitchen a long time, trying to steel herself to return to the bar – it was her only way upstairs. At last, nervously, she went back to the kitchen door which she had slammed shut in her terror. She opened it gingerly. The bar was as before – not stopping to turn out the kitchen light, not stopping for anything, she ran swiftly across the room, through the door she could now see at the end of the room, into the hall and up the stairs. Seconds later she was in her own room, in her own time, safe. She undressed slowly, already beginning to wonder whether she had dreamed the whole incident, yet she knew she had not. Not only had she seen the bar as it had once been but

253

it was not the first time she had seen it thus. She climbed into her side of the bed and looked at the empty space where Jonathan should have been. Yet it was not of Jonathan she thought, but of Charles. She could not think of the night she had spent with Charles as being unfaithful to Jonathan, but of course she had been. Her mind was muddled, her emotions confused, she was very tired. Gradually, she calmed down and began to feel drowsy and no one's fears and sorrow's troubled her again as she slipped into sleep.

'I'm sorry, I shouldn't have come,' Prue said. 'But I needed to talk.'

Charles emerged from behind a desk full of papers, his face lighting up with obvious pleasure. 'Prue! How wonderful to see you. Don't apologize.' He came round from behind the desk, bent and kissed her briefly on the lips.

Mrs. Plum, hovering in the doorway, cleared her throat. 'Will you be wanting coffee?'

'No, thank you,' said Prue. 'I can't stay long, I must be back at the inn for the lunchtime session.'

'As you wish.' She sniffed and disappeared.

'I don't think you should have kissed me in front of Mrs. Plum,' Prue said.

'Nosey old bat, at least it will give her something to think about.' Charles smiled. 'I'm spending the morning going through the accounts again and I was feeling very dreary until you arrived. Come and sit down, you look tired.'

'I am tired,' said Prue.

Charles's library was a lovely room. Oak-panelled bookshelves lined three sides and the fourth wall, consisting mainly of a large window, overlooked the park, in front of which stood his desk. At the opposite end of the room was a large fireplace and a couple of easy chairs, leather-bound like in a man's club. Prue sank gratefully into one of these now.

'You may have refused coffee but you can't refuse a drink. I think a glass of sherry is what you need.' She didn't argue. Charles poured two glasses and came and sat beside her. 'So, to what do I owe the honour of your visit?'

'A strange thing happened to me last night,' Prue said, 'and I need to talk it through.' She told Charles, as carefully and as unemotionally as she could, about what had taken place on the previous evening. He listened in silence, questioning her occasionally. When she had finished, she looked up at him anxiously. 'You don't think I'm going mad, do you?'

'No, I don't,' said Charles. 'But I think it is becoming increasingly important that we find out what happened to Elizabeth – until we know that, you can't very well exorcize the ghost, can you?'

'If that's what I have to do,' said Prue, wearily.

'But surely it is – isn't that the whole point?'

'Yes, yes I suppose you're right. Certainly I would like to give her some peace.'

Charles stared at her curiously. 'Do you honestly believe you can?'

'I don't know. I just feel she's a poor, miserable soul, still wandering around and it's up to me to do something in my century to ease the pain of whatever it was she suffered in hers. After all, I am, her great-great-great-great-great-granddaughter. How many greats is that, have I got it right?'

Charles smiled. 'More or less, I think.'

'You're laughing at me,' said Prue.

'A little, perhaps, but I do understand what you're saying. Whether you believe in ghosts or not – whether you see them as headless phantoms or merely sense their emotions as you clearly do – there has to be a reason why nearly two hundred years later, Elizabeth is still around and, as I've said before, I do believe she is your ghost simply because you do.'

'It is Elizabeth, Charles, I know it is. When I spoke to her last night, when I called out her name, it was then that she conjured up the past for me, I'm sure of it.' It was only as Prue put her thoughts into words that she realized how much she believed them.

'Then we must find out what happened to her,' said Charles. 'You're leading a much busier life than me at present, let me do some more digging around. I don't quite know where I'll start but perhaps the local library might produce something. Will you let me?'

'Of course, gladly,' said Prue. 'I have to admit that this whole business seems to be taking me over,' she looked away, 'and I feel I have enough emotional upheavals of my own to cope with at the moment, without having to take on board someone else's, particularly from another century.' She tried a smile but it didn't really work.

'Meaning me and Jonathan?'

'Meaning you and Jonathan,' said Prue. 'But I don't want to talk about that, not this morning, Charles, I really don't.'

'But we have to talk about it sometime,' said Charles. 'I didn't sleep much last night either, tossing and turning, thinking that he

255

might have returned, that you might be in his bed – I couldn't bear the thought. *Is* he back from New York?'

'No,' said Prue.

'If he had been, what would have happened last night?'

'Oh Charles, I don't know. Please, you must give me some breathing space to try to work out how I feel. I've no idea how I would have reacted.'

'But surely . . .' Charles began.

'Please, Charles, please drop it.'

'I can't,' he burst out. He stood up and began striding about. 'Look, I thought I loved Evette, I'm sure I did in a sort of adolescent way, but this thing with you is different. I appreciate we haven't known each other very long and even then we've spent most of the time trying to piece together the story of our ancestors rather than building a story of our own. Nonetheless, we have something, something very precious. I know it, I know it as strongly as you know the feelings you experience at the inn belong to Elizabeth. We're meant to be together, Prue, we're meant to marry and have children. I don't know whether I, too, have been affected by what happened in the past, whether it's influencing me at all, or whether I'm just simply Charles Chadbrook in love with Prue Mansell. But I am in love with you, Prue, and I want to marry you, and the thought of you spending your life with that idiot Jonathan appals me. I know it's not meant to happen.'

'It's not fair to start abusing Jonathan, Charles. You don't even know him, you've never even met.'

'He's not making you happy.'

'But that's not his fault,' said Prue. 'He's not making me happy because he's married to somebody else at the moment. If I'd met you a year ago the same would have applied to you, wouldn't it?' There was an angry silence between them. 'In any case I must go,' said Prue. 'I shouldn't have come.'

'You should have come, you must always come to me if you need anything, however great, however small. Can I take you out to dinner tonight?'

'No,' said Prue, 'I have to work and I must contact Jonathan and find out what's going on.'

'Then tomorrow night?'

'No, Charles, I need time to think.'

'But I love you.'

Prue raised tired eyes to his. She was standing too now, leaning heavily on the back of one of the chairs as if needing the support. 'I know you do, Charles, and I'm flattered. No, a horrible word, I'm honoured that you do care about me, but for pity's sake, if you really love me, leave me alone, let me work this thing out on my own.'

'I can't,' said Charles. 'I can't take the risk.'

Prue gave a weary sigh. 'Then I'll just have to order you out of my life. Don't contact me again, Charles, I mean that. I'll be in touch with you when I have something to say.' She turned and left the room.

He was about to follow her when commonsense prevailed. Instead, he walked to the window, and craning his neck he was just able to see a patch of drive. In a moment or two, he was rewarded by the sight of her little blue Fiat as she drove round the bend in the drive, out of his sight, perhaps even out of his life, if he let her.

If he let her . . . the words seemed to hang in the air. All his life, to date, Charles had let life happen to him, making no attempt to alter events, to influence his destiny in any way. When Evette had told him she was leaving him, he had made no effort to fight for her. He thought of that now – was it because he had not loved her enough, because he recognized the futility of trying to change her mind, was it lack of confidence in his own persuasive powers or simply inertia? What a bloody idiot he had been, just at the moment when Prue had come to him for comfort and reassurance he had blown it, pressurizing her when her mind was already a mass of confusion. What had he expected . . . that she would fall into his arms declaring undying love? He had always prided himself on being reasonable, in tune with other people's feelings. As a writer, he made a good listener – yet when he had needed to be at his most sensitive, he had messed things up.

He sat down heavily at his desk again, pushing the columns of figures away. What was it that made him feel so desperate about the relationship when they knew each other so little – *was* the past influencing him in some way? He looked around the room. Thomas Chadbrook must have sat here at this very desk thinking of Elizabeth – it was a strange notion. He relaxed a little, leant back in his chair and studied the desk. It was a wonderful old piece of furniture, pockmarked with cigar burns, scratches and knocks. Slightly to the right, there was a huge ink stain which presumably had been caused by the knocking over of an inkwell sometime in the desk's history. Probably it had been a child. He smiled slightly – there must have been a row about that.

257

Thomas . . . what would he have done in these circumstances – would he have waited for Prue to come back to him or would he have pursued her? Would he perhaps have confronted Jonathan? He dismissed the idea. What could he possibly say to the American, presuming he could even find him? Jonathan Lindstrom of Lindstrom's Bank – it would not be difficult, he realized. A call to the bank either here or in New York should elicit his address without too much of a problem. The idea began to take hold. If he wanted Prue, really wanted Prue, it was clear he was going to have to fight for her. For the first time in his life, he needed to be the one to take action. He would go to New York, talk to Jonathan, persuade him to stay where he belonged, to leave Prue alone. Fleetingly he wondered how Prue would feel when she found out that he had meddled in her relationship – and then again, perhaps Jonathan was already on his way back to England. It was a risk, but then life was a risk and, in a moment of clarity, Charles realized that all his life he had simply been an observer, not a player. The time had come to change all that.

CHAPTER TWENTY-EIGHT
New York – April 1982

The approach to Manhattan from Newark airport was a new experience for Charles. He had been to New York only once before and on that occasion had flown in to Kennedy. Now as he sat in a yellow cab, watching the Manhattan skyline come up to greet him, he felt a surprising tinge of excitement. The time for self-doubt was over, he had made his commitment to find Jonathan Lindstrom and now the indecision had gone he felt a surprising degree of self-confidence and calm. This trip to New York was very different from his last when he had come with a group of friends as an impoverished student, during the summer vacation of his second year. Then he had slept on the floor of an attic in Greenwich Village, now he was booked into a suite at the Carlyle. The decision to stay at arguably New York's best hotel was quite deliberate for he had decided to play the Earl of Clare for all it was worth, recognizing it could be his winning card. It was strange really, he had never anticipated either the need or the inclination shamelessly to use his title yet he felt perfectly justified in exploiting his position in any way that would help Prue.

Having checked into the hotel, feeling tired and more than a little jet-lagged, he ordered room service – a bottle of champagne and a plate of smoked salmon sandwiches. What the hell, he felt justified in spoiling himself. Then he lay back on the bed, television turned low to watch the flickering images, his mind a million miles away. He had told no one but Mrs. Plum of his whereabouts, fearing that somehow Prue might come to hear he was in New York and instantly guess the reason for his visit. Mrs. Plum had handled the privileged information surprisingly well, accepting his explanation of a business meeting and promising faithfully to tell no one, absolutely no one of his whereabouts.

He had not the least idea what he was going to say to Jonathan Lindstrom. He was very clear on his objective – his aim was to stop him returning to England and ensure that he left Prue alone in the future – and while he did not know what he was going to say, he did know what he was going to do. A little research had told him that the bank was still run by Jonathan's mother, Harriet, and it was with her he was going to start.

At ten o'clock the following morning, Charles presented himself to Lindstrom's main branch on Wall Street. He approached the enquiry desk. 'I would like to see Mrs. Harriet Lindstrom, please,' he said.

'Do you have an appointment?' the girl asked, in a bored voice.

'No.'

'I'm sorry, I'm afraid Mrs. Lindstrom sees no one without an appointment. If you would like to tell me the nature of your business, I will see if I can arrange for someone else to talk with you.'

'No,' said Charles. 'It's Mrs. Lindstrom I wish to see. Would you kindly tell her that my name is Charles Chadbrook, Earl of Clare, and I've come all the way from England quite specifically to see her.'

The girl stared at him, open-mouthed. 'Yes, sir,' she said, 'right away.'

It works, Charles thought, trying to suppress a smile, and sure enough, within a few minutes he was escorted up to the palatial Lindstrom president's suite and to Harriet Lindstrom herself. She was tiny, a little sparrow of a woman with a clever face and unusual pale blue eyes. She came out from behind an enormous desk and extended a hand. 'Welcome to Lindstrom's Bank, Earl,' she said. Then she smiled, 'Oh dear, I don't know how to address you. Do I call you Sir or Your Highness or what?'

Charles laughed, he liked her instantly. 'Charles will do.'

Harriet smiled. It was a surprisingly warm smile. 'Charles it is then. Come and sit down. Coffee?'

'No thanks, I've just had some at my hotel.'

They sat in easy chairs opposite each other and regarded one another in silence for a moment. 'I'm rather hoping you've come to see me because you wish to move your account to Lindstrom's Bank. I have to confess a quick referral to *Who's Who* informs me you have a large estate in Suffolk. Are you perhaps planning a move to America?'

Charles laughed aloud, greatly admiring her direct manner. 'No such luck, I'm afraid.' He hesitated; his plan had been to pretend that he wished a financial involvement in The Lady in Waiting and therefore required Jonathan's address in order to discuss the matter. Suddenly he realized that this excuse was not going to work. Harriet Lindstrom was too shrewd – only the truth would do. 'Mrs. Lindstrom I'm here because I need your help on a personal matter. I've . . . fallen in love with a girl named Prue.'

It was Harriet's turn to laugh. 'Have you now? Well congratulations, Charles.'

He ignored her flippancy. 'Prue Mansell runs The Lady in Waiting in Long Melford, Suffolk.'

'Ah,' said Harriet. The smile left her face. 'Jonathan's Prue,' she said.

'My Prue, I hope,' said Charles.

'Go on,' said Harriet. She shifted uneasily in her chair; clearly the mention of her son had touched a raw nerve.

'As I understand it,' said Charles, 'your son, Jonathan, is in New York at the moment. The reason for his visit, or so he told Prue, is to seek a divorce from his wife. While he has been away, Prue and I – who have been friends for some time – have recognized our relationship could be more than that. Prue, however, is a very loyal and honourable person and as far as she is concerned, she has made a commitment to Jonathan. I am here, to be honest, because I hope to be able to release her from that commitment. I don't believe Jonathan is right for her because he makes her unhappy and I'm very sorry if you find this an offensive thing to say about your son but it's the truth. They come from two very different worlds, they seem to have very different expectations of one another and ever since Jonathan has been in New York, he has made no attempt to contact Prue and so she doesn't know what's going on. I love her and I wish to make her my wife. All I'm asking you to do is to give me your son's address, so that I can go and see him and try to persuade him to give her up.' He smiled disarmingly. 'I was going to tell you quite another story but having met you I can see that nothing but the truth will do.'

Harriet sighed, stood up and walked to the window. She stared out of it for some moments – Charles held his breath. 'Of course I'll give you my son's address,' she said at last. 'But I can save you a lot of time by telling you he's here, in the bank, right now. We patched up our differences and he has started working for Lindstrom's again.'

'Really!' Charles did not know how to react – whether to be pleased at his good fortune or apprehensive of the meeting which now clearly was going to take place.

'I think perhaps I should tell you a little about what's been going on here, Charles, to forewarn you certainly, and perhaps help you, I don't know.' She came back and sat down in the chair opposite

Charles. 'Jonathan, to all intents and purposes, is back with his wife, Jo.'

Charles felt his heart leap. 'Really? Are you sure?'

'Yes, of course I'm sure,' Harriet said, 'I'm his mother.' Her sudden flash of irritation made Charles realize that Harriet must be a very formidable woman when angry.

'Of course, I'm sorry,' said Charles, 'I'm just well . . . pleased and relieved. I wonder if he's told Prue yet?'

'Wait a moment,' said Harriet. 'It's not that simple. Jonathan's back with his wife because . . .' she hesitated. 'I don't want to make you privy to the problems of our family but we have a few skeletons in the cupboard and, to be frank, Jo has blackmailed him into going back to her.' Charles was shocked and Harriet noted his expression. 'Oh, don't get me wrong, she loves the guy but she's a tough lady and in order to keep him she has taken out some insurance – it's as simple as that. As for Jonathan, just because he's my son, it doesn't mean to say I don't recognize his weaknesses. He goes for the easy life. Jo is a very attractive woman and a businesswoman in her own right. Her home is beautiful, she entertains very well and she doesn't want the complications of children which I think pleases Jonathan because in many ways he's still a child himself. Having said all that, I don't think he's about to give up your Prue either and I don't think it worries Jo too much – if you like, Prue is Jonathan's insurance. I think he has come to really like English country life, it's such a contrast from Manhattan. He's obviously very taken with your Prue and it's my belief he'll string her along, for a while.'

'But that's terrible!' said Charles.

'It's terrible to a man like you – to Jonathan it's simply a way of life.'

They were both silent for a moment. Charles stood up abruptly. 'Then the sooner I see Jonathan and force him to be honest with Prue, the better.'

'Yes,' said Harriet. 'I'll call him right now and tell him you wish to see him. I won't tell him what it's about. Surprise will help your cause.'

Charles smiled at her. 'You're being very kind.'

Harriet went over to the telephone and dialled. 'Jonathan. I have someone here I would like you to see. Yes now, right now. No I'm not going to tell you what it's about. He'll tell you himself, but believe me it's in your own interests to see him.' She listened for a moment. 'The Earl of Clare. Yes, that's right, a real English Earl. He's on his

262

way up.' She put down the phone. 'That's fixed him,' she said, smiling.

'I don't like using my title but it's useful on these sort of occasions,' Charles admitted.

'You use everything you can to win your Prue. She's a lucky lady to have you caring for her this much. Please God she doesn't waste any more time with Jonathan.'

'That's a strange thing for a mother to say,' Charles said.

'Yes . . .' said Harriet, a little wistfully. 'But to be honest, Charles, I . . . well, I could do with a man like you for a son, rather than the one I've got.'

Charles smiled. 'It's interesting,' he said, 'but my life would have been a lot different if I'd had someone like you for my mother.'

'Touché,' said Harriet, delightedly. She held out her hand. 'Good-bye and good luck.'

Charles took her hand. 'I don't know what the hell I'm going to say to him, to persuade him.'

'You'll think of something,' said Harriet. 'You've come this far.'

He was a good-looking man, Charles was forced to admit, with his mother's pale blue eyes in stark contrast to his dark hair. He was slightly shorter than Charles but more thickset and instantly made Charles feel scruffy in his old tweed jacket, for Jonathan was immaculately dressed in a dark grey Italian silk suit. They shook hands and Jonathan motioned Charles to a chair. 'Would you care for a coffee or something stronger?' Charles shook his head. 'My mother was most mysterious about you,' said Jonathan, obviously at ease. 'I'm very honoured to have a real live Earl in my office. How may I help you?'

'I want you to leave Prue Mansell alone,' said Charles. He watched the surprise come into Jonathan's face but there was no real sense of disquiet. It was a scene he must have played before, Charles thought bitterly.

'Why should I do that?' Jonathan asked, carefully.

'Because I understand from your mother that you are now back with your wife and that you've taken up the threads of your old life, by rejoining the bank. There is obviously not going to be much time for you to spend in Suffolk. I love Prue and want to marry her.'

'Ah, so that's how the land lies.' Jonathan smirked, and Charles had the over-riding desire to hit him, hard. 'Prue and I have been together a good long time and I don't think she's about to jack in

263

our relationship for you or anyone else. She's never mentioned you and I have to say I think you're wasting your time – she belongs to me.'

'So, you feel perfectly justified in having a woman either side of the Atlantic?' said Charles, in disgust.

'The *rapprochement* with my wife is only on a trial basis. Things may not work out, in which case I will make my home permanently in England and marry Prue.'

His arrogance infuriated Charles. 'That's not what I understand from your mother,' he said. 'She tells me that your wife is holding you to some sort of ransom, that she's blackmailing you against the disclosure of some skeletons in your cupboard you'd rather keep locked away.'

'She told you that?' said Jonathan, clearly rattled for the first time.

'Yes, she did,' said Charles.

'Well, that only goes to prove what kind of a woman my wife is and why I am sure you understand I would prefer to spend my life with someone like Prue. I'm sorry if you've come all the way to New York to talk me out of this relationship, because you're wasting your time.'

'Have you been in touch with Prue yet, to tell her what's happening?'

'I rather think that's my business not yours.'

His reply lit the fuse that Charles needed to galvanize him into action. 'I understand you're back working for the bank,' he said.

'On a part-time basis,' said Jonathan. 'Obviously I'm keeping a watching brief on The Lady in Waiting and my mother recognizes I will have to visit Suffolk several times a year.' Again he smirked. 'However, it's very important I keep abreast of events at the bank since I will be taking over as president when my mother retires, in the not too distant future.'

This disclosure was just what Charles needed. Suddenly, from nowhere an idea flashed into his mind. 'If you don't leave Prue alone, you won't have a bank to be president of.'

'On come on,' said Jonathan, laughing.

'I know the aristocracy plays no part in the American way of life, which is all income,' said Charles. 'But in England, as I am sure you will have noticed, it's still a major influence. I can finish Lindstrom's Bank in the City, within a week. My god-father is Governor of the Bank of England, and my word in the City can wrap up your London operation in days. I can't imagine that you can cut your losses in

London without serious detriment to the overall financial structure of the bank, not to say the general lack of confidence the collapse of the London end would engender in your whole operation. If you don't believe me, Mr. Lindstrom, try me. I'm flying out of New York this evening. By the time I reach Suffolk tomorrow, if you haven't telephoned Prue and ended your relationship, then I'm going to start making some calls.' The threat was a complete lie – Charles did not even know the identity of the Governor of the Bank of England, but he was so enjoying Jonathan's obvious discomfiture that he found himself slipping quite naturally into the role of a City whizzkid.

There was a long silence. 'OK, OK,' said Jonathan, with a sigh. 'Supposing I go along with you, what do you propose I do about The Lady in Waiting?'

'Sell it,' said Charles, 'Prue won't be needing it. She'll be coming to live at Chadbrook as my wife.'

'I wouldn't be too sure of that,' said Jonathan. 'She doesn't know you're here, I presume.'

'No,' Charles admitted.

'She's an independent lady, I'm not sure she's going to take too kindly to you meddling in her private life.'

'I have a right to meddle in her private life,' said Charles.

Jonathan shrugged his shoulders as the two men rose. 'England's a godforsaken country anyway,' he said, as they reached his office door.

'It's a hell of a lot better than this jungle,' said Charles. He opened the door. 'We have a deal, then?'

Jonathan nodded. 'OK, but I still reckon you're going to be the loser, and if Prue comes running back to me, you're just going to have to accept it.'

CHAPTER TWENTY-NINE
Chadbrook – October 1789

The boy did not look well, Thomas was forced to admit. He was unusually pale and appeared much thinner than when he had arrived five weeks before. There was a sadness about him – he had done some growing up. 'So, how do you fare, Guy?' Thomas asked gently.

The boy stood stiffly before him. His joyful spontaneity had gone and he was clearly no longer relaxed in his father's company. 'I am well, thank you sir.'

'You do not look well. Are you eating?'

'Yes, sir.'

'Perhaps you are not having enough exercise. Would it suit you to spend less time in the school room and more out riding that pony of yours?'

Guy brightened a little. 'Yes, sir, that would suit me very well.'

'Then I shall arrange it. And tell me, are you becoming acquainted with my wife and Christopher?' Guy's eyes slid away from where they had briefly met his father's. For some time he said nothing. 'Tell me, Guy, tell me the truth,' Thomas insisted.

'They do not like me,' Guy managed at last.

'I am sure that is not true,' Thomas began and then instantly regretted the platitude. Of course they did not like him. 'It is not easy for them,' he said, after a pause. 'You are so like me in many ways and Christopher is not. It is hardly surprising that he is jealous of you. As for my wife . . . she understandably is not happy about the relationship I shared with your mother.'

Guy took a deep breath and squared his shoulders. 'I am very grateful, sir, for your hospitality, but I would like to go home now. I must search for my mother. I do not believe she is dead and it concerns me that she may come home and find me absent. I have to find her, sir, I have to.' His voice betrayed his desperation.

'Goddammit,' said Thomas, jumping to his feet. 'You are but a child, it is not your job to find her, it is mine.' He slammed his fist down on the table. He was angry not with the boy but with himself. His thumb caught the edge of the open inkwell, turning the pot on its side. The ink gushed out and for a moment father and son watched as the stain crept into the woodwork. Thomas righted the inkwell, trying hard to calm himself. 'Guy, it is I who have been remiss. I am your father, it is my responsibility to find your mother. I have been very much lacking in my duty in recent weeks, both in tending to your welfare and in seeking your mother. It is a busy time of year, the harvest. . .' His voice trailed away. None of the excuses he could conjure up, he knew, would sound true to Guy's ears. He had been avoiding yet another confrontation with Beatrice, telling himself that it would not be in Guy's best interests to anger her further. She had always been a difficult woman and now she was deeply suspicious of his every move. It would be impossible to go searching for Elizabeth without admitting what he was doing. 'I will start making enquiries tomorrow, Guy, trust me. Within the week I will find your mother if she can be found, though I think you should prepare yourself for the possibility that she has died.'

'I must know, sir, one way or the other.'

'I understand that,' said Thomas. 'But in the meantime I would like you to stay here at Chadbrook. The inn is no place for a boy on his own. Do not worry, everything is well there. Betsy is running the tap room for your mother and caring for your grandmother. Should your mother return, Betsy will tell her immediately where you are and that you are well and safe.'

'Thank you, sir, thank you very much.' Guy turned to go.

'Guy,' said Thomas, gently.

Guy turned. 'Yes, sir.'

'When we are alone, completely alone, such as this, I would like it very much if you would call me Father.'

The boy ran to him, arms outstretched. Thomas caught him and, returning to his chair, he sat down and cradled him as if he was a baby. Guy began to sob. 'I am sorry, I am sorry, Father.'

'Do not fear,' Thomas murmured, gently brushing back the hair from his forehead, rocking him, soothing him. 'Let out your grief, you will feel the benefit of it.' They stayed thus for some time, father and son, drawing comfort from one another.

After Guy had left, Thomas summoned his spring spaniels and set out across the park. It was a cold day for early October, more like winter than autumn, but he was grateful for the chill for he needed to clear his head. Where would Elizabeth have gone? Immediately after her disappearance, he had seen to it that Long Melford was thoroughly searched. He had also sent his servants to Sudbury to make enquiries. Being the nearest large town, it had seemed the obvious place that she would go to. When there had been no trace of her there, he had instituted a search of the local villages, such as Cavendish and Lavenham in case she was residing with friends, but all to no avail. He had tried to convince himself she had simply taken a ride that morning to clear her head, but in his heart he knew she had set out on a journey – but a journey to where? As far as he knew she had been nowhere beyond Sudbury, except for that one occasion when he had taken her to Bury St. Edmunds, to the pleasure gardens. He stopped short in his tracks, startling the dogs. Of course, Bury – it had to be right. Whenever one was in a state of unhappiness turning to a place where one had been happy always helped, just as he now was heading towards the larch wood, where he had always sought solace as a child. They had been happy, those three days in Bury. It was after the death of Eleanor, during their honeymoon period, when he was free to see Elizabeth as often as he wished, when trade at the inn had been excellent, before his marriage to Beatrice and the conception of another child. . . He had given no instructions for anyone to check along the Bury road. It was a long way, fifteen, no, nearer twenty miles from Long Melford. Of course it was madness to consider such a ride in her condition, but then Elizabeth was more than a little mad. He would go to Bury that very afternoon, he decided, and mercifully he needed no excuse, for his lawyer who dealt with estate matters had offices in Bury. The decision brought a degree of relief.

After a comfortable night, passed at an excellent inn in town, Thomas presented himself at his lawyer's offices at nine o'clock. The two men exchanged a friendly greeting. They could not have been more different – Jacob Lessing was a tiny, spare man, stooped, myopic and with thinning hair. In fact he was several years younger than Thomas but he could have passed for twenty years older. He was a Jew, an astute, clever man. Many people in the county shunned him but he had been a good friend to Thomas, particularly during the dark days when money was short.

'Well, sir,' said Jacob, pouring a customary glass of Madeira. 'What brings you to Bury so soon after our recent business?'

'It is a personal matter,' said Thomas. 'One over which I would like to ask for your absolute discretion.'

'You can always rely on that,' said Jacob. It was a mild rebuke.

'I know,' said Thomas. 'But in this case, as I am about to reveal, it is particularly important.' The two men raised their glasses in silent toast. 'For some years,' said Thomas, 'I have enjoyed a relationship with the young woman who runs The Lady in Waiting, the inn at Long Melford.'

'I know that,' said Jacob, 'Mistress Elizabeth Monson.'

Thomas, despite the circumstances, threw back his head and laughed. 'I cannot believe that gossip could travel this far. Is there anything you do not know, Jacob?'

Jacob smiled, his eyes twinkling behind his pince-nez. 'Precious little,' he said. 'The lady in question has borne you one son, Guy, and recently she appears to have vanished and I believe she is with child again. The story has it that you had already abandoned her. Is that true?' There was a slight edge to his voice.

Thomas frowned. 'You disapprove of the liaison, I can tell.'

'Not disapprove, it is not my place to do that,' said Jacob. 'I have been blessed with a long and happy marriage and I did not have the pressures placed upon me to marry for money that you have had. I married for love, not the most original motive but the best, I swear. Nonetheless, it gives me no right to sit in judgement on others. I apologise, I digress – what can I do for you in connection with Mistress Monson, or is it her children who trouble you?'

'The boy, Guy, now lives with me at Chadbrook.'

Jacob let out a whistle. 'That was a brave decision, sir.'

'Yes, indeed,' said Thomas, ruefully. 'The boy pines for his mother and I, too, am concerned for her welfare. The rumours are true, Mistress Monson and I have ended our liaison, but that does not mean I feel no responsibility towards her, nor indeed the child she bears. I need to find her, Jacob, and I have reason to believe she may be in Bury.'

'Why is that the case, sir?' Jacob asked.

'We spent some days together here seven or eight years ago. She was very happy – it was a happy time for us both.' His voice was suddenly full of longing, Jacob recognized, though he doubted Thomas was aware of it. 'I have established that she resides nowhere local to Long Melford and as far as I know Bury is the only other place she has ever visited.'

Jacob nodded. 'Your thinking would seem to be logical, sir.'

'I am most grateful you think so,' said Thomas with a slight smile.

'How near to her time was she?' Jacob asked.

'I think the babe was due very shortly,' said Thomas. 'It would be born by now, I believe.'

269

'Then it would be best, I would think, if we made contact with all the local doctors and midwives – the chances are she needed the ministrations of one of them. How long can you stay in Bury?'

'Two days,' said Thomas.

'Let us just hope she did not suffer too much on the journey,' said Jacob. 'It must have been hard on her and the baby.'

'I do not think she cared very much about the baby,' said Thomas. 'I am only speaking from hearsay but on talking to her servant at the inn, I understand that she did not want the child, indeed she blamed it for our parting.'

'I see . . .' said Jacob. 'Well, that suggests yet another possibility.'

'Does it?' said Thomas.

'Yes, the orphanage. We have a large orphanage here in Bury. If I had a child I did not wish to keep, then the orphanage would be the obvious place to take it. I think perhaps as your time is short, we should start our enquiries there. I will send my clerk directly. At which inn are you staying, sir?'

'The George,' said Thomas.

'Shall I meet you there at noon? Perhaps by then I shall have some news for you.'

'You are a good man, Jacob, I am most grateful.'

'It is an honour to serve you, sir,' said Jacob. The words were not hollow. To have such an influential client was of enormous value to Jacob Lessing, but he liked and respected Thomas and would have been happy to serve him, regardless of his rank.

Thomas could settle to nothing that morning. He went to the saddlery, intent on buying a new pair of hunting boots but could find none to his liking. He next visited his tailor, but there again he could not make a decision as to which cloth was the most suitable. At last, with a sense of mounting frustration, he returned early to the inn, ordered a bottle of brandy and sat by the fire to wait for Jacob. His mind was clouded with apprehension for he knew now, somehow without a shadow of a doubt, that Elizabeth had come to Bury, and he cursed himself for not realizing earlier.

Jacob Lessing was late which was completely out of character and one look at his face told Thomas the news was bad. 'I must apologize, sir, for my tardiness. I have a hansom waiting outside, I think it best you accompany me to the orphanage.'

'You have news?' said Thomas.

'Yes,' said Jacob, awkwardly. 'But I think it best if you hear what they have to say at the orphanage.'

The two men travelled the short distance to the orphanage in silence. It was a dirty, grey, dilapidated building in which could be heard the wails of children.

Thomas was very tense. 'Did you have to bring me here, Jacob?' Jacob nodded.

They knocked on the great oak door which was answered by an elderly woman in squalid clothes which could barely pass as a nurse's uniform. She ushered them up a short flight of stairs to a small office. A tall, slender man stepped forward to greet them. 'Good morning, sir,' he said to the Earl. 'Good morning again, Mr. Lessing.'

'This is Dr. Bateman,' said Jacob, 'the governor of the orphanage. He and his wife share responsibilities for . . . how many children, were you telling me?'

'Over four hundred at the last count.' Dr. Bateman gave a tired smile. He looked a good man, Thomas thought, and instantly warmed to him.

There was a knock at the door and a young woman entered. She would have been strikingly good-looking if she did not look so tired and care-worn. She was dressed shabbily in an old gown, over which she wore a stained apron. Her dark hair was pinned back untidily, her eyes were a vivid violet. 'May I introduce my wife, Mistress Anne Bateman,' said the doctor.

'I am pleased to meet you,' said Thomas.

'It is my wife who tended the young woman about whom you seek information. I think it is possibly best if she tells you herself of the events of that night.'

Thomas looked questioningly at Jacob. Jacob nodded for him to sit down. He felt strangely awkward, as if on some sort of trial.

'The young woman came to us four, no it must be five weeks ago,' Anne began. 'She arrived late at night – it was nearly midnight. My husband and I were abed and we would not have heard her but for the desperate banging on the door. She was in an advanced state of labour. We took her in, of course, it would not have been Christian to do anything else. We made her as comfortable as possible. There was no point in calling for either doctor or midwife, they would not have reached us in time. The baby was born alive, but she lived for just a few minutes. She was born too early . . . six, perhaps eight weeks before her time and she was a tiny child. The young woman . . . she haemorrhaged shortly after the birth. We tried to save her, we did everything we could, but she died, too, within the hour.'

271

'Are you telling me that this was Elizabeth?' Thomas's voice sounded strange even to his own ears – a strangled desperate sound.

'I am afraid so,' said Jacob, gently.

'How – how do you know?' said Thomas.

'We know her name was Elizabeth,' said Anne, her voice strangely devoid of emotion. 'She would not tell us from whence she came, though she said she had been travelling alone for two days. Her horse was lame, which was why she reached Bury so late. She was a beautiful woman with hair the colour of copper beeches and green eyes.' Anne searched Thomas's face and saw him wince. 'And when she knew she was dying she spoke of her son, Guy, fearing what would become of him, hoping that his father would take him in.'

'Guy is a common enough name,' said Thomas, angrily. 'There could be other women in similar circumstances. This does not prove it was Elizabeth; she may still be alive. You have made too many assumptions, Jacob.'

'There is more,' said Jacob.

'As she died,' said Anne, 'the last word she spoke was "Thomas".'

There was silence in the room for some time. 'I see,' said Thomas. He seemed to be in perfect control, there was no outward sign of grief. 'I am most grateful for what you did for Elizabeth and the child. I would like to know how much I owe you for your services.'

'You owe us nothing,' Anne burst out. 'Nothing at all. All I hope is that you learn from this experience and do not treat other poor women this way.'

'My dear, please.' Dr. Bateman put a restraining hand on his wife's arm.

She shook herself free and stood up, her eyes blazing, her pale skin flushed. 'Someone has to tell him. You enjoyed that poor woman, took from her what you wanted and then left her. She was not just sick in body when she arrived here, she was sick in mind, destroyed by your rejection of her, weighed down by the thought of trying to support two children alone. It is always the same with men of your rank. You treat lowly women as if they were no more than cattle with no thought for the consequences. This orphanage is full of bastard children sired by men such as you. They will grow up deprived in mind and body, with a grudge against the world, and who can blame them, while men continue to pay no heed to the results of their folly.'

There was a shocked silence in the room. Thomas was very pale. Jacob winced inwardly. For all that he greatly admired his client,

Thomas's short temper was legendary – he waited anxiously for the explosion – none came.

'I accept your criticism, young woman,' Thomas said at last. 'You are right to chastise me. When I return home I will arrange a banker's draft for five hundred guineas to be sent to your orphanage, to improve at least the facilities and care that you offer these poor unfortunate children. I know it cannot make amends for the loss of Elizabeth and my daughter, but it will help other children and perhaps indicate to you the sincerity of my regret.'

Anne said nothing but Dr. Bateman rose to his feet. 'This is most generous, but unnecessary. I must apologize on behalf of my wife – she is very tired and care-worn, but she should not have spoken to you in such a manner.'

'Your wife spoke nothing but the plain truth,' Thomas said. He hesitated. 'Where is . . . where are they buried?'

'We could do no better for them than to put them in the paupers' graveyard, I am afraid,' said Dr. Bateman. 'We buried the mother and child together.'

'Do you know the spot?' He nodded. 'Then I would like to arrange for the bodies to be exhumed.' He turned to Jacob. 'I would like you to deal with this matter for me, Jacob.'

Thomas refused Jacob Lessing's offer of dinner that night. He could not bear to be surrounded by the little man's happy family. He spent the evening alone in his room with a bottle of brandy, but the liquor brought him neither relief nor pleasure. Images of Elizabeth when he had first met her – the beautiful, golden girl of sixteen – kept flashing through his mind. He did not need telling that if she had not made the fateful journey to Bury, Elizabeth's baby would have been born at its due time and they would both have survived. A daughter . . . he would have liked a daughter. Poor Amy, she had brought him no pleasure, but Elizabeth's daughter – beautiful perhaps like her mother, a sister for Guy . . . Mistress Bateman's words had shocked him in a way that had never before occurred in his life to date. He realized, with surprise, that no one had ever spoken to him in such a manner, except perhaps when he was an erring child. In his position as the Earl of Clare, he was beholden to no one. He meted out justice, as he saw it, to those below him in station but nobody sat in judgement on him, no one until Anne Bateman. He realized how true her words were and he found in his mind he had already made a commitment to the orphans of Bury. He would do more than just give them the draft he had promised. He would try to help the children to learn a trade, perhaps even receive some schooling. It was what the young Elizabeth had longed for, a chance to learn, a chance to better herself. She would have approved of such a scheme. The notion brought him temporary comfort, until his thoughts turned to Guy. He could only guess at the grief his mother's death would cause the boy.

CHAPTER THIRTY
Chadbrook – April 1982

She would not come to the phone. On the two previous occasions that Charles had called he assumed she was genuinely out or busy. Now, he recognized that she was quite deliberately avoiding him. While she had told him to leave her alone, he had not expected this, particularly since, if Jonathan was to be believed, he would by now have telephoned her and ended the relationship. It made no sense to Charles. Why was she not turning to him, now when she must need him, when her world had come crashing round her ears? Perhaps Jonathan had not kept his part of the bargain but somehow Charles doubted it – not because he had any faith in Jonathan's ability to keep his word, but because he knew that Jonathan had believed him, had really thought he had the power to finish Lindstrom's. Clearly after whatever trouble there had been between Jonathan and his mother, Jonathan was anxious now not to make a mess of his new position at the bank. He obviously did not love Prue, not in the accepted sense, and so it was a comparatively small sacrifice for Jonathan to make to ensure that there were no ripples on his particular pond.

Charles felt very depressed. He had come back from New York with such high expectations, imagining that Prue would fall into his arms, thank him for clarifying her life and accept his proposal of marriage. Now it appeared she would not even see him. He loved her, loved her enough to want her to be his wife, but still that did not seem to help him understand how her mind worked, particularly how she truly felt about Jonathan. He gazed despondently out of the window, across the parkland to the larch wood, an old childhood haunt which he had always loved. The sun was shining, it was a beautiful spring day with a light, fresh breeze. Skip, his father's old black labrador, sat mournfully by the desk. 'Come on, Skip, let's have a walk,' said Charles, suddenly. 'Neither of us is doing ourselves any good by sitting around moping.'

In the park he felt better and he realized for the first time that he was starting to love his home. The thought gave him pleasure.

Throughout his childhood he had seen Chadbrook only as a place where his father bullied him, his parents fought and he was outshone by his elder brother – a place where he simply did not fit in or belong. Now that Chadbrook was his, he was beginning to appreciate the splendours of the house and the beauty of the parkland. So many of his ancestors must have rambled across this land with a dog at their heels, on a fine spring morning. On the one hand it was a humbling experience, on the other it was oddly comforting. Chadbrook had seen it all before – loves found, loves lost, birth and death, the drama of life itself with all its tragicomedy. He approached the larch wood and then abruptly decided to steer away from its dark eeriness – today he needed to keep in the sunlight to buoy up his spirits. 'Come, Skip.' He turned away towards the lake, gazing around appreciatively, and it was at that moment he made his decision. . . It would not be him who lost Chadbrook for the Earls of Clare. Whatever the outcome of his relationship with Prue, he would do as she suggested and find a way of turning the old house into a paying concern. It would have to be done well, with style and care. He would have to be commercially astute, something which he knew would not come to him easily, but it could be done and he would do it. He might have lost Prue but he would not lose Chadbrook, too.

For nearly two hours Charles strode around plotting and scheming the future. He returned in better spirits, left Skip in the scullery for his lunch and hurried to the library, intent on a glass of sherry to warm him.

The figure sitting in a chair drawn up to the fire was so unexpected that for a moment he did not react at all. 'Hello, Charles.'

He stared at her. 'Prue! What on earth are you doing here?'

She smiled slightly. 'You told me to visit you whenever I felt like it.'

'Yes, I know, but you have been avoiding me.'

'I've been busy,' she countered.

'Not that busy.'

'I'm sorry.' She was instantly on the defensive and Charles regretted his words. 'I've just had a rather difficult couple of days.'

'I'm sorry, too, I'm badgering you,' said Charles. 'Would you like a sherry?'

'That is a good idea,' said Prue, wearily.

He poured two sherries, with a shaking hand. Would she raise the question of Jonathan or should he? Had Jonathan told her about his visit? He handed her a glass and came and sat in the chair beside her. 'So, how are things?' he asked, casually.

'Not very good, as I imagine you know.'

His heart sank – it was not just what she said but the way she said it. 'Go on,' he said.

She took a sip of sherry and stared into the fire. 'It's over between Jonathan and me. He's gone back to his wife and . . . I understand, I understand the basis for this decision was largely your doing.'

The rat, Charles thought. He couldn't just concede defeat, he had to try to mess things up. 'The decision had nothing to do with me,' said Charles.

'Oh, I see,' said Prue, turning to him. Her eyes were cold, she looked drained and exhausted. 'So are you telling me you haven't even been to New York?'

'I've been to New York,' said Charles. 'I've seen both Jonathan and his mother, but the decision Jonathan took to stay with his wife was nothing whatsoever to do with me – it was already made before I even climbed out of the aircraft.'

'That's not what Jonathan said.'

'It wouldn't be,' said Charles. 'He doesn't take kindly to the idea that you and I might have some sort of future together.'

'I'm sorry,' said Prue, 'I never thought I'd say this to you, Charles, but I'm not sure I believe you – I can't imagine why you should go to New York except to try to persuade Jonathan to leave me.'

Charles rose to his feet. 'I'm no saint, Prue, but for God's sake surely you can appreciate that I'm more likely to be an honest man than Jonathan. That man doesn't have a decent bone in his body. He's totally shameless about the fact that he was quite prepared to continue his relationship with you and with his wife and fob you off for as long as it suited him.'

'I don't believe that,' said Prue.

'It's what he told me himself,' said Charles. 'I don't know whether he's told you anything about it but the main reason it seems he is staying with his wife is because she's blackmailing him.' He had struck a chord, he saw it instantly.

'Yes, I do know something about that,' Prue admitted.

'I was told about it by Jonathan's mother, Harriet, who incidentally is a very decent old girl, and very much on our side.'

'I didn't know we had a side,' said Prue, coolly.

'OK,' said Charles, with a sigh. 'Very much on my side. Jonathan was encouraged, shall we say, to resume his relationship with his wife, and because he is basically a weak man, it was the easiest thing for him to do. However he had no intention of giving you up. Prue, put yourself in my position. I love you, forget for a moment my personal ambitions concerning *our* future, I couldn't bear to see you humiliated in this way, being strung along by that bastard, pretending he was going to marry you when he clearly had no intention of doing so.'

'You don't know anything,' Prue stormed. 'You don't know anything about it.'

'I know this,' said Charles, 'that Jonathan Lindstrom would never have made you happy. If I've done nothing more, I have at least saved you from more years of unhappiness, from a half life, never knowing where you stand.' He tried to lighten the moment. 'After all, you of all people should know better than to put yourself in that position.'

'Why?' Prue asked.

'Look at Elizabeth, it didn't make her happy.'

'We don't know that,' said Prue.

'Oh come on,' said Charles. 'What about all these terrible feelings you've been experiencing, they're hardly the ecstasy of love's young dream. From what you've told me, Elizabeth was miserable to the point of desperation. Can't you learn from what she went through?'

'It is extraordinary,' Prue admitted after a moment, 'the parallel between our two stories. Don't you see, both Thomas and Jonathan had to remain married for money.'

'So it's essentially money that his wife is blackmailing Jonathan about?' Charles asked, grimly.

'Yes,' said Prue.

'Then if he can put money before happiness, surely you can see that Jonathan's not worth having.'

'Thomas did the same,' Prue reminded him. 'And I seem to remember your saying that he was one of your favourite ancestors.'

'It's different,' Charles said. 'He had Chadbrook at stake.'

'Jonathan has Lindstrom's. One is a grand old estate, one is an old-established bank employing hundreds of people who would lose their jobs if things went wrong – there's no difference, no difference at all except two centuries.'

Charles fell silent. She was right of course. He tried again. 'I know you must have suffered a great shock but please let me help you pick up the pieces. You could become involved in developing Chadbrook.

I've decided to take your advice and I have all sorts of plans. It would take your mind off your troubles and. . .'

'Charles,' Prue interrupted, 'I'm going away.'

'Away?' He stared at her blankly.

'There's no future for me at The Lady in Waiting. Jonathan is going to put it on the market and although he wants me to stay until it is sold, I can't continue working there in the circumstances. I have to get away, away from him, away from you and away from Elizabeth.'

'Please don't go,' Charles said, desperately. 'Stay with me, here.'

'No, Charles,' Prue said.

'When are you going and where?' He felt a sense of rising panic – to lose her after all this, it was as Jonathan had predicted.

'I'm not telling you where I'm going. As for when . . . today.'

'No!'

'Yes,' said Prue. 'It's why I'm here, to say goodbye.'

Charles knelt down by her chair and seized her shoulders. 'I won't let you.'

'You can't stop me.' Her voice was harsh, uncompromising. 'Charles, it's not fair to put this pressure on me. I didn't have to come here to see you.' Her voice was shaking. 'I could have just left. In many ways it would have been a great deal easier – in fact I'm starting to wish that's what I'd done. I felt I owed it to you to try to explain but you're not even prepared to listen.'

'I am prepared to listen,' said Charles. 'I just don't understand. You can't deny what happened in Brussels was special.'

Prue turned her face away. 'It was special, but not enough to build a lifetime upon. I've just finished with one serious relationship, I'm not ready to move on to another. Surely you can see that.'

'I can see that,' said Charles. 'That's the whole point. I'm not asking you for some major commitment now, I'm simply asking you to come and live with me. God knows we needn't be in each other's pockets in a house this size. You can have the East Wing and I'll have the West, seriously. We'll meet at meal times or not even then, if you wish, and I won't touch you if you don't want me to. I'm just saying don't run away from us, from me.'

'I'm sorry,' said Prue, 'I have to, my mind's made up.' She ducked under his arm and stood up.

'You're doing the wrong thing,' said Charles, 'for both of us.'

'I'm doing the right thing for me,' said Prue.

'I'll wait for you, however long it takes,' he said – anything to delay her. For a moment she seemed to hesitate. He took advantage of the situation. Taking the two strides that separated them, he pulled her into his arms and kissed her fiercely, passionately, willing her to feel his love. She did not resist him, she was passive which was worse. At last he released her, defeated.

'You're very special, Charles, and I won't forget you,' she was shaking, 'but I'm going and I'm going now.'

'You're not safe to drive, not like this. Let me drive you.'

'I'm all right. In any case I'm only going as far as my parents' house tonight.' She gave him one long searching look, 'Goodbye,' she whispered. In an instant she was gone, leaving Charles lonelier than he had ever been in his life.

That night Charles got very drunk and the following morning he woke late with a thick head, a raging thirst and an evil temper. Uncharacteristically, he snapped at Mrs. Plum all through breakfast and afterwards shut himself away in his study, where he did nothing but sit hunched in an armchair, going over and over again the scene with Prue and his own mismanagement of it.

By midday, desperate for a diversion, he drove to Sudbury. The hair of the dog was the only answer – he would have a good lunch in a pub. With a stab of disquiet, his reaction reminded him of how he used to seek solace in the cafe in Antibes – history, it appeared, was repeating itself.

As the road dipped down into Sudbury, he passed, as he had done thousands of times before, Chalmers Brewery. Today as he drove by, a thought suddenly struck him. Chalmers, he knew, had been brewing beer since the late 1600s. Perhaps they had some record of The Lady in Waiting, perhaps they could throw some light on the period during which Elizabeth had run the inn. Instead of the leisurely lunch he had anticipated, he stopped at the first pub he came to, ordered a pint of beer and a rather unappetizing sandwich, and sat in a corner of the bar thinking through this sudden development. Prue, he had lost – at any rate for the time being – but not so Elizabeth. Of course the rational way to think of it was that there was no point now in pursuing Elizabeth's story, but somehow he felt it held the key to his relationship with Prue. It was a fanciful notion, he recognized, but the quest to find Elizabeth's fate would at least keep his mind occupied. In any event, he realized that for his own sake, as much as Prue's, he had to know what happened to Elizabeth.

A second pint of beer made him feel a great deal better and at two o'clock sharp he presented himself at the brewery. He was in luck.

Not only was Sidney Chalmers, the managing director, in the office, he was also free. 'It's very kind of you to see me,' said Charles, extending a hand.

'A great pleasure,' said Sidney Chalmers, a pleasant man in his early fifties, with a large ruddy face suggesting he enjoyed his own product. 'How may I help you?'

'I'm doing some research for a book I'm writing on local history,' said Charles, who had prepared the excuse while still in the pub. 'I'm trying to find some information about The Lady in Waiting at Long Melford in the late eighteenth century. It occurred to me that your brewery might hold some records concerning the inn – perhaps details of deliveries which might specify the name of the landlord.'

'Yes, of course, though we may be able to do rather better than simply look up deliveries. We owned the inn for many years, you know. In fact we only sold out about twenty years ago to a Gerry Jackson. The inn had become very run-down and we could see no way of refurbishing it in a cost-effective manner, so we were happy to offload it onto someone who wanted to turn it into a free house. It seems we made a mistake – I gather it's a roaring success now.'

Charles smiled. This was better news than he could have dared hope for. 'That's wonderful, what luck.' He hesitated. 'I'm not so much concerned with whom you sold out to, but I would be very interested to know who you bought it from.'

'Ah, now you're asking,' Sidney Chalmers smiled. 'Still, there's nothing like presenting a challenge to the filing system. Would you mind waiting – I'll go down to the vaults where we hold all our records. I'll arrange for my secretary to bring you a cup of coffee in the meanwhile.'

Twenty minutes later, Sidney Chalmers reappeared, triumphant, with a pile of documents. 'I have the information you want, at least I hope it's what you want. We acquired The Lady in Waiting in 1821. We purchased it from the Naylor family, the Naylors of Brundon, who were a very important family in those days. They owned the big mill at Brundon and much else besides.'

'I know a little about the Naylors,' said Charles. 'One of my forebears, Thomas, was married to a Beatrice Naylor.' He frowned. 'I wonder why on earth the Naylors owned The Lady in Waiting and how they came by it.'

Sidney Chalmers sighed. 'There I'm afraid I am unable to help you. The first and only reference we have to The Lady in Waiting is our purchase, as I say, in 1821. We bought the property for one hundred and twenty pounds, a tidy sum at the time I should think.'

'You've been most helpful,' said Charles. 'Tell me, do you know if there are any Naylors still left in the district?'

'I'm sorry, I'm afraid I have no idea.'

On his return to Chadbrook, Charles looked up Naylor in the telephone directory. It was all so childishly simple, there they were – Frederick Naylor, Brundon Mill, Sudbury. It was not, after all, so surprising that they had not moved. The Earls of Clare were still at Chadbrook, the Mansells were still at Thurston Hall and Prue had returned to The Lady in Waiting. Nothing really had changed in two hundred years – it was an odd thought. He telephoned immediately and spoke to Sally Naylor. Her husband, Freddy, was a stockbroker and away in London all week, but she said she knew a fair amount about The Lady in Waiting and 'our family scandal', as she referred to it. She at once asked Charles to come and join her for lunch the following day.

Brundon Mill was at the end of a long, leafy lane. The mill itself had been converted beautifully into a large, family house through which the millstream flowed. The big house – Naylor Hall – the former Naylor residence, appeared to have been sold off. It was an extremely pleasant setting – chickens scratched in what had once been the mill yard, there were doves on the roof and an old sheepdog sat in the sun and barely glanced at him as he walked up to the front door. There were children's bicycles littered about.

Sally Naylor was pretty, vivacious and about thirty-five. Charles liked her instantly. 'Come along in,' she said. 'I feel very honoured to be entertaining a real live Earl – you're much younger than I expected.'

'You realize we're related?' said Charles, following her through to an attractive conservatory at the back of the house.

'Oh yes,' said Sally. 'It's our one claim to fame, our marriage into the nobility.'

'Hardly your one claim,' said Charles. 'From what I understand your family had a finger in every pie in the commercial life of this area.'

'Yes, and we didn't have a particularly attractive reputation. Still, I console myself with the fact that I'm only a Naylor by marriage and not by blood.' She smiled. 'A drink?'

It was not until they sat down to lunch that Charles unfolded his story of Prue and Elizabeth, of their research to date and of their trip to Brussels. Sally heard him out in silence. When he finished she refilled his wine glass thoughtfully, her early vivaciousness suddenly dampened. 'Well, I can help you,' she said. 'In fact I can fill in most, if not all of the gaps, but it's not a pretty story. As I suspected, it is our family scandal, or rather one of them, you're after. We acquired the inn because the Earl of Clare insisted we took responsibility for it. "Blood money" he called it in a letter he wrote to Harry Naylor, Beatrice's brother, after Elizabeth's death.'

'Go on,' said Charles, hardly able to contain himself.

'As you know, or suspected, Elizabeth Monson, the first Lady in Waiting, had an affair with Thomas, the then Earl of Clare, which lasted for some years – in fact I think it probably began when he was still married to his first wife, Eleanor. When he married for the second time, to Beatrice Naylor, he acquired an annual income from her father, which was sufficient to dig Chadbrook out of financial trouble. It was also Elizabeth's undoing.'

Charles smiled and inclined his head. 'Thank you kindly for the financial support.'

Sally smiled faintly and continued. 'I don't know when exactly things began to go wrong for Thomas and Elizabeth, but the story has it that the relationship became too public and was proving embarrassing from the Naylors' point of view. Beatrice did not like being cuckolded and so the family started to get heavy. They threatened to withdraw Beatrice's income and ruin Chadbrook, and also to reroute the coaches unless Thomas and Elizabeth stopped seeing one another.'

Charles frowned, 'I'm sorry, I don't understand the significance of the coaches.'

'The Lady in Waiting was essentially a coaching inn,' said Sally. 'It relied for its trade almost entirely upon the coaches travelling to Bury St. Edmunds and on into Norfolk. The Naylors owned most of the coaches and threatened to have them bypass The Lady in Waiting unless Elizabeth and Thomas ended their relationship.'

'Wow,' said Charles. 'When you Naylors pack a punch you certainly do it properly.'

'You won't be so flippant when you hear the outcome,' said Sally. 'Of course, no one knows the full details but Thomas must have decided that there was no alternative but to give in to the blackmail. Elizabeth was expecting a child, their second, and she just couldn't cope with being parted from Thomas. So, she ran away, travelled alone and on horseback while heavily pregnant. She got as far as

Bury, where she and her child, a daughter, died in the orphanage there. Elizabeth was only twenty-five.'

'That's terrible,' said Charles. 'A dreadful story – poor girl.' He was deeply shocked but could find no words to express his feelings properly.

'Yes,' said Sally. 'It was tantamount to suicide. OK, so she didn't throw herself into the river or under a passing coach, but she must have known she was putting herself in considerable danger by travelling alone, and that the journey itself would probably kill her.' There was a lengthy silence between them. 'There was another child,' Sally said at last. 'A boy. He must have been six or seven at the time of his mother's death. Thomas took him in and raised him at Chadbrook. I don't know his name.'

'Guy,' said Charles, quietly.

'Oh, so you know about him. Let's at least hope that father and son drew comfort from one another,' said Sally. 'One imagines that Thomas must have felt very guilty about Elizabeth, even if the affair was over. He can't have been indifferent to her or their children or he would never have taken Guy into his home. He must have cared very deeply for the boy. It was certainly not standard practice to give one's bastards such recognition in those days.'

'They may have been good friends while Guy was a child,' said Charles, heavily, still reeling from the news of how Elizabeth had died. 'But it appears there was some kind of rift between them when Guy grew up. They fought alongside one another at Waterloo but although Guy accepted a grace and favour house at Hawkedon from his father, it appears that in later life, there was no communication between them.'

'That's very sad,' said Sally.

'It is,' said Charles. 'And of course we'll never know the reason for it.'

CHAPTER THIRTY-ONE
Chadbrook – August 1815

Thomas was nervous, he realized, far more nervous than he had been on that terrible morning two months ago, when he had stood beside Wellington in the pouring rain, waiting for the moment when one of the bloodiest battles in history would begin. After all, the only thing he had to lose then was his life, what he was threatened with losing now was his son. He stood up from his desk and looked out of the window. By craning his neck he could just catch sight of the driveway leading up to Chadbrook. He thought he had heard the approach of a horse but there was no one in sight, he must have imagined it. He turned back to the room. He loved this library at Chadbrook, it was his sanctuary, his place of refuge, but even here, there was no escape from his agony of mind. He must not lose Guy, he could not bear to lose Guy, but was his tongue persuasive enough, his argument subtle enough, his ammunition good enough? He looked at the papers laid out on the desk before him and gave a grunt of approval. The ammunition at least was not insubstantial. At his own recommendation, the King was to grant Guy a knighthood. There was a personal letter from the Lord Chamberlain confirming the honour. Beside the letter, he had placed the deeds of Thurston Hall. It was not a big house, at least not by Chadbrook standards, but it was a very comfortable property, set in four hundred acres of excellent farmland. Until now, it had been part of the Chadbrook estate, the house having been leased. Thomas had rehoused the tenants, refurbished the house and was ready to offer both the Hall and the land to Guy and his new bride. It was a handsome gift by any standards and Thomas intended to accompany it with an annual income of four hundred pounds, to ensure that Guy could live in comfort. Would he even accept it? Thomas sat down heavily at his desk again. Surely he had to, for his bride's sake. Little Marcelle was used to great luxury – the de Villefranche family lived extremely well, but while she had brought with her to the marriage a dowry, it was not over-generous. Guy desperately needed financial support – he would have to accept.

Thomas sighed heavily. If only the events of the last few months could have been averted. He had managed to keep the truth from Guy all these years, all through his boyhood, and then fate had dealt them this blow from such an unexpected quarter. Yet surely now Guy was a man, and a very brave one, Thomas thought proudly, he would understand, having recovered from the initial shock. It had all happened so many years ago, it was no longer relevant . . . was it? Elizabeth with her wild, red hair, her bright green eyes, her creamy skin, her beautiful body . . . there had never been a woman in his life like her. He closed his eyes, how could he ever say she was irrelevant? She could never be irrelevant, not to him, for as the years passed he realized with a continuing ache just how much he had truly loved her. And had she not given him his beloved son? Yes, she had freely given him everything a man could want, and what had he given her . . . He shook his head, to clear away the thoughts. If only Guy had accepted Marie-Claire's invitation to the opera that night, everything would have been very different.

The atmosphere in the days leading up to the Battle of Waterloo was quite extraordinary. Wellington arrived in Belgium on the 4th April and was not entirely happy with the men under his command. Many were raw recruits and there was a large number of foreign troops – Belgians, Dutch, men from various German states. It was therefore very heartening to be joined so early in the campaign by Thomas, Earl of Clare, and a few weeks later by his ward, Captain Guy Monson, who had served him so well during the Peninsular Campaign. It was well known, of course, that Guy was Thomas Chadbrook's illegitimate son but this bothered Wellington not at all. The drawing rooms of London could tittle-tattle to their hearts' content. So far as he was concerned, Guy was made in the image of his father – a strong, brave man, who could command respect and loyalty from his men, and be relied upon to equip himself well whatever the outcome of the battle.

It was a good time for Thomas and Guy, who were billeted at the house of La Comtesse de Villefranche. Guy had known them only as friends of the family and was amused to discover that the effervescent Comtesse Marie-Claire was also his father's mistress. Father and son did not discuss the matter but any pleasure his father could find away from his shrew of a wife, Beatrice, his son did not begrudge him.

The hospitality of the de Villefranche household, the party atmosphere in Brussels, the air of anticipation as Napoleon moved nearer and a large battle seemed imminent, were exhilarating. For father and son, away from the restrictions of English society, they provided the perfect opportunity to get to know one another all over again, after Guy's years away in the army. While still little more than a child, Guy had been enrolled in His Majesty's service, and it had proved to be the right answer for him. He had never been happy at Chadbrook – Beatrice had seen to that – and he had been in a no-man's-land as far as class and position were concerned. Beatrice had ostentatiously excluded him from every social occasion she could manage and it had led to a lonely childhood. In the army young Guy found his feet and soon acquired a commission, and the notice of his commanding officer. Thomas was immensely proud of him. Christopher, his heir, had improved a little in health and spirits since his sickly childhood but there was still no question of him joining his father at Waterloo. In later years, Christopher was to grow into a subtle, clever, artistic man with a fine and sharp wit, but under his father's shadow, at present he was nothing but a pallid youth – in such stark contrast to Guy.

La Comtesse Marie-Claire was a widow and had been for some years. She and Thomas had met in 1801, at a ball in London, and had begun a passionate affair which they had pursued with as much vigour as their frequent Channel crossings allowed. Thomas was not Marie-Claire's only lover and he was well aware of it but it did not bother him. It was not so much an affair of the heart as a strong physical attraction, although he was enormously fond of her and found her immensely amusing. She was a woman of class and breeding, who knew all about good food and drink, and he enjoyed her charming, if somewhat frivolous conversation. She had two children – a young son, Paul, who was twelve and a daughter, Marcelle, who was at seventeen an exceptional beauty. She was a quiet girl, modest and shy, no doubt kept well under her mother's thumb, but Guy provided an excellent escort for her and the four of them were much in social demand.

On the evening of the 14th of June, the night before the Duchess of Richmond's Grand Ball, Marie-Claire had arranged that the four of them should go to the opera. Guy loathed opera and made the excuse that he was required on the line to check his men.

Thomas took him to task. 'The opera rarely pleases me, Guy,' he said, out of the women's earshot. 'But I think as a matter of courtesy you should attend. La Comtesse has arranged a seat for you in her box.'

'I am sorry, sir, but I really cannot be with you. I have already extended my apologies to La Comtesse and she has accepted them most graciously.'

Thomas eyed him shrewdly. 'You're missing the camaraderie of army life, are you not?'

Guy had the grace to blush a little. 'Perhaps,' he said, cautiously.

'I do not condone your decision but I will own a night with my brother officers in a local tavern does have a certain appeal.'

'I will be on the line, sir.'

'Initially, I have no doubt . . . but later?' Thomas smiled and left him.

Guy watched him go, affectionately. His father, now over sixty, had worn well – he still had all his hair and it was only sparsely flecked with grey. He stood as tall and erect as any young man and while he carried a little more weight than he had done, he appeared to have boundless energy.

Thomas, of course, had been correct in his view as to how Guy intended to spend the evening. A brother officer of Guy's from the Peninsular Campaign had arrived just two days before in Brussels and a group of young officers were planning to give him a night to remember in Brussels. They began with an excellent dinner and, as Thomas had predicted, later moved to a local tavern with a lively floor show. The evening became progressively more drunken and more out of hand and the guest of honour, William Copeland, was seen accompanying a young lady upstairs and was presumed to have left the party for good. Guy found himself talking to a man named Major George Martin. He was not from Guy's Suffolk regiment but was an officer in Sir Thomas Picton's Infantry Division. He was a friendly man, an army officer born and bred, who had seen a great deal of action in his forty-three years. As the party began to break up, George and Guy sat on, drinking port and discussing the likely battle ahead.

'That is enough of war,' said George, after a while. 'Tell me a little about yourself. I see you're with a Suffolk regiment, where do you come from?'

'I was born in Long Melford,' said Guy, uncomfortably. He never liked inquisitions into his past, it was so difficult to explain.

'Long Melford, I know it well. There was a wonderful inn there, run by a quite amazing woman.'

Guy felt his heart begin to beat. 'Do you mean The Lady in Waiting?'

'Yes, indeed I do, the very one. Do you know it?'

'Yes, I . . .' Guy began.

'Splendid place, splendid. Elizabeth, that was her name. Flaming red hair and a temper to match, mind. It was extraordinary, a woman on her own like that could keep control of an inn, with all nature of travellers passing by. There was never any trouble, never, no one dared cross her. Oh, I had some good times there, some very good times. It was a pity it should all end like that.'

Something in his tone made Guy hesitate from immediately disclosing his own identity. 'What went wrong?' he asked, casually. As he said the words he regretted them but it was too late to retract.

'Why, the poor woman as good as killed herself, didn't you know?'

There was a sudden humming sound in Guy's ears, as if he was about to faint. He stared at George as though he was a madman. 'What do you mean, killed herself?'

'I don't know the details of the story,' said George. 'But they say she was involved in an affair with a local nobleman and things went wrong between them. She was with child and I suppose he would not stand by her. In the end the whole situation became too much for her and she rode off one night – deranged, she was or so the story goes. She died in Bury, her and the babe – she simply rode until she dropped – she wanted to die, poor soul.'

Guy said nothing and George was encouraged by his silence. 'Of course her lover was to blame – he drove her to it. She was a strong woman but not that strong – he destroyed her. For my part, I hope he rots in hell, whoever he is. I say, are you feeling ill?'

'No,' said Guy, faintly.

'Can I fetch you another drink?'

'I rather think we have drunk too much already, but why not?' Like a sleepwalker, Guy called the barman and ordered another bottle of port.

'Why don't we raise our glasses to The Lady in Waiting,' George suggested, 'God rest her soul.' Guy joined in the toast in silence.

Guy was very drunk indeed by the time he left the tavern and began weaving his way through the unfamiliar streets in the general direction of the de Villefranche chateau. His mind was whirling. There was no doubting the truth of what George Martin had said – he had been quite clear, quite lucid – he knew too much detail to have been mistaken. In essence the story was much as his father had told it – only the emphasis was different. He could remember every detail of that terrible day when his father had called him to the library to tell him his mother was dead. An accident, his father had said – she had gone for a ride and clearly fallen – a foolish thing to do to travel alone. His father had not mentioned the baby and until now Guy had forgotten there was to have been another child. Indeed, then as now, he had never sought details of his mother's death – the subject was too painful.

All through his life Guy had suffered from a sense of insecurity and uncertainty. He dimly remembered life with his mother at the inn. It had been exciting and eventful but always uncertain for his mother was given to violent changes of mood. Life at Chadbrook, after his mother's death, had been considerably worse. He did not fit in and knew he never could. The servants laughed at him because of his awkward ways – he was one of them, elevated to a position above them by an accident of birth. What had made his childhood bearable had been his father – his father was a great man, an Earl, a man other men respected and looked up to with awe, and his father loved him, he was sure of that. In Guy's life to date Thomas had done nothing wrong, he was a hero in the truest sense of the word and now, in one single evening, George Martin had sent the pedestal toppling. His father had sent his mother to her death, that was clearly the truth of it, and he had twisted the facts to cover his responsibility. A great wave of guilt swept over Guy. He should have known, he should have stopped her leaving. His mother would not have left him if he had begged her not to, if he had understood her state of mind. He was as much to blame as his father. He was crying in earnest now as he blundered along. He heard the wheels of a carriage and stepped aside to let it pass, lolling against the stone wall which ran along the edge of the road.

It was a hansom cab and the driver drew it to a halt by Guy's slumped body. 'Can I help you, sir? May I take you home?'

'Oh yes, yes indeed,' Guy managed. 'To the de Villefranche residence.'

'Very good, sir.'

With a sigh of relief, Guy slumped back in the seat. The guilt was fading now and was being replaced by anger, anger at his father for the way he had treated his mother, anger at his mother for, as it now appeared, deliberately leaving him. How could she have left him alone, when there was no one else?

Outside the chateau, Guy paid off the driver and then unsteadily climbed the steps to the front door. A footman must have been waiting up for him for the door opened as he reached the top step.

Guy nodded at the man, entered the hall and started up the mahogany staircase. Half-way up he lost his footing and suddenly he was clawing at the air, falling backwards and finally striking his head as he rolled the full length of the staircase.

The footman was beside him in a moment. 'Are you hurt, sir?'

'I think not,' Guy groaned. The footman bent down, picked him up and half carried, half dragged him across the hall towards the drawing room.

There were light footsteps running down the stairs. 'What is happening here? What is wrong?' It was Marcelle, her dark hair hanging down to her shoulders, a wrap clutched tightly around her nightshift.

The footman helped Guy onto a couch in the drawing room and then began speaking with a strong Flemish accent which Guy could not understand. 'I am not hurt,' he said. 'Just leave me alone. Let me lie here, I will be well in the morning.' If only they would leave him to his thoughts.

'We will give you some brandy,' said Marcelle. She sat down beside him and took his hand. 'What has happened, are you really not hurt?'

'You should not be here,' said Guy, trying hard to focus on her face. The room was in darkness, except for the firelight. She looked very beautiful and very young, in the reflection of the flickering flames.

'It is no matter. Please tell me what happened?' she urged.

'I went drinking with some brother officers. It is shameful, I had rather a shock during the evening and as a result I drank a good deal too much.'

'What sort of a shock?' Marcelle asked.

'It is of no consequence,' Guy said, dismissively.

The footman arrived with a bottle of brandy. Marcelle poured a glass and slipping an arm under Guy's shoulders, lifted him slightly so that he could sip at the brandy. As she did so her wrap slipped, revealing creamy shoulders and gently swelling young breasts barely concealed by the thin muslin of her nightshift.

Guy felt lust rise in him like a monster. He closed his eyes, fighting for control, but the rage was returning, rage at his fate, rage at his father, rage at his mother for leaving him. In a single gesture he knocked the brandy glass from Marcelle's hand, and pulled her down on top of him.

She did not stand a chance. Frail and young, with little experience of life and none of men, she had no weapons with which to fight. He kissed her savagely as he would a whore and together they tumbled from the couch onto the floor before the fireplace. In a single gesture, he tore the shift from her body. She moaned in terror but he did not hear her.

Just for an instant, as she lay naked before him, he hesitated, not because of her trembling sobs, nor the whispered, 'Please, no, Guy, no, I beg of you.' He saw before him perfect beauty – her young body, smooth, untried, untested, glowing by the light of the fire and, just for a second, it humbled him. Then with a curse, he tore at his britches and forcing her legs apart, plunged into her again and again in a desperate, hopeless attempt to blot out the horror in his mind.

'Get to your feet, you scoundrel.' The angry voice filtered through Guy's consciousness but it did not disturb him. Used to army life and the constant background of noise, he could sleep through anything. 'Do you hear what I say? Get to your feet, Guy!' A hand seized his shoulder and shook him vigorously. He tried to brush it away but the grip was strong and firm. 'Get up now, or, by God, I swear I will kill you where you lie.' There was no mistaking the emotion or the sincerity of the threat, nor indeed the identity of the voice – it was his father's.

His eyes opened abruptly and stared in amazement at his father's face – Thomas was white with fury. For a moment Guy could remember nothing. Then, like a nightmare, the previous night returned to him and the colour drained also from his face. He stumbled to his feet. 'Marcelle . . .' he began.

'Yes, Marcelle,' Thomas thundered, his voice shaking.

'Is she, is she . . . ?'

'She will live, if that's what you mean,' said Thomas. 'But I doubt she will ever fully recover from what happened last night. A seventeen-year-old child, Guy, and you raped her in her own home where she has every right to feel safe and secure. I cannot believe what has happened. If it were anyone but the Comtesse who had broken this terrible news to me I would have dismissed them as a liar, so sure was I of your honour. But Marie-Claire has never lied to me, besides which I only had to see that poor distraught girl, with bruises on her neck and shoulders, to know that she spoke the truth. I thought I knew you, I thought you were my son. You are nothing but a beast.' He turned away and put a hand over his eyes and Guy realized, as shock was heaped upon shock, that Thomas was crying.

He tried to pull himself together. 'I am truly sorry, sir, it was not

292

meant to happen. I was very drunk when I arrived at the chateau. Marcelle was very kind, she is also beautiful and she was wearing very little. It is a long time since I have been close to a beautiful woman, or any woman. I – I just lost control.'

Thomas turned back to him, his face a mask. 'I am a red-blooded man,' said Thomas, quietly. 'There have been many women in my life but I have never forced myself on any one of them – however lowly their birth, whatever the circumstances; even if they were a paid whore, I have not forced myself on them. I am so ashamed, so disgusted by what you have done. Why, your mother was only sixteen when I met her and I a married man well into my twenties, but I waited until she was ready, I would not have had it otherwise.'

At the mention of his mother, Guy's mind cleared and the whole evening came back to him. 'You may not have forced yourself upon her,' said Guy, coldly, 'but what you did to her was worse – you killed her.'

Thomas stared at his son. 'What do you mean by that?'

'It is no small wonder I was so drunk last night. I met a major in Picton's Infantry Division at the tavern. He knew Suffolk well and Long Melford and The Lady in Waiting – he used to drink there. He remembers my mother as someone to be much admired for the way she ran the inn. He did not realize I was her son, so he did not hesitate to tell me how sad it was the way in which she died – how she as good as took her own life and that of her unborn child because a member of the aristocracy, with whom she was in love, rejected her. Why did you reject her, Father?'

Thomas let out a great sigh and slumped down in a chair. He put his head in his hands for a long moment. There was a terrible silence in the room. 'It seems, Guy, I owe you an explanation,' he said, looking up at last. 'But I do not propose to give it to you now. Whatever you may think of me and the circumstances of your mother's death, it gave you no cause to rape the innocent young daughter of your hostess. There is a battle to be fought and a decision to be made regarding your future. We must deal with these matters first.' Guy opened his mouth to protest but he could not. He was as much sickened by his behaviour towards Marcelle as his father. 'I have talked at length to La Comtesse since Marcelle came sobbing to her room last night,' Guy winced, 'and we think it is best that you should marry the girl.'

'Marry her! But surely she will not have me, not after the wrong I have done her.' Guy was astonished at the suggestion.

'I am not asking for either your views or wishes, I am simply telling you what we consider to be in the best interests of Marcelle. You have behaved like an animal, you should be drummed out of the army, you sicken me, but none of these things will help Marcelle. For all we know she could be with child.' It was something that had not occurred to Guy and he flinched at the suggestion. 'There is every chance that you or I, or both of us, will be killed in our tussle with Napoleon and therefore it is vital that you marry Marcelle before the battle, so that should she be with child, there will be no disgrace attached to her. If you are killed, then she will be a widow. When her child is born, and she is fully recovered, then she will be free to marry again, without any hint of scandal. If you live, then you must devote the rest of your life trying to put right the wrong you have done her.' Guy said nothing. 'Have you anything to say for yourself?' Thomas asked.

'Only that I cannot imagine that she will have me.'

'Marie-Claire believes that she was in love with you in the first place, poor child. Maybe it will be possible to rekindle that love, but I do not think in the circumstances she has any more choice than you – she cannot take the risk of not marrying you. If she is with child, her future would be finished. This is the only . . .' He paused. 'I hesitate to use the word . . . honourable way out of the situation.'

'I will do as you suggest, sir,' Guy said, stiffly. 'But only if I may have a few moments alone with Marcelle, so that I may establish her true feelings.'

'I very much doubt that La Comtesse will allow you to be alone with her.'

'She will have to once we are married,' Guy said. 'However, you can assure them both that I shall do nothing to offend either of them.'

Father and son eyed one another in silence for a moment. If Thomas had expected to see nothing but guilt and sorrow in Guy's eyes, he was disappointed. There was still anger there and resentment. 'I shall discuss it with them,' he said. 'In the meantime, I suggest you wash and change and generally prepare yourself for the day.'

Marcelle was sitting in the window-seat of the little morning room when Guy entered. She had her back to him and appeared to be looking out of the window. 'Marcelle.' His voice was almost a whisper. She turned and studied him in silence. She seemed quite composed and a great deal older than the girl of yesterday. The sight of her shook him to the core. 'There are no words that can express the horror of what I have done to you,' Guy said, stumbling over the words. 'It can be of little comfort to you that I am the most wretched of men. I am most humbly sorry. I will not insult you by seeking your forgiveness because there can be none, but I beg you to believe that I shall suffer for the rest of my life for what I did to you last night.'

'Why did you do it? Why did you not stop when I begged you?' Marcelle asked, her voice surprisingly steady.

'Oh, do not speak so.' Guy turned away, unable to bear the hurt and bewildered expression in her face, nor the sight of the livid bruise on the lovely skin at her neck. 'I am so sorry, so terribly sorry.' Misery burst in on him and once again he found himself losing control. He tried to hide it from her, turning away so that she should not see his tears.

She was beside him in a moment, her hand on his arm. 'Guy, what is it, what is it?' He could not speak, and as the sadness and shame engulfed him, the tears poured down his cheeks. Yet in his grief something astonishing happened, bringing him instant comfort. Marcelle slipped her arm around him and buried her face in his heaving chest. 'Do not grieve, I cannot bear it,' she whispered.

His arms were about her. They were not lover's arms – he clung to her for support, desperate for comfort. They stayed thus for some minutes until at last Guy had control of himself once more. 'What must you think of me?' he murmured.

'I do not know, except that I cannot bear your unhappiness,' Marcelle replied, honestly.

He drew away a little. 'You treat me so kindly, I cannot understand how you can bear even to speak to me.'

She dropped her eyes. 'I do not believe that you intended to do what you did last night. I do not believe it is something you have ever done before. Am I right?' Her voice trembled slightly.

Guy marvelled at her courage at being able to talk of it. 'You are right,' he said. 'It is not something that I have ever done before nor have ever imagined doing to you or to anyone, but especially to you. I was very drunk, as I am sure you were aware, but there was something else – a shock I sustained during the evening and I think it must have addled my brain. It is no excuse but I ask you to believe that I was not really in my right mind.'

'What kind of shock?' Marcelle asked.

'It is of no matter,' said Guy. He released her and turned away.

'I think,' said Marcelle, more confident now, 'that it is your duty

295

to explain to me why you behaved as you did. You can be assured that I will never tell a living soul, if that is what you wish, but I deserve an explanation.'

Guy turned to her. 'Yes, of course,' he said. 'You had better sit down.' They sat together in the window-seat where Guy had found her earlier. She was composed and silent.

At first he struggled with his explanation, finding words difficult, his own feelings still so raw and exposed. Gradually, though, as the story of his mother's life and death unfolded, he felt a sweet relief begin to take hold of him and he realized that this was the first time he had ever spoken of his mother to anyone.

There was a stunned silence when he had finished. It was Marcelle who spoke at last. 'Poor Guy, no wonder you were so drunk.'

'I do not deserve your understanding,' Guy said, gently. 'But as you said, I did owe you this explanation. At the moment I hate my father for what he did to my mother, but in a curious way I feel almost more hurt by my mother. We were very close, she and I, or so I thought. I dream of her often, even now. Yet she left me, abandoned me deliberately – I would never have believed she could have done that.' He was close to tears again. 'You must think I am very weak, a grown man crying for his mother.' He drew a sleeve across his face, the gesture of a child, to stem the tears that threatened again.

'Oh Guy.' Marcelle stood up and flinging her arms about his neck, she held him close to her. 'I understand now how you felt. You were angry with all women, you avenged yourself and your anger on me, because I was there. Your explanation leaves nothing to forgive – what you did was completely understandable.'

At her words, Guy felt a tightening around his throat and a pounding of his heart, so strong was the emotion that gripped him. This young girl, whom he had thought very pretty but whom he had never given a second glance before now, not only understood him, but loved him, too. Mistreated and abused, she still wanted to comfort him. He was not worthy of her and yet all his life, since his mother's death, he had been unconsciously seeking someone to whom he could belong. He drew away and kneeling down before her, took her hand. 'I have no right to ask this, Marcelle. I know it is what our parents wish but I am not asking you for that reason. I wish for your hand in marriage because you are the most lovely and wonderful woman I have ever met. With you, and only with you, I think it possible that my life can be made whole again, and I can promise that if you accept my hand in marriage, from this day forth I will devote my life to your happiness and wellbeing.'

Marcelle regarded him in silence for a moment and then she smiled, a delightful smile. 'It is as well that you have asked for my hand in marriage, Guy, for from the first moment I saw you, I promised myself that I would make you love me and so I shall.' She hesitated, the smile disappeared. 'I will do my best to be a loving and devoted wife to you, and we will forget all that passed between us before this moment.' They embraced and Guy kissed her gently, carefully, desperately anxious to demonstrate his desire to cherish her.

A special licence was acquired and they were married at four o'clock that same afternoon. Marie-Claire and Thomas were still grey and tight-lipped with shock but after the brief ceremony they drank champagne in the drawing room and attempted to celebrate. The young couple's happiness was short-lived however, for the same evening Thomas and Guy were recalled to the line to play their part in the bloodiest battle in history.

If only there had been time to talk, Thomas thought as he sat alone at his desk awaiting the arrival of his son. Everything had been so hurried, set as it was against the drama of Waterloo. Thomas winced when he thought of the battle. Being the age he was, he had seen little of the action as his role had been to stay close to Wellington. Guy, however, had been in the thick of the fighting and it was only afterwards that he learned of his son's valour during the French cavalry charge. During that long day, Thomas had been heavy in spirits, sure that he would never see his son alive again, cursing himself for allowing them to part so bitterly. In fact it was Thomas who was wounded, taking a shot in the arm at the end of the battle, when Napoleon's Garde Impériale attacked. Wellington by then was becoming short of men and it had been necessary for him to marshal all his available troops, including Thomas. The wound was not serious but it was left untreated for some hours, resulting in an infection and a fever which had nearly killed him. Mercifully it had meant that he had little memory of the aftermath of Waterloo.

Guy, however, had not rested on his laurels following his bravery during the battle. For two days he had toiled to help the wounded, a terrible task, during which Guy had spared neither himself nor his men. Indeed, the carnage had been so dreadful, no one could find it in their hearts to rejoice at the victory. Again and again, while still

297

convalescing in Brussels under the tender administrations of Marie-Claire, and later when he returned to England, Thomas heard the name of Guy Monson hailed as a hero. But Thomas could not rejoice or take pride in his son's achievements. During the whole of Thomas's illness and brush with death, Guy had not been near him, despite Marcelle's pleadings. He had only consented to come to Chadbrook today, at Thomas's specific request, and how the meeting would fare Thomas could not even imagine. Even Guy's valour worried him. He had never doubted that his son was an excellent soldier and a brave man but it seemed that at Waterloo he had almost courted death, to the point where Thomas wondered whether he had actually wanted to live at all.

This time Thomas's sharp ears heard the unmistakable sound of a lone horseman coming up the drive. Once again, he leaned out of the library window and caught a sight of a rider on a dapple grey mare he did not recognize – it had to be Guy. He sat down at his desk and waited with mounting apprehension.

The two men eyed each other in silence. 'Would you care to sit down?' said Thomas. 'And will you take some refreshment?'

'No refreshment,' said Guy. 'And I would rather stand. I will not be staying.'

'As you wish,' said Thomas. 'There are three reasons I invited you here today, Guy. I will deal with the speedier matters first. I have in my possession a letter from the Lord Chamberlain confirming that a knighthood will be bestowed upon you for your valour at Waterloo. I wrote to the King, at Wellington's request, recommending you for the honour. It seems the King had already received reports of you. You are to be congratulated, you are a very brave man and well deserve the honour.' Guy said nothing and seemed totally unmoved. He had aged considerably, Thomas noticed, there were few traces left of the boy he had once been. 'The second matter is with regard to your future home. I have here the deeds of a property known as Thurston Hall. You will probably never have seen it for it is at the extreme west of the Chadbrook lands. It comprises a fair-sized house and three hundred acres of good agricultural land. I have gifted this property to you, in order to provide you and Marcelle with a home. There are no conditions attached to it, Guy, the house is yours irrevocably and I intend to grant you an income of four hundred a year, to help maintain your wife and future family.'

'I would like to be in a position, sir, to refuse your offer,' Guy said.

298

His tone and his words shocked Thomas. 'However,' he continued, 'I am patently aware that I am not a man of means or position and it is necessary that I support my wife, if not in luxury, at least in comfort. For that reason I will accept your offer of Thurston Hall on her behalf but I will not accept the annual income. Marcelle and I will manage on the income from the land, and her dowry.'

'You speak too hastily,' said Thomas. 'Marcelle is not a country-woman and you have little enough experience of husbandry. It is not a large estate and it may be many years before you will be able to work it sufficiently to bring you a reasonable income.'

'We will manage,' said Guy, uncompromisingly.

Thomas sighed and walking over to the window, stared out into the parkland, to the ha-ha and beyond to the larch wood. 'Before you finally refuse my offer I think you should hear the third part of what I have to say. I owe you an explanation concerning your mother's death and I will do my best to explain what happened.' He turned to Guy. 'Please sit down, you make me feel uncomfortable and this may take some time.' Guy did as he was asked. 'As I told you in Brussels, I fell in love with your mother when she was sixteen. I was forced to stay at The Lady in Waiting one night on a return journey from London, the weather conditions making it impossible for me to travel further. We parted, never to meet again or so I thought, but by chance we happened upon one another at a horse fair at Long Melford. I am not going to try in any way to hide from you the motives behind the relationship – they were simple enough. I was then married to Christopher's mother, Eleanor. The marriage was not a happy one, but because I was so short of funds I had little opportunity to go to London and perhaps seek comfort in other female company. When I happened upon your mother and clearly she reciprocated my feelings, I began what I thought was simply a casual affair with a local girl.' He looked at Guy hoping for under-standing but his son's eyes were devoid of warmth. 'As it happened, it was not that simple,' said Thomas. 'Your mother was an extraordi-nary person. Her parents were from very lowly stock and yet she had something different about her – quality, breeding.' He struggled for words. 'The way she walked, bore herself, she had natural grace, her looks – she was an extremely beautiful woman, I am sure you will remember that yourself. She also had an aptitude and an interest in book-learning which, considering her background, was truly marvel-lous. Her mother told her once that she had indulged in a passing relationship with a nobleman visiting the inn and Elizabeth was the

299

result. Elizabeth always hoped it was true, for her father was nothing more than an uncouth, dirty peasant. For my part, I am as sure as I can be that the story was true, for I do not believed that couple could have conceived such a beauty as your mother. I helped her with her learning over the years and taught her correct manners and how to dress. She was very quick to learn and it gave me pleasure. It was also useful to her as the inn prospered.' Again Thomas looked at Guy, hoping to see if he had made some impact. It appeared not.

'Why did you marry Beatrice Naylor, after your first wife was killed in the hunting accident? Christopher told me once that the marriage took place on the day of my birth. Is that correct?'

'Yes.' Thomas shifted uneasily. 'I had to, Guy, for the sake of Chadbrook. My father had gambled away all available capital and indeed had put the whole estate in debt. Either I had to sell the estate or marry a rich woman and your mother was certainly not that.'

'How did my mother feel when she learnt of your decision?'

'She was very angry and sad,' said Thomas. 'In fact we were estranged for nearly four years. Then we met again by chance, in the spinney at Long Melford.'

'I remember that,' said Guy. 'I remember everything from then on, every detail – when you visited us, the presents you gave me.'

'I loved your mother very much and I love you, too. Perhaps this is something I should not say to you. . .' He hesitated. 'Though Christopher is my heir, he is not the man after my own heart that you have been.'

Guy said nothing for some while. 'You have not explained why you abandoned my mother again. Was it because another baby was to be born?'

'No,' said Thomas. 'I cannot tell you the details without dishonouring my wife but we were blackmailed, your mother and I. We had to give up the relationship or we would both have been ruined.'

'After all that has passed between us, you are not going to tell me the reasons why you abandoned her?' Guy shouted, standing up.

'It is not possible for me to give you the details. I have just explained that. It involves my wife's family and it would be dishonourable for me to disclose them. However, I can tell you that not only would Chadbrook have been ruined but so would your mother if we had persisted in our affair.'

'If it was so impossible for you to continue to see one another, then why did she die?' Guy asked. 'Clearly, she could not have agreed with your decision. If she had done, she would have made the best of her life without you as she did after I was born.'

For the first time Thomas caught a glimpse of the hurt Guy must feel. It was not only he that was discredited in his son's eyes – Guy clearly resented his mother, too, for leaving him, and Thomas could understand this. He sought quickly to reassure. 'Your mother was always a very volatile woman, she was quick to anger, quick to laugh, but there was a slightly unbalanced side to her nature. For example, on the day you were born. . .' He got no further.

Guy was on his feet, crimson with fury. 'How dare you insult my mother! She was not mad. This is just a pathetic excuse to try to cover your own blame. I agree, my grandmother was simple in the head but there was nothing wrong with my mother, nothing at all. You drove her to her death.'

'I did not, Guy.' The two men stood facing one another, either side of Thomas's desk. 'Her mind was deeply disturbed – it had to be for her to ride off as she did.'

'I agree but it was you who disturbed her mind. God in heaven, I will hear no more of your pathetic excuses.' The air between them was thick with tension and shock. There was a long silence and when at last Guy spoke again, he was a little calmer. 'I will accept your offer of Thurston Hall because I have no alternative. I will not accept one penny from you in income, and I would ask that from this moment forth we never meet again, for I swear to God I cannot be held responsible for my actions if we do.' He turned and left the room.

'Guy. . .' Thomas began. The door of the library slammed. He had failed, he had lost him. Thomas slumped into his chair, put his head in his hands and began to weep. 'Elizabeth, Elizabeth,' he moaned. 'Why did you leave us?' There was no answer, only silence, save for the sound of the wind blowing through the larches.

301

CHAPTER THIRTY-TWO
Vancouver Island, BC. Canada – January 1983

The snow was not like English snow – not damp and cloying – it was powdery and sparkling with frost. When you picked it up in armfuls, it did not leave you wringing wet, it fell through the fingers like newly sieved flour. Prue stood in an enchanted world, the forest around her shining in the afternoon sun. Each twig, each leaf was picked out individually in a layer of snow, hardened by frost. The light through the trees was warm and golden, the sky, only just visible, was a deep blue. She let out a sigh of pure joy and then shivered slightly. It was time to be going home; darkness came very quickly to Vancouver Island and when the sun set it would be bitterly cold. She pulled her coat tightly around her ungainly figure and started trudging back in the direction of Richard and Anna's cabin.

It had been an extraordinary coincidence, the letter from Richard. It had arrived on the same day as she had received the call from Jonathan to tell her their relationship was over. Richard Sinclair was her old flatmate – the photographer who had shared her life in the days before Jonathan. When she had first left London they had corresponded quite frequently but in recent months it had lapsed. Richard's fortunes had changed dramatically – he had been on an assignment in Vancouver Island and while there had met a British nurse called Anna. He had fallen in love with both Anna and the island and, as he said in the letter, was never coming home. Richard and Anna had married just weeks before and as was the way with young people on the island, they had bought a plot of land in the middle of the forest, just outside Chemainus, and had built their own cabin. It sounded impossibly romantic. 'Why not come and visit us?' Richard's letter had said. 'It's a very unhealthy life, running a hotel. If you must bring Jonathan with you, fair enough, but I'm hoping you'll come on your own.' Richard had never liked or trusted Jonathan, Prue remembered. If only she had listened to him in those early days in London.

She had made the decision to go, immediately, and had never regretted it. Richard's home was as perfect as he had described it in his letter. It was a large log-cabin, fashioned round an old mobile home – primitive, but with plumbing and an electricity supply. The forest was all about them and the peace and tranquillity of the place was inspiring. Anna became an instant friend. She was a little older than Prue, a British-trained nurse who had come to Vancouver Island for no reason other than she had tired of the English climate. She was a very practical girl, full of humour and fun. In many ways she and Richard were rather alike. They made Prue feel not only welcome but also useful, allowing her to join them in the decorating of their now completed cabin and showing enormous appreciation of the splendid meals she cooked them.

Briefly, when alone Richard had picked her up from the airport, he had asked her about Jonathan, and when she told him that it was over and that she had come to Canada to recuperate, he had accepted her explanation with the rejoinder that she must stay with them as long as she wished. That had been seven months ago and a great deal had happened to her in the intervening period.

Prue had been staying with Anna and Richard for only two weeks when she realized she was pregnant. The child, without a shadow of doubt, was Charles Chadbrook's, conceived in Brussels in the de Villefranche chateau. The shock was enormous and coming as it did, hard on the heels of losing Jonathan, it had the effect of numbing her brain, so that she seemed incapable of making any form of decision. Driven half mad by trying to keep the pregnancy to herself she had eventually admitted her condition to Anna and Richard, who accepted it with kindly concern and then left her alone to come to terms with what had happened. The weeks slid by in a haze and then one Sunday morning Anna urged Prue to come out for a walk and had carefully but firmly pointed out that if Prue wished to terminate the pregnancy, she would have to make a decision within the next week.

'What do you mean?' Prue had asked, apparently scandalized.

'It's none of my business,' Anna had said. 'But I am a nurse and I think it would be irresponsible of me not to point out to you that unless you have this pregnancy terminated within the next two weeks, you cannot have it done legally, either here or in England.' Prue said nothing. Anna tried again. 'From what you say, you know who the father is but there's no question of a permanent relationship, at least not for the time being. In the circumstances, do you honestly feel able to bring up a baby on your own and is it even fair to try? You seem to be very uncertain as to what you want from life at the moment. There's no doubt about it – a baby's going to be a consider-able complication.'

'How dare you!' Prue had said. 'How dare you suggest that I should kill my baby.' She had burst into hysterical tears and sobbed on Anna's shoulder for a long time. The tears were not just for herself or for the baby, they were for Jonathan, for Charles, perhaps even for Elizabeth. She had been emotionally pent-up for months yet quite unable to grieve. It was inevitable that at some point the dam had to burst.

Later that evening, after supper, Prue had apologized for her outburst and said she would like to discuss her future with both Richard and Anna. 'I can't have an abortion,' she said. 'It's not just that I'm against it, which I am, it's something else. I feel I have to have this child, I can't explain why. Equally, though, I don't think I can go back to England, not yet anyway. I can't face my parents' concern and I don't know what to say to Charles, the baby's father, as I don't know how I feel, let alone how he does.'

'You can stay with us,' said Richard promptly. 'For as long as you like.'

'It's not fair,' said Prue. 'You're newly married, you must have the place to yourselves. I can't stay here any longer.'

'You can and you must,' Anna insisted. 'At least until the baby is born. Neither of us feels right about your being on your own and pregnant in a strange country. We would be a great deal less happy if you moved out than if you stayed.'

Their kindness overwhelmed her. 'I'll have to start earning my keep, then,' Prue said.

'Why don't you try to do a little catering,' said Richard, 'for parties and special functions, like you used to do? It's not worth trying to get a work permit if you don't know how long you're going to stay in Canada. We can put the word around and I am sure you can earn enough to satisfy your need for independence. I do understand that but I must insist you stay with us.' He slipped an arm round her and gave her a hug.

And so Prue had stayed and the months had been happy ones. She had found plenty of work as Richard had suggested and the money she earned was good for her self-esteem. She was able to pay her way properly with Richard and Anna, rather than accept their hospitality, and still save a little towards the time when the baby was born.

It had been an easy pregnancy and, despite the circumstances, surprisingly untroubled. At some time during the months of her burgeoning figure Prue had realized, with a shock, that she was very glad the child was Charles's and not Jonathan's and yet still the whole situation was tinged with unreality. She shivered again; the wind was getting up, a cold north-east wind blowing snow from the trees, giving the illusion that it was snowing again. The sky was clouding over but nothing seemed to shake her happiness. There was no reason for it really – she was an unmarried mother with no proper job, no home, no future, no man, but none of it seemed to matter. The previous week she had gone shopping in a store in Victoria to purchase the bare essentials for the baby. She'd had a wonderful time but it was as if she was shopping for someone else. When friends of Richard and Anna's had presented her with a teddy bear, her instincts had been to hand it back because it was not relevant, as if they had muddled her with someone else. It was crazy considering it was weeks since she had been able to see her feet . . . presumably it was the baby who was responsible for her sense of wellbeing, but still she did not seem able to grasp the reality of it.

Suddenly, she saw ahead of her through the trees the light of the cabin. 'Nearly home,' she said aloud and the words brought swiftly to mind her parents, and with the thought came a stab of guilt. Following a hospital scan two months previously which confirmed the baby was doing well, Prue had finally written to her mother, to tell her of the pregnancy. Margery Mansell's reaction had not been unexpected. She had been shocked and surprised but what had really concerned her was Prue's welfare and she had urged her daughter to return to England immediately. She had sent a cheque for the fare and promised that neither she nor Robert would be critical in any way as long as Prue came home. But Prue could not do that, not yet. Several times in her letter her mother had mentioned how she and her father had struck up a friendship with Charles Chadbrook. She wondered whether her parents would tell him of the pregnancy and if so what he would think – that the child was Jonathan's, that it had been conceived in Canada? Would it even occur to him that it was his? Somehow, though, she doubted her parents would ever tell him, or anyone else come to that, unless they were forced to do so. In response to the letter, she had telephoned her mother and promised she would return soon after the birth. While Margery had been tearful and pleading, reproachful even, Prue also sensed she was also slightly relieved.

That night after her walk through the forest, for the first time Prue had a disturbing dream. It was of a little boy running through a wood apparently lost. She never saw the child's face but his back view looked like Charles's. She longed to bring him comfort and she woke distressed, with a pounding heart and tears on her face which reminded her of her terrible nights wrestling with Elizabeth's misery. Since coming to Canada her nights had been undisturbed. She had enjoyed deep, dreamless slumber which made her realize just how short of sleep she had been during the period she had lived at The Lady in Waiting. The relief at being free from Elizabeth was considerable but Prue felt extremely guilty, guilty for having abandoned her with her misery unresolved. This new dream of the child disturbed her greatly. She tried to convince herself that the child was Charles, the lonely little boy whose father preferred his elder brother, but she knew that was not the case. The child was Guy, and the wood, the larch wood at Chadbrook. From that night on, the dream became a recurring feature, gathering intensity and causing her such distress that the thought of going to sleep began to frighten her. Gradually, her new-found happiness began to flow from her and all the old feelings of unease and foreboding she had experienced at The Lady in Waiting began to return. Yet she could confide in no one, and as the time drew near for her baby to be born, the lost child began to upset her quite as much as his mother's misery had done.

CHAPTER THIRTY-THREE
Thurston Hall – January 1983

Robert Mansell and Charles Chadbrook sat in contented silence before the drawing room fire, sipping at an excellent port and puffing on the cigars which Charles had brought with him. The basis for the friendship which had sprung up between the two men was never discussed. If asked, they would have said it was the discovery that they were related and both interested in their families' past. In reality it was their mutual love of Prue which bound them together, although neither was aware of it.

They had met at a cocktail party within a few weeks of Prue leaving for Canada. Charles, discovering who they were, had introduced himself thinking that contact with Prue's parents might relieve the pain of her absence. In fact they rarely spoke of her though Charles sensed that her sudden departure had caused her parents considerable pain. Since he had no intention of admitting his true feelings for their daughter, it was difficult to find an excuse to ask about her but every so often he coaxed from them little pieces of information about her which kept him going. The friendship prospered and the Mansells dined at Chadbrook on several occasions although, more frequently, Charles had taken to dropping in for an evening drink with Robert, and often stayed on for supper.

Charles's plans for developing Chadbrook were going well and he, genuinely, found that talking through his problems with Robert helped him a great deal. He had very few friends in the area; mostly they lived in London, frequenters of the Chelsea Arts Club – writers and painters mostly – charming people but absolutely useless in helping him with the commercial considerations of Chadbrook. At Prue's suggestion he had obtained planning permission to build a restaurant on the banks of the lake. He had constructed a landing stage and bought a selection of hire boats. The restaurant was due to be opened in the spring and the old walled garden was in the process of being converted into a garden centre, also due for a spring opening. The final stage was the riding school. Charles had become friendly with the Naylors. He had discovered that Sally Naylor was a fine rider and was looking for an opportunity to start a riding school for children in the area. She had jumped at the chance of going into partnership with Charles and starting a school at Chadbrook. The stabling was considerable and an indoor school was being built.

'I just hope we won't cause Thomas to do handsprings in his grave at the thought of a Naylor coming back to Chadbrook,' Sally said, only half joking.

Charles was very pleased with the nature of his commercial ventures to date. He was taking advantage of the natural resources of Chadbrook without spoiling the beauty and tranquillity of the place. At all costs he was trying to avoid model railways and funfairs and was desperately hoping that these three enterprises alone would persuade the taxman that sufficient income could be raised to allow the taxes to be paid off on an instalment basis. If only Prue was with him, he would feel more confident about the success of his ventures. Although he was working hard he felt as if his life was on hold, that he was only half a person. The only thing that seemed to keep him going emotionally was these frequent visits to Thurston Hall. He glanced up at Robert now, who was gazing into the fire. He had been quiet, unusually quiet all evening. Charles noticed there was a worried frown on his face. Instantly his heart lurched – was something wrong with Prue? He had been so wrapped up in his own affairs he had not really given much thought to the Mansells that evening, but now he thought about it there had been tension in the air at supper and Margery had retired very early.

'You seem a little preoccupied tonight, Robert,' Charles suggested.

'Do I, my boy? Sorry.' Robert jerked his attention back to Charles. 'I'm getting old,' he said. 'And worn out – the older one gets, the more one needs one's sleep.'

'I'll go,' said Charles. 'I'm sorry, I didn't mean to keep you up.'

'No, no, don't go.' Robert picked up a decanter and refilled Charles's glass. 'I'm sorry I'm such poor company today but I've one or two things on my mind.'

'No serious problems, I hope,' said Charles.

'No, no,' said Robert, dismissively.

Charles took a deep breath. He was going to lose the thread of the conversation unless he was a little pushy. 'There's nothing wrong with Prue, is there?'

Robert looked at him sharply. 'Why do you say that?'

Charles shrugged his shoulders. 'I'm not a parent myself but

308

watching you just now, you have the preoccupied look of someone who is worrying about their child. I have enough friends with children to know that one's offspring cause a very complicated mixture of pleasure and pain.'

Robert smiled slightly, took a sip of his port and then seemed to be considering the question. Charles held his breath. 'I shouldn't really talk to you about it, Margery would be furious, she has sworn me to secrecy.'

'Talk to me about what?' Charles asked, quickly.

'As a matter of fact you are right, it is Prue I am worried about. You see she . . . well, she seems to have got herself pregnant.'

The shock was complete. It was the very last thing Charles had expected. So she had been right to go, she could not have loved him if she had formed a new relationship and was already pregnant. He felt as though someone had kicked him in the stomach. At all costs he must hide his feelings. Luckily, Robert, clearly embarrassed by the disclosure, was staring fixedly at the fire. 'Has, has she met someone in Canada?' Charles managed to say, surprised at how normal his voice sounded.

'Oh no, no, I don't think so.' Robert seemed vague. 'She can't have done – the baby's almost due, any day now.' So the baby was Jonathan's, that at least made Charles feel slightly better though not much. He dared not press Robert further – he was clearly very uncomfortable about discussing the subject. 'You see,' Robert volunteered, after a pause, 'Margery wants her to come home, understandably she's worried sick about her. Prue sounds very down in her letters and she is having difficulty sleeping. She's not ill, it's just bad dreams she says, but she should be at home given all the circumstances.'

Dreams . . . Surely Elizabeth had not followed her to Canada. Elizabeth belonged at The Lady in Waiting, Prue had always said that. She had never been troubled here at Thurston Hall, nor the time they had been in Brussels together. As the thought of Brussels came into his mind, at the same moment Charles realized that the baby could be his. This second shock sent him from his chair. He walked over to the window, desperate to collect his thoughts. 'So you assume the baby is Jonathan Lindstrom's?' he said, at last.

'Yes,' said Robert. 'The scoundrel, he's caused all this trouble. Prue wouldn't have gone to Canada but for him, he messed her about terribly you know. She didn't realize he was married. When she found out, he said he was seeking a divorce but, of course, he wasn't'.

309

So she ran away, to have his baby, but how she'll feel about the child I don't know.'

It was like an echo, a terrifying echo from the past. 'So she ran away, to have his baby.' Elizabeth had run away to have a baby she did not want, by a man she could not have . . . and Elizabeth had died. For a moment Charles shut his eyes, resting his head on the windowpane.

'Are you all right, old boy?' Robert called from the fireplace.

'Yes, I'm fine,' Charles said hastily. 'Why don't you and your wife go out to Canada to be with her when the child is born?'

'Margery suggested that to her but Prue is absolutely dead against it. In any case Margery is terrified of flying. We'd have to go by sea and it's too late now, the baby will be born before we could get there. I could go alone, of course, but it's not me she wants. I imagine if she wants anyone, she wants Jonathan, but of course it's hard to tell – young people these days are a mystery to me.'

'Someone should go to her, someone should be with her,' said Charles, desperately.

'Perhaps,' said Robert. 'But as things stand, we'll just have to sit here and wait . . . There's no reason why she shouldn't be all right, she's a healthy young woman.'

'So was Elizabeth,' Charles found himself saying.

'What?' said Robert. 'What on earth do you mean by that?'

Instantly Robert regretted his words but it was too late to retract them. He shrugged his shoulders and returned to the fire. 'I'm sorry, I was being fanciful, forget what I said.'

'No, you weren't,' said Robert, shrewdly. 'What did you mean, what has this got to do with Elizabeth?'

'Nothing whatsoever,' said Charles, desperate now to change the course of Robert's thinking. It was too late.

'So, you're suggesting that because Elizabeth ran away to have the child of a married man and Prue has done the same thing, that Prue could come to an equally sticky end – is that right?'

Robert sounded calm enough but Charles was not fooled. 'No, of course not,' he said. 'I didn't mean that at all.'

'You did,' said Robert. The two men stared at one another in silence for a moment.

'I could go out there and stay with her until the baby is born,' Charles suggested.

'You?' Robert was surprised. 'But you barely know her.'

Again Charles rose to his feet. He felt weak with tension but he

310

needed to put some distance between himself and Robert. He chose his words carefully. 'I haven't been quite frank with you in the last few months, Robert. It's true I haven't known Prue very long but in fact I'm in love with her. I'm not sure how she would receive me, because she ordered me out of her life when she decided to go to Canada, but I do know her rather better than I have led you to believe.'

'I see,' said Robert. The silence now was charged with tension. 'I'm sorry,' said Robert, 'but I'm afraid I have to ask you this question though, of course, you don't have to answer it.' Charles winced inwardly, sensing what was coming. 'Could this child be yours, rather than Jonathan Lindstrom's?'

Charles took a deep breath. 'Yes,' he said. 'Yes it could.'

'I see,' said Robert, 'or rather, I don't see. What the hell has she been playing at? I thought I knew my daughter yet she seems to have been behaving no better than a tart. I can't believe it. You, Jonathan, who else has she slept with?' He sounded almost hysterical.

It was not the reaction Charles had expected. The anger should have been directed at himself, not Prue. 'There hasn't been anyone else, Robert,' Charles said quietly. 'I want to marry her. I believe she and I are meant to be together. However I do accept now – although I didn't when she first went away – that she couldn't come straight to me from her relationship with Jonathan.'

'But if the child is Jonathan Lindstrom's, presumably you will not want to have any more to do with her? You won't want to bring up another man's child.'

'The child isn't Jonathan Lindstrom's, it's mine,' said Charles.

Robert stared at him curiously. 'How the hell do you know?'

'I don't know,' said Charles, 'I don't even know what made me say that.'

'I don't know what to think,' said Robert, with a heavy sigh. 'I like you, Charles, you know that, but it's come as a shock to realize that you've been more than just a friend with my daughter. I wish you'd told me before . . . but no matter, if you think you can help her then for pity's sake do so. I daren't give the notion that history is repeating itself any credence or I think I'd go out of my mind, but if you think your presence might help Prue, then go to her, go now.'

It took Charles just a few hours to organize a flight to Canada the following day and it was five o'clock in the morning local time when finally he landed at Vancouver airport. He was uncertain how to

311

make contact with Prue. Robert Mansell had given him Richard's address and telephone number but although telephoning her to say he was on his way might be practical, it was also dangerous. Supposing she refused to see him? Good manners suggested that she would not do so, his having travelled so far, but it was a risk he did not feel he dared take. He took a cab across the city to the small local airport which services Vancouver Island and caught a plane which took him to the island in just over twenty minutes. By now the sun was up and although it was a cold, January day the sky was blue and the light golden. At the airport he managed to hail yet another cab and gave the driver Richard's address. 'How long will it take to get there?'

'About twenty-five minutes, half an hour, no more.'

He tried to sleep in the cab but in his mind he kept rehearsing again and again what he was going to say to Prue. Perhaps he had reacted too hastily but he could not escape the terror that clutched at him when he thought of Elizabeth and her death. It was a crazy notion but all through the last months, Prue had seemed to helter-skelter through life, almost slavishly following the path of destiny which Elizabeth had once taken. Charles shuddered. And what of the child?

'This is it, buddy,' the driver called. 'These folks surely live in the back of beyond.'

They drew up outside a log-cabin. Charles stepped shakily from the cab and climbed the steps; his heart was pounding in his chest. He felt like a small boy.

A tall, pleasant-looking man opened the door. 'Hello, can I help?'

'You must be Richard,' said Charles.

'Yes, I am.'

'My name's Charles Chadbrook. I've come to see Prue Mansell and have been given this address. Is she here at the moment?'

Richard stared at him for a moment. 'No, she's not. She's at the hospital.'

'Why, what's wrong?'

'Calm down,' said Richard, hastily. 'Everything's OK – it's just that the baby has started. There's no problem. It was due in a week anyway. My wife's with her. Come along in and have some coffee. Prue's told us a little about you.'

'No, no I can't stop, I must get to the hospital,' said Charles.

'I shouldn't think there's much of a hurry,' Richard replied. 'Anna, that's my wife, expects it to be a fairly long labour.'

If his words were intended to bring comfort they had the opposite

312

effect. 'No, I have to go,' said Charles. 'W-which hospital is it? Can you give directions to my driver?'

'Would you like me to come, too?' Richard asked.

'No, no I'll be fine. I just have to go to Prue, quickly.'

Within moments they were heading back down the track again. Charles leaned back in the seat and stared out of the window at the forest with unseeing eyes. Had it been like this for Thomas? he wondered. Thomas had arrived too late, please God let him not do the same.

CHAPTER THIRTY-FOUR

The maternity hospital at Chemainus was a relaxed and friendly place. There were sprigged curtains at the windows of the delivery room and in the distance, as the sun rose, Prue could see the forest trees, the life blood of Vancouver Island. In truth though, she was in no mood to admire the view on this particular morning for she had been in labour for fifteen hours. She was both exhausted, and terrified for her baby. She shifted uneasily in the bed. Her stomach was wired up with monitors to regulate the baby's heartbeat and her own contractions, and a nurse was keeping a constant vigil. On the other side of the bed, slumped in a chair, was Anna. Poor Anna, who had insisted on staying by her side but now, at last, had passed into an uneasy sleep. An alarm bell rang on the monitor, jerking Anna awake and bringing the midwife to her feet.

'What's wrong?' said Prue, unbearably tense.

'It's OK, honey, I'll just fetch the doctor.'

Dr. Roberts, when he arrived, looked more like a lumberjack than a doctor, dressed as he was in check shirt and jeans. 'Sorry about my appearance,' he said. 'I've just got out of bed. What's the trouble here?' He smiled reassuringly and began his examination.

'Miss Mansell's been in labour for nearly fifteen hours,' said the midwife. 'And the baby's becoming very distressed.'

Prue turned a weary head to look at the doctor. He seemed kind, with a big, open face. 'Please help my baby, I'm so frightened. It's all been going on for too long – it can't be right.'

'Don't worry, sweetheart, you're right, you've struggled long enough, I should have been called long ago.' He glared at the midwife. 'Never fear, we'll soon have you a bouncing baby though I guess it will mean forceps.'

Things moved very quickly, Anna was banned from the room, despite her protests. An anaesthetist was called and Prue was given an epidural injection. She sighed in wonder as the pain left her, her legs becoming floppy and numb. 'Not long now,' the doctor assured her. 'Don't you fret, it won't hurt. You'll feel nothing, I promise.'

There was a sudden commotion at the door, raised voices and what appeared to be a scuffle. 'What the hell . . . ?' said Dr. Roberts.

A man erupted into the room. 'Prue, Prue! Are you all right, what's happening?'

The voice was unmistakable. Prue turned her head to see Charles struggling to free himself from an orderly. The shock was total, numbing her senses, just as surely as the injection had numbed her body. Charles here, at this moment – how had he known? She did not speak, but simply stared at him in disbelief. 'Prue, for God's sake, tell them who I am, they wouldn't let me in. I have to be with you.'

'Out,' said Dr. Roberts. 'Get this lunatic out right now.'

'One moment,' said Prue, suddenly coming to her senses. 'This man is Charles Chadbrook, the Earl of Clare. He also happens to be the baby's father.' Their eyes met. They stared at one another in silence and such was the tension between them that it silenced the medical team. Everyone seemed to be waiting.

'I knew it,' Charles said, his voice croaking. 'I'm so sorry you had to go through all this alone, what can I say, what can I do?'

'The very best thing you can do now,' said Dr. Roberts, 'is to get the hell out of here, if I am to produce a healthy son or daughter for you.'

'But is she going to be all right?'

'Not unless you let us get on with the job, buddy.'

'I'll wait just outside, Prue. You'll call me if anything goes wrong.'

Charles caught Dr. Roberts's arm, the expression on his face was desperate. The poor guy's a basket case, Dr. Roberts thought. 'Nothing will go wrong, if you just let us get on with our job,' he said, trying to sound reassuring. It worked – reluctantly Charles allowed himself to be escorted from the room.

Prue turned to Dr. Roberts. 'Please don't be so hard on him, he's just flown all the way from England to be with me, without even knowing if the child was his.'

'OK, I just don't like people busting in on me, Earl or no Earl.' He smiled. 'I'll be Mr. Nice Guy when this is over, OK?'

Prue smiled back. 'OK.'

'Right then, here we go. Push only when I say.'

Within minutes, almost seconds it seemed to Prue, she heard a cry. 'There you go, young lady, a boy, a fine son for you.'

Prue felt the strange sensation of a slippery little body being placed on her stomach. Then before she could put her arms around him he was gone and she had not even seen him. 'My baby,' she called out.

'We'll just have him weighed and checked,' said Dr. Roberts. 'Don't worry, he looks fine, a big boy, just a little reluctant to be born. Not surprising really – he was very comfortable in there and it's a wicked old world out here.'

Prue dissolved into tears at his words. 'I'm sorry,' she said, 'I just want to hold him.'

'Would you like your friend to come in now?' Dr. Roberts asked. 'I can't see any reason why he shouldn't be with you while I sew you up.'

Prue hesitated. Charles's extraordinary appearance at such a moment held absolutely no reality for her – there were so many emotions to handle. Instinctively she knew suddenly that it was important to be alone with her son for just a few minutes before she tried to tackle the implications of Charles's arrival. 'I think I'd like a little time with the baby on my own first,' she said, apologetically.

Dr. Roberts smiled. 'I can understand that. Here he is then, let's help you into a more comfortable position. I'll just go and have a word with the proud father – and I'll even buy him a coffee, how about that?'

The midwife handed Prue a small, white bundle. She parted the blankets, stared down at the crumpled little face and gasped aloud. 'What is it?' said the midwife anxiously. 'What's wrong?'

'Nothing,' said Prue. 'Nothing at all.'

The baby was indeed perfect – bright blue eyes, a wisp of dark curls, a dimple on one cheek. The shock of seeing him though was profound . . . for she knew him, knew him instantly, had always known him, from a long time ago. She stared into his eyes, he met her gaze and she saw the same startled expression in his own face. There was no doubt in her mind. Tears began to pour down her cheeks.

'It's all right, sweetheart, he's fine, don't worry.'

'I know, I know,' said Prue, tearfully.

'Do you want me to take him now?'

'No, it's all right,' she said. 'I'm sorry about the tears.'

The midwife looked at her concerned. 'You did want the baby, didn't you?'

'Oh yes,' said Prue.

'That's good then,' she said, a little uncertainly. There was a silence between them for a minute. The midwife was clearly still anxious at Prue's reaction. 'So what are you going to call the little fellow?' she asked, with forced cheerfulness.

'Guy,' Prue replied, promptly. 'It has always been his name.'

The flight to Heathrow was ahead of schedule because of a tail wind which suited the parents and their young baby very well indeed. It was only five days since Guy's birth, but the feeling . . . the need to return to England was something of an obsession with them both. They were shell-shocked emotionally and without expressing it to one another in so many words, they knew that their lives could not take on any form of normality until Guy was home.

In the hours immediately after his birth there had been no time to talk properly. The inevitable cleaning-up process of mother and baby meant that they had not spent a second alone. Then there had been visits by the paediatrician, nursing staff to help Prue feed the baby, and even the hospital chaplain to see if they would like the baby blessed. After such a long labour, Prue was exhausted and, much to her later shame, fell into a deep sleep without exchanging more than a few words with Charles, and none alone.

It had been the following day before they had found any sort of privacy and conversation between them initially was still stilted and awkward, both being so uncertain as to the feelings of the other. 'I would have come earlier,' Charles said, anxiously. 'Only I didn't know, your parents didn't tell me. It was only last night, no the night before . . . I was having dinner with them and your father suddenly blurted out that you were pregnant. Because of Elizabeth, I was so worried. The identity of the father wasn't really relevant – I just thought you might . . .' his voice tailed off.

'What do you mean, because of Elizabeth? Might have what?'

It was only then that Charles realized that they had not met since he had learnt from Sally Naylor the ending to Elizabeth's story. He told her there and then everything he knew, carefully, gently, aware that so soon after the birth of her own child, he could scarcely have chosen a worse moment. She cried when he had finished, clutching Guy to her as if afraid someone would take him away. At last, he took the baby from her and returned him to his crib. Then he put his arms around her for the first time since their parting and held her while she sobbed. 'It's all right,' he murmured against her ear. 'We've all been given a second chance.'

Prue leant back on her pillow, a wave of relief flooding through

317

her at his words. So he knew . . . She eyed him, uncertainly, still cautious. 'You mean, you, me and Guy?'

'I suppose so.' He stood up abruptly and walked to the crib where his son lay. 'Hell, Prue, I don't really know what I mean – it's just that . . .'

'It's all right,' she said. 'It's Guy, isn't it, you recognized him when you first saw him?'

He raised his eyes to meet hers and she could see her own relief mirrored in his face. 'Yes,' he said. 'Yes I knew him.'

'What do you think it means?' said Prue.

Charles came and sat down on the bed again. 'I don't know. All I do know for certain is that this time we must do the right thing for him. If . . .' he hesitated over his words. 'If this isn't his first visit . . . oh hell, it sounds crazy doesn't it?'

Prue shook her head. 'Not to me.'

'If this isn't his first visit then we have to do better for him than we did on the last occasion. We'll never know what went wrong between father and son but something must have happened to drive them apart, and now we know about Elizabeth, just think how Guy must have felt – rejected by his mother, no rightful claim to his father. He was born illegitimate then, and now it has happened again. I want you to marry me, Prue, but it's not just for Guy, it's for us. We have to marry . . . it's part of our destiny. I can't be without you, I love you, life is meaningless without you.' He spoke defiantly, expecting the old Prue to come back to him, full of practical common-sense reasons why as yet they could not make a commitment to one another.

'I agree,' she said, simply. He stared at her incredulously and then wordlessly drew her to him. The strain and stresses of the last months faded away. They held one another close and gazed at the baby, not kissing or speaking, just savouring the moment and recognizing at last the complete understanding between them. 'When did you realize?' Prue said at last. 'Was it when you first saw Guy?'

'No,' said Charles. 'It was several months ago. I've taken your advice – Chadbrook is coming along very nicely as a tourist centre. I can't wait to show you what I've done.' He hesitated. 'Last June I decided to lay down some tracks for walks around the estate, to avoid people messing up all the pasture. After a great deal of soul-searching I decided it would be sensible to put a path through the larch wood – you know, the larches you can see from the library window.' Prue nodded. 'I've always had a special feeling about that place, it's very private, solitary, but it didn't seem right to put the path round it so I set some chaps to work to clear a footpath. I was in the library messing about with planning applications when Roger, the foreman, came in and said they had found something I ought to see.' He drew away a little so that he could watch her expression as he spoke. 'Prue, you'll think I'm mad but I knew even then what it was they'd found. I followed Roger like a sleepwalker. Where they had cleared the undergrowth, I suppose it was about a third of the way into the wood, they had uncovered a stone, a gravestone. I bent down to look at it and do you know the engraving was as clear as if it had just been done. "Here lies Elizabeth Monson 1764–1789, and her infant daughter".'

Prue gasped. 'So Thomas brought her to Chadbrook.'

Charles nodded. 'He buried her in the larch wood because he could see it from the library, which was his favourite room, as it is mine.' His words were a statement.

'You're sure of that, aren't you?' Prue said.

'Yes, I am. I just stood there staring at Elizabeth's grave and then . . . oh God, it was so embarrassing, I began to sob. Roger hurried the workmen away and left me to it. I felt, suddenly, this terrible burden of grief, and just as has happened so often to you at the inn, I knew they were not my own feelings but someone else's. You probably think I'm crazy but . . .'

'Of course I don't,' Prue said, gently. She smiled. 'You are preaching to the converted, after all.'

'It is extraordinary, isn't it, that we should both have had such similar experiences?'

'What's even more strange is that it should be the larch wood where she was found. Before Guy was born I kept having these terrible dreams. They were always the same – a little boy lost in the larch wood at Chadbrook. I never saw his face, but his back view was so like you. They have haunted me for weeks – I even became afraid to sleep.'

'Your father mentioned bad dreams. I supposed that Elizabeth had somehow followed you,' Charles said.

Prue smiled slightly. 'Elizabeth didn't follow me but her son certainly did, and not only in my dreams. When they handed Guy to me for the first time, not only did I recognize him – he knew me, I'm sure of it.'

'Then are we Thomas and Elizabeth?' Charles asked.

Prue considered the question for a moment. 'I don't think so, but

I'm equally sure that it doesn't matter whether we are them or whether, as their direct descendants, we have been chosen to set the record straight. All I am sure of is Guy. Guy hasn't changed. This is his second chance and we have to put things right for him.'

'I know,' said Charles, with utter conviction. 'While we may understand very little of what has happened to us, Guy is our one certainty.'

'Ladies and gentlemen, we are now making our final approach to Heathrow. Would you please fasten your seatbelts and extinguish all cigarettes.'

'Shall I take the baby while you sort yourself out?' said Charles.

'Thanks.' Prue fastened her seatbelt. 'I'm glad we didn't ask my parents to meet us at the airport. I don't feel ready for them somehow.'

'Nor I,' said Charles. 'I don't really feel I can face anybody at the moment. I suppose we could stay the night in London, telephone to say our plane had been delayed and see them in the morning.'

'I have a better idea,' said Prue. 'A much better idea.'

Outwardly the inn had changed not at all. For some reason Prue was particularly relieved to see the sign had not been altered. Still uncertain as to what they were doing, Prue and Charles, Prue clutching the baby to her with a bag of his possessions over her shoulder, struggled through the door, travel-worn and disorientated.

The bar, too, was unchanged. Everything was as it had been, as she had created it, except there was no Terry. A pleasant-looking girl in her early twenties smiled a greeting. 'Good evening. Can I help you?'

'We would like a room, please,' Charles said. 'Just for one night.'

'We are rather full,' the girl said.

'It's important,' said Charles. 'Please try to squeeze us in somewhere.'

'I'll go and find the manager and see what I can do.'

'I'd like to change the baby, if I may,' Prue said.

'Of course, the ladies' cloakroom is through this way.' Prue followed the girl in a daze. She opened the cloakroom door and was ushered in. Nothing had changed there either – the same carpet and curtains which Prue herself had chosen. It was at once familiar and yet strange and disorientating. She spread a towel on the floor and laid Guy upon it. He was awake but quiet, staring around him as if he, too, was waiting for something to happen.

'Elizabeth,' Prue whispered. 'Are you still here?' There was no answering sensation, there was nothing at all. Ridiculously, Prue felt a keen sense of disappointment. It was madness to miss Elizabeth's misery when in the past it had frightened her so often. She changed the baby's nappy quickly, washed her hands, ran a comb through her hair and went back into the bar.

'They've managed to find a room for us,' said Charles, with a smile, taking the baby from her.

'I'm afraid it's not one of our best rooms, there's no bathroom,' the girl said apologetically. 'I'm particularly sorry as you have the baby.'

'It doesn't matter,' said Prue.

In the privacy of their room, Prue fed Guy and put him in his carry cot. 'Are we mad?' she asked Charles.

He shook his head. 'It feels right.'

'What shall we do now? It's as if we're waiting for something to happen.'

'I don't think a sleep would do us any harm,' Charles said.

They undressed and lay together on the bed, their arms about one another. 'Does it worry you at all, knowing that in all probability we're some sort of puppets of destiny?' Charles asked.

'Not at all,' Prue replied.

'You do know, don't you, that whoever we are and however much we may be influenced by the past, I love you for yourself, not for who you might have been.'

'I know that, Charles, and I love you, too.'

'I will make you happy this time, I won't let you down again. Do you trust me?'

'Yes,' she replied.

The baby woke Prue. She struggled to sit up in the bed, momentarily uncertain where she was. Then she remembered and smiled. She reached over and plucked the child from his crib and put him to her breast. Charles stirred beside her and then slipped back into sleep. The curtains were wide open, it was dusk, the sky still tinged pink from what had obviously been a wonderful sunset. The room, which naturally Prue had never slept in before, looked out over the kitchens and stableyard. The view, however, was spectacular, for beyond the village you could see the fields and the hill on which stood the spinney, a favourite picnic place in the area. Prue gazed down at Guy, his dark head resting in the crook of her arm, and as she did so she felt a fluttering in her mind and then a rush of such pure joy and happiness that it made her gasp aloud.

The noise woke Charles. 'What is it?' he said. 'Are you all right?'

'Yes, fine,' said Prue. 'I'm just feeding the baby. Oh Charles, I'm so happy.'

'Me, too.' He drew closer to her, snuggling against her, one arm flung round both her and their son.

She would tell him later, of course, that now she knew why they had come. To lay the ghost, to give Elizabeth peace at last . . . the words in her head sounded trite, a cliché, like some bad old Hollywood horror movie. Yet this was surely what had happened. For Elizabeth had returned – not this time to tell of her misery and suffering but to make Prue aware of her joy that all was well with Guy at last. There was no room for doubt. Prue was happy for herself, for Charles and for Guy, but the emotions she had just felt with such a force had not been hers. They had belonged to someone else entirely.

EPILOGUE

Prue Mansell and Charles Chadbrook were married by special licence six days after their return to Suffolk. Afterwards they were blessed at Shrimpling church, where two hundred years before Thomas and Elizabeth had parted for the last time. It was a simple service, attended only by Prue's parents and a few local parishioners. After the blessing, the ceremony continued with Guy's baptism. For everyone present it was a moving scene – the young couple were so obviously devoted to one another and their new-born baby. Not the most conventional of marriages perhaps, but no one doubted the love that was there for all to see.

And after the ceremony was over, and the guests had dispersed, the proud parents took their son home to Chadbrook.